The orchestra struck up a waltz.

"We must also find you a dance partner, Ria," Lady Thornborough said.

"I think I would like that," Lizzie replied. She was truly enjoying herself this evening, in a lighthearted way that she had not experienced in a long time.

And then she heard Geoffrey's voice behind her. "Will I suffice?"

Lizzie turned around. How had she gone almost an entire hour without thinking about this man? Now as he stood there, looking alarmingly handsome, she could think of little else. His black coat and white shirt drew attention to his dark eyes and the fine angle of his jaw in a way that took her breath away. He flashed one of his rare smiles and extended his hand.

Her heart lost several beats as she felt the warmth of his touch through her thin gloves. A joyous, heady feeling pulsed through her—one she had not known for too many years. Yes, she would dance. How had she even considered not coming tonight? How had she not realized she might have given up an opportunity to be in his arms again—if only for a dance?

"Jennifer Delamere sets a new standard in Victorian romance, with characters who shine and a plot that'll keep you guessing."

—Abby Gaines, author of *The Earl's Mistaken Bride*

"A sweetly rendered tale of discovery and forgiveness with a refreshing touch of innocence."

—Cindy Holby, bestselling author of *Angel's End*

An Heiress
at Heart

Jennifer Delamere

FOREVER

NEW YORK   BOSTON

Forever

Hachette Book Group

237 Park Avenue

New York, NY 10017

www.HachetteBookGroup.com

Printed in the United States of America

RRD-C

First Trade Edition: November 2012

10 9 8 7 6 5 4 3 2 1

Forever is an imprint of Grand Central Publishing.

The Forever name and logo are trademarks of Hachette Book Group, Inc.

The Hachette Speakers Bureau provides a wide range of authors for speaking events. To find out more, go to www.hachettespeakersbureau.com or call (866) 376-6591.

The publisher is not responsible for websites (or their content) that are not owned by the publisher.

LCCN: 2012942491

ISBN: 978-1-4555-1995-8 (pbk.)

In memory of my mother

Margaret Wayt DeBolt

Who believed we ought to follow our dreams

Acknowledgments

I owe a very large debt to the Romance Writers of America for opening so many doors in publishing and, most important, for giving me the tools to make the most of those opportunities and to grow as an author.

Many thanks to my local RWA chapter, the Heart of Carolina Romance Writers, who continue to provide an astonishing amount of wisdom and inspiration.

Thanks to my agent, Jessica Alvarez, and to my editor, Lauren Plude, who both got me to the fast lane rather quickly and have thus far managed to keep me on the road.

Thanks to my critique partners for this book, Sarra Cannon and Karen Anders: to Sarra for insight and encouragement, and to Karen for being the very best example of a mentor.

Thanks to Elaine Luddy Klonicki, my first ever beta reader, for being so excited about my book and providing valuable input.

I am most especially grateful to all my friends and family. Not once did anyone tell me it couldn't be done: everyone cheered

Acknowledgments

me on from the beginning. I am thankful every day to have such amazing support.

Thanks to Frank DeBolt, Sr., my wonderful dad, who has given me so much over the years.

Last, and most, thanks to Jim Harrington for love, laughter, and believing—in short, for being a husband *extraordinaire*. Any resemblance to my books' heroes is not entirely coincidental.

As far as the east is from the west,
So far hath he removed our transgressions from us.
Bless the Lord, O my soul.

— PSALM 103

Ever the wonder waxeth more and more,
So that we say, "All this hath been before,
All this hath been, I know not when or where."
So, friend, when first I look'd upon your face,
Our thought gave answer each to each, so true—
Opposed mirrors each reflecting each—
That tho' I knew not in what time or place,
Methought that I had often met with you,
And either lived in either's heart and speech.

— ALFRED, LORD TENNYSON

An Heiress at Heart

Prologue

Beyond this breach, my friends, lies the great Bathurst Plains!"

This announcement came from a man on horseback who was leading the procession of four bullock drays—large two-wheeled carts piled high with supplies and pulled by oxen.

From her perch atop one of the drays, Lizzie Poole strained to catch her first glimpse of the valley beyond the Blue Mountains.

It had been a long journey from Sydney. For three days they'd traveled the narrow road painstakingly cut through the mountain pass. The road had risen and fallen sharply and taken countless turns through narrow gorges. Lizzie thought they might never escape the dense woods, which were at times so thick she could barely see the sky above. And she did not care at all for the bird they called the kookaburra, whose call sounded to her like maniacal laughter.

But they were at last moving into bright sunshine. The drivers brought the rigs to a halt at the point where the road crested a ridge, and the western valley opened before them in a breathtaking vista. Beyond the steep cliffs with their dramatic rock formations, the land stretched away for miles: trees and plains making a tapestry of green and brown, dotted here and there with colorful flowers. Lizzie even glimpsed a sparkle of blue from a distant river. Although she had spent four months looking at the ocean's endless horizon, the world never appeared as large to her as it did now.

"Tom, isn't it magnificent?" she called down to her brother, who had been walking beside the dray.

"Aye," agreed Tom. "It looks bigger than all of England."

Lizzie could see the same awe she felt reflected on the faces of the other newcomers: there were three single men who had been hired straight off the ship in Sydney to work on the sheep farms, and a clergyman, Rev. Greene, who had traveled with his wife and two children to preside over the small church in Bathurst.

Their guide, Mr. Edward Smythe, appeared pleased at their reactions. He spread his arms wide and proclaimed in theatrical tones:

> *"The boundless champaign burst upon our sight,*
> *Till nearer seen the beauteous landscape grew,*
> *Op'ning like Canaan on rapt Israel's view."*

Lizzie smiled. She was not surprised that Mr. Smythe should be spouting poetry at a moment like this. He was a handsome man, with dark hair and expressive brown eyes, and Lizzie could easily picture him as an actor on the stage. He was young, too; like Lizzie and her brother, he looked to be still in his twenties. What intrigued Lizzie most, however, was that although his accent revealed him to be an English gentleman, he seemed perfectly at home in this rough and untamed land.

"Canaan," repeated Mrs. Greene, who was seated on the dray with Lizzie and cradling an infant in her arms. "I suppose the Promised Land was indeed as beautiful as this."

Lizzie considered these words as the drays once more took up their slow, steady advance. She and Tom had left behind everything in England. Would they really find a new beginning here, as Tom had promised her? She desperately hoped so.

After another hour or so, they came within sight of a group of men digging a ditch along the edge of the road. There were ten of them, and Lizzie thought she had never seen such miserable-looking creatures. Dirty and ragged, they worked with grim determination under the oversight of three men—the master of the crew, shouting orders from horseback; a tall man with a sunburned face, who was holding a shotgun; and a third very large fellow, who was wielding a whip.

When the master saw the caravan, he immediately rode up to meet them and exchanged greetings with Mr. Smythe, riding along with him for a few minutes as the caravan kept its forward pace. The other two men, Lizzie noticed, kept the road crew mercilessly at work.

"This is Captain McCann," Mr. Smythe announced to the travelers. "He is in charge of keeping this road maintained and safe."

"Welcome," said the captain, riding his horse up the line of oxcarts so he could greet everyone. "I am happy to see more immigrants to the valley." When he saw Lizzie, he lifted up his eyebrows in surprise, then turned and said over his shoulder,

"What's this, Smythe? Did you take your wife with you all the way to Sydney and back again?"

Mr. Smythe's eyes glinted in amusement. "No, sir," he said. "This is Miss Poole. Lately arrived from England with her brother."

A look of confusion crossed the captain's face. After a moment's hesitation, he replaced it with an apologetic smile and raised his cap to Lizzie. "I beg your pardon, miss."

"Are those...convicts?" the minister's wife asked timidly, pointing to the workers.

"Indeed they are, ma'am," the captain responded. "We've brought them up here to repair the culverts."

Two of the convicts turned from their work to watch the drays as they passed, but a flash of the whip from the burly man sent them back to their labors once more.

"Poor creatures," she said, echoing Lizzie's thoughts.

"Do not give them too much pity, ma'am," the captain said. "They brought it upon themselves by their evil ways. 'Twas no more than they deserved."

"Why, what have they done?"

"Thieves, mostly," he replied coolly. "Some are murderers, too. You'll do well to stay clear of them."

As their cart passed the convicts, two others managed to throw them dark glares without their overseer being aware of it.

Rev. Greene's son turned to him and said, "Papa, do you suppose God has forgiven those fellows?"

"He has if they have repented and asked Him for forgiveness," he replied.

"Do you really believe it is that simple?" Tom asked him. "Wouldn't a just God exact vengeance?"

The minister gave Tom an inquiring look. Tom's impassive face gave little indication of what he was thinking. But Lizzie knew what must be on his mind. Four months had passed since Tom had killed Freddie Hightower in a duel, exacting his own vengeance on the man who had seduced his sister, taken her to Europe, and abandoned her there. The memory of that cold, miserable morning when Tom, still bloody from his duel, revealed to her what he'd done still sent a chill to Lizzie's heart. Even though Freddie had cruelly mistreated her, she had never wished for his death—certainly not at the hands of her own brother.

"Perhaps after we are settled, you might visit me at church," the minister suggested to Tom. "Then we might have leisure to discuss these matters more fully."

"Thank you, sir," Tom said with a nod of his head. But Lizzie doubted such a meeting would ever take place. Tom had made it clear to her that he felt justified in acting as he had. He had done it "for her sake," he said, and he would not allow anyone to change his mind. Despite his words, Lizzie knew his actions had left a stain on his heart and given him no real peace. She was in no better condition herself, she reflected bitterly. Her foolish actions had brought on those terrible events. Surely there was no pardon for that.

"It's for certain the Crown is not so forgiving," the captain said to Tom. He gestured dismissively toward the convicts. "These men will be paying for their crimes for the rest of their lives. It's a fate worse than death. Be glad you've come to Australia as a free man."

The captain could not have known how close he was to the truth. If Tom had been arrested for what he'd done to Freddie, he might well have arrived in Australia in chains. But Tom had escaped. He'd arranged the duel for the morning they left for Australia, not telling Lizzie of his plans until the deed had been done. They had been out to sea within hours of the duel, their trail untraceable to anyone who might wish to follow. No one here was aware of the sordid tale that caused their departure from England.

It all seemed as a dream now, as they began moving across the open valley, full in the light of the brightly burning sun. Odd, too, that it was February and yet they were in the heat of summer. Everything was different here. The world she had known was gone.

Would she ever feel at home in this strange new land?

Mr. Smythe had insisted they would. He had seen them as they disembarked from the ship at Sydney harbor, and had immediately worked his way through the crowds in order to meet them, offering work on one of the largest sheep ranches in the Bathurst Valley. He said that he'd been sent by the owner to hire able-bodied laborers from the immigrant ship, whose arrival had been keenly anticipated. With transportation of criminals now limited to other parts of Australia, the region of New South Wales was in dire need of free workers.

"My wife will be overjoyed to meet you," Mr. Smythe had said upon their agreeing to go.

Lizzie had lost count of how many times he'd repeated this sentiment over the course of their journey. "Are there no other ladies to keep her company?" Lizzie had asked.

"None have given her the close friendship she craves. But something tells me you two will be very close."

Lizzie had asked for more particulars, but he would say no more. It would have to remain a mystery until she met this Ria Smythe.

The day was far advanced when they finally reached the town of Bathurst and pulled up to the place where they would lodge for the night. A sign above the door proclaimed this to be the *Royal Hotel*. It seemed far too grand a name for the two-story wooden building. And yet, after three nights of sleeping on the ground, Lizzie was sure it would feel as grand as a palace.

Tom helped Lizzie descend from the oxcart. At the front of the caravan, Mr. Smythe dismounted from his horse and was immediately met by a lovely young lady. "Eddie, you're home!" she cried happily. She tossed back her bonnet as she ran toward him, giving Lizzie a clear view of her face before the woman threw her arms around him and kissed him.

"Blimey," Tom remarked to Lizzie. "If that lady ain't the spittin' image of you!"

Lizzie could only stare. The woman did look *amazingly* like her. She was a match in so many ways, from her pale blond hair to her face and figure. Lizzie could not see the woman's eyes from this distance, but she was certain they were blue like her own. She had the oddest feeling she was looking in a mirror.

Tom grinned. "Now I see why Smythe asked us so many questions about our family!"

"It might also explain why he seemed so disappointed that I had never had a sister," Lizzie observed. "He must have thought there was a connection."

Mr. Smythe gently set his wife at arm's length to get a better look at her. "How well you look. I cannot believe you came all the way to town to meet me. But, my dearest, I fear you have scandalized these good people with your actions just now." He spoke as if he were chiding her, yet it was clear he was pleased by her enthusiastic greeting.

"Why, Eddie," she answered, "you know I could not wait even one more day to see you."

They gazed at each other with such loving affection that Lizzie's heart twisted in envy. She had once felt love like that. But she had never known such happiness. Falling in love had brought her only ruin and heartache. She would never again dare to open her heart in that way.

"Ria, my darling," said Mr. Smythe, "aren't you going to ask me what I brought you from Sydney?"

"Have you brought me a present?" she asked gaily. "What could it be?"

"Come and see," he said, and began to draw her toward Lizzie. The moment Ria saw Lizzie, she pulled up short. Her mouth fell open and her eyes—blue, as Lizzie had known they would be—lit up with wonder and joy.

"Indeed I have brought you a present," Edward said with a satisfied smile. "I have brought you a sister."

Chapter 1

London, June 1851

I f you've killed her, Geoffrey, we will never hear the end of it from Lady Thornborough."

Geoffrey Somerville threw a sharp glance at his companion. The man's flippancy annoyed him, but he knew James Simpson was never one to take any problem too seriously. Not even the problem of what to do with the young woman they had just accidentally struck down with his carriage.

The girl had been weaving her way across the street, seemingly unaware of their rapid approach until it was too late. The driver had barely succeeded in steering the horses sharply to one side to keep from trampling her under their massive hooves. However, there had not been enough time or space for him to avoid the girl completely, and the front wheel had tossed her onto the walkway as easily as a mislaid wicker basket.

Geoffrey knelt down and raised the woman's head gently,

smoothing the hair from her forehead. Blood flowed freely from a wound at her left temple, marring her fair features and leaving ugly red streaks in her pale yellow hair.

Her eyes were closed, but Geoffrey saw with relief that she was still breathing. Her chest rose and fell in ragged but unmistakable movements. "She's not dead," he said. "But she is badly hurt. We must get help immediately."

James bounded up the steps and rapped at the door with his cane. "First we have to get her inside. People are beginning to gather, and you know how much my aunt hates a scandal."

Geoffrey noted that a few people had indeed stopped to stare, although no one offered to help. One richly dressed young lady turned her head and hurried her escort down the street, as though fearful the poor woman bleeding on the pavement had brought the plague to this fashionable Mayfair neighborhood. At one time Geoffrey might have wondered at the lack of Good Samaritans here. But during the six months he'd been in London, he'd seen similar reactions to human suffering every day. Although it was no longer surprising, it still saddened and sickened him.

Only the coachman seemed to show real concern. He stood holding the horses and watching Geoffrey, his face wrinkled with worry. Or perhaps, Geoffrey realized, it was merely guilt. "I never even seen her, my lord," he said. "She come from out of nowhere."

"It's not your fault," Geoffrey assured him. He pulled out a handkerchief and began to dab the blood that was seeping from the woman's wound. "Go as quickly as you can to Harley Street and fetch Dr. Layton."

"Yes, my lord." The coachman's relief was evident. He

scrambled up to the driver's seat and grabbed the reins. "I'm halfway there already."

Geoffrey continued to cautiously check the woman for other injuries. He slowly ran his hands along her delicate neck and shoulders and down her slender arms. He tested only as much as he dared of her torso and legs, torn between concern for her well-being and the need for propriety. Thankfully, nothing appeared to be broken.

James rapped once more on the imposing black door. It finally opened, and the gaunt face of Lady Thornborough's butler peered out.

"Clear the way, Harding," James said. "There has been an accident."

Harding's eyes widened at the sight of a woman bleeding on his mistress's immaculate steps. He quickly sized up the situation and opened the door wide.

Geoffrey lifted the unconscious girl into his arms. She was far too thin, and he was not surprised to find she was light as a feather. Her golden hair contrasted vividly with his black coat. Where was her hat? Geoffrey scanned the area and noted with chagrin the remains of a straw bonnet lying crushed in the street. Something tugged at his heart as her head fell against his chest. Compassion, he supposed it was. But it was curiously profound.

"She is bleeding profusely," James pointed out. "Have one of the servants carry her in, or you will ruin your coat."

"It's no matter," Geoffrey replied. He felt oddly protective of the woman in his arms, although he had no idea who she was. His carriage had struck her, after all, even if her own careless-ness had brought about the calamity. He was not about to relinquish her, not for any consideration.

He stepped grimly over the red smears her blood had left on the white marble steps and carried her into the front hall, where James was again addressing the butler. "Is Lady Thornborough at home, Harding?"

"No, sir. But we expect her anytime."

Geoffrey knew from long acquaintance with the Thornborough family that Harding was a practical man who remained calm even in wildly unusual circumstances. The childhood escapades of Lady Thornborough's granddaughter, Victoria, had developed this ability in him; James's exploits as an adult had honed it to a fine art.

Sure enough, Harding motioned toward the stairs with cool equanimity, as though it were an everyday occurrence for an injured and unknown woman to be brought into the house. "Might I suggest the sofa in the Rose Parlor, sir?"

"Excellent," said James.

As they ascended the stairs, Harding called down to a young parlor maid who was still standing in the front hall. "Mary, fetch us some water and a towel. And tell Jane to clean the front steps immediately." Mary nodded and scurried away.

Another maid met them at the top of the stairs. At Harding's instructions, she quickly found a blanket to spread out on the sofa to shield the expensive fabric.

Geoffrey set his fragile burden down with care. He seated himself on a low stool next to the woman and once again pressed his handkerchief to the gash below her hairline. The flesh around the wound was beginning to turn purple—she had been struck very hard. Alarm assailed him. "What the devil possessed her to step in front of a moving carriage?"

He was not aware that he had spoken aloud until James

answered him. "Language, Geoffrey," he said with mock prud-ishness. "There is a lady present."

Geoffrey looked down at the unconscious woman. "I don't think she can hear me just now." He studied her with interest. Her plain black dress fit her too loosely, and the cuffs appeared to have been turned back more than once. Her sturdy leather shoes were of good quality, but showed signs of heavy wear. Was she a servant, wearing her mistress's cast-off clothing? Or was she a lady in mourning? Was she already sorrowing for the loss of a loved one, only to have this accident add to her woes? "If she is a lady, she has fallen on hard times," Geoffrey said, feel-ing once again that curious pull at his heart. He knew only too well the wretchedness of having one's life waylaid by one tragedy after another.

A parlor maid entered the room, carrying the items Harding had requested. She set the basin on a nearby table. After dipping the cloth in the water, she timidly approached and gave Geof-frey a small curtsy. "With your permission, my lord."

Something in the way the maid spoke these words chafed at him. He had been entitled to the address of "my lord" for sev-eral months, but he could not accustom himself to it. There were plenty who would congratulate him on his recent elevation to the peerage, but for Geoffrey it was a constant reminder of what he had lost. Surely nothing in this world was worth the loss of two brothers. Nor did any position, no matter how lofty, absolve a man from helping another if he could. He held out his hand for the cloth. "Give it to me. I will do it."

The maid hesitated.

"Do you think that is wise?" James asked. "Surely this is a task for one of the servants."

"I do have experience in this. I often attended to the ill in my parish."

"But you were only a clergyman then. Now you are a baron."

Geoffrey hated the position he had been placed in by the loss of his two elder brothers. But he would use it to his advantage if he had to. And he had every intention of tending to this woman. "Since I am a baron," he said curtly, motioning again for the cloth, "you must all do as I command."

James laughed and gave him a small bow. "Touché, *my lord.*"

The maid put the towel into Geoffrey's hand and gave him another small curtsy. She retreated a few steps, but kept her eyes fastened on him. Geoffrey suspected that her diligence stemmed more from his new social position than from the present circumstances. It had not escaped him that he'd become the recipient of all kinds of extra attention—from parlor maids to duchesses—since he'd become a baron. The years he'd spent as a clergyman in a poor village, extending all his efforts to help others who struggled every day just to eke out a meager living, had apparently not been worth anyone's notice.

Geoffrey laid a hand to the woman's forehead. It was too warm against his cool palm. "I'm afraid she may have a fever in addition to her head injury."

James made a show of pulling out his handkerchief and half covering his nose and mouth. "Oh dear, I do hope she has not brought anything catching into the house. That would be terribly inconvenient."

Harding entered the room, carrying a dust-covered carpetbag. He held it in front of him, careful not to let it touch any part of his pristine coat. "We found this near the steps outside. I believe it belongs to"—he threw a disparaging look toward the prostrate figure on the sofa—"the lady."

"Thank you, Harding," James said. He glanced at the worn object with equal distaste, then motioned to the far side of the room. "Set it there for now."

That bag might be all the woman had in the world, Geoffrey thought, and yet James was so casually dismissive of it. The man had a long way to go when it came to finding compassion for those less fortunate.

He turned back to the woman. She stirred and moaned softly. "Easy," Geoffrey murmured, unable to resist the urge to comfort her, although he doubted she could hear him. "You're safe now."

James watched from the other side of the sofa as Geoffrey cleaned the blood from her hair and face. "What a specimen she is," he remarked as her features came into view. He leaned in to scrutinize her. "Look at those high cheekbones. And the delicate arch of her brow. And those full lips—"

"This is a woman, James," Geoffrey remonstrated. "Not some creature in a zoo."

"Well, it's clear she's a woman," James returned lightly, unruffled by Geoffrey's tone. "I'm glad you noticed. Sometimes I wonder if you are aware of these things."

Geoffrey was aware. At the moment, he was *too* aware. He could not deny that, like James, he had been taken by her beauty. Except her lips were too pale, chapped from dryness. He had a wild urge to reach out and gently brush over them with cool water...

"Good heavens," James said, abruptly bringing Geoffrey back to his senses. He dropped his handkerchief from his face. "This is Ria."

Geoffrey froze. "What did you say?"

"I said, the young lady bleeding all over Auntie's sofa is Victoria Thornborough."

No. Surely that was impossible. There were occasions, Geoffrey thought, when James seemed determined to try him to the absolute limit. "James, this is not the time for one of your childish pranks."

James shook his head. "I am absolutely in earnest."

"But that's preposterous."

"I think I should know my own cousin. Even if it has been ten years." He bent closer as the woman mumbled something incoherent. "You see? She heard me. She recognizes her name."

The room suddenly became quite still. Even the servants who had been hovering nearby stopped their tasks. All eyes turned toward the sofa.

Was this really Ria? Geoffrey had to take James's word on it for now; he had never met her. He had been in Europe during her brief, clandestine courtship with his brother. This woman, to whom he had been so curiously drawn—for some reason he could easily believe her to be a lady, despite her dirty clothes and bruises. He had no trouble believing Edward could have fallen in love with her—had he not been taken with her himself? *No,* he told himself again. It had been mere compassion he'd been feeling. And it was utterly incomprehensible that his sister-in-law should appear like this out of nowhere.

"If this is Ria," Geoffrey said, "then surely Edward would be with her?"

"So one would expect," James replied. "I agree that the situation is most unusual."

"Unusual," Geoffrey repeated drily. The word might describe everything about what had happened between Ria and his brother. Their elopement had taken everyone by surprise, causing a scandal that was bad enough without the embarrassing fact that Ria had been engaged to his other brother, William, at the time.

"At least we can surmise that they were not aboard the ill-fated *Sea Venture*," James said. "Where *did* they go, I wonder?"

"That is only one of the many things I'd like to know," Geoffrey said. He'd exhausted himself with searches and inquiries after Edward and Ria had disappeared without a trace. The best they could discover was that the couple may have booked passage on a ship that had sunk on its way to America. And yet all was conjecture; there had never been answers.

Geoffrey took hold of the woman's left hand and began to remove a worn glove that was upon it. He heard the maid behind him gasp, but he was beyond worrying about the possible impropriety of his actions. If this was Ria, he wanted evidence that Edward had made an honest woman of her. He did not think his brother would deliberately trifle with a woman's affections, but he also knew Edward was prone to rash whims and irresponsible actions. Anything might have kept him from carrying out his plans.

With one last gentle tug from Geoffrey, the glove came off, revealing a hand that was rough and calloused. It was a hand that had done plenty of manual labor. Though she was not wearing a wedding band, she was wearing a gold and onyx ring that Geoffrey recognized as having once belonged to Edward. The sight of it nearly devastated him. He could think of only one reason she would be wearing it instead of his brother.

"Why?" Geoffrey asked roughly, as his concern melted into consternation. "If they were in dire straits, why did they stay away? Why did they not ask us for help?"

"If you were in their shoes," James answered, "would you

have wanted to face William's wrath? Or Lady Thornborough's?" He looked at the woman thoughtfully. "Perhaps they were not always so destitute. Look at her, Geoffrey. Look at what she is wearing."

Geoffrey allowed his gaze to travel once more over the slender figure in the plain black dress that seemed to declare her in mourning. "No!" Geoffrey said sharply. How could she have survived, but not Edward?

Geoffrey rose and gave the towel and the glove to the maid. He walked to the window and peered through the lace curtains to the street below. It was filled with carriages moving swiftly in both directions, but he could see no sign of either his coach or the doctor's. He knew it was too soon to expect their return, but he could not quell the anxiety rising in him.

Which was worse: the continual pain of not knowing what had become of his brother, or the final blow of discovering he really was dead? If anyone had asked him that question before this moment, he might have given an entirely different response.

He had to get Ria well again. And he had to get answers.

Chapter 2

S he was dimly aware of voices speaking above her, of a soft, cool cloth against her burning face.

A sweet scent of roses kept urging her to inhale deeply, trying to lure her back to consciousness. But a piercing pain shot through her side with every breath, and the pounding behind her right temple kept forcing her back into a gauzy daze, unable to open her eyes.

The murmuring paused, seemingly stilled by a rustle of skirts and a quick tread upon the floor. A woman's sharp voice said, "Have you done nothing to bring her around?"

"We have sent for Dr. Layton," a man replied.

"Tut, tut. You are as useless as your father was."

"My dear aunt, I must protest. I am sure I am a good deal more useless than he was."

Another disapproving noise, then a curt order. "Quick, Mary. Bring my smelling salts."

More rustling, followed by the assault of an acrid smell under her nose. She sneezed hard, wincing as a bolt of pain surged through her head.

Gradually her eyes focused on an elderly lady dressed in a heavy silk gown of very dark green. The woman was looking down at her with a mixture of shock and astonishment.

And then she remembered.

She had been standing across the street from Lady Thornborough's house, trying to make up her mind whether or not to approach it. Even now, after coming so far, she had hesitated. Could she carry out her plan? Would they believe her story?

It had to be done. She had made a promise to a dying woman, and she would keep it. Both fever and chills had plagued her during the long walk up from the docks, compelling her to keep moving lest she faint dead away on the pavement.

"You must go," Ria's voice had echoed in her ear. *"I am counting on you."*

Gathering her courage, she had stepped into the street. Her aching head had blurred the multitude of sounds on the busy thoroughfare, and the glare of the late afternoon sun had hidden the approach of a swiftly moving carriage.

Now, Lizzie Poole lay motionless as she returned the gaze of the lady standing before her. The woman's gray eyes matched the color of her hair, which was pulled back in a tight bun. Her regal manner indicated she was the lady of the house. This must be Lady Thornborough—the stern, implacable woman who had raised Ria.

Would Lady Thornborough believe she was now looking at the granddaughter whom she had last seen ten years ago, when the girl was just seventeen? Or would she instantly recognize Lizzie as an imposter? *Not entirely an imposter,* she corrected herself.

Ria had convinced her they were half sisters and told her where she could find proof. This made Lizzie a granddaughter of Lady Thornborough, too, although the old woman did not know it.

And if Lizzie pretended to be Ria, what of it? Ria was dead now. Her relationship with Lady Thornborough had been a stormy one, and Ria had begged Lizzie to help her make amends. What better way to do this than to *become* Ria—to be the dutiful granddaughter Lady Thornborough had always wished for? As an illegitimate granddaughter, Lizzie could do nothing; as Ria, she could claim everything. Ria had given her blessing to the scheme; in fact, it had been her idea.

For several long, agonizing moments Lizzie watched as Lady Thornborough's face remained stern and inscrutable. Then she frowned and shook her head.

Lizzie closed her eyes. *I have failed,* she thought. *She knows I am not Ria.* She fought a surge of disappointment. Ria had so thoroughly described the family, the house, and the servants that Lizzie believed she could walk through the door and take up the life her half sister had left behind. Now she was seized with fear that they would toss her into the street before she even had a chance to explain.

At last, Lady Thornborough spoke. "Ria, where have you been?"

Her words were crisp, but not unkind—and sweet to Lizzie's ears. Relief washed over her, for one blessed moment stemming the pain that wracked her body. Lady Thornborough believed her to be Ria. She could stay. She reached for the cloth on her temple and sat up, despite the fresh round of pain this set off in her throbbing head. So many things she had planned to say, yet all she could do was answer Lady Thornborough's question:

Where have you been? "Why, Australia, of course...," she murmured, her voice trailing off.

"Australia?" Lady Thornborough repeated in mortified surprise. She sat down and put her arms around Lizzie. "Oh, my dear girl."

This was not at all what Lizzie had been expecting, but she accepted it gratefully. She relaxed into the woman's comforting embrace, thankful for the way the cool silk of Lady Thornborough's dress soothed her burning cheek. Soft whispers of guilt stirred within her, awareness that this plan could hurt the woman whose love and respect Ria had so longed for. But Lizzie was ill and exhausted, and her body ached everywhere. She had set her course, and she would stick with it. And in any case, she had nowhere else to go.

Slowly she became aware of a man sitting on a nearby footstool. He leaned his chin on a gold-handled cane and examined her with curiosity.

"You have changed, Ria," he said. "I don't remember your eyes tending so much to the violet. You are certainly much thinner, and your skin is brown as a farm girl's. But you remember me, don't you, my girl?"

He gave her an encouraging smile. Lizzie studied him carefully. He was a slender man of about thirty, with curly brown hair and cornflower blue eyes. And well dressed. He wore a fine gold vest and white shirt under a tailored blue coat that showed off his square shoulders to their best advantage. A cravat of the same color as his waistcoat was tied in an expert knot at the base of his crisp shirt collar. The only thing marring his handsome features was the tiniest bump on his nose—a souvenir, Ria had called it, of a day long ago when he had fallen out of a tree.

The man must be James Simpson. He met every one of Ria's

descriptions of her favorite cousin. His clothing proclaimed that he was still a dandy, and Lizzie wondered if he was also, as Ria had said, *"a wastrel and a wild one, the sort who was always getting into the kind of trouble that requires 'hushing up.'"*

Certain as she was, Lizzie was still anxious as she answered him, hoping fervently that her instincts were correct. "It appears you have not changed, James."

"That's a girl!" He laughed and slapped his knee. "You see, Geoffrey, it *is* Ria."

This last remark was addressed to a man standing on the opposite side of the parlor. Lizzie could just see him beyond the large round table in the center of the room, upon which sat a brightly painted vase of yellow roses.

Geoffrey?

The only "Geoffrey" that Ria had ever spoken of was her husband's younger brother. Ria had never met Geoffrey, but Edward had once described him as staid and scholarly, destined for a life in the church. Given this description, Lizzie had envisioned a short and nondescript man, perhaps wearing spectacles, shabbily dressed, and stooped from too much studying.

The man watching her from the fireplace was nothing like that. He stood tall and straight. His fine brown hair was clean and expertly cut; his short side whiskers trimmed a face that was pleasantly intriguing, if not classically handsome. His dark eyes, unguarded by spectacles, watched her intently. His black suit was far more understated than the royal blue coat James was wearing, but it was new and fit him well.

No, this could not be Ria's brother-in-law. And yet James had called him by his Christian name. Was there someone else in the family by that name? Was Lizzie not as well prepared as she thought she was?

She tried not to panic, telling herself he was probably not a family member. Ria had said that James had a wide circle of acquaintances. Given his easy and irreverent manner, he might well refer to his close friends so familiarly. But this thought did not reassure her. How many of James's social set might Ria have known? How many would Lizzie be expected to "remember"?

Lady Thornborough gently moved the hair back from Lizzie's face. "Ria, I have worried myself sick," she said. "I have no doubt you've taken some ten years off my life."

"Years off your life, Aunt?" James repeated. "I doubt it. You'll live to be a hundred; that's my wager."

Lady Thornborough gave him a disapproving look. "Do not speak of betting in this house. I will not have that shameful language used here."

James tilted his chin in acquiescence. Once his aunt had turned her attention back to Lizzie, he gave Geoffrey a smile and a wink.

The man by the fireplace did not respond to James's playful gesture. He was studying Lizzie—taking in every inch of her with an expression that hovered somewhere between curiosity and contempt.

Who was he?

Lizzie's face burned—whether from the fever or the man's unwavering scrutiny, she could not tell. She found herself riveted to his dark eyes as she tried unsuccessfully to regulate her breathing. Suddenly the room seemed quite close.

Lady Thornborough's cool hand on her forehead provided some relief. She inspected Lizzie's wound. "And now James has managed to run over you as though you were a dog in the street."

"It was not I," James protested.

Lady Thornborough ignored him. "Why were you alone and on foot, like a common servant? And why, in all these years, did you never contact us? Do you realize what agonies we have been through on account of you?"

"I will explain everything, Grandmamma," Lizzie said, trying out the word for the first time. It came off her tongue easily enough. Surely this was a good sign. She was Ria now, and she would soon discover what secrets this family was hiding. The Thornboroughs held the keys to her own history, one she had never dreamed of until the day she met Ria.

Kind, sweet, silly Ria. Given to impulsive actions, yet resolute once she'd made up her mind on something. Yes, they had shared those traits as well as their looks. When Lizzie had agreed to this plan so far away in Australia, she had thought it was a good one. Now that she was here, the magnitude of what she was doing washed over her with more force than her fever.

Lizzie fought to keep her mind in the present, here in this room. One misstep could be disastrous. But she was so hot. Her head was pounding and the room was beginning to spin again. She sank back heavily on the sofa.

"Ria!" Lady Thornborough cried.

"I'm terribly sorry...I did not plan to arrive this way..."

She was assailed by a rush of heat from her fever, followed by a rising tide of nausea. She closed her eyes, willing her stomach to stay put. Her plan was going well, she thought. Except for the fact that she had nearly gotten herself killed on the way in. And except for the man staring at her whom she could not identify.

The room was once again spinning dangerously out of control...

Geoffrey crossed the room and knelt beside her, his eyes

fierce. "Please forgive me—I can see you are not well, but I must ask you. I have to know. I have waited ten years with no news. What is this talk of Australia? Where is my brother?"

Lizzie pulled together a few remaining threads of thought. "You are my brother-in-law?" she asked dazedly. How tall he was. How striking. How different from what she expected. And yet...how like Edward. She could see it now, see vestiges of Edward's confident bearing and the way he looked at people— really observed them—when he was talking to them. How odd, she realized now, to think it could have been anyone else.

"But where is he?" Geoffrey demanded, as though he wanted to drag the information out of her. "What has happened to him?"

"He..." She shut her eyes. Now that she saw the resemblance, it was too painful to look at him. Too many memories. Her mind was drifting, she knew. All she could say was, "He...described you...quite differently."

She had just enough time to see his look of frustration and anger before the darkness enveloped her.

Chapter 3

Geoffrey strode briskly down the street, glad to be free to move and to think. The walk to his home was not far, and he had left his coachman with instructions to take Dr. Layton wherever he needed to go after he had finished tending to Ria.

Ria.

Geoffrey's pace quickened, giving much needed vent to his irritation. She'd been on the verge of giving him the answers he desperately wanted, only to lose consciousness before she could make any sense.

Dr. Layton had confirmed that Ria's injuries were not life-threatening, but that her fever could be. This pronouncement had set off a maelstrom of panicked activity. Lady Thornborough had been beside herself, dispatching all the servants on multiple errands, from preparing a room to heating water and bringing food—all the while commanding them to stop and give the doctor whatever assistance he needed. She'd been far from her usual steady calm, issuing contradicting orders and expecting them to be carried out with unrealistic speed.

Geoffrey was glad to be away from the chaos, if only for a few hours. He needed time to recover from the shock of the day's events. Time to reflect upon what they signified.

William's death last winter had forced Geoffrey to confront the question of the family estate and the title. He had been compelled to resign his small parish in order to assume the barony and all the responsibilities that went with it. He had been uneasy about doing this, not wanting to take the necessary step of having Edward declared dead for legal purposes. It struck him as traitorous to his brother's memory. He'd never been able to shake the belief that Edward was alive.

Geoffrey pulled up short and squeezed his eyes shut, fighting back the frustration that threatened to overtake him. Australia! Why had Edward gone to such a harsh and dangerous place? And where was he now?

He blinked and took a deep breath, considering the sad irony of his situation. His official period of mourning for both his brothers had ended weeks ago. If Edward's death was now confirmed, no one would expect him to begin the process again. But he knew he would be doing just that—in his heart, if not publicly.

As Geoffrey turned onto his street, he bowed a greeting as he passed those he knew, but did not stop. He moved swiftly up the steps to his town house and let himself in through the front door.

As he set down his hat on the small side table, he noticed that the silver tray for receiving calling cards was piled high. A stack of letters and notes lay next to it. He did his best to stifle a groan. All of society, it seemed, was taking the first opportunity to cultivate the acquaintance of the new Lord Somerville.

Geoffrey lifted one of the cards to read the name printed on it. His nose crinkled as a rich fragrance wafted up from the card, signaling the real reason for his sudden popularity. Women who had ignored him before were now angling to fill the position of baroness.

Did any of these elegantly engraved cards hold the name of someone who would understand his aspirations and share his dreams? Not likely. It had been difficult enough trying to find such a person among those willing to marry a clergyman with a modest living. Although the ranks of ladies desiring to become a baroness were considerably larger, Geoffrey had no illusions that the search would become any easier. Frowning, he returned the card to the pile. He would not have a marriage that was based solely on the dictates of society. He would take a wife whom he could truly love and cherish, as the Bible commanded. No woman who cared only for his title or his wealth could gain his heart.

He turned at the sound of footsteps to see Mrs. Claridge, the housekeeper, coming down the stairs. "Oh, Reverend, I beg your pardon for not opening the door. I didn't hear you come in."

Mrs. Claridge was a sturdy and sensible woman who had known Geoffrey since he was five. She should now be addressing him as Lord Somerville, but she preferred "Reverend," and he was glad of it. To be a member of the peerage was so contrary to his former way of life that he appreciated having someone who could remind him of his true calling. "You were listening for my carriage, I expect. However, I walked home."

He consulted his pocket watch. Six o'clock. Less than two hours since Ria had walked in front of his carriage and turned his life around completely.

Something in his tumultuous thoughts must have shown on his face, which Mrs. Claridge was an expert at reading. "Is everything all right, sir?" Before he could reply, she spotted the blood on his shirt and exclaimed, "What has happened? You've been injured!"

"I'm fine," he assured her. "The blood is not mine. I was... helping another."

"How very like you, sir," she said with pride. Her kindly face looked up at him with concern. "Shall I have tea brought up? You look as though you could use a bit of food, if you don't mind my saying so."

Geoffrey was sure the news of Ria's arrival would spread quickly, and he wanted Mrs. Claridge to be among the first to know. She had been loyally serving the Somervilles for over twenty years, and she deserved to be kept abreast of such important family news. "Would you be so kind as to bring it yourself in about half an hour? There is something I must relate to you, but I should like to have time alone first."

She gave him a sympathetic smile. "Of course, sir. I'll make sure you are not disturbed."

Mrs. Claridge bustled off to the kitchen as Geoffrey took the stairs to his study. He sank into a leather chair by the fireplace, glad to finally be alone. The weather was too warm for a fire, but this was still his favorite spot to relax and think.

He let his thoughts move freely, with memories of his brothers coming to him in random order. He recalled the games they'd played as children and the fights and childish arguments that sometimes ensued. It had often come down to two against one, but which two against which one had been different on any given day. Sometimes it was Geoffrey who was outnumbered. More often, it was Edward or William. Geoffrey had usually been the peacemaker.

As they grew older, William became more distant. He'd been caught up in learning his duties as a future baron. He'd spent hours in discussions with their father or accompanying him on visits to nearby landowners, enjoying the honors and privileges of being the heir.

Edward had been the first of the three to develop a keen interest in women. He had learned how to dance, how to behave at social events, and how to speak in ways that were pleasing to the ladies. And Edward had pleased them. They found his good looks and warm demeanor irresistible. Many a time Geoffrey had seen a young lady casting her gaze around a crowded ballroom, searching for Edward while trying not to appear to do so.

Geoffrey recalled their whispered conversations together, late at night, when Edward described the very interesting things he was discovering about women. Things their father certainly had never told them.

Edward could have had his pick from among every eligible lady in England. Instead, he ran off with William's betrothed. Their speedy courtship and subsequent elopement proved that Ria was just as headstrong and reckless as Edward.

William had been furious, of course. But Geoffrey soon discovered that the cause of his elder brother's anger was not lost love, but hurt pride and concern for his family's reputation. Within a few months he had simply found another woman upon whom to bestow his favor. William had evidenced the exact attitude toward marriage that Geoffrey detested: all that mattered was a lady's position in society and her willingness to play by its rules.

Geoffrey shifted in his chair, idly setting one foot on the iron grate and staring moodily at the dark fireplace. Women were still an enigma to him. He never had the smooth magnetism of Edward, nor William's cool detachment when it came to affairs of the heart. He was still trying to thread his own way.

Above all, his thoughts kept returning to Ria. Why did she appear in such reduced circumstances? If Edward was dead—God forbid—what would she expect from his family? Would she demand a widow's dower of some kind, even though there had been no prearranged settlement?

What had she and Edward been doing all these years? There was no telling how many days it would take for Ria to recover enough to give them a complete account. There was nothing to do but wait—and this was infinitely more frustrating than not being able to take action of some kind. Of *any* kind. Geoffrey stood and began pacing the room. The wait was going to be very hard indeed.

Chapter 4

Lizzie pushed her way up through deep, cold water, desperate to reach the shaft of sunlight that glittered down through the shadowy depths. *Reach the top, find air...*

She awoke with a start. Turning her head toward the source of the light, she realized sunlight had indeed been teasing her eyelids. It poured through a gap in the window curtains and bathed her bed in light and warmth. She breathed in deeply, drinking in the room's tranquil stillness. Gradually, the noise and confusion of her dreams faded.

Violent nightmares of storm and shipwreck were nothing new to Lizzie. She'd been plagued with them ever since Tom's death, as though some part of her were constantly trying to imagine her brother's terror when his ship was breaking up in that savage gale. The things she'd been through during the voyage from Australia had only increased their severity.

It had taken all of Lizzie's determination to set foot on a ship back to England, when Tom had been lost on a mere trip from

Sydney to Melbourne. Her fears had been justified. They'd been battered for days on end by rough seas and bad weather, and more than once Lizzie was sure she would meet the same fate as her brother.

Mercifully, the ship reached England, but not before many of its passengers had succumbed to illness. Day after day the burials at sea grew to a horrifying number. Lizzie had somehow kept well while aboard the ship, but in the end the influenza found her, too. She had been told the symptoms could come without warning, but she had not expected them to strike with such force. The fever had come upon her during her walk up from the docks and left her staggering in the street, close to fainting—only to be run down by a carriage.

Raising a hand to her temple, Lizzie pressed tentatively on the bandage covering it. The wound was still tender, but no longer throbbed in agonizing pain. She tried to piece together what had happened after the carriage struck her.

She had a vague memory of being taken up into warm, strong arms. After that, brief snatches of conversation had somehow drifted into her consciousness. She'd heard Ria's name. Then she'd been pulled back to her senses and found herself face-to-face with Ria's family.

That had been a revelation. Even in the midst of her pain and confusion, Lizzie had instantly recognized Lady Thornborough. The knowledge had burst upon her with startling clarity. Ria's descriptions of her grandmother had certainly been accurate, but Lizzie sensed a deeper reason for the connection. It was a curiously powerful sensation—as though she'd been waiting her whole life for a reunion with someone she'd never met.

Her encounter with James had followed a similar pattern. He had looked and acted exactly as Lizzie had pictured he would.

Only Geoffrey had taken her utterly by surprise.

The memory of Geoffrey brought Lizzie's heart to a quicker pace, much as the shock of meeting him had done. He was no retiring cleric; in fact, he could not have been more different from the man Lizzie had imagined. As she recalled his tall form, his powerful presence, his urgent questioning, another image pressed itself on her memory as clearly as if she were seeing it now.

There had been bloodstains on his shirt and collar.

Her blood.

He had carried her.

His arms had provided a warmth and comfort that she had not seen later in his eyes.

What must he have thought of her? She could easily guess. His look of contempt had been clear enough. There could be no doubt what he thought about the woman who had run off with his brother, and who now returned home in such an embarrassing state.

And yet, Lizzie reminded herself, the critical thing right now was not so much *what* he thought of her as *who* he thought she was. Somehow, despite such a bad beginning, she had convinced them all that she was Victoria Thornborough. She had managed to step into the life Ria had left behind.

But had she really done it? What if they had somehow discovered their error while she'd been lying here, unconscious? Although she was alone right now, a wooden chair close by the bed gave evidence that someone had been sitting with her. Had they been keeping vigil because of her illness, or because they planned to confront her as soon as she awoke?

Fighting a rush of fear, Lizzie pushed herself to a half-sitting position, trying to ascertain where they had brought her. Her bed was a large four-poster, with a counterpane of rose-patterned chintz. Through the partially opened window curtains she could see a cozy window seat lined with a deep red cushion. On the far side of the room stood a dressing table covered with an assortment of perfume bottles and a wooden box inlaid with ivory.

It was Ria's room, exactly as she had described it. Lady Thornborough must have kept it unchanged during all these years. More important, they had brought Lizzie here. Despite her illness, the accident, and a few missteps, they seemed to have accepted that she was Ria. Lizzie sank back into the pillows and let out a long sigh. She hoped this boded well for what was to come.

The bedroom door opened and a large, round woman entered the room. She was dressed as a servant, yet she settled herself on the chair beside Lizzie with an easy familiarity. "So you are awake at last," she said with a smile, which showed a small gap between her front teeth. "You gave us a hearty fright, collapsing like that the moment you come through the door."

Lizzie quickly reviewed the woman's features. Her rosy face was framed with graying hair just showing from underneath a white cap. A faded scar was barely visible under her left eye. Ria's former nursemaid had a scar like that. Whenever Ria used to vex Martha—which, to hear Ria tell it, happened often—the old scar would stand out clearly.

A surge of excitement ran through her, similar to what she'd experienced before she'd taken the risk of addressing James by name. It was like walking off a cliff and yet somehow knowing there would be a bridge there. It gave her a heady feeling, and she liked it. "You see that you have your Ria to fuss over again, Martha." Lizzie spoke in a higher tone of voice, copying Ria's inflections. She had always been an excellent mimic of the wide variety of accents she'd heard every day in London. It was a skill that she and Tom had once used to entertain themselves for hours—now her future depended on it.

The old servant beamed. "Bless my soul!" She took one of Lizzie's hands into her own, fleshy and calloused ones. "We were afraid we'd got you back after so many years only to lose you to a fever." She let go of Lizzie's hand to wipe away a tear. "I beg your pardon, miss. But we are so very happy to have you back."

"Are you really glad, Martha? And Lady Thornborough— Grandmamma—is she happy, too?"

"Why, of course!" Martha replied without hesitation. "She was naturally very angry when you left as you did, with no word and so much bad blood between you. But time heals all wounds, they say. I have often seen her sitting alone in the garden, all pensive-like, and I know'd she was a-thinkin' of you."

So Lady Thornborough had been pining for Ria's return. Half a world away, Ria had been longing for the very same thing. During the final weeks of Ria's illness, when she'd shared so much about her life with Lizzie, Ria had often voiced the fear that everyone here had forgotten her. Clearly she'd been mis- taken. The entire household, Lady Thornborough included, had been holding their collective breaths, hoping that Ria might someday come home to them. Tears stung Lizzie's eyes at the thought that Ria would never know.

Martha gave her a comforting smile, and then placed a hand on Lizzie's forehead and nodded in satisfaction. "Dr. Layton told us yesterday that the worst was past and you would be coming around again soon. All a matter of time, he said."

"Martha, how long have I been here?"

"Five days, miss."

"Five days!" Lizzie tried to sit up, but Martha gently restrained her.

"Easy, miss," she said. "You're not fully recovered yet."

Lizzie took note for the first time of the soft linen nightdress that fell loosely against her skin. She scanned the room for evidence of her clothes, but could find none. "Martha, where are my clothes?"

"Not to worry. Her ladyship has ordered four new dresses for you. Yours was too worn, and not in keeping with the latest fashion, she said."

These words were meant to be reassuring, but they only brought a new fear—that the precious heirloom Lizzie had come so far to return might now be lost. She had visions of her petticoat being sold cheap in the used clothing stalls, its new owner unaware that a diamond and sapphire bracelet was sewn into the waistband. She grabbed Martha's arm. "Who undressed me?"

Martha beamed complacently. "I did, miss. Just like in the old days." Martha leaned in close. "Rest easy," she said softly. "The bracelet has not been lost."

Relief washed over her. "I suppose you recognized it?"

"Indeed I did, miss."

"I have every intention of returning it to Grandmamma."

Martha patted her hand. "I know my Ria is an honest soul and would never keep what weren't hers. I'm sure her ladyship will be overjoyed when you give the bracelet to her."

"You have not already done so?"

Martha shook her head. "That was not my place." Her voice dropped to a conspiratorial whisper. "However, I did not want any of the other servants to find it, so I put it away for safekeeping. I put it in your secret hiding place."

Lizzie stared at her blankly.

Ria had described a hiding place at Rosewood, their country estate in Kent. That was where Lizzie would find the love letters that had been written years ago between Lizzie's mother and Ria's father—letters Ria insisted would prove Lizzie was a blood relation. But Ria hadn't mentioned a hiding place in the London house. How could Lizzie admit to Martha that she didn't know where it was?

Martha gave her a reproving look. "Come now. There have been many years and many miles gone, but you must remember that."

Was Martha deliberately testing her?

Lizzie gave her a coaxing smile, imitating the one Ria had often used to wheedle Edward into anything she wanted. "Martha, you are such a clever old thing. But you know I haven't the strength to get out of bed, and I would like to return the bracelet to Grandmamma right away. Would you be a dear and get it for me?"

Martha remained seated. "Her ladyship was crushed when you ran away. She will be too proud to say so, but she has wished for nothing else all these years but that her dear Ria would return to her." She gave Lizzie a deep, questioning look. "I do hope that you will not do anything to cause her more suffering."

Lizzie was taken aback by Martha's words. She had never in her life had servants, but she was fairly certain they did not question their employers in such a way. Did Martha suspect her of being a fraud?

No. For the moment she must assume that Martha was simply a faithful old servant who was secure enough in her position to chastise her charge. Especially one for whom she cared so much. "Martha, there are many things I must set straight. And

I will." She pursed her lips into an exaggerated pout. "Don't be such a weeping willow."

These last words, a common retort of Ria's, seemed to have the desired effect. The shade of doubt in Martha's eyes lifted. "I'll get the bracelet for you straightaway, miss."

Martha left through a door that most likely led to the old nursery. That would, of course, be the perfect place for Ria to hide something, Lizzie thought. She sighed. In her mind's eye she saw herself picking her way, rock by rock, across a rushing stream. One misstep and she would be carried away by the current.

The door to the hallway opened, and Lady Thornborough entered. The next step across that stream, Lizzie thought.

"You are awake. Thank God." She crossed the room to the bed. "Where is Martha? I instructed her to stay with you."

"Don't be cross, Grandmamma. I sent her on a small errand for me, that's all."

Martha reentered through the nursery door. "I'm here, my lady." She made a show of straightening the bedclothes, and quietly placed a folded white handkerchief into Lizzie's right hand as she did so. Lizzie guessed from its weight that the bracelet was wrapped inside.

Lady Thornborough placed a hand on Lizzie's forehead, just as Martha had done. "How are you feeling?" Lady Thornborough's hand was cool and dry, like a piece of parchment. But Lizzie found it soothing.

She took a deep breath. Just a few days before, her lungs would have been screaming in pain from the effort; now she felt only a whispering ache. "I feel as though I've just come up for air."

The old woman's brow wrinkled. "I beg your pardon?"

"I dreamed I was in the ocean, swimming upward but never able to break the surface."

"Do not talk of oceans," Lady Thornborough said sharply. "They have done nothing but separate people who should have been together."

Her words and her rigid exterior seemed to illustrate Ria's claim that her grandmother was harsh and unyielding. Ria might once have responded with an angry defense of her most excellent reasons for crossing those very oceans. But that was long ago, and Ria had gone to her grave with an unfulfilled desire for reconciliation. Armed with the knowledge Martha had just given her, Lizzie was determined to find a softer spot in Lady Thornborough's heart. She gave her a tiny smile. "Then I shall just say that I am much improved. And hungry, perhaps."

"Martha," said Lady Thornborough, "tell Cook that we are in need of her special broth."

"Right away, my lady." Martha hastened out of the room, closing the door behind her.

Lady Thornborough took the chair next to Lizzie's bed. "You know we are so very anxious to hear all about what has happened. Lord Somerville has been calling every day to inquire after you."

Lizzie frowned. *Lord Somerville.* That would be William, of course. As head of the Somerville family, he would naturally want to question her about Edward. No doubt Geoffrey had already filled him in on the particulars of her disgraceful arrival. She wondered if Geoffrey had been round to ask about her, and was suddenly quite anxious to know. She felt a particular urge to see him again—a need to explain why she had been in the street, and to thank him for his kindness in bringing her in, even if he seemed much colder to her later. What if he wished to have nothing to do with her? It was an unsettling thought. "I'm sure that *both* my brothers-in-law are desirous to hear everything," Lizzie said, in an effort to subtly draw out the answer from Lady Thornborough.

"Both...," Lady Thornborough repeated, clearly perplexed. A pained expression crossed her face, and she cleared her throat. "Yes, of course." The guilty way she looked away as she spoke seemed to contradict her answer.

It was disappointing, but really, not so surprising. After all, Geoffrey would have plenty of reasons for disliking his sister-in-law. His feelings toward her were based, Lizzie knew, on his belief that she was Ria. It was yet another obstacle that Lizzie would have to overcome. By taking up Ria's identity, she would also have to accept responsibility for all the hurtful things Ria had done.

The weight of so many lives pressed upon her. The joys and sorrows not only of her own life, but of Ria's and Edward's, too. She had thought she would be leaving behind her burdens in order to step into a new life. Now she realized she must carry the burdens of both.

Lizzie dropped a disheartened gaze to the ring on her left hand. Edward's ring. Ria had insisted she take it.

Lady Thornborough lightly touched the ring. "You and Edward *were* married, weren't you?"

"Oh yes."

"And Edward? Is he..."

For a moment, Lizzie could not answer. Two graves, side by side in a small churchyard at Bathurst, filled her mind's eye.

"Yes," she said at last with a shaky sigh. "He is dead." She contemplated the ring, thinking of the two people who had worn it before her, knowing their loss was beyond regaining.

After a few moments' silence Lady Thornborough said, "We were concerned when you appeared at our door in widow's weeds. But I refused to believe the worst until you confirmed it. Even though I did not wish you to marry him, I want you to know how deeply grieved I am about his death. I know how hard it is to lose a husband."

The words were simple, but heartfelt. Lizzie could see it in the old woman's eyes. She was offering both forgiveness and solace.

"Grandmamma...," Lizzie began. The word came out a little easier each time she said it. "I know I have behaved wickedly. But please understand that I acted out of love for Edward. It was not my intent to bring scandal upon the family."

"Intended or not, that is what happened," Lady Thornborough said. "But it cannot be undone now."

Lizzie's hand closed around the wrapped bracelet in her hand. She knew it had a sentimental value that was higher even than the worth of the precious stones. It had been a gift to Lady Thornborough from her husband on their wedding day. She held it out to Lady Thornborough. "There is perhaps one thing I can set to rights. I have wanted to return this to you for a very long time."

Lady Thornborough's hands trembled as she opened the small bundle. The cloth fell away, and the diamonds and sapphires sparkled in the light. "My bracelet," she murmured, her rigid exterior softening visibly. "I was sure you had broken it up and sold it years ago." She shook her head. "I cannot believe you kept it all this time."

Lizzie knew the words Ria wanted her grandmother to hear. She had practiced them many times during the interminable voyage from Australia. "I was unforgivably selfish to take this bracelet, but I hope that by returning it, you will find it in your heart to forgive me anyway. I took it because I was so afraid of being destitute, but Edward insisted that we would never sell it. And we never did. Somehow we always managed."

The same could be said for Tom, Lizzie realized. He had given everything to protect and care for her, working tirelessly in a harsh land to give her a new life. She would have no difficulty playing the part of a bereaved widow. She *was* bereft, her loss felt no less deeply because it was her brother and not a spouse. "He said he would be my provider," Lizzie found herself saying, "and he was."

And then, the tears came.

Lady Thornborough wrapped her arms gently around Lizzie, murmuring soft words of comfort. "You have come home, my dear child, and we will muddle through together."

She spoke with a tenderness that might have amazed Ria herself.

Lizzie let the tears spill, unheeded, that she had held back for far too long. In Australia, she'd been required to be strong, to soldier on as Edward, Tom, and finally Ria were taken from her. She'd had no time to grieve as she faced one tragedy after another.

The three people who had once meant the most in the world to her were gone. Lizzie clung to the woman now offering her comfort. This was her home now, she thought fiercely. This was her family.

Chapter 5

Geoffrey sat at his desk, trying to focus on the papers in front of him. As a board member of the Society for Improving the Condition of the Labouring Classes, he was responsible for arranging the dedication ceremony of the newest building, a block of flats in Spitalfields.

Normally such a task would readily consume his thoughts. After years of service as a clergyman, he refused to take up the dissolute and careless lifestyle that many of the peers were living. Having a title didn't prevent him from continuing to do at least some good in the world.

Today, however, despite his best intentions, all he could think of was Ria.

He could not forget her pale face as she lay unconscious on the sofa, nor the way he had been riveted to her violet-blue eyes when they had finally opened. She had been weak from fever and exhaustion, but Geoffrey thought he had seen a glimpse of the spirited woman who had captured Edward's heart.

He assured himself that his thoughts kept returning to Ria solely because he wanted information from her. He had to know what had become of Edward. Nearly a week had passed, and she had yet to regain consciousness. Geoffrey had spent most of that time consumed with worry. If she should slip away before telling him what had happened to Edward...

No. Surely the Lord is too merciful for that. He shook his head to clear his thoughts. He looked down and noticed his pen had left a blot of ink on the paper where his hand had been resting, unmoving. He quickly placed the pen back in the inkstand and wiped his hand on a cloth.

Mrs. Claridge entered the room. "I beg your pardon, sir, but Lady Thornborough is downstairs."

Lady Thornborough would not have come in person unless the news was either very good or very bad. Geoffrey dropped the cloth and rose from his desk. "Please show her up."

Geoffrey paced the room as he waited, praying that the news was good.

Lady Thornborough breezed through the study door ahead of Mrs. Claridge, not waiting to be announced. She crossed the room and took both of his hands in hers. She did not even bother with formalities but simply said, "Her fever broke last night. She's awake."

Geoffrey found himself exhaling a deep breath that he had not been aware he'd been holding. "Have you spoken to her?"

A shadow crossed Lady Thornborough's face. "Yes. We had quite a little chat."

"And?"

Lady Thornborough gently withdrew her hands from his and glanced around the room for a place to sit. Belatedly remembering his duties as host, Geoffrey motioned to a chair by the window. "Would you be so kind?"

Lady Thornborough seated herself, taking a few moments to arrange the folds of her gown. She looked up at him expectantly. "Won't you sit down, Lord Somerville?"

Geoffrey would have preferred to stand, to pace the room if necessary. Movement always helped when dealing with difficult matters. But Lady Thornborough appeared unwilling to speak until he was seated. With great effort he acquiesced and took the chair next to hers. "What other news do you have for me, Lady Thornborough?"

He did not have to elaborate. She would be perfectly aware that the question of Edward's fate was uppermost in his mind.

Her gray eyes held his. "I fear you already know what I have to tell you."

He did. He could see the pity written on her face. His last shred of hope on the matter was now gone. In spite of Lady Thornborough's uncharacteristic gentleness, pain shot through him as surely as if she had wielded a knife. "How did he—" Suddenly his mouth was parched, his voice dry and brittle. "When?"

"Nearly two years ago."

"Two years!" All his anguish about having Edward declared dead, and the man had gone to dust long ago. The absurdity of it was too painful even to contemplate.

"As to *how*," Lady Thornborough continued, "I do not have the particulars. Ria asked that we all be assembled together so that she need only tell the tale once."

"Is it really so bad, then?"

"I gather it is most unpleasant. In spite of the time that has passed, it is clear to me that she still suffers deeply."

Geoffrey tried to remind himself that he was not the only one mourning. It did not help. Whatever Ria was feeling, Geoffrey was certain he could match it. He was numb and nauseous at the same time, having both an urgent desire to run and a complete inability to move. A dull ache pulsed through every part of his body. "Oh, Edward," he moaned.

Lady Thornborough pulled a handkerchief from her reticule and gently held it to her nose. Somehow, through all of his warring emotions, Geoffrey was dimly aware of the scent of lavender wafting from it.

What could have possibly befallen his brother? All sorts of possibilities began to enter his head. A terrible accident, a mortal illness... "She gave you no clue?"

"None, I'm afraid."

"Were they really in Australia? Or was the fever making her confused?"

"They were in Australia. Like you, I am anxious to know how they came to be in such a wretched place." Lady Thornborough returned the handkerchief to her reticule. "Dr. Layton says she should be well enough to get out of bed within a few days. I will contact you as soon as she is able to receive visitors."

More days to wait. More interminable days. He would have preferred to get all the details quickly, rather than in this excruciating fashion.

"Lord Somerville, you must not think me unaware of the poignancy of our situation," Lady Thornborough said earnestly. "Although I am overjoyed at Ria's safe return, I am also deeply grieved at the loss of your brother."

Geoffrey could only acknowledge her words with a nod, not trusting himself to speak.

"You must be feeling alone in the world," Lady Thornborough went on. "However, even though Edward is dead, we can never forget the tie that has been so closely bound. You must always consider yourself a member of our family." Her gaze, though kind, held more than a trace of her usual imperious manner, an expectation that her wishes would be carried out.

Geoffrey searched for his voice. "You are very kind."

His response seemed to satisfy her—for now. She seemed to know better than to press him. She stood up, and Geoffrey did likewise, more out of thankfulness to be on his feet than from mere custom.

"I will trouble you no more for the present." The decisive, brusque woman Geoffrey knew was once again in evidence. She checked her reflection in the mirror over the fireplace and readjusted her hat before turning toward the door. "I must be going."

"I'm sure you are anxious to return to Ria."

"Indeed I am, although I must go to Regent Street first."

This pronouncement took Geoffrey by surprise. Regent Street had many of the more fashionable shops. It was odd to think Lady Thornborough would be shopping today.

"I must order new dresses for Ria. She has not brought back anything that is suitable for either the current fashion or her position."

Geoffrey paused in the act of opening the drawing room door. "Her *position*?"

"Yes. She is a young widow in half-mourning now. She must have clothing appropriate to this season of her life."

With more assurances that she would contact Geoffrey as soon as possible, Lady Thornborough left the room with as much speed and purpose as she had entered it.

Leaving Geoffrey to speculate over just what season of life Ria's return had put *him* in.

Chapter 6

Lizzie sat at the dressing table, looking at herself in the mirror, as Martha put the finishing touches on her hair.

Her face was looking fuller. The fever and the months of deprivation had been assuaged by rest, quiet, and so many bowls of Cook's special broth that she thought she might never care to eat soup again.

In a few minutes she would be going downstairs for the first time as Victoria Somerville. She certainly looked the part. The gown Lady Thornborough had bought for her was a deep gray silk with muted pinstripes. It was expensive, flattering, and perfectly suited to the occasion.

Her hair had been pulled up and curled into ringlets behind her head. A tedious process, but she knew Ria would have loved nothing better, and so she did her best to bear it patiently.

In the week that had passed since her fever broke, Lizzie had found it simple enough to be Ria. She spent most of her time resting, speaking to no one except Lady Thornborough,

Martha, Dr. Layton, and, occasionally, the young housemaid who cleaned Lizzie's room. The real challenges of her masquerade were just beginning—and the greatest of these would be facing the Somervilles. Perhaps she had been able to fool Lady Thornborough and Martha because they so desperately *wanted* to believe Ria had returned. William and Geoffrey were far less likely to be won over so easily.

Geoffrey must be a lot like William, Lizzie thought. Ria had described William as a dispassionate man with an implacable eye for detail. Apparently the man noticed *everything*. Lizzie had known before she even set foot in England that William could easily become suspicious of her if she spent too much time in his company. She now had the same concerns about Geoffrey. Many things about the day she arrived were hazy in her memory, but she could not forget how his eyes never seemed to leave her, how he seemed to be taking in everything about her—disbelieving, untrusting. Clearly, she would have to tread carefully.

As Martha placed a few last pins, Lizzie mentally reviewed every piece of information she could remember about the layout of the house and the names of the servants. Martha had confirmed that, yes, Mr. Harding was still the butler, and Mrs. Travers was still the housekeeper. And Cook (whose real name no one bothered to remember) was the same dear woman who had fed Ria far too many sugar cakes as a child.

Lizzie thought no one would be suspicious if she did not know the names of the lesser servants. It would be only natural that she could have forgotten these details, given Ria's reputation for flightiness and after so much time had passed.

She stood up, shooing Martha away. "I believe I am as ready

as I shall ever be." She was careful to speak with Ria's higher-pitched voice.

"May I say you look lovely, Miss Ria." Martha's hand flew to her mouth. "I beg your pardon, madam. Even though you are Mrs. Somerville now, I confess I will always think of you as Miss Ria."

Martha's words gave her pause. Martha seemed to have accepted her, and Lizzie hoped she would be able to rely on her help in the future. "I am glad you think of me that way. I would never reprimand you for that."

Martha's eyes twinkled, even as she gave a respectful nod of her head. "Indeed, madam."

Lizzie took one last look in the mirror before turning toward the door. Martha made as if to follow, but Lizzie held up her hand. "I would like to go down by myself."

Martha dropped a small curtsy. "Certainly, madam."

Lizzie stepped into the hallway. Now she would become truly acquainted with this house, not just from Ria's descriptions but from actually exploring it for herself. To her left would be Lady Thornborough's room and several guest chambers. Lizzie turned right, toward the staircase.

The rose designs in the wool carpet and on the wallpaper were all as Ria had described. Lizzie walked slowly, running one hand along the fine oak trim on the wall. She was still achy, but she was relieved to find she was steady on her feet.

Near the end of the passage, Lizzie found another object Ria had told her about—a lovely gilt-framed painting of a manor house in midsummer. Ria had loved the painting because it had been painted by her mother, who died when Ria was just three. For Lizzie, it provided the first tantalizing view of Rosewood—

the Thornborough estate where she would find the letters proving the truth of her parentage. She eagerly scanned the picture, taking in every detail. The stately home was depicted in a bucolic landscape of rolling hills and a profusion of blooming roses and lilacs. The canvas was warm and effervescing with life, painted with a sure hand of someone who clearly cherished the place. Lizzie was already in love with it, too.

Seeing that Martha stood at the bedroom door, watching her, Lizzie said, "Oh, Martha, how beautiful Rosewood is. I cannot wait to go there!"

Martha gave a wry smile. "You used to prefer to stay in town."

This took Lizzie by surprise. Ria had always spoken rapturously of Rosewood. Perhaps homesickness had elevated her appreciation of it. One of the endearing things about Ria was that once she had changed her mind about something, she categorically denied she had ever felt any other way. This was the tack Lizzie decided to take for her reply. "Nonsense, Martha," she said playfully. "I always said Rosewood was the most wonderful place in the world."

Her teasing brought a chuckle from Martha. "Indeed you did, madam."

Lizzie continued along the passage and made her way down the staircase to the second floor, where the library and the parlor would be located. She moved past a collection of family portraits, pausing in front of the one she wanted most to see: Sir Herbert Thornborough.

The painting showed a man of imposing stature, richly dressed, with fair hair and blue, almost violet eyes. He was brimming with confidence, the combination of a wealthy upbringing and a strong will. How different he looked from the one day, long ago, when Lizzie had seen him. He had been older and heavier then. Lizzie had not known at the time who he was.

Her father.

Lizzie had been only five years old on that day. She had forgotten the incident until many years later when she and Ria were comparing their family histories. This was the one childhood memory they'd both shared.

Lizzie had been standing outside the dry goods store owned by Sam Poole—the man she had always thought of as her father. She'd been idly watching the street while waiting for him to close up shop so they could walk home together. She saw a little girl, the same age as herself, coming out of the apothecary shop across the street. The girl ran over to Lizzie and excitedly asked her name. Before Lizzie could answer, Herbert Thornborough came rushing out of the shop. He took Ria by the elbow and said to come away, that they did not have time to stand in the street gossiping with shop people.

About that time, Sam had come out and drawn Lizzie close in a protective way, glaring at Sir Herbert as though he suspected the man might attempt to do her harm.

Ever since Ria had brought this meeting back into her mind, it had left Lizzie with conflicting emotions. Ria had said her father had gone frequently to that apothecary shop, claiming the man's ointment was the only thing that relieved his gout. The truth of the matter, Ria insisted, was that he must have gone there only to catch glimpses of Lizzie. He must have known who she was.

Why, then, had he shunned her when they were face-to-face?

Was she really the product of a love affair he'd had with another woman, even while his own wife was nursing his child?

Choking back a quiet sob, Lizzie stared at the man in the portrait, wishing she could find the answer there. She saw nothing but pride and self-satisfaction in those eyes, which were so very like her own—and so different from Sam Poole's. Sam had been a swarthy man, and Tom had grown to look just like him. But Lizzie favored neither Sam nor her mother, Emma, a melancholy, distant woman with soft brown hair and hazel eyes. Now she knew why.

"They are all assembled in the Rose Parlor, madam."

Lizzie nearly jumped at the unexpected sound of a gravelly voice. She turned to see Harding standing at her side. She had not even heard his approach. No wonder Ria had always been afraid of him. His manner was diffident, but Lizzie saw him trying to decipher the play of emotions that must have been going across her face.

"Thank you, Harding," she said archly. "I will be there presently." She spoke too haughtily, perhaps, but Harding's sudden appearance unnerved her. She had been less formal in her dealings with Martha, but she had to be careful to keep her guard up with the other servants. It was important, if she was to become Ria, that she address the servants in a manner befitting her station. Lizzie hoped her words conveyed to the butler that she would move at her own leisure, not his.

He nodded and gave a brief bow before turning away.

She made her way down the hall, stopping in front of the second door. She could hear the low murmur of voices. Despite her moment of bravado with Harding, Lizzie was aware of a cold lump of uncertainty growing in the pit of her stomach. She closed her eyes and breathed deeply. She had promised them a full account of what had happened in Australia, and she was prepared to give it—omitting a few significant details, of course.

She had so far been able to bluff her way in by her looks and by a general knowledge of the family. But how long could she keep this up? How long would it be until her ignorance of tiny details that Ria would know began to surface and alert the family that something was amiss? Lizzie hesitated, fighting a sudden urge to flee.

Then she called to mind a vibrant image of Ria. They had shared the days of hard work, the mundane evenings, the celebrations. She thought of the long hours they had spent together, talking about their families, their childhoods. She knew as much about Ria as one person could possibly know about another, as though Ria were indeed a part of herself. She had heard that twins often experienced this kind of bond. Ria and Lizzie were not twins, but they *were* sisters. Herbert Thornborough was her father. She would prove it.

These thoughts and resolutions circled in Lizzie's brain, pushing away the uncertainty. Anticipation coursed through her like a Thoroughbred at a race. She knew what she had to do, and she firmly told herself she had the ability to do it.

With a final shoring up of her resolve, she pushed open the parlor door.

Chapter 7

William was not there.

The only Somerville present was Geoffrey. He stood alone by the fireplace, in exactly the same position as when she had first seen him. He was looking at her now with a tightly guarded intensity, reminding Lizzie of a banked fire that requires scant fuel to become a blaze. With great effort, she turned her eyes from his and scanned the parlor again.

She had been barely conscious the last time she'd been in this room. Now, despite her preoccupations, she could appreciate how lovely it was. A large vase of roses sat on the round tea table in the center of the room, and Lizzie recalled how the scent of roses had been one of her first memories upon regaining consciousness here. Beyond the tea table, Lady Thornborough was seated on the sofa, and James was draped lazily across a wing-backed chair. Lizzie's heart eased a little at the sight of them— another sign, perhaps, that she was beginning to think of them as family.

But where was William?

"Ria," Lady Thornborough said, "there you are at last."

"I'm sorry to have kept you waiting, Grandmamma."

James rose and crossed the room to give her a kiss on the cheek. "Well, cousin, we never knew you to be on time. It's no more than we expected."

A smile rose naturally to her lips. "Whom do you suppose I learned that from?"

James grinned. "I can't imagine."

Geoffrey approached and gave her a stiff, somewhat formal bow. "I am happy to see you fully recovered...Ria." Again Lizzie had the sensation that he was working to hold some part of himself in check. "I confess it seems strange to address you by your Christian name upon our first meeting."

"Ah," said James, "but it is not really your first meeting, is it?"

No, it was not their first meeting. Geoffrey had picked her up off the street, bruised and bloody, before he even had an inkling of who she was. Or rather, who she was *supposed* to be. "You must call me Ria, of course," she said. "We are family, are we not?" Lizzie truly wished—as Ria herself had done—to gain his good opinion, to somehow repair the breach. She was well aware that it would not be easy. She held out her hand, hoping her smile wasn't wavering too much.

Geoffrey's touch was pleasant, immediately bringing Lizzie's mind back to the moment he'd taken her into his arms. The memory sent heat to her cheeks. She had an unsettling notion she might forever experience that visceral memory when she was near him. His expression was cold, however, and that, too, she had witnessed at their first meeting.

From this close vantage point Lizzie was struck once again

by the resemblance between Geoffrey and Edward. However, she would never have imagined Geoffrey was the younger of the two. He was far more reserved than Edward had been.

Edward had always displayed the easy grace and fine manners of a man raised in the best circles and used to making friends easily. But he was also a man unbridled, looking for adventure, discontented by the strict rules of society and welcoming to members of any class if they were honest and kind. His acceptance of Lizzie, despite her disgraced past, had been proof of that. It had made him a dear friend.

Geoffrey was showing her no friendliness, even though he believed her to be his brother's widow. He might well be bitter about Edward's departure from England on account of her. And what would he do if he knew she was *not* Ria? What if he truly knew the shameful woman she was? Lizzie's sins were far greater than anything Ria had done. She could only imagine once more that banked fire becoming a blaze and somehow destroying her utterly.

The complete subjugation of her life into Ria's was the only possible course. As Ria, she might at least find a way to make peace with this man. That would be her goal. She found she wanted to win this man's respect. Only as Ria did she have a chance of making that happen.

*

She is lovely, Geoffrey thought. He could not deny it. Her gray gown, supposedly the dress of a young widow, only served to accentuate her violet-blue eyes. The area around the cut on her forehead was still bruised and purple, but even that could not detract from her beauty.

Her skin was clear, but not pale. She had spent time in the sun. He dropped his eyes to inspect the cool hand in his. It was softer now than when he'd first held it. The calluses had begun to fade as Ria had been given time to rest and heal.

Her polite and collected demeanor was a sharp contrast to the last time he had seen her, barely conscious and flushed with fever.

She seemed to be working hard to make a good impression on him. "I must thank you for what you did for me." She smiled at him, no doubt attempting to win him over with her beauty, as she had done with Edward.

He steeled himself against its effects. He was not so easily taken in as his brother. He said, "You wish to thank me for running you over?"

"I was at fault, since I walked into your path," she responded with self-composure. "I'm grateful that you acted as swiftly as you did."

There was strength behind those riveting eyes—something Geoffrey certainly had not anticipated. He had a sudden flash of understanding of why his brother left everything behind to be with her. He was stunned as the thought came, unbidden, that he, too, might follow those eyes halfway around the world and not regret it.

Geoffrey quelled the thought with a stern reminder to himself of the hard facts. Edward had allowed his passions to get the better of him, and Ria had been just as guilty for leading him to do it. Perhaps they had been enthralled with the idea of relinquishing all else for the sake of "true love." In truth, what they had left behind were honor and propriety, and they had gained nothing for it but heartache and disaster. Geoffrey had many shortcomings, as he was well aware, but falling prey to foolish fancies was not one of them. He would not allow it to be.

He let go of her hand and stepped back.

Ria must have perceived the coldness behind his withdrawal. Undaunted, she straightened her shoulders and lifted her chin. He was utterly unprepared for what she said next. "William must still be very angry, I suppose."

Geoffrey took a sharp intake of breath. "I beg your pardon?"

"I hope he is not still bitter about what happened between us. I believe he knew as well as I that we would not be happy together. No doubt he is glad he married Annabel Harris instead."

Geoffrey stared at her.

Evidently she misunderstood the reason for his stunned expression. She said, "I know about the marriage. I read about it in the society columns."

Geoffrey threw a confused look at Lady Thornborough. "Did you not tell her what happened?"

"I thought it better to wait until today," she replied. "Ria has been so frail. I thought the news could wait until we were all together."

Ria looked back and forth between them. "What have you not told me?"

Lady Thornborough put a handkerchief delicately up to one eye. Even James cleared his throat and looked away.

Geoffrey knew it was his duty to say it. "William is dead, Ria. He died last summer of scarlet fever. I suppose you missed that tidbit in the society columns."

Ria moaned softly, bringing a hand to her chest. The apparent depth of her grief was more than Geoffrey would have expected, given her cavalier treatment of William all those years ago. Perhaps she was realizing that by not returning to England sooner, she and Edward had given up the opportunity for a grand title.

She swayed a little. Afraid she might faint, Geoffrey stepped forward and took her arm in his. Instantly he regretted the move. She was too close to him now, her nearness more powerful than he could have imagined. Her warmth radiated through the silk sleeve of her dress and spread like a thunderbolt through his body. Her bowed head came just to the level of his chin, and he found himself taking in the gleam of her blond curls. She smelled of fresh roses—a scent he had never found intoxicating until now.

Lady Thornborough held out a hand. "Come and sit down, Ria. You must be mindful of your health."

Geoffrey knew he should help Ria to the sofa, but he found himself unable to move.

James stepped forward and gently took hold of Ria's free arm. "Please. Allow me."

Ria released her hold on Geoffrey. As she moved away from him, all the warmth seemed to go with her, leaving him chilled and yet somehow freeing up his mind to work again.

He watched as James led Ria across the room to join Lady Thornborough. Even now, in a subdued mood, she moved with a grace that did not appear conscious or affected. He had always pictured Ria as a silly and headstrong girl. She had, after all, thrown away the opportunity to become a baroness in order to run away with a man whose prospects were far from certain. It was difficult to match that image with the woman in front of him. Perhaps maturity had been forced upon her by the events that had followed.

On the other hand, he reminded himself with a mental shake, given the wildly unorthodox way she'd arrived on Lady Thornborough's doorstep, perhaps she was not so changed after all.

When Ria was seated, she asked, "What has become of Annabel?"

"My sister-in-law preceded her husband in death by about twelve hours," Geoffrey said uncompromisingly. He'd been hit hard by these deaths, and he saw no point in trying to soften the blow for Ria.

Her mouth fell open in shock. "William *and* Annabel are dead?"

Lady Thornborough patted her hand. "I knew you would take the news hard, my dear. That is why we waited."

"William and Annabel are dead," Ria repeated quietly, as if trying to convince herself of the truth of it. She looked at Geoffrey, understanding dawning in her eyes. "*You* are Lord Somerville."

"That's right, cousin," James said. "He has been so for several months now."

"Several months?" Ria's eyes narrowed. "How could that be? You did not yet know what happened to Edward."

"It was a conundrum," Geoffrey acknowledged, unable to keep the sarcasm from his voice. "What to do about a missing baron? A man whom no one has seen nor heard from in ten years? A man who by all accounts was dead. What do you suppose I should have done?"

"Did you not even attempt to find him—to find *us*?"

"Would you like me to give you a detailed account of the time and money we spent searching for you? Shall I describe each painful step we took, searching towns, cities, and ships' manifests? Or will you have the decency to spare me on this point?"

"If only we had known," Ria said, her expression wavering between anger and compassion.

"You most certainly would have," Geoffrey returned, "*if* we had known where you were."

Ria dropped her eyes. "Yes, I suppose that's true." Her tone did not match the affirmation of her words.

"Do you doubt me?" Geoffrey demanded, irritated at being put on the defensive. After the hell he'd been through, he was not about to let this woman judge him. "Do you think I wanted this? Do you think I take pleasure in the title? I most certainly do not."

"That much is evident," James said. "I must say you are taking entirely too slowly to the benefits of your position."

Geoffrey ignored James's attempt to lighten the situation. He kept his gaze squarely on Ria. "Edward was already dead in the eyes of the law. Upon William's demise, there was nothing left to do but to make it official. It is not what I would have wished. But it was what I had to do. Duty comes first. You would benefit by remembering that in the future."

Ria's mouth set in grim determination. "I am fully aware of my duty. That is why I am here."

"Then do it," he snapped. After all the years that had passed without knowing what had happened to Edward, he thought he would go mad if he had to wait even one hour longer. "Tell us where you've been, and what has brought about Edward's death. And why, in all this time, you never *once* saw fit to contact us."

Chapter 8

R ia's gaze was locked on him now. The smiles she had given
him earlier had vanished.

James dropped into the wingback chair. "I do believe Ria
is willing to tell us everything, Geoffrey, if we will give her the
opportunity." He leaned forward and propped his chin on his
hands, looking at Ria as though he were at the theater and an
exciting play was about to begin.

Lady Thornborough motioned Geoffrey to another chair.
"May I suggest that you sit down as well, Lord Somerville? We
must allow cooler heads to prevail."

She phrased it as a request, but Geoffrey did not miss the implied
command. This was a woman who was used to being obeyed—
especially in her own home. Geoffrey did his best to suppress his
agitation as he moved to the chair she indicated. He chided himself
for allowing his anger to overrun the normally charitable aspects
of his nature. Patience was a virtue, but the high demands of the
previous weeks had caused him to run short on supply.

"I will begin with your question, Geoffrey," Ria said, her voice steady. "You asked why we didn't contact you. But we had. Edward and I did send word from Scotland that we were married."

"We never received such a letter," Geoffrey said.

She frowned. "I know that now. The letters must have gotten lost, or were never posted."

"You didn't post them yourself?"

"No. We were rushing to board the ship, and had no time. Edward gave the packet of letters to a man on the docks—a sailor from another ship, I think it was. He seemed to me a rather disreputable-looking fellow, but Edward gave him the letters and the money, and he said he would post the letters for us. For all we know, he may well have discarded the letters and pocketed the money for himself."

"Once again we see Edward's spectacular ability to make bad decisions," Geoffrey said. "Was that the only time you wrote to us?"

"Yes. We were stunned not to hear from you. We had left instructions where to reach us in Sydney. I suggested to Edward that maybe something had happened to the letters. I felt we should write again, but Edward was too proud. He said we would wait until we were properly established. He knew his family thought him incapable of succeeding on his own, and he wanted to prove them wrong."

"But, Ria, how on earth did you end up in Australia?" James asked. "You must tell us every detail."

"Of course." She took a deep breath. "Edward and I eloped to Scotland, as you all surmised, even without our letter."

James smirked. "Married by the blacksmith at Gretna Green, were you?"

"That is a vulgar expression," Lady Thornborough said archly. "James, you will mind your manners today, if only for one hour."

"I beg your pardon, Aunt," James said, although his eyes were still filled with mirth. "However, I believe a touch of levity can sometimes aid in the discussion of difficult subjects."

As if to prove his point, Ria laughed softly. "It's all right." She gave James an adoring look that, for some reason, Geoffrey found disconcerting. "In Scotland, of course, it would have been legal even if the blacksmith *had* done it. However, we were married properly—in the church, by special license." She looked pointedly at Geoffrey as she said those words.

"That is a comfort," Lady Thornborough said.

"Please continue," Geoffrey said, anxious to get to the meat of her story. "We thought we had traced you as far as Edinburgh."

Ria nodded. "We had originally planned to go to Liverpool and take a ship to America. But we met a man who convinced Edward he could find better opportunities in Australia. So we left Edinburgh on a ship bound for Plymouth. From there we boarded a ship to Australia."

James leaned forward. "Did you plan to take the *Sea Venture* from Liverpool? That ship sank and all aboard were lost. When we never heard from you, we began to fear you had been aboard. Your names were not on the ship's manifest, but we thought you might have used an alias."

"I'm glad we were not on that unlucky vessel," Ria said with a shiver. "We might have been, if we'd kept to our original plan." Again she looked pointedly at Geoffrey. "I suppose Edward made the *correct* decision in that instance."

Geoffrey would not respond to the goad. He would keep on

the offensive. "I'm guessing it is true, however, that you were not using your real names."

"That is true. We were, in fact, traveling under the name of Mr. and Mrs. Smythe."

"Smythe?" James smirked. "How original!" But upon receiving a cold frown from Lady Thornborough, he said no more.

"It served our purpose," Ria said. "When we arrived in Australia, we met a man by the name of Mr. McCrae. He owned a large sheep farm in New South Wales, just beyond the Blue Mountains. He immediately offered Edward a position. They are so very short of free workers there."

"I'm sure they are," James said. "As I understand it, most of the men over there are convicts. Or ex-convicts. The *taint* and the *stain*."

Lady Thornborough sniffed. "To think that the granddaughter of a knight and the son of a baron should take it into their heads to form associations with the criminal classes."

Geoffrey bristled. Years of working with the lower classes had taught him they were not "criminal" by nature. Many a good man was forced into disreputable acts owing to the grinding forces of poverty and the willful blindness of those more fortunate.

"Are you telling me you did manual labor on a farm?" James said, incredulous. "How on earth did you survive?"

"It was difficult at first," Ria acknowledged. "Perhaps more for me than for Edward. He really threw himself into it." With a frosty look at Geoffrey, she added, "He was determined to succeed."

"No one ever accused Edward of lacking in determination," Geoffrey said. His brother was not lazy by nature, but he had been brought up in such ease and luxury that Geoffrey still had a hard time imagining him at work on a sheep farm.

"Eddie soon became one of Mr. McCrae's most trusted hands. He frequently traveled the road over the mountains, taking wool to Sydney and bringing back supplies. It was an important job." She paused. Her eyes closed briefly, her face pinched with pain. "It was dangerous, too. On one of the trips, they were met about halfway through the mountains by bushrangers. In England we would call them—"

"Highway robbers," James finished for her.

Ria nodded.

"Edward was attacked by bushrangers?" Geoffrey asked. He had imagined Edward's death might be due to accident or illness, but Ria's tale was tending in a much different direction.

"Three of them." She took a shaky breath. "And that was Edward's last trip across the Blue Mountains."

*

For a moment, nobody breathed. The silence in the room was palpable. It seemed even to overpower the bustling street sounds wafting through the open windows.

Geoffrey was watching her so closely that Lizzie thought he might bore a hole right through her. "Are you telling us Edward was *murdered*?"

"I do not believe they intended to commit murder. They would have taken the money and gone, leaving the men tied up, to be found by other travelers on the road. But they didn't plan on the way Eddie and Tom would fight back. They—"

"Wait a minute," James broke in. "Who is Tom?"

"Tom was another of the ranch hands." She did not add,

Tom was Edward's best friend. The friendship the four of them had shared was closer than many families. It was precious, and for her own sake, Lizzie wished to speak of it as little as possible. "The bushrangers thought they had an easy mark. They were all on horseback, and Eddie and Tom were driving a bullock dray."

Perplexed, Lady Thornborough said, "I beg your pardon?"

"A bullock dray is a very slow-moving oxcart," Lizzie explained. "There was no way they could outrun the men on horses. However, Eddie and Tom were not willing to be parted from their money and their goods so easily. Shots were fired, and there was much confusion. At the end of it, Edward was..."

"Dead," Geoffrey supplied, his voice flat.

Lizzie shook her head. "Not dead. But he was grievously wounded."

She did not need to draw them a picture. She knew they could well imagine Edward bleeding on the dry ground. Geoffrey's face contorted, as though he felt his brother's suffering.

No one spoke. Lady Thornborough put one hand to her heart and held a scented handkerchief to her face with the other. The clock ticked loudly in the silence.

"Go on," James encouraged gently. "What happened next?"

"When he saw that two of his fellows were dead, the third bushranger got on his horse and raced away."

"Edward and this man Tom killed two bushrangers?" James's voice was filled with admiration. "Incredible."

Geoffrey's hands clenched. "What happened to Tom?"

"He was injured, too, but he managed to get Edward onto one of the horses, and rode to the farm as quickly as he could. Eddie was in a bad state. He was bleeding profusely from his left side. Tom had been hit in the thigh and nearly fainted along the way from loss of blood. But he was determined to bring Eddie back."

"Why did Tom take him to the farm?" Geoffrey asked. His voice was sharp, holding an edge of accusation. "Surely it would have been better to go to town for medical help?"

"That was what Tom wanted to do. But Edward insisted on going home."

"The fool!" Geoffrey stood and began pacing the room. "He may have brought about his own demise." He glared at Lizzie. "What kind of man is this Tom? Why didn't he insist on the proper course of action?"

Lizzie glared back. "I believe he did the right thing."

Geoffrey made a scoffing noise and continued pacing.

"There was a man on the farm who had medical skill," Lizzie said, her voice defensive. "He tended to their wounds admirably. But he confirmed what Edward and Tom already knew—that it was futile. No town doctor could have saved him." Lizzie wanted to make Geoffrey understand what an honorable man his brother was. "Edward's greatest desire was to get home so he could say good-bye. There was never a man so devoted to his wife." Tears stung her eyes.

"Yes, we can see you loved him, dear," Lady Thornborough said, patting her arm gently.

Geoffrey halted his pacing. "We *all* loved him," he said. "The fact remains that if you had not taken Edward away from England, he might still be alive today."

Lizzie had known there would be a possibility of this accusation, but that did not lessen the sting when it came. She stood up. "Tell me, *Lord Somerville*," she said, placing wry emphasis on his title, "how does it follow that Edward would be alive today if he were here? William never left England. I suppose he had the best doctors money could buy. But he, too, is dead." She stopped, gasping for breath. She was unused to heavy corsets, and finding air was difficult.

"Ria, you must sit down," Lady Thornborough ordered. "You will make yourself ill again."

But Lizzie would not sit down. She advanced toward Geoffrey. "Edward was determined to go to Australia. He knew the hard work it would entail—and the risks. He believed it was the way to build a new life. How many men would face any obstacle, and go to the ends of the earth for love?"

"I certainly have never flung myself off the map for someone else," James interjected. "It sounds terribly uncomfortable."

"The ends of the earth," Geoffrey repeated with scorn. "For love. What foolishness."

At this moment, the memory of Ria and Edward was so vivid that Lizzie could practically see them in the room. How many times had she observed them with their heads bent together, speaking low, smiling and whispering words only for themselves? They had a love few people find in a lifetime, and Lizzie would defend their actions with all her might. "How many people can truly say they are happy? How many women can say they are married to the man they love, desperately and passionately, and that her husband *worships* her?" She used the word deliberately, and was perversely glad to see Geoffrey scowl in response. "It's all very well for you to pronounce judgments. You were not there. You were here in England with your books. What do you know about true love?"

Geoffrey reached out and gripped her shoulders so tightly that she was forced to bite back a cry of pain. "I can see you know all about my life," he said caustically. "You also claim to know about *duty*. Well, let me tell you something about that. If a man truly understands his duty, he will not neglect it for something so fleeting as romantic love."

"Lord Somerville," Lady Thornborough remonstrated. "You are hurting her."

Geoffrey released his hold, but Lizzie's arms continued to burn from his touch. She reached up instinctively to rub the spot where his hands had been.

"I apologize for hurting you," he said. "I do not apologize for what I said."

"Nor do I," Lizzie shot back defiantly. She had wanted this meeting to go well, to show Geoffrey he could be proud of his brother, to find some way to reconcile him to what had happened. But she could see there was no point in further discussion.

His judgmental comments about Tom angered her, too, and made her decide that there was one more thing she would not tell him.

She would not tell him that her own brother was dead because he had gone after Edward's murderer.

Chapter 9

For the second time in as many weeks Geoffrey found himself marching away from the Thornborough home, his thoughts a bundle of agitation about Ria. He was overwhelmed with an urgent need to escape, to find a quiet place to sort out his tangled thoughts.

He had left as soon as propriety would allow, after assuring Lady Thornborough that, yes, he would return again. But truly, there had been nothing more to say. His brother was dead, and Ria, though heartbroken, was unrepentant. Her years in Australia had taught her nothing.

Sorrow and shock buffeted him, as did the gut-wrenching knowledge that his brothers were gone from him forever. He had no other family now. His last, tenuous connection to his long-lost brother was this woman to whom he was legally bound as a sister, and yet how could he bring himself to forgive her for all she had done?

Forced to stop at a busy street corner, he waited for a break in the stream of carts and carriages, still pondering their acrimonious exchange about love and duty. While he stood there, a crossing sweeper boy approached him. "A penny clears the path for you, good sir." The boy couldn't have been more than twelve. His face was black with dust and his clothes were filthy. He held a battered broom in one hand; the other was outstretched for money.

Geoffrey was more than capable of making his way across the street without help, but he had a desire to help the lad. He reached into his pocket and gave the boy double what he asked. To cover his act of charity he said sternly, "Quickly, if you please."

The boy's face lit up. "Yes, sir!" Imitating a soldier, he saluted and added, "At the double!" He dashed into the street, pushing his broom expertly, dodging horses and vehicles, clearing a path through the debris and animal dung.

While Geoffrey waited, a carriage pulled up next to him and a woman's shrill voice cried, "Lord Somerville! Is that you?"

He knew that voice. It was loud enough to be heard in three counties. It belonged to Lady Cardington—one of the many fine matrons with marriageable daughters who had been hounding Geoffrey since his return to London.

A comparison arose in his mind between Ria and Lady Cardington's eldest daughter, Lucinda. She was a wan young lady, pleasant enough, but painfully awkward in polite society and completely pliable to her mother's wishes.

The exact opposite of Ria.

Geoffrey pushed these thoughts from his mind. He acknowledged Lady Cardington with a bow, even as he regretted having accepted the street sweeper's services. As they exchanged the standard greetings, he was grateful for the litany of civilities that crowded everyday life. It prevented him from having to think of anything genuine to say.

He had a dim hope that a few words would be enough, and that Lady Cardington would not linger. However, he resigned himself to the inevitable when she signaled to her footman to help her descend. She would speak to him further, and he, being a gentleman, had no choice but to remain.

Getting Lady Cardington down from the carriage was no easy feat, for she was a portly woman. Geoffrey was impressed by how smoothly her footman managed it. No doubt he'd had a lot of experience. Geoffrey had never seen a woman who was so large and yet so constantly in motion.

Once she was set down, the footman closed the carriage door and retreated. Lady Cardington smiled at Geoffrey. He suppressed a grimace, knowing what was to come.

"How fortunate that I should see you, Lord Somerville! I have not yet received your reply to our invitation for the charity gala. I do hope you have had an opportunity to consider it?" The loose folds under Lady Cardington's chin wiggled as she nodded her head up and down.

"Indeed I have." Geoffrey served on the board of directors for the organization that would profit by this gala. His involvement most likely influenced Lady Cardington's choice, rather than the worthiness of the cause. She was looking for another chance to parade her daughter in front of him.

"I apologize for my delay in responding," Geoffrey said. "I have been somewhat deluged of late."

Indeed, *deluged* was the correct word. Ria had come upon him like a sudden storm, and he found himself without shelter from the flood of her effects.

"So I hear." Lady Cardington's look turned confidential, and she lowered her voice. "Is it true that the widow of your brother Edward—God rest his soul—has returned to London?"

Her words stunned Geoffrey. He had known there would be gossip, of course, but had little realized how quickly it would spread. Lady Cardington had used the word *widow*, so the reason for Ria's return was already known.

There was no point in denying it. He had no doubt everyone would soon know the truth for certain. "Yes, it is true."

"Please allow me to express my deepest condolences on your loss." Lady Cardington's face twisted as she did her best to emulate grief.

Geoffrey was not fooled. The lady must be overjoyed at this news. It removed any lingering doubts about his standing in the peerage. Most likely she would press her daughter's suit even harder. The emphasis on social status and the cold-blooded marriage market that was known as London's social season sickened him. "Thank you, Lady Cardington. You are very kind."

"Of course, I am so relieved to hear that Mrs. Somerville has returned safely."

Geoffrey had not thought of Ria as "Mrs. Somerville" until now. It was disconcerting to think that now he must be forced to hear that appellation whenever someone made mention of her—which was bound to be often. He cleared his throat and managed to say coolly, "Yes, we are all thankful to divine Providence that she has come home."

"What a time she must have had in that wretched, uncivil place!" Lady Cardington's jowls wagged as she shook her head. "And to lose her husband, too. But am I right in understanding that some time has passed? I have heard that she is nearly out of mourning."

"Yes. It has been nearly two years since..."

He could not bring himself to finish the sentence. For once, he thought he saw a glimmer of genuine sadness in Lady

Cardington's face. A tear glistened in her eye, and she gave him a sympathetic look. Perhaps social climbing had not managed to wholly squelch her more tender instincts.

In an instant it was gone. "I have, of course, added Mrs. Somerville to the invitation list for the ball," she said, as though he would be glad to hear this.

Ria at the ball? In society? "She has been ill," Geoffrey said. "Despite the time that has passed, she still mourns her husband deeply." There could be no doubt of that, Geoffrey added to himself, feeling an odd pang as he remembered the way she'd spoken of Edward.

"She cannot sequester herself forever. She is still young. Getting out can only do her good."

Geoffrey suspected that once again Lady Cardington was covering her more selfish plans under the guise of doing good. She might want to ask Ria all manner of impertinent questions about her life in Australia.

"I am not the only one who thinks so," Lady Cardington added. "In fact, I have heard that she has also been invited to Lord Beauchamp's ball at the end of the month."

Apparently no one in London had wasted any time in issuing invitations to the exotic new arrival. For a moment he was almost sorry for Ria, knowing the intense scrutiny she was about to undergo.

With this realization came the clear certainty that he must speak to her again soon, before people like Lady Cardington could get hold of her. Perhaps he could give her some guidance— help her navigate the waters that were more treacherous than any ocean. Lady Thornborough might have the foresight to offer similar advice; nevertheless, Geoffrey felt he had firsthand knowledge to offer in a way that the long-established society matron did not.

As he reflected on these things, Geoffrey concluded that he must be at Lady Cardington's charity gala for the same reason, and told her he would be most honored to attend. Having been thus appeased both in her curiosity about Ria and her desire to bring Geoffrey to her home, Lady Cardington lost no time in departing.

As he watched the carriage pull away, Geoffrey tried once more to place his thoughts about Ria into some kind of coherent order. Trouble was, she crowded his thoughts so completely that finding any way to arrange them was nearly impossible. Something in her look and her manner kept perplexing him. She seemed almost to be two separate people, with her defiant pluck and self-reliance warring against something more vulnerable and uncertain.

Hadn't he been going through something of the same thing himself? He'd been pulled from the country backwaters into the pressures and expectations of the peerage. He knew he'd been the subject of endless discussion and speculation. Perhaps he understood Ria better than he had at first believed.

He still took issue at many of the things she had said. And yet, how could he not extend Christian charity to a member of his own family?

Her marriage to his brother had bound them together. He should find a way to help her in her new life. A few minutes ago he had left in anger, wishing only to put distance between them. Now he realized he wanted very much to see her again—and soon.

There were still plenty of reasons why to be sorted out. But he would have to trust to the Lord and go one step at a time.

Chapter 10

"Ria, my dear, are you sure you are feeling well?" Lady Thornborough was studying her from across the breakfast table. "Shall I call the doctor?"

Lizzie set down her fork, her food untouched on the plate before her. She was brooding over yesterday's meeting with Geoffrey. Although Lady Thornborough had attributed her listlessness to a physical complaint, it was merely an illustration of her vexed heart. "I'm fine, Grandmamma. A doctor will not be necessary."

The butler entered, carrying a silver tray with a small stack of letters on it. Still keeping a concerned eye on Lizzie, Lady Thornborough scanned the letters before choosing one to open. A footman hovered at Lizzie's elbow with more tea, and she nodded at him to refill her cup. To allay any further questioning from Lady Thornborough, Lizzie picked up her fork and made another effort to eat.

She could not stop thinking of yesterday's meeting. She had defended Edward and Ria as passionately as if she had truly lived their life, not merely viewed it from the vantage point of a friend. Was she truly losing herself so completely in the role of Ria? It was her goal, and she should be relieved that it was coming to pass. Yet it left her anxious and unsettled.

The eggs were no doubt cooked to perfection, but they were not sitting well in Lizzie's stomach. She gave up all attempts at eating, and settled for a sip of tea. She would have loved a more bracing cup of coffee, but Ria had always abhorred it and so Lizzie made do with the tea.

Her lackluster movements were not lost on James, who was sitting beside her. "You are looking rather peaked this morning, cousin. I've noticed that Geoffrey has that effect on people."

He *would* bring it up, Lizzie thought darkly. Of course he would. Lizzie had gone straight to her room after Geoffrey's abrupt departure, requesting to be left alone to rest. James and Lady Thornborough had complied, but Lizzie suspected neither of them was going to let the matter rest for long.

Sure enough, Lady Thornborough looked up from the letter she was reading and said, "For once, James has gone to the heart of the matter. You are distressed at the harsh words you exchanged with Lord Somerville yesterday."

What had truly distressed Lizzie were Geoffrey's callous words. "You heard what he said yesterday about Edward!" she exclaimed. "How could I let his remarks go unchallenged?"

"You must remember that he has just learned of his brother's death," Lady Thornborough remonstrated. "His grief is still fresh. I have no doubt he will see things differently in time, and regret his bitter words. As will you." She reached out to pat Lizzie's hand. "You must mend the rift that is between you. He is your brother-in-law, after all, and you must not forget how important he is."

"Important? Do you mean because he's a peer?"

"Yes. You have married into a titled family. Even as a widow, this will help you in your return to society." She indicated the letter in her hand. "You have already been included in the invitations."

"Invitations have arrived for *me*?" Lizzie asked incredulously. "How could that be?"

"The news of your return has already spread all over town." Lady Thornborough looked pointedly across the table at James as he calmly dropped a lump of sugar into his coffee, his face a picture of innocence. "Therefore, we must act. If you feel strong enough, I should like for you to accompany me today on a few morning calls."

Morning calls. Ria had enjoyed such visits, but to Lizzie it sounded like little more than trotting around from house to house for short, meaningless conversations with pompous society women. Lizzie knew she might be called upon to do this, but she had hoped it would not be so soon. "But I do not know these women," she objected.

"Precisely. It's time you did. Lord Beauchamp's ball is just a fortnight away, and things will go more smoothly for you if introductions have already been made."

Lizzie's earlier unease was now erased by alarm. Morning calls were one thing, but a formal ball was another matter altogether. She had expected her status as a widow would delay her having to appear at the grander social events. She needed time to establish herself, to learn the finer points of living as a woman of high status. The sooner she went out, the more likely she would be to make some gaffe that could give her away. "But, Grandmamma," she protested, "I couldn't possibly go out so soon."

"I know what's troubling you," Lady Thornborough said.

"You are concerned that others will feel there is some impropriety involved. However, Edward has been dead for nearly two years. No one can accuse you of not spending enough time in mourning." Her look was sympathetic, despite the pragmatism of her words. "It is perfectly respectable for a young widow to go back into society after such a space of time."

"Not so young, Aunt," James put in. "She is eight and twenty."

"There is still time for her to make a good match."

A match? As in marriage? Lizzie's teacup clattered loudly as she set it down with a shaky hand. She was most certainly never going to marry. So long as she was Ria, she would not need to. She would have Ria's inheritance to support her, and marrying for love was out of the question. Her heart was sealed in that matter.

She would remain the grieving widow, and that would be her unassailable protection against any pressure or argument. "Grandmamma, I will never remarry," she declared. "It would be untrue to Edward's memory."

Lady Thornborough's expression was kind, but unyielding. "You need to view your circumstances with a clear eye. You know the Rosewood estate is entailed to James. You cannot live there forever."

"She can stay there as long as she wants," James said. "I have no objection. And besides, it is still your home, too."

"So you see, the need is not really so pressing," Lizzie said.

"I am only speaking of taking the first step. You need time to rebuild your reputation. Your actions ten years ago tarnished the reputations of both our families. You must allow others to see the responsible woman you have become, and that you are living up to your good breeding."

Good breeding. The words pierced Lizzie's heart. "I will think on it," she said quietly.

Her attempt at equivocation did not escape Lady Thornborough. "There is no time to waste," she said. "The season is already half over. If you make some appearances now, you will increase the probability of securing a good match in the future."

Lizzie looked at James, trying to judge whether appealing to him might help her cause. He gave her a brief but understanding smile before turning to his aunt. "I must say that all this talk about making matches is beyond tedious."

"That would explain why you are five and thirty and not yet wed, I suppose?" Lady Thornborough said dryly.

"No, it is because I have been pining all these years after Ria." He took Lizzie's hand and gave it a gallant kiss. Despite her worries, Lizzie smiled.

"You may stop your pandering," Lady Thornborough huffed. "You are fooling no one."

"You are right, as always, Aunt," James said with a playful gleam in his eye. "However, since I can fool no one, I shall almost certainly never marry. It seems there must be a good amount of fooling people in order to make a *good match.* Isn't that right, Ria?"

Lizzie was startled by this. Was James making some kind of veiled reference to her deception? He was giving her a frank appraisal, looking as though he genuinely expected an answer to his rhetorical question. For a long moment she stared at him, unable to speak, wondering if he had somehow worked out that she wasn't Ria.

No, she decided. Even James would not speak in such a light and teasing way if he intended something more serious. She touched a finger to her chin, an imitation of one of Ria's gestures. "I cannot think what you are talking about, James. Eddie and I *never* kept secrets from one another."

The laugh lines around James's eyes crinkled as he smiled broadly. "Undoubtedly." His reaction gave Lizzie a measure of relief, although he held her gaze for a moment or two longer than was strictly necessary. He leaned back in his chair. "In any case, I *hope* I shall never marry. When I enjoy the company of so many ladies, why should I settle for a lifetime with just one?"

Lizzie reached for her tea, grateful that his words had taken the focus of the conversation off her. Her reprieve was cut short, however, by James's next remark.

"Unfortunately, I do not think I would make the best sort of husband for our dear Ria. She needs a man with a title and a good position. A man who can guide her with a firm hand... someone like Geoffrey, for example. In fact, she *ought* to marry Lord Somerville."

Lizzie nearly choked on her tea. She set down her cup, coughing. James gave her a gentle pat on the back.

Marry Geoffrey? It was unthinkable. The man was cold and hard and took all those ideals of "duty and honor" to the extreme. He blamed her for the death of his brother. More provoking was that he blamed *Tom* as well.

And yet...

Could Lady Thornborough be right—that Geoffrey had only been lashing out in grief and pain? Was he really so intractable as she imagined, or was there a better man beneath that anger?

Images arose in her mind of the first day she had seen Geoffrey. The way he had carried her, the blood on his shirt, the cool cloth on her forehead that must have been administered by him.

Lizzie brought her napkin to her mouth, glad her coughing

fit gave her the excuse to cover the blush that was slowly spreading up her face.

Lady Thornborough said, "Don't be ridiculous, James. She could never marry Lord Somerville. It is against the law."

"Against the law?" Lizzie rasped. The blood that had been spreading pink across Lizzie's cheeks now began to drain from her face. "How so?"

Lady Thornborough gave her an exasperated look. "You know the law says a widow cannot marry her brother-in-law."

"Oh. Yes, of course. I had…forgotten," she stammered. *Forgotten that she was Ria, forgotten that, therefore, Geoffrey was her brother-in-law.* How utterly stupid she was to let thoughts of this man put her in such a turbulent state.

"It seems to me, Aunt," said James, "that the law is contrary to biblical precepts."

If Lady Thornborough had not been such a woman of unflappable poise, her jaw might well have dropped upon hearing this pronouncement by her nephew. She looked sternly at him. "And what, pray tell, do you know of biblical precepts?"

"I'm no scholar, like Geoffrey, of course," James acknowledged. "But every week he takes me to lunch and tries to convert me to better ways. At the same time, I try to subvert him to more wicked ways. We both enjoy ourselves immensely, although neither of us is likely to attain our objective." He picked up his toast and began to spread orange marmalade on it. "Nevertheless, dining with him every week has caused me to learn a few things. I distinctly remember a passage about marrying one's brother's widow and raising up seed."

"Don't be vulgar, James."

James allowed a sly grin to cross his face. "It's biblical, Aunt. How can it be vulgar?"

Lady Thornborough had no answer to this.

James passed the toast under his nose and inhaled gently, taking in the tart fragrance of the marmalade in a way that struck Lizzie as almost sensual. He popped the toast into his mouth and chewed it with undisguised satisfaction.

Lizzie could see why Ria had adored her cousin. He approached everything in life with humor and zest. He had the same lighthearted playfulness that she had adored in Ria. Wouldn't it be wonderful, she thought, if she could tell James the story of how she and Ria had met? He would take immense pleasure in the sheer improbability of it. She regretted that she would never be able to fully confide in him.

"Of course, the idea of marrying someone out of obligation is simply not appealing," James went on. "Even if it were our charming Ria. I shall wait until perfect love falls upon me. Or knocks me over."

"Do not wait too long," Lady Thornborough advised. "You have a duty to marry and produce an heir."

"I suppose I shall have to give in sometime," he replied with an exaggerated sigh. He lifted his cup as though raising a wineglass for a toast. "In the meantime, I propose that we live in the present and make ourselves *merry*, rather than worrying about whom we shall *marry*."

Lizzie found herself trying to hide her smile from Lady Thornborough's disapproving eyes.

James drained his cup with a flourish. A serving girl instantly came forward to refill it. He smiled his thanks to her and she blushed. This girl might be serving him, but he had her eating out of his hand.

Lady Thornborough shot an expression of severe disapproval at the girl, and she bowed her head and withdrew quickly. James saw it, too, but he must have known better than to try his aunt's patience too far. He gave Lady Thornborough a conciliatory smile. Then he turned to Lizzie and said, "I am afraid, cousin, that we have come full circle, right back to what Aunt has been urging. You must attend Lord Beauchamp's ball."

Lady Thornborough's eyes narrowed at his abrupt change in tactic. "You agree with me?"

"Oh, yes." James nodded at Lizzie, as if to verify the truth of what he was saying. "I'm sure it is a trial to move forward, dearest, but you must make the effort. I believe it will do you good."

"So even you are against me, James?"

"No, I am completely on your side." His bright blue eyes held hers. "I will help you in every way I can."

Once again Lizzie wondered whether James was communicating more than his words held at face value.

"And just how do you plan to help her?" Lady Thornborough asked.

"To begin with, I'm taking her on a walk in the park. She could use some fresh air, I think."

"How can you be so energetic? You were not in bed until a very late hour."

"Oh, no," he corrected her. "It was not *late* when I went to bed." Seeing his aunt's incredulous expression, he clarified, "It was *early*. Early this morning. I believe I passed the flower men on their way to Covent Garden as I was making my way home."

"You will not be young forever," Lady Thornborough warned him. "One day your riotous living will catch up with you."

"No, I shall keep running very hard. It will never be able to catch up." He turned to Lizzie. "How about it, my dear? Shall we take a turn together in Hyde Park?"

His enthusiasm was contagious. "I would like that," said Lizzie. "However, do we have time? If I'm to go on morning calls with Grandmamma…"

Lady Thornborough laughed. "Gracious, you have been too long out of society. We won't leave until two o'clock."

Lizzie bit her lip. Another blunder. She was glad the woman was attributing it to her years away. She rose from the table and said to James, "I can be ready in a quarter of an hour."

Chapter 11

Geoffrey strolled down the path beside the twisting lake in Hyde Park known as the Serpentine. He breathed deeply of the fresh morning air, which today was thankfully crisp and clean. A stiff breeze the day before had blown much of the smoke away from London. He knew it was only temporary, but he was glad for the reprieve.

It was a far cry from his morning walks in the little seaside town in northern Devonshire, where he had lived for five years tending to the needs of his parishioners. The rocky track that followed the rough coastline was steep and sometimes treacherous, but the views of the ocean from the high cliffs were staggeringly beautiful. He had done some of his best thinking there as he picked his way along those narrow paths. He'd planned his sermons or contemplated ways to help his people with problems they were facing, both great and small.

His family estate where he would now be spending most of his time was far away to the southeast, in Kent. The place was

beautiful, to be sure—a stately mansion surrounded by mani-
cured lawns and gardens, situated among gently rolling hills and
lush hedgerows. But Geoffrey would miss the unencumbered
feeling of the untamed landscapes and the constantly changing sea.

A group of about twenty men and women hurried past him,
walking three abreast in a line. They were chatting excitedly to
one another, and he could tell from their accents that they were
not from London. Under normal circumstances, the park would
have very few people in it at this hour. One might perhaps see
workmen tending to the shrubs, or nannies watching their young
charges at play. The society people came out in the late afternoons to parade their finery and well-appointed carriages along
a popular path known as Rotten Row.

The recent opening of the Great Exhibition of the Industry
of All Nations had changed all that. London had become the
center of the world. Like the group that had just passed him,
people had been drawn here from all over England and from too
many foreign countries to count. They were on their way to view
the astounding show of items housed in a giant building made of
glass and steel, the likes of which had never been seen before. It
was so magnificent that the newspapers had dubbed it the Crystal Palace.

Across the Serpentine, the park was filled with activity as
men, women, and children made their way to the Exhibition.
Today was one of the cheapest admission days, when entrance
cost only a shilling.

Only a shilling.

Geoffrey smiled, amused to catch himself thinking that way.
A shilling was not so much to him now, but not too long ago he

had just as great a need to watch over every penny. He thought back to the people of his parish, many of whom were in poorer circumstances than he had been. They were farm laborers and factory workers—much like the people who filled Hyde Park today. One shilling represented a good part of their weekly income.

The "better classes" had feared that the influx of so many "common" folk in London would lead to riots and increased crime. But nothing like that had occurred. Everyone was on their best behavior. Here on a Tuesday morning they were dressed in their Sunday best, laughing and chatting among themselves as they hurried toward the Crystal Palace. Many carried small baskets filled with food and drink, prepared to spend the day inside that grand building.

Geoffrey tried to set his thoughts on the duties of the day. He had promised to see Lord Ashley, the chairman of the Society for Improving the Condition of the Labouring Classes, and he had also been asked to meet that afternoon with two potential patrons for the next charitable building project.

Somehow he had to find time to call upon Ria. Yesterday's meeting had been disastrous. He had allowed his anger and hurt to get the better of him. Perhaps a bit of pride, too. And yet she had been goading him with her single-minded insistence that love was more important than family duty and honor. Her intense devotion to Edward was touching, to be sure. It might have been a good thing, if it could have led them down more honorable paths. His opinions on that subject had not changed, but he vowed to himself that today he would keep his emotions tightly in check. He must find a way for them to reach some kind of peace.

*

Lizzie and James walked arm in arm at a comfortable pace along the Serpentine.

"I must say that despite your recent illness, you are much more vigorous than you used to be," James remarked.

"Oh?" Lizzie shortened her stride and slowed her steps.

"No, no, it's a good thing!" James assured her with a laugh. "When we used to walk in the park, you would hang back and complain that your shoes would get ruined."

Lizzie raised one foot a few inches off the ground for their mutual inspection. The well-worn black leather boot looked very much at odds with the soft folds of her heavy silk gown. "Perhaps it's because I have learned to wear something more practical than satin slippers when going for a walk in the park."

"I see," said James. "You are older and wiser now."

"Older, certainly. As for wiser…" Lizzie shrugged, and James grinned.

"Nevertheless, those boots are hideous," James admonished. "I cannot believe you are willing to be seen wearing them in public."

"I'm getting fitted for new shoes tomorrow. Grandmamma has arranged that."

As they rounded a bend in the path, they saw an elderly couple tottering slowly toward them. "It's old Mr. Walburton and his wrinkly wife," said James. "Do you remember them, Ria?"

Lizzie murmured something noncommittal as she watched the approaching pair. The man stooped heavily over his walking cane, and his wife clung to his arm for support. Their clothes, though well cared for, had gone out of fashion years ago. Lizzie and James nodded to the couple as they passed. They returned the greeting cordially, their wrinkled faces opening to vague smiles, giving no indication that they truly recognized either Lizzie or James.

When they were out of earshot, James said, "Those two have been old since the beginning of time. You used to call them Mr. and Mrs. Prune. Do you remember?"

"Did I? James, you must not hold me to all the things I said back then."

"But you always used to say the most delightfully silly things. If you *are* older and wiser, I shall find you quite dull."

Since James appeared to be in a mood to discuss childhood memories, Lizzie considered this a perfect opportunity to ask him some questions. Ria had only a few clues as to what might have happened between Sir Herbert and Lizzie's mother. One such clue concerned some information that James had shared with her once years ago.

Not wanting to arouse his suspicion, Lizzie thought it best to approach the subject in a roundabout manner. "Tell me, James, what do you remember most fondly about our childhood?"

James looked pleased at the question, and took a few moments to consider it. "I loved the way you would pout when Auntie would not let you eat all the tea cakes." He turned to look at her, as though admiring her bonnet, and studied the line of blond hair that showed from underneath it. He lightly touched one of her curls with his gloved hand. "I loved how it was so vitally important that the ringlets around your face be arranged just right."

Those things did indeed sound like Ria. Lizzie chuckled, her mind filled with sweet, sad thoughts of her dear friend. "Was I really so vain?"

"Oh yes, truly," James affirmed. "But you were so beautiful that your vanity was understandable, and so of course we all forgave you for it."

They were approaching two nannies seated on a park bench. Each had a perambulator in front of her and would peer into it from time to time, ensuring that the baby inside was still sleeping comfortably. One of the nannies looked old enough to have brought up several sets of children, but the other looked younger than Lizzie. She kept stealing glances at Lizzie as she and James approached. She was not staring openly—she was too well trained for that—but Lizzie saw her surreptitiously studying her gown and bonnet.

James lifted his top hat. "Good morning, ladies."

The younger nanny's eyes opened wide at being thus acknowledged by a gentleman. She gave a half smile and blushed deeply, then dropped her eyes as the elder woman whispered something to her—probably chastening her for allowing her feelings to show.

James replaced his hat and they moved on. "Do you remember," he said to Lizzie in an offhand manner, "how you and I used to make up stories about what the servants did on their days off? How we used to discuss whether or not they had any actual feelings?"

It was hard on Lizzie whenever she was confronted with one of the less charitable aspects of Ria's nature, which were bred no doubt by the selfish and privileged life she'd led in England. Lizzie had seen glimpses of it from time to time in the things Ria had said or done in Australia, but she was only now beginning to realize how deeply ingrained it had been.

James, for all his good-natured jests and fine manners, seemed as staunchly uncaring about the lower classes as anyone of his station. He was her avowed friend now, but what if he knew she'd held no higher station in life than the women they had just passed, or the servants whose "feelings" he'd dismissed so casually? She shivered at the thought.

"Are you cold?" James asked with concern.

She shivered again, this time intentionally. "I'm just dreading the prospect of accompanying Grandmamma on her calls."

He grinned. "I understand. I am sure I would find it perfectly dreary to listen to women's idle chatter all afternoon."

Lizzie reminded herself that she must not allow her feelings about Ria—good or bad—to sway her from her goal of finding out all she could. James's remark about idle chatter helped her approach the question she most wanted to ask. "Perhaps I should just spend the afternoon below stairs, like you used to do. I believe you once said that servants' gossip was much more interesting than anything discussed in drawing rooms."

James gave her a sidelong glance. "So I did. I still feel that way."

"But didn't that get you into trouble sometimes? Like the time you repeated something you'd overheard about Father's valet? Do you remember that?"

"Let me see…I am an absolute repository of servants' gossip…" He made a show of thinking very hard. "Yes," he said finally, with a nod. "I do remember. It seemed the man had gotten a young milliner with child, and the two ran away to London together. The servants said they had been guilty of *criminal conversation*. I thought, of course, that meant they'd been speaking with criminals! But when I asked Auntie about it, she made me wash my mouth out with soap and told me never to utter those words again."

"A good thing," Lizzie said. She tried to say it in jest, but she truly meant it. Those terrible words had once been cruelly leveled against her, too. "Did Father know—about the woman, I mean?"

"I have no idea. By the time I heard about it, which was seven or eight years later, he had just passed away."

"Is it possible that when he died, and people were reviewing his life the way it normally happens after a person dies, that something might have brought that gossip back into people's minds?"

"Ah," he said. "Are you worried there is a connection—that the servants' gossip was not entirely correct, and that perhaps he was somehow *personally* involved in the affair?"

"Might he have been?" Lizzie asked, trying not to show how desperately she wanted to know. "I was only seven when he died. You remember him better than I do. Might he have been that sort of man?"

He took both her hands in his and gave her an encouraging smile. "Don't you worry—no one ever accused Sir Herbert Thornborough of being less than the most blameless and stalwart member of society."

Lizzie looked at him askance. "You always have a way of not answering questions while appearing that you are."

He laughed. "You are more perceptive than you used to be, cousin. But why are you trying to dredge up bad things about your father after so many years? Surely you have enough good memories of him to dwell upon?"

Phrased as it was, the question took Lizzie off guard. She had only the one memory of her father, and it was *not* a good one. But Ria had adored him.

James's bright blue eyes were actually twinkling. Did he enjoy her evident discomfiture? Probably, she thought wryly. It was part of his teasing nature.

"Let us not dwell on such things now," he said. "Here is something far more interesting to talk about." He led her around a bend in the path and pointed across the Serpentine.

The worries on Lizzie's mind receded for the moment as she took in the sight before her: it was the largest building she had ever seen.

A building made entirely of glass.

It was shaped like a cross. The shorter section had a rounded roof, giving the appearance of an oblong dome. The longer section seemed to stretch for a mile. The building gleamed in the sun, its roof higher than the surrounding trees and trimmed with hundreds of colorful flags.

"It's like something from a fairy tale," she said with awe. "Is it truly made of glass?"

"It is." James smiled at her thunderstruck expression. "It's called the Crystal Palace."

"But how does it keep from collapsing?"

"A steel framework holds it up. Inside there are wooden floors, balconies, and even whole trees. There was such an outcry against the possibility of our stately elms being cut down that they simply erected the building around them."

"You've been inside?" Lizzie hurried up the path to find a better view.

"Indeed I have. It's filled with hundreds of displays, from heavy machinery—tedious, although it is the best in the world—to exquisite gems. You'll be interested to know that two of the largest diamonds in the world are in there." He looked at her askance. "Did you not hear anything about the Great Exhibition while you were living in the wilds of Australia?"

"I don't know when I last saw a newspaper. It must have been at least six months ago. I remember reading about an exhibition that was spearheaded by Prince Albert, and that there was some controversy surrounding it. I don't remember any details."

"That 'controversy' you speak of was the decision to hold the Exhibition in Hyde Park. It was vehemently opposed by many of the fashionable set. They gave dire predictions that the building would be hideously ugly and leave our beautiful park a treeless, barren landscape. But as you see, the result is—"

"Dazzling," Lizzie finished for him, staring at the building with admiration. "When were you there?"

"Oh, I've been several times. I bought a season ticket, of course. It was the only way to get in for the grand opening last month."

She turned to him eagerly. "Can we go there now?"

James laughed. "I'm afraid not. You will need at least a full day to see everything. Auntie wants you home in time for luncheon. I'll take you there soon, if you feel strong enough for such a venture."

"I'm sure I shall."

"I'm so glad you have returned to London," James said. "What fun we shall have."

Lizzie tried to envision whole trees inside a building filled with fine objects on display. She was sure it would be grander than anything she could imagine. How she wished Tom could have seen it. He had loved London, with all its crowds and business and majestic monuments; he'd even loved its dirt and fog. How thrilled he would have been to see this incomparable sight.

At these thoughts, the Crystal Palace seemed to blur before her. She blinked several times and murmured, "He would have loved it."

"How thoughtless of me," James said. "Here I was thinking only of the joy of having you back, and not of the sad circumstances that brought you here." As he turned to pluck a bloom from a flowering bush, he added, "I know I am no match to your dear Edward for company." He presented it to her with a flourish. "Will you forgive me?"

She accepted the bright red bloom with an attempt at a tiny smile, and took a moment to savor its delicate scent, not trusting herself to speak.

"Oh, dear," James said, glancing down the path. "Just when I thought I had succeeded in brightening your mood, here comes Geoffrey."

Lizzie looked up. He was about fifty yards away, moving in their direction. His tall form stood out among the reeds that grew along the water's edge. He caught sight of them and quickened his pace, causing Lizzie's heart to quicken as well. It was her anger over yesterday's events causing it, she knew. She had not forgotten his harsh words.

Yet she could not help noticing how well he looked in his dark coat and cravat. Black might look drab on other men, but it seemed to suit Geoffrey's jet-black eyes and hair better than any bright color could have done. She would have preferred it for her own composure if he had not looked quite so handsome.

As his long strides rapidly closed the distance between them, Lizzie found herself locked in that intense gaze of his, rooted to the spot, unable to move and strangely light-headed.

Chapter 12

Geoffrey had caught sight of them just as James had been presenting her with a flower.

Even from a distance he could see the dramatic gesture James had used, as flowery as the bloom he'd been flourishing. But it was the grace with which Ria had accepted it that most riveted him.

What was the point of James's overwrought gallantry? Geoffrey hoped James was not sincerely wooing her. Ria was too good for James. Startled to find himself thinking this after the way she'd irritated and unsettled him, he amended to himself that, despite her many faults, she was too good for James.

James was a womanizer and a wastrel. He did not know how to keep two shillings in his pocket. It was rumored that his family fortunes were low and James would have to procure a rich wife in order to maintain the lifestyle to which he was accustomed. That would leave Ria out of the running. Ria had clearly returned from Australia without a shilling to her name. She was due an inheritance from her father, but it would not be large enough to support opulent living.

Ria stood still as a statue as he approached. The bright red flower in her hand set off the dark gray gown she wore. Behind her, the Crystal Palace glinted in the sun. She had been smiling at James, but as her eyes met Geoffrey's, the smile had faded, to be replaced with the same wariness he had seen yesterday. He had the impression that he was literally watching walls spring up around her.

When he reached them, James shook his hand. "I should have known you'd be up early, rambling about the park."

"I must say I never expected to see you," Geoffrey replied. "Isn't it a bit early for the smart set to be out?"

The implied criticism rolled off James as smoothly as the water off the ducks in the Serpentine. "It makes no difference nowadays," he said easily. "All the hubbub from the Exhibition has ruined the afternoon walks on Rotten Row. And in any case, I am sacrificing myself for our dear Ria. We thought a walk might be good for her health."

Geoffrey turned to Ria and gave her a bow. He wanted to speak, but even the commonplace pleasantries managed to escape him. Seeing her made each scar on his heart hurt afresh. And yet she stood there so still, so beautiful. Not looking at all like a woman capable of bringing scandal and heartache to two families.

She nodded in return, but said nothing.

The frostiness of this exchange did not appear to escape James. "Come, come," he said. "You two cannot still be angry with each other?" He gently disengaged Ria's arm and held it toward Geoffrey. "You must at least shake hands."

Geoffrey took her hand. She seemed reluctant to leave it there, but made no move to pull away.

"I decree," said James, "that from here on out, we shall remember the dearly departed with love and reverence, but we shall not let it interfere with what we are about today. Life goes on, you know."

Geoffrey did not trust himself to look at Ria's face just then, so he studied her hand. The black glove upon it was new, and the workmanship was fine. Even through his own gloves he could feel the leather was soft and supple. The thought crossed his mind— wildly inconsequential to this moment—that Lady Thornborough's visit to Regent Street had yielded excellent results.

He raised his gaze and found himself once again captive to those violet-blue eyes. "Yes," he said quietly. "Life goes on."

The tense wariness holding her body seemed to subside a little.

James grinned his approval. "Thank goodness that's done," he said. "Now, Geoffrey, give her your arm." He took Ria's hand and placed it on Geoffrey's arm.

They began once more to follow the path by the Serpentine, with Ria walking between the two men.

"It is so pleasant to walk together," James remarked to no one in particular. "Don't you agree?"

Geoffrey was keenly aware of Ria's nearness. Every nerve telegraphed how close she was to him. It was the same curious sensation he'd felt when he'd taken her arm in Lady Thornborough's parlor. This time, however, his limbs managed to function, and he was grateful for it.

He was barely conscious of James's animated remarks about some aspect of the Great Exhibition and the effect of the crowds on Hyde Park. He was glad Ria was making enough replies to James so that the conversation could continue without his help.

He was startled back into the conversation when James said, "Do you have a carriage nearby, Geoffrey?"

"Yes. I told my driver to meet me beyond Kensington Gardens."

"Excellent." James stifled a yawn. "I have reached my limit for walking today. I must find my bed before I keel over from exhaustion. Ria is still filled with energy, however. I'm sure she would love to walk with you as far as Kensington Gardens. Might I prevail upon you to drive her home?"

"James, you cannot be leaving me," Ria protested. No doubt she preferred James's company to his. After yesterday, he could not blame her.

James was already extricating himself from her grasp. "You two have much to talk about, and I would only be in the way."

"But—"

"Don't worry, my dear," James interrupted with a smile. "You'll be in good hands. He'll protect you from the teeming masses."

Yes, Geoffrey thought, *but who will protect me from her?*

They watched him stride swiftly down the path that led back to the eastern entrance to the park. "James seems to have a great deal of energy for a man who is exhausted," Geoffrey remarked.

"I'm sorry if he has put you out," Ria said. "He is a dear, but he is a bit like a shooting star—taking you by surprise, delighting you, and then disappearing."

Despite the weightier things pressing on his mind, Geoffrey found himself amused at this description. "I'm well aware of this quality of his, although I'm sure I never heard it described quite like that." Perhaps James's joie de vivre was something Geoffrey should cultivate, too.

Although he had wanted to talk to Ria, he thought he would have more time to organize his thoughts beforehand. Perhaps it was for the best, however. They could speak privately now, without interference from Lady Thornborough or James.

He was intensely aware of Ria's hand on his arm as they walked. The scent of her hair was sweeter than any of the flowers trimming the path. This would have been far easier, Geoffrey reflected, if they had been sitting in a parlor at a respectable distance from each other.

It had been easier to think of Ria in the abstract, when he could picture her as a headstrong girl who needed to be reined in. It was far more difficult when he was confronted with her in person, walking placidly beside him.

"Ria," he began. "I'm glad we have a few minutes to speak together. I was planning to call on you today."

She tensed, her walls rising back into place. She kept her eyes focused across the river, on the people coming and going from the Crystal Palace. "I'm sure you have many questions. I am willing to answer them, of course. But first, I hope that you will allow me to apologize for my behavior yesterday."

Geoffrey looked down at her, startled. This conversation might go more easily than he had imagined.

"Please understand," she continued, "that I do not apologize for our decision to go to Australia."

Naturally not. "I see."

"However, it *was* rude of me to speak so harshly. I know you cared deeply for your brother." She regarded him earnestly. "I'm sorry that we began our acquaintance on such a sour note. Edward was so desirous that you and I should be friends."

"Yes, that sounds like Edward. He always wanted to be friends. With everyone."

"Are you implying it was a failing? As faults go, it's not such a terrible one to have."

"I suppose that's true," Geoffrey acknowledged. Friendships came so easily to Edward. Geoffrey had secretly envied him for that. Geoffrey was more guarded about whom he took into his circle of friends.

"Edward often spoke proudly of you and William," Ria said. "He believed his own life had fallen far short. He wanted to be worthy of your love and admiration."

"He always had my love," Geoffrey pointed out.

"But not your admiration."

Geoffrey did not answer. Ria's point was true enough, although there were qualities in Edward that Geoffrey might have wished he had in stronger measure.

"He wanted to prove that he could be successful on his own merits, without help from the family," Ria said. "He wanted to make you proud."

"Well, it was an insanely foolish way to go about it," Geoffrey said. "He would have made me much more proud if he had—"

"Please." Ria took both his hands in hers. "Let us not quarrel about the past. We cannot change it."

Her eyes searched his, her face open and appealing, and any further words of recrimination died in Geoffrey's throat. Perhaps she was teaching *him* about forgiveness. The silence lengthened, broken only by a soft rustle of leaves in the trees overhead. Geoffrey sighed. "You are right. And I must apologize to you for speaking in anger yesterday."

She smiled. A cool breeze moved across the Serpentine and teased a stray curl of hair at her neck. Once again Geoffrey had the same absurd notion as he had at yesterday's meeting: that it would be hard to deny this woman anything.

He stepped back, dropping her hands, although not in anger as he had done the day before. This time he moved away because it was too difficult to think clearly when she was so close.

Propriety, however, dictated that he offer her his arm, and once again they began to stroll along the river path. Even with her nearness, her hand gently resting on his arm, movement was preferable to standing there, spellbound, unable to see anything beyond her lovely countenance.

He found his breath returning as they moved. "Ria, you were correct in saying that we should not dwell on the past. As it happens, the present is exactly what I would like to discuss. What are your plans now that you have returned to England?"

Chapter 13

Lizzie stumbled on a root. Geoffrey's hands tightened on her arm to keep her from falling. She found her balance and smiled her thanks, and his grip relaxed.

She was thankful for those few extra seconds to consider her response. She reminded herself of one of Ria's maxims: *If you are going to tell a lie, put as much truth in it as possible. Tell the truth and you can forget it; tell a lie and you must remember it forever.*

The advice was sound. "I hope to live as quietly as possible," Lizzie said, which was the absolute truth. "I need time to regain my strength."

"And then?" Geoffrey pressed.

"I am eager to get to Rosewood."

"But you will remain in town for the rest of the season, will you not?"

"Yes." Lizzie sighed. "I would have been happier to leave for the country right away. I'm sure it would be better for my health." *And keep me away from prying eyes and questions.*

"Lady Thornborough is not of that opinion?"

"No. Dr. Layton says I am out of danger, and Grandmamma is adamant about staying in town."

"I think it only fair to warn you that you will have a difficult time leading this 'quiet life' of which you speak. All of London knows you have returned. You will be invited everywhere."

Lizzie recalled the uncomfortable conversation at breakfast. "I've tried to explain to Grandmamma that I have no desire to go out into society at all."

"No?" Geoffrey looked unconvinced. "I would have thought you'd be excited about getting back to dinner parties and soirees. William said you enjoyed such things."

She gave him a reproving look. "Believe me, I am not the same light-headed society girl who left England ten years ago." Once again, Lizzie considered she was speaking the truth. But it went beyond the fact that she wasn't actually Ria. When she'd run off with the handsome and debonair Freddie Hightower, she'd been young, naïve, and in love, just as Ria had been. She was far different now. She'd learned that exterior refinements were not the real measure of a man.

"You should prepare yourself for what will happen. Everywhere you go, people will be asking you all manner of impertinent questions about your life in Australia. You will be scrutinized and discussed as if you were a fascinating exhibit at the zoo."

Lizzie thought nervously of interacting with all those people, of facing the whole spectrum of social situations. She felt unprepared, despite her long conversations with Ria and the social graces she'd acquired during her months with Freddie. She had not been expecting Lady Thornborough to push her out into society so quickly. She'd thought she'd have more time.

"When you are subjected to these questions," Geoffrey continued, "you must be careful. You must not say or do anything that will injure the reputation of either of our families."

"Is that what you are concerned about? You think I will do something further to disgrace you?" Despite her own concerns on this subject, she could not prevent a note of indignation from creeping into her voice.

Geoffrey shook his head. "That is too harsh. I am merely reminding you of the need to act with discretion."

Lizzie was painfully aware of the need to watch every step. "I had hoped my words today might have given you some confidence on this subject. I am as concerned as you are to preserve your family's good name." Indeed, Lizzie realized that she wanted to give Geoffrey a higher regard not only for Ria but also, somehow, for *herself.*

He considered her thoughtfully for a moment. "I do believe you are telling the truth."

The truth.

She wished he had chosen any other words but those.

They walked together in silence. Lizzie was searching for a safe topic of conversation when her attention was caught once more by the people and carriages on the other side of the Serpentine. "Have you been to the Great Exhibition?"

This was definitely the right choice, as she discovered from Geoffrey's cheerful response. "I was involved in its planning, actually."

"Were you? Have you met Prince Albert, then?"

"Indeed I have."

"Is he..." Lizzie lowered her voice, even though no one was near enough to overhear them. "Is he really such a stiff German bore as the newspapers make him out to be?"

Geoffrey laughed. The sound of it startled Lizzie because it was so full and pleasant. Instantly she hoped to hear more of it.

"Prince Albert has a rather wicked sense of humor when you get to know him. He is a fine man—and I'm not just saying that because he is married to our Queen. He has high ideals and a real concern for every person in the realm, both rich and poor."

Lizzie shook her head in disbelief. "I've never yet seen a prince who was genuinely concerned about the poor, except for how to wring more work or taxes from them."

He tilted his head. "That's a fairly cynical statement—especially from a member of the privileged class."

Lizzie stared at him, nonplussed, trying to think of an explanation for her statement. Once again Ria's advice to *tell the truth as much as you can* came to her aid. "For the past ten years I have hardly been living as a member of the privileged class. I've seen firsthand what it's like to struggle for a living."

Her statement was reasonable, and Geoffrey accepted it easily. "You would have a different view of things now, I suppose." His voice seemed to hold a touch of approbation. "And your assessment is probably true, as far as most monarchs are concerned. But Albert has found himself in a unique position. He is married to the Queen, but he is not the King. He has time and many resources at his disposal, and his active mind is searching for ways to make use of them."

He motioned toward a stone bridge spanning in elegant arches across the Serpentine. "May I show you one of the projects spearheaded by the Prince himself? It's not far from here."

Lizzie was intrigued. "I'd like that very much."

They crossed the bridge and took a path leading to Kensington Palace. Geoffrey quickened his pace, but Lizzie kept up with him easily, buoyed by his enthusiasm.

They approached a long row of nondescript wooden buildings, home to a garrisoned army regiment. Lizzie recalled seeing these barracks years ago when she came to the park to watch the gentlemen and ladies taking their afternoon rides along Rotten Row.

Something new had been added to this area of the park. A two-story building of polished white stone stood in stark contrast to the brown barracks nearby. Everything about the structure was symmetrical. Two doors on the ground floor framed twin large windows. A wrought-iron staircase led to an open landing on the second floor, where two more doors and windows formed an exact copy of the layout below.

"What is this place?" Lizzie asked.

"There are actually four dwellings in this building," Geoffrey replied. "They are known as the Prince's Cottages."

Lizzie said incredulously, "The Prince wishes to live here?"

"Good Lord, no," Geoffrey said, smiling. Lizzie was discovering that she liked his smile. When the hard edges fell away, he seemed warmer and not so formidable.

"These dwellings are designed for the working classes," Geoffrey explained. "They are not grand enough for a prince, but no ordinary person would be ashamed to live here."

"Surely the Prince does not intend for working people to take up residence in Hyde Park?" The building was just within view of Kensington Palace. Although it was not currently a royal residence, it was Queen Victoria's birthplace and had been her childhood home. "Perhaps the Prince has a unique sense of humor after all."

"The building is temporary," Geoffrey said. "After the Great Exhibition ends, it will be torn down and rebuilt south of the river."

Two dozen or so people milled about, admiring the structure from every angle. A portly gentleman with a stiff cravat and tall top hat stood near the doors, handing out pamphlets and encouraging the visitors to tour the inside. Spotting Geoffrey, he smiled and bowed. "A very good morrow to you, my lord," he said. "Lord Ashley told us to expect you."

Geoffrey shook his hand warmly. "I see you have a lot of business, Mr. Lang."

The gentleman beamed with pride. "Forty-five visitors today, by my count, sir. We've been getting a fair share of working-class folk, as well as the upper classes." Perhaps in deference to Geoffrey's background as a clergyman, he added, "As it says in Proverbs, 'The rich and the poor meet together, but the Lord is the maker of them all.'"

Geoffrey smiled. "Right you are, Mr. Lang. I am confident the efforts we've made here will ultimately benefit everyone." He looked around. "Is Lord Ashley still here?"

"Indeed he is, sir." Mr. Lang motioned to the staircase. "He is upstairs at present, giving a tour to two gentlemen from the *Illustrated London News*."

"Lord Ashley, the Earl of Shaftesbury, is the chairman of the Society for Improving the Condition of the Labouring Classes," Geoffrey explained to Lizzie. "You will enjoy meeting him."

He had no sooner spoken than they heard a bustle on the landing as several men exited one of the upstairs rooms. "There you have it, gentlemen," a voice boomed out. "Dwellings that are sanitary, safe, and cost no more for the laboring classes to rent than the wretched hovels they live in now."

The wrought-iron stairs vibrated and a tall, silver-haired gentleman with a prominent nose and chin came into view. He moved briskly, his polished boots clanking with authority on the metal steps.

Two men carrying small notebooks and pencils followed in his wake. "This five percent return you spoke of," one of the men asked. "Is that really what you are seeing?"

"Do you doubt my word?"

The second man kept writing in his notebook, even as they descended the steps. "But can you really expect to receive money on a regular basis from this low sort of people, my lord?" he persisted. "Isn't it too risky to allow your capital to be dependent on them?"

Lord Ashley turned as he reached the bottom step. He examined the men, who had been forced to a halt on the steps after his abrupt stop. With his walking stick, he gave a light poke to the chest of the man who had asked the question. "Let me give you an example," he said. "Over at Whitechapel, another such building has been in use for several years. Excepting a few shillings, there are *no* arrears due on a rental of more than two thousand pounds, paid by more than one hundred tenants."

The earl's commanding tone easily garnered the attention of everyone within hearing distance. A few men and women even looked over the railing, listening from the landing above. Clearly he attracted notice wherever he went. "These are reliable working men, who deserve what we can provide for them, which is the capital to build these dwellings. They pay the rent, and the investors benefit." He looked pointedly at the second man, who continued to take notes. "The most important thing to remember, however, is that we have used our money to benefit our fellow man."

There was an approving murmur from the crowd.

Lord Ashley caught sight of Geoffrey. "Lord Somerville, there you are."

"I apologize for being late. I was unavoidably detained."

There was no rancor in Geoffrey's voice, but Lizzie felt chastened anyway. James had foisted her upon Geoffrey's care, not even considering that he might have had other plans.

Lord Ashley's gaze lit upon Lizzie. "Detained, eh? So I see! One could hardly blame you, if attending to a lovely young lady delayed your arrival."

Lizzie looked away in embarrassment, but Geoffrey seemed unperturbed.

"Lord Ashley, may I present my sister-in-law, Mrs. Edward Somerville."

"Mrs. Somerville?" The earl's bushy white eyebrows lifted. "Why, yes, of course." He took Lizzie's hand, assessing her with interest and a bit of pity. "Lord Somerville has already apprised me of the situation, of course. Such ghastly business. Thank God that you, at least, have returned safe and sound." The earl's expression showed genuine sympathy as he surveyed the two of them. "Perhaps you can be a comfort to one another, eh?" To Lizzie he said, "I have no doubt that Lord Somerville will take good care of you."

The earl could only be referring to Geoffrey's role as a loving brother-in-law, of course. Even so, the concept of being under his care left her oddly breathless.

"The lady is well provided for," Geoffrey told the earl. "She is living with her grandmother, Lady Thornborough, at present."

Throughout this exchange, the men from the *Illustrated London News* had maintained a polite distance. Although they sent only occasional glances in her direction, Lizzie saw that one of the men kept scribbling furiously in his notebook. She concluded that they must be well trained on how to watch and listen without overtly appearing to do so. Lizzie shifted uneasily. She did not like the idea of their taking down the details of this conversation.

Lord Ashley saw her troubled notice of the men. "Gentlemen," he called out in his booming voice, "I believe you have seen everything you need?"

He spoke it as a question, but his intent was plain. The men came forward and thanked the earl for his time, giving several bows to both Lord Ashley and to Geoffrey before tipping their hats to Lizzie and taking themselves off.

Lord Ashley watched as they walked away. "Did you hear that man's remark, Somerville, questioning whether we could truly rely upon the common man to pay his rent?"

"I did, sir."

"Did you not find it highly impertinent—especially coming from a man who is probably not so far removed from the so-called laboring poor himself?"

Geoffrey nodded. "I have often noted that the common working man is far more reliable at paying his debts than many a dissolute member of the upper classes."

"An astute observation," said the earl with approval. He fixed a gaze upon Lizzie that was friendly, despite his imposing appearance. "Since Lord Somerville has brought you out today, would you like to view our little project?"

Lizzie instinctively liked this man. Although his manner was as self-assured and commanding as any man in his position, he seemed approachable, too. "Thank you, Lord Ashley," she replied, returning his smile. "I'd like that very much."

"Splendid, splendid." He turned once more to the staircase.

"You really must see the upstairs to fully appreciate the exquisite design of the coal and dust chutes."

As they went up, Geoffrey took gentle hold of Lizzie's elbow, bringing his solid frame close to hers on the narrow steps. By the time they reached the top of the steps, she found herself curiously out of breath. Geoffrey made no move to pull away but waited for her breathing to even out. He said gently, "Everything all right?"

She managed a nod. "Fine, thank you."

She had forgotten about the other people on the landing, those who had been watching while Lord Ashley addressed the newspapermen. She was brought to heart-stopping remembrance, however, when a nearby voice cried out, "Why, bless my soul! If it ain't Lizzie Poole!"

Chapter 14

Waves of heat and ice rushed over Lizzie all at once.

She turned to find herself looking into the wrinkled face of a very old man. The coat covering his stooped back had been patched and mended dozens of times, but was probably his best. His mouth broadened into a wide, nearly toothless smile. "Lizzie Poole! We thought you was gone forever! But here you are, plain as day, and dressed in such fine clothes! Wouldn't your dear father 'ave been knocked right over if he coulda seen you!"

The old man's voice was wheezy and raspy, as if he was bothered by a lung ailment. But his words were terrifyingly clear.

Fear kept Lizzie rooted to the spot. She had known there might be people in London who could recognize her, even after all these years. But she had convinced herself she could not possibly cross paths with them since she would be moving in London's best circles. Who could have guessed that the Great Exhibition would bring all levels of society into such close contact?

The rich and the poor meet together ...

Lizzie was unable to speak. Geoffrey stared at the old man in frank surprise. Even the boisterous Lord Ashley seemed at a loss for words.

"It's me!" the old man said as he drew a step closer to Lizzie. "Ben Weathers! You can't 'ave forgotten me."

Lizzie examined his face. He had a wide, fleshy nose that was decidedly red, and watery blue eyes that were so faded it was as if the color had been rinsed out of them. He was older and more wrinkled to be sure, but Lizzie could not mistake the face of one of her father's dearest friends.

She fought to keep her expression impassive, even as a multitude of conflicting desires warred within her. Her father had died while she was in Australia, and she knew nothing about his last days. She was sure Ben Weathers could answer all the questions she craved to ask. Weathers continued to watch her with anticipation. Had he seen a flicker of recognition in her eyes? He even opened his arms slightly, as though expecting her to approach him for a warm embrace. It took every ounce of her strength not to rush into those arms. She forced herself to concentrate on the solidity of Geoffrey's arm as she clung to it. This was her path now. She must deny any knowledge of the man standing before her.

Lizzie leveled a flat, disinterested stare at the old man she had once loved as dearly as her father. Somehow she dredged up the same haughty tone that she had employed with Harding, saying coldly, "To whom are you referring, *sir*?"

She laid an extra bit of ironic stress on the word *sir*, reasoning that a lady would be affronted at being thus addressed by a stranger who was so obviously beneath her station.

Weathers drew back, as though she had literally slapped him.

"Why, Lizzie! What…" Confusion and doubt crossed his features. "You mean, you ain't Lizzie Poole?"

Lizzie's throat constricted. She choked out, "I am sure I can be no one of *your* acquaintance."

In her anxiety to appear adequately offended, she over-reached and spoke too harshly. She regretted it the moment she saw Weathers's look of shame.

She was inwardly thankful when Geoffrey said in an appeasing tone, "You are confused, old man. You are, in fact, addressing Mrs. Edward Somerville."

Weathers squinted as he studied Lizzie's face, trying to reconcile Geoffrey's statement with the contradicting evidence of his own eyes. Lizzie stood very still under his intense scrutiny, not trusting herself to move a muscle.

Finally he seemed to accept Geoffrey's words. His gaze dropped to the ground, and his face took on the self-effacing expression any poor man would use when addressing his betters. He bowed deferentially. "I beg your pardon, ma'am. I meant no harm by it, I'm sure."

Lizzie's heart squeezed so tight she thought it might burst. She said nothing.

"No harm done," Geoffrey said kindly. "Perhaps your aged eyes are playing tricks on you."

Lizzie would have laid bets that Ben Weathers's eyes were sharp as a hawk's. But his humble posture never changed. He nodded and said, "Indeed, sir, I am sure that is what happened." He bowed again. "I shan't trouble the lady any further."

Geoffrey gently pulled Lizzie away from the staircase to clear the way for Weathers. She looked away then, pretending to peer with interest through one of the windows that opened onto the landing. She hoped Weathers would take this as a sign that he was already out of her thoughts.

Even with her back to him, she could feel his curious gaze resting on her as he made his way toward the stairs. She let out a sigh of relief when the sound of his steps on the staircase faded away.

"How extraordinary!" Lord Ashley exclaimed. "What do you make of that?"

"I'm sure I couldn't possibly guess." Lizzie tried to speak nonchalantly, but to her dismay, it came out as a croak.

"Clearly he thought he knew you," Geoffrey said.

"Yes, well..." She swallowed in an effort to loosen the knot in her throat. "As you said, his eyes were playing tricks on him."

Geoffrey shook his head. "I only said that to spare the old fellow some embarrassment."

"Why should you want to do that? It was impertinent for him to address me that way."

"Perhaps you resemble the daughter of someone he used to work for," Lord Ashley offered. "He mentioned something about her father."

"That's a reasonable guess," said Geoffrey.

Both men were taking the event far too seriously. Lizzie had to find a way to make the whole thing seem preposterous. What would Ria say? "I must say I find the whole thing horribly distressing." She spoke lightly and punctuated the remark with an exaggerated pout.

This brought a look of consternation from Geoffrey.

Lord Ashley said, "Distressing? How so?"

"I am horrified to think there may be someone out there who resembles me. It is so unflattering." She tilted her head proudly. "I should like to think I am undeniably unique!"

"Right you are, my dear!" Lord Ashley said with amusement. "It was unpardonable of us to discuss any other possibility."

She gave him a sunny smile. "I forgive you." She peered once again through the window with a show of curiosity. "Shall we go inside? I am all anticipation to discover everything about this quaint little cottage."

Lord Ashley motioned her toward the open door. "You will be impressed, no doubt of that..."

Lizzie thought she expressed a credible amount of interest as the earl showed off the modern conveniences in the simple dwelling. He pointed out the bedroom for the husband and wife, and two smaller rooms for the children.

"Separate bedrooms!" he exclaimed happily. "To encourage modesty and high morals."

In the tiny scullery, he bubbled with pleasure as he demonstrated the separate chutes for coal and waste.

Lizzie smiled and nodded appreciatively. She even managed to ask a few pertinent questions, although her mind kept returning to her encounter with Ben Weathers.

Her actions had hurt and disappointed the old man, and she was sorry for that. It must have been at least ten years since he had last laid eyes on her. He wore those years plainly on his hunched figure. Yet he had recognized her. How many more of London's lowliest denizens could still identify her?

Only an hour ago she had been excited about attending the Great Exhibition. Now she was uneasy to think of spending hours in that vast building with hundreds—perhaps thousands—of people from every corner of London. *The rich and the poor meet together...*

She would have to be very careful.

*

Geoffrey sat opposite Ria, watching her as the carriage skirted the southern edge of Hyde Park, heading east toward Mayfair. She sat with her head tilted back and her eyes closed, sinking more deeply into the cushioned seat with each rock and sway of the carriage. Everything in her face and posture indicated utter exhaustion. She had not spoken for some time.

Geoffrey chastised himself for keeping her out so long, adding to her exertions by taking her to see the Prince's Cottages. At the time she had seemed up to it, and had even shown a genuine interest. It was not until they had parted from Lord Ashley that signs of Ria's fatigue began to surface. She had become subdued and watchful, carefully scanning the faces of everyone they passed as they returned to Geoffrey's carriage. Perhaps she was looking for the old man who had spoken to her earlier.

He was still mulling over the strange event. The fellow was convinced he knew Ria, though he had called her by another name. Ria had dismissed the incident out of hand, yet Geoffrey sensed that it upset her more than she acknowledged.

Ria must have realized that he was studying her. She opened her eyes. Geoffrey thought he saw a certain vulnerability in her look, a sadness that he was tempted to think he understood. Her brows drew together, as though she were trying very hard to remember something. He wanted to reach out and take her hand, as one might comfort a lost child.

He was glad he resisted the urge, because in an instant Ria's expression changed to something altogether different. A mischievous smile wiped away any trace of the quiet, lost girl. She brought her hands to her cheeks and said, "Oh, dear—do I have a smudge on my face?"

Geoffrey forced a smile and shook his head. "I was merely wondering whether you are well."

"Oh, yes. Perfectly well." She reached up to check the placement of her bonnet and tucked back a stray lock of hair. "I confess I am tired, but that is no matter. It has been such an *interesting* morning."

The carriage stopped. Geoffrey peered out the window and saw that they had paused at the intersection with the wide avenue leading to Lady Thornborough's home. Carriages, carts, and wagons streamed up and down the busy street. The driver must be waiting for an opportunity to enter the fray.

"The Crystal Palace is such a marvel!" Ria said sprightly. "I cannot wait to see the inside."

"When will you go? Tomorrow?"

"Oh, no. James says we must wait until Saturday, when the crowd is smaller due to the higher admission fee."

Ria was speaking in a light, silly tone, like so many of the society misses he'd met in London this season, and it chafed him. "You plan to avoid persons of the baser sort," he said with a touch of sarcasm. "A brilliant plan. After all, you would not want a repeat of what happened today. Someone mistaking you for a commoner."

Ria's face reddened. She must have caught the reproof in his tone. He was, therefore, taken aback when she nodded as though his words were perfectly sensible. "Quite right. I certainly would not want another such incident. That would be—"

She was cut off in mid-sentence when the carriage lurched forward without warning. The driver must have found an opening and raced to take advantage of it. The unexpected movement threw Ria from her seat and she fell forward, landing on the floor of the carriage.

"—awkward," she finished.

Instantly Geoffrey moved to help her up. His hands found their way around her slim waist, which sent an unpardonable array of sensations through him. "Are you hurt?" he asked, his voice hypocritically cool.

Her face was mere inches from his. "I ... I don't think so," she stammered.

Slowly she managed to get her feet back under her. They both had to struggle for balance against the movement of the carriage as Geoffrey helped her back to her seat.

When she was settled, Geoffrey dropped back into his own seat. The carriage continued to make its way briskly up the avenue, and Geoffrey was glad of that. It would be a relief to get Ria safely home and be on his way. She had stirred up entirely too many emotions today.

Ria gave a little tug to her gloves and rearranged her shawl as the carriage pulled up to Lady Thornborough's home. Her cheeks were tinged with pink—a vivid contrast to the day he first laid eyes on her, sprawled unconscious on those white marble steps.

The coachman opened the door. Geoffrey descended from the carriage and turned to help Ria. Once she was safely down she stood unnervingly close, looking up at him, making no effort to move away. Every time she drew near like this, he found their surroundings seemed to fade, and only Ria was in sharp outline. The subtle scent of roses reached out and enveloped him.

"Thank you for bringing me home, Geoffrey. I know it was an inconvenience for you."

Her tone was subdued.

Again he felt that strange need to console her. "I think we can safely blame James for any inconvenience."

"Then we must also 'blame' him for affording us an opportunity to resolve some of our differences." She smiled. "I know I chatter on like a silly woman sometimes, but I am glad we had this time together today."

"So am I." He meant it, for here was another glimpse of the Ria he wished to know better. He cleared his throat. "Might I come round tomorrow?" Somehow he felt like a fool for asking, as though he were some sort of suitor, so he added, "I would love to hear anything you can tell me about Edward."

She seemed genuinely pleased at his request as she replied, "Of course. I shall enjoy it."

Like everyone else in London, Geoffrey found himself eaten up with curiosity about how Edward had spent his final years. Although *unlike* most of London, he had a right to know. There were other things Geoffrey knew he should discuss with Ria as well, although he did not say so. Certain legal matters would need to be addressed regarding her status as Edward's widow. But these could wait until tomorrow.

The door to Lady Thornborough's home opened. Harding stood there, watching them expectantly. Geoffrey led Ria up the steps.

"Until tomorrow, then," she said with a smile, and disappeared inside.

In spite of his earlier urge to be gone as soon as possible, Geoffrey stood for a moment, unwilling to move, watching as the door closed behind her.

Chapter 15

L ady Thornborough looked up from her writing desk as Lizzie entered the drawing room. "Goodness, child, where have you been? I was beginning to worry."

"I'm sorry I'm late." Lizzie gave her a kiss on the cheek. As she did so, she noticed that the writing desk was covered with invitations. Lady Thornborough was probably arranging a dinner party—with Lizzie as the guest of honor. "I was with Geoffrey. Did James not send word?"

"No, he did not. That's just like him. He probably went to his club and didn't give it another thought." She set her quill into its stand. "You were with Lord Somerville, did you say?"

"Yes." Seeing the multitude of questions in the woman's eyes, Lizzie turned away. She was not ready to answer them. The memory of what had passed between her and Geoffrey in the carriage was still too fresh. The surprising jolt of pleasure she'd felt at his touch still coursed through her. He'd caught her and held her close, steadying her feet but unsteadying her heart.

She caught a glimpse of herself in the mirror over the fireplace and saw that her face glowed pink. This fact did not escape Lady Thornborough either. "Are you well, my dear?" She rose from the desk and rang for the butler.

"I am tired," Lizzie admitted. She sank slowly into a chair. Her legs were dangerously wobbly.

"I have ordered more of Cook's special broth for luncheon. That should help you recover from your exertions."

Lizzie did her best to keep from making a sour face. It was possible to have too much of a good thing, she decided. Cook's broth was proof of that.

Harding entered. His gaze rested for only the briefest of moments on Lizzie, but she was sure he had missed nothing. He had heard her farewells with Geoffrey on the front steps, seen the look on her face that most likely belied her formal words. She did not have a "poker face," as Tom had called it. A term he had learned from the Americans who had come to Sydney.

"Harding, you may tell Cook that we are ready for luncheon," Lady Thornborough informed the butler.

"Right away, madam."

Harding withdrew and closed the door, and Lizzie found herself breathing a sigh of relief. He managed to bring about the same kind of schoolmaster's terror in Lizzie that Ria had suffered.

Lady Thornborough turned her attention back to Lizzie. "Did things go well with you and Lord Somerville today?"

Lizzie carefully smoothed her gown. "Of course."

"Are you on amicable terms, then?"

"You could say that." Lizzie did not aim to be coy with her, but the powerful reaction she'd had to Geoffrey was not something she could divulge. She continued to move her hands slowly over her gown, attempting to draw strength from its silky coolness.

"Well, that's a relief," Lady Thornborough said. "I am glad you took my advice to heart. We are all family now, after all."

Family. Lizzie had come back to England in search of her family, and she'd certainly found one in Lady Thornborough and James. Her feelings toward Geoffrey were harder to define. It had been too easy today to forget that he was supposed to be her brother-in-law. "He's going to call again tomorrow," she said. Geoffrey wanted to see her again, and no matter the reason for it, she was undeniably glad.

"Excellent," Lady Thornborough said with satisfaction. "I believe it will be a good thing for you to spend time together." She laid a cool hand on Lizzie's hot cheek. "Are you sure you are up to making calls with me today?"

Lizzie took a deep breath, hoping it would settle the quick, shallow beats of her heart. "Of course. Cook's broth is bound to give me all the strength I need."

*

"It's incredibly exciting," Lady Cardington declared, her voice filling the ornate and overstuffed drawing room. The other women who were present nodded in agreement.

This visit to the home of Lady Cardington was the last call Lizzie and Lady Thornborough would make today, and Lizzie was counting the minutes until they could leave. It was a tedious business, getting in and out of carriages, being led upstairs into drawing rooms, being announced, and making introductions— all for the sake of a trivial fifteen-minute conversation.

The only relief for Lizzie was that she was not the primary topic of interest after all. It was Geoffrey who could claim that honor. Everywhere they went, the talk was the same: society matrons and their daughters vigorously discussed Lord Somerville and how he was the unexpected bounty of the season. Somewhat of an oddity, to be sure, but undeniably the biggest and best catch nonetheless.

Hearing Geoffrey reduced time and time again to a mere prize to be won was sorely trying to Lizzie's nerves. Surely he was more than that. During their time together this morning, she began to see the man beneath the labels that had been heaped upon him. She realized she'd been just as guilty of shallow assumptions as everyone else. He was not the critical clergyman she had initially thought him to be; neither was he simply the most eligible peer in this season's marriage market. Lizzie was beginning to suspect he'd make a fine husband, although not for the reasons she'd heard bandied about thus far.

Geoffrey had told her at their first meeting that he did not take pleasure in titles. She believed that now. He'd been forced to change his life's plans, to fulfill a role he'd never prepared for. He must be struggling under a load of pressure. Perhaps they could help each other, as Lord Ashley had said. Her position as his sister-in-law would allow them to spend a lot of time together if they wished. Lizzie found she was happy at this prospect. She might just have to guard against caring for him *too* much.

"My husband is of the opinion that Lord Somerville intends to marry as soon as possible," said one of the ladies, who had been introduced to Lizzie as Mrs. Paddington. She was a tall, slender woman who wore a gown with a garish red-and-green tartan design. Lizzie had learned during an earlier house call that plaids were all the rage this season. Her eyes were nearly crossed from the varieties of plaid she had been subjected to this afternoon.

"My husband spoke to Lord Somerville at the club last week," Mrs. Paddington related with a superior smile. "Of course, he badgered the poor man for the particulars—you know how my husband is such an incorrigible gossip!" Several women tittered at this remark. "But even my Stanley could get no details out of him."

"He has been very careful not to show a preference for any particular lady," Lady Cardington said with a knowing air. "But I can tell where his eye is heading…" She let her voice trail off dramatically as she looked pointedly toward Lucinda, her eldest daughter.

Lady Cardington was in a position to speak candidly. All the women present, except for her two daughters, were either elderly or already married. Or out of the running, Lizzie amended to herself, thinking of her own situation. Lizzie thought wryly of the previous visits they had paid that day. In those drawing rooms there were other women who had been just as sure where Geoffrey would be casting his favor—and it was not at the eldest Miss Cardington.

"We anticipate his offer any day," Lady Cardington said. "I'm quivering all over, as though I were sitting on pins and needles." She made several sharp movements up and down in her chair to dramatize this pronouncement.

Lady Cardington was the wrong person to imagine quivering all over. Lizzie quickly turned her eyes away, hoping she could prevent the image from lodging in her head. As she did so, she found herself staring right into the large brown eyes of Lucinda Cardington.

She proffered the teapot in Lizzie's direction. "More tea, Mrs. Somerville?"

Having never *actually* been married, Lizzie was finding that to be continually addressed as Mrs. Somerville was unnerving. She told herself she would get used to it in time—the way a callus grows over skin that is repeatedly chafed. She extended her cup. "Yes, thank you."

Lucinda's eyebrows knit together as she concentrated on pouring the tea. When the cup was full, she turned just as carefully to lower the teapot onto a small table in front of them. Despite her efforts, the teapot clattered loudly as the china made jarring contact with the silver tray, causing the poor girl to wince in embarrassment.

She seemed to have a difficult time controlling her movements. Lizzie was still trying to sort out whether this was her natural tendency or if she grew awkward only in the presence of guests. Perhaps it was her own presence that was making Lucinda so nervous. She was, after all, the sister-in-law of London's *most eligible bachelor.* Perhaps Lucinda was desperate to make a good impression so Lizzie would give a good word to Geoffrey for her. It was not a scenario Lizzie cared to contemplate.

She did seem a good sort of person, however. Honest and kind, and reasonably well educated. She had even managed some interesting conversation when she was not fretting herself into knots about the tea service. Lizzie sympathized with her on that account; like Lucinda, Lizzie was not comfortable with the stiff formalities of society. Unfortunately, it was nothing she could confess to Lucinda to make her feel any better. They might both feel like outsiders, Lizzie thought, but for completely different reasons.

At Lizzie's other elbow was Emily, Lucinda's younger sister. Emily could not have been more than sixteen years old, yet her conversation was so centered on "marriage prospects" that she might as well have been out of the schoolroom and presented into society. Perhaps she already was. Lizzie had heard of girls whose parents allowed them to come out at such a young age.

Emily studied Lizzie with intense curiosity, as though she were some strange, otherworldly creature. It was a bit unnerving.

"Emily, where are your manners?" Lady Cardington said sharply. "I'm sure Mrs. Somerville does not appreciate being stared at so rudely."

Emily gave Lizzie a smile that was intended to appear apologetic and said a bit too sweetly, "I beg your pardon, Mrs. Somerville."

"That's better," her mother said, somewhat appeased.

"I should like to know all about Lord Somerville," Emily went on cheerily, undeterred by her mother's scolding. "Lucinda thinks it would be heavenly to have such a man in the family." She gave a mischievous smile. "Perhaps *heavenly* is not the correct word, now that he no longer has a parish." She giggled at her silly joke.

Emily's frivolous words sent a chill down Lizzie's spine. These ladies were discussing Lucinda's marriage to Geoffrey as a foregone conclusion. But what were Geoffrey's thoughts on the matter? She had no doubt that he would fulfill his familial duties and take a wife. But how soon would he do it? Was it really imminent, as Lady Cardington implied? Unlike these women, Lizzie was concerned for the man himself, that he might be genuinely happy—not merely providing a big society wedding for their entertainment.

Lizzie sipped her tea and sent another surreptitious glance toward the clock. Just a few minutes more and they could leave. She would be glad to get away and get back home. And tomorrow, she thought with a smile to herself as she watched these uselessly chattering women, she would be seeing Geoffrey again.

Chapter 16

The bright summer sun bathed London in a particularly fine light. Geoffrey was glad for the clear weather as he rode in his open carriage toward the Thornborough home. He would have preferred to walk, but he anticipated offering a ride to Ria today. It would be an agreeable way for her to become reacquainted with the city.

It was astounding, really, how continually she had been in his thoughts, although he had yet to completely comprehend her. He had been pleased at how easily they had reached a reconciliation, at her genuine desire that they should be friends. This was a good thing, surely. But she could irritate him, too. Her silly words yesterday after meeting that old man in Hyde Park were a case in point. In fact, Geoffrey was disappointed at the way she had handled the entire episode.

Then there was the moment in the carriage when she had fallen into his arms. He had no idea why his reaction had been so uncomfortably strong. Certainly he had held women before—

dancing with them, escorting them. But never had it felt like that. It was perhaps one thing he would be safer *not* to dwell upon.

Today he was ready to ask her for details about Edward. Certain things she'd told him at their first meeting kept returning to him, and he wanted to know more. He wondered what the trajectory of Edward's life might have been if it had not been cut short. Geoffrey hoped he could find some consolation in knowing his brother had been content with the life he had chosen. He hoped Ria could shed more light on this, and help him find peace.

As the carriage came to a stop, he found himself praying, *Thank you, Lord, for helping me to heal—and for helping Ria to heal, too.* And as a quick addendum as he walked up the steps to the Thornborough home, he added, *Lord, please help me understand her better. Help us know what we should do in the future.*

The butler showed him up to the parlor. Ria stood by the window, the sunshine illuminating her face. Geoffrey paused, transfixed. A deep burgundy gown beautifully set off her features, and her hair was set in ringlets in the back that edged her graceful neck.

Only days before, he had viewed her as the cause of so much misery. Now he knew he could not allow it to overshadow all of his thoughts and actions. There was no changing the past; he and this woman must make the best of the present.

She walked over and clasped his hands warmly. "I'm so glad you could come."

He was inordinately happy to find that neither Lady Thornborough nor James was present. "Are we all alone, then?" he asked.

"I'm afraid so. Grandmamma had another engagement this morning. She hopes you will forgive her absence."

He nodded. "Of course."

Ria looked uncertain about what to say next, and Geoffrey also felt suddenly tongue-tied. He sensed they were both growing embarrassed as the silence lengthened. Finally he said, "Would you like to take a drive? It is a fine day, and I brought an open carriage."

Ria smiled, and Geoffrey was glad to see the tension subside from her manner. "That sounds marvelous."

A few minutes later they stepped out of the town house. Geoffrey handed Ria up into the carriage and was relieved to find this task a shade less disconcerting than it had been yesterday. He hoped that, as he grew more familiar with Ria, he would not always find her nearness so diverting to all his senses. As soon as he sat down next to her, however, he realized he still had a long way to go.

"Where to, my lord?" the driver asked.

Geoffrey turned to Ria. "What would you like to see? Shall we go north to Regents Park, or down toward the river? Perhaps a visit to Saint Paul's Cathedral?"

Her face lit up at the mention of Saint Paul's, which was located in the original part of London still known as the City. "It would be lovely to see the City again."

"Excellent." To the driver he added, "Take us by way of Buckingham Palace," and was gratified to see Ria's look of delight.

The streets were filled, as always, with carriages, carts, and even livestock. There were a great many pedestrians, too, their ranks swelled by the visitors who had come for the Great Exhibition. Ria seemed to take it all in with fascination. "How busy London is," she observed. "The noise and activity never stop."

"It's a far cry from a sheep farm, I'm sure," Geoffrey said.

She nodded. "It is also, I think, very different from your quiet little parish in the country?"

How kind, he thought, *that she should think of that.* "Yes," he agreed. "I wonder if I shall ever acclimatize to it."

"I feel the same way," she replied with a melancholy air.

They were alike in that respect, Geoffrey reflected. They were both facing extraordinary life changes. "A lot has changed since you were last in London, I expect."

She gave a little laugh. "Yes, much has changed." She cast him a teasingly critical look. "Have you perchance changed as well? I confess you are not at all like I had pictured you'd be."

He should not have been surprised to hear this; after all, hadn't he felt the same way about her? Even so, it gave him pause. "No doubt Edward's descriptions did me no credit. What did he tell you about me, to give you such low expectations?"

"It's not that Edward spoke ill of you," she protested. "He just said that all three brothers were very different people. In his opinion, William was too bullheaded, Eddie himself was too easygoing, and you were too short on patience for either of them."

"No doubt he was right," Geoffrey said, shaking his head. "I only wish he might have confided in me before leaving England."

"Perhaps he feared you would talk him out of it."

"Undoubtedly. He knew I would vigorously remind him of his duties and urge him to do the right thing."

"But would it have been right to stay in England? It would have meant seeing the woman he loved married to his brother. And she would have been forced into a loveless marriage."

This seemed an odd way for her to phrase it. "Why do you speak of yourself in the third person?"

"I..." She faltered. "I...was merely attempting to lay the question out logically."

Logic was not a word Geoffrey would once have used to

describe either Ria or Edward, but he thought it better not to say this. There was a time, he thought, for discretion.

Their carriage was forced to a stop while a man drove several cattle across the road. Geoffrey tried to imagine Edward in such a role. It still seemed incredible to him. "Ria, you said Edward was one of Mr. McCrae's most trusted hands. What were his duties exactly? Did he truly enjoy the work?"

It was like a dam had broken—in a good way. Ria began to speak freely of the life she and Edward had led in Australia. She was so animated as she spoke, and Geoffrey took pleasure in watching her as she described caring for the sheep, the intensive days of shearing in summer, and Edward's vital role getting wool and supplies across the Blue Mountains. Edward's excellent horsemanship, a hallmark of the Somerville family, had been his first greatest asset. His energy and leadership had been the second.

"I confess that you are giving me a picture of Edward I never had before," Geoffrey told her.

"I'm not surprised. He never had the chance to prove himself in England. He was always just the second son—the 'spare.' In Australia it was like he became unbound." She gave him a misty smile. "You would have been so proud."

He took her hands, happy to hold them, happy to be able to share these moments with her. "I wish I might have known him then. Seen him..." He broke off. It was difficult to put in words his sense of loss, his regret that he had missed out on sharing what must have been his brother's finest years.

Ria squeezed his hands gently. "He would have loved that, too," she said.

"Were you happy there, too? Is that why you stayed so long after his death?"

She glanced away, looking at the passing buildings. "I believe I was content—so long as Edward was alive. We had some dear friends, too." She paused to briefly touch a handkerchief to her eyes. "I did not want to leave Edward at first. Leave his grave, I mean. Even though he is dead, I felt like it would be abandoning him."

"What made you change your mind?"

"I…" She looked at him apologetically. "I knew there was unfinished business here. I had to return."

"Thank you for that," Geoffrey said. "I know it cannot have been easy for you."

"It was no easy thing to cross those mountains again, I can tell you," she said with feeling. "To retrace the steps Edward had taken…There was a small group of us traveling together. Our guide knew where Edward had been attacked, but I specifically asked him *not* to point out that location to me."

She dabbed again at her eyes, and Geoffrey felt it would be a shame to give in to sorrow now. "Let us not dwell on his death today," he proposed. "Today, let's rejoice in the life he lived."

"Thank you," she said. "That is a wise suggestion."

There followed a moment of silence, however, when there seemed no good way to begin speaking of anything else.

Geoffrey saw that they were approaching Buckingham Palace. "I can see the royal standard," he said, pointing to the ornate red, blue, and gold flag flying high atop the palace. "The Queen is in residence today."

*

Lizzie marveled at how well Geoffrey received the things she told him about Edward. It was another important milestone, she thought, that she had been able to increase his appreciation for his brother. It was one way she was keeping her promise to Ria, and her heart was a little lighter because of it. "Thank you for bringing me out today," she said.

"Thank *you*," Geoffrey replied with a smile.

She loved his smile. It did not come as easily as Edward's, but it was just as attractive. She wondered if Geoffrey was aware of the effect it could have on women. She suspected he did not. Lizzie turned her face toward the sun, basking in its warmth and in the satisfaction she'd already received from being with Geoffrey this morning.

They drove through Saint James's Park and began to head east. This was her first real opportunity to see the city since her return. Her brief forays with James and Lady Thornborough had been limited to Hyde Park and a few fashionable homes in Mayfair and Belgravia. What a treat it was, too, to see it all from the comfort of a carriage. In the past when she'd lived in London, she usually traveled on foot, and had rarely come this far west.

The traffic grew denser as they approached the heart of the city. The famous dome of Saint Paul's Cathedral had been visible from a great way off. As they drew near to the cathedral, Lizzie saw many people milling about, admiring the two rows of double pillars and the two tall towers that framed the front of the edifice. She had fond memories of this place. In some ways, it was like seeing an old friend.

"Would you like to go in?" Geoffrey inquired.

She readily agreed.

The interior of Saint Paul's was refreshingly airy and cool after the heat of the summer day. There were plenty of people inside, but they quickly dispersed among the smaller chapels and alcoves of the enormous cathedral. As she and Geoffrey walked slowly down the long nave, Lizzie enjoyed the hushed calm that pervaded the place—so quiet after the noisy confusion of the streets outside.

When they reached the center, they paused to look up at the inside of the giant dome. Lizzie saw at least a dozen people looking down at her. These were the intrepid visitors who had climbed the many stairs leading up to the whispering gallery, an area ringing the base of the dome. Lizzie turned to Geoffrey. "Can we go up?" she asked eagerly.

"Are you sure you want to do that?" he replied with surprise. "I believe there are over two hundred steps."

"It's two hundred and fifty-seven, to be precise," said a man who happened to be walking by them at that moment. "The missus and I just came down." He indicated the lady he was escorting. Both were well into middle age, and they were looking a little red-faced, as though from heavy exertion. Lizzie instantly recognized the man's American accent. "It's quite a hike, I can tell you," the man declared. "I was so tuckered when I got to the top, I thought I'd peg out. But the view is bully." Lizzie tried to suppress a smile at the look on Geoffrey's face. Was he more surprised at the man's colloquialisms, or at being thus addressed without an introduction?

She soon had her answer. After they had parted from the couple and found the entrance to the gallery steps, Geoffrey asked Lizzie with amusement, "Do you have any idea what that gentleman said?"

"Oh, yes," Lizzie replied. "I had occasion to meet some Americans in Sydney. Their expressions can be quite colorful." She translated for him as they proceeded up the steep and narrow staircase. They paused on a small landing halfway up. It was warmer up here, and Lizzie was still adjusting to the extra layers of clothing she was now required to wear. Dressing in Australia had been much simpler. She leaned on Geoffrey's arm as they took a moment to catch their breaths, and she was happy to see that he seemed to take as much pleasure in this as she did. Thus fortified, they took the last flight of steps and at last exited through a door onto the whispering gallery.

Lizzie went straight to the iron balustrade and surveyed the immense nave far below. She had been up here once before as a child. She and Tom had enjoyed testing the peculiar characteristic for which the gallery got its name. Tom had circled the walkway to the other side, and the two had been able to talk to one another in a normal voice despite the great distance separating them. "Have you been here before?" she asked Geoffrey as he joined her at the railing.

"Oh, yes," he answered. "My brothers and I first came here as children, and we were naturally intrigued by the way the sound travels around the walls."

"I can definitely picture that," Lizzie said. How odd to think that they had all, in a way, crossed paths up here. What different courses their lives had taken since then.

She turned to look up. From here they had a closer view of the murals decorating the inside of the dome. "What do they represent?"

She was sure Geoffrey would know the answer to this question, and he did. "These are scenes from Saint Paul's life. There are eight in all, as you see. This first one," he said, pointing to the mural just above them, "shows Paul's conversion on the road to Damascus. There is Paul on his knees, with the bright light of the Lord shining round about him."

Geoffrey gave her a brief background of the stories illustrated in each of the paintings. When he reached the last one, he said, "And this is the shipwreck, when Paul's ship was broken up during a fierce storm."

"A shipwreck?" The word brought unsettling things to Lizzie's mind: she could almost feel, as well as visualize, waves that were endlessly rolling, never ceasing. And then to be thrown into wild waters, taken away by a reckless sea, just as Tom had been. Her heart broke afresh at the thought of it. "It must have been horrifying," she said, her voice strained.

"It was described vividly in the Book of Acts: '*All hope that we might be saved was lost.*'"

Lizzie gripped the railing. She looked across the open expanse to the other side of the whispering gallery, remembering how her brother had stood there, alive with the joy and excitement of youth. Now she saw that he had been standing beneath that mural of a shipwreck. "All hope lost," she repeated sadly.

Seeing her expression, Geoffrey added, "The Bible says that all two hundred and seventy-six people aboard the ship made it safely to land. God protected them."

He intended this as a good thing, Lizzie knew, and she said, "What a wonderful miracle." But in her heart she sinfully wondered why the Lord could not have saved Tom. Of course, Paul had worked tirelessly to win others to Christ. Tom had boarded a ship with far different intentions. He felt he knew where Edward's murderer was, and he was going after him.

"I've always admired Saint Paul," Geoffrey mused. "He went from being a persecutor of Christians to becoming their leader. He had a complete change of heart. He later wrote that one must forget things that are behind and reach forth for those things that are before."

"Forget the past?" Lizzie shook her head in disbelief. "Do you think that is ever really possible?"

"I believe the lesson is that we must not allow past sins to keep us from living for the Lord today."

Lizzie had never thought about "living for the Lord." She had always attended church, like everyone else. But with all that had happened in her life—brief periods of joy overwhelmed by grief and disappointment—God had remained distant to her.

Nor could she even consider forgetting the past. With each new day, Lizzie was becoming more and more successful in her new life, and yet she was discovering that the past never receded. She could never forget who she truly was. No, the past was something she lived with each and every day. She would never be able to leave it fully behind.

She turned back to see Geoffrey looking at her. She knew how easily her morose thoughts could show on her face. She did not wish him to see her discomfort, so she giggled, fanned herself, and said in a perfect imitation of the American gentleman, "I believe I am tuckered." She looked over the railing. "But the view is bully!"

Chapter 17

Geoffrey stood in his library, thoughtfully staring at a large portrait of himself with his two brothers. Although it was painted when the three boys were in their early teens, their individual personalities were already quite evident. William was standing looking rather imperious, Edward was kneeling, playing with their favorite dog Buck, and Geoffrey was seated in an armchair, looking at both his brothers with an expression that today he could only describe as bemused. For a long time it had been too painful for Geoffrey to spend any time looking at this portrait. Today he found instead that the memories it brought back cheered him.

"How well you look, sir."

He turned to see Mrs. Claridge standing in the doorway. "Do I?"

She nodded. "You must have had a good morning out with Mrs. Somerville."

Geoffrey found to his surprise that it was not as jarring to hear Ria referred to by that name as he had once feared it would be. "Yes," he said. "I believe it was a good morning." He was still marveling at how much he enjoyed Ria's company.

"Your heart seems a bit lighter now—if you don't mind my saying so," she added deferentially.

Once again, her perception amazed him. "Does it seem odd to you that my heart should be, as you say, lighter, after I am more fully aware of all that has happened?"

"Not at all," she replied. "I always say that knowing the worst is not as terrible as fearing it."

"In some ways, though, it's not the worst. Mrs. Somerville told me fascinating things about Edward, things I never knew about him. She showed me some of his best aspects." *And some of hers,* he added silently to himself. Despite her occasional missteps, he found his esteem for her was growing.

"Perhaps that's why her return has been so good for you," Mrs. Claridge said.

Had Ria been good for him? Perhaps so. "I shall invite her over here soon. I would like for you to meet her."

Mrs. Claridge beamed. "That's kind of you, sir. I'm sure I would like that very much."

"She can tell you some of the things she told me about Edward." He turned to look again at the portrait. "Edward accomplished many things in Australia that would have astounded us all."

"Not me," Mrs. Claridge returned. "I always knew Mr. Edward was a resourceful and enterprising young man."

"Did you?" he said in surprise. "Somehow that fact escaped the rest of us."

"It's hard, sometimes, to see these things in your own family members."

He pondered this. There was certainly truth in it. "Edward was

146

a natural leader—I can see that now. He would have performed his duties very well if he had taken up the barony. Perhaps even better than William did." He sighed. "Perhaps even better than I can."

Edward certainly could have carried out the social responsibilities of the peerage more deftly than Geoffrey had been doing. And now Ria had shown him Edward could have handled a leadership role as well.

"All three of you were and *are* leaders, sir," Mrs. Claridge declared. "Just in your different ways. I have no doubt you will live up to the Somerville title as well as anyone—better even."

He smiled gratefully at his housekeeper. "You have always been my greatest advocate."

He turned toward the mirror over the fireplace. "Mrs. Claridge, do you think this coat looks too serious?"

"Serious?" she repeated, perplexed. "How do you mean?"

"Well, I don't know exactly," he said truthfully. "It's something Mr. Simpson told me once."

"That Mr. Simpson," she said with a chuckle. "He is a dandy."

Geoffrey's evening attire was just as "serious," and he was secretly wondering if he should get something more stylish to wear to the Beauchamps' ball. It was unlike him to worry about such things, but as he recalled how Edward always conducted himself so well at parties, he was suddenly seized with a foolish notion that he wanted to look good for this event. He wanted to please Ria.

"I would not say the problem was with your coat," Mrs. Claridge observed. "Perhaps it was only your expression that was too serious. You don't need a tailor to improve upon that. Only yourself. And that seems to be on the mend."

How true, Geoffrey thought. Perhaps some of the peace he'd prayed for was coming to pass.

*

"Mrs. Dodd, we must be absolutely sure to get this right. I want my granddaughter to be above reproach."

Lady Thornborough's special clothier had come to the Thornborough home to measure Lizzie for the gown she was to wear to the grand ball at Lord and Lady Beauchamp's home. Lady Thornborough was anxious that the color and style of the gown be exactly proper for a young widow reentering society.

Mrs. Dodd gave a crisp bob of her head. "Indeed, Lady Thornborough, I concur wholeheartedly. This event calls for just the right display of delicacy and protocol." She was a small, trim woman, dressed impeccably from head to foot. She exuded confidence in her profession and was a perfect model of it. It was easy to see why Lady Thornborough had chosen her for the task. "I promise we will design a dress that is both stylish and appropriate."

Mrs. Dodd and her assistants were thorough. Lizzie was pushed, prodded, and measured from every angle. They draped sample after sample of beautiful silks over Lizzie's shoulder to see how well they would complement her complexion. There were so many samples that a small army of assistants was needed to bring them in. The silks covered a range of dark hues, from rich maroon to vibrant midnight blue. Even the dark gray was enticing. Lizzie admired the way it shimmered as it moved, reflecting the light like silken water.

Her initial worries about going out into society were dropping away with each successful day. Her calls with Lady Thornborough had been successful, as had a dinner at the home of a baronet. She had also been "refreshed" on etiquette by Lady Thornborough. Since Ria had left before her debutante year, it was understood that she would need instruction on deportment and the niceties of behavior at fancy balls. Geoffrey would be at the ball, too, giving her any needed advice. She was beginning to look forward to events where Geoffrey was present, feeling that somehow she could always rely on him to help her if necessary.

Lizzie had been easily caught up in the excitement of the gown's preparation. Of the many fine dresses she'd been privileged to wear since her arrival in London, this would be the most special—an elegant gown to be worn for only the finest occasions. Drawn to beautiful clothes for as long as she could remember, Lizzie had spent many afternoons in Hyde Park watching the beautifully dressed ladies as they rode by in their carriages or strolled along the Serpentine.

Freddie had dressed her well, too. That was one of the first things that had led to her downfall. He promised her silks and fine linens and jewelry. He made good on the promise, too—in the beginning. When he ran out of money, he sold everything without her knowledge to buy his way home. She'd been left with only the clothes on her back. And her wits.

"Ria, stop frowning," Lady Thornborough said. "You know that will give you wrinkles. Is something wrong?"

Lizzie pulled herself out of her cloud of black thoughts and relaxed her face into a smile. Those days were far behind her now, she reminded herself. She was no longer mending other people's clothes to scrape out a living, as she had in Vienna for those months before Tom had come for her. Now the fine clothes were being tailored for *her.* "It's just that I'm so vexed because I can't make up my mind which material to choose. They are all so lovely."

"That is why Mrs. Dodd is here. She has made dresses for the Queen's ladies-in-waiting. She knows what will suit you best."

Mrs. Dodd beamed. "Your confidence in my judgment is most flattering, my lady."

"Ah," returned Lady Thornborough with a smile. "But the question remains: which color is the most flattering on my granddaughter?"

"Midnight blue," replied Mrs. Dodd without hesitation. "She will be stunning."

One of Mrs. Dodd's assistants immediately retrieved the blue silk from a chair and draped it once more around Lizzie.

Lizzie stood, looking at herself, delighted at how her eyes deepened and glittered, set off by the beautiful material.

Lady Thornborough rose and walked over to her. They stood, side by side, studying her reflection in the mirror. "See how it brings out your father's eyes," she said with admiration. "How proud he would be."

"Would he?" Lizzie basked in these words. She *was* showing her true colors as a Thornborough, she thought. Fine clothes were no longer her downfall, as they had once been with Freddie. Nor were they the reason she was here. Yes, there were times when Lizzie wished she could stand here free of her deceptions, where she belonged, with her family. Since she could not, she took solace in the fact that she was fulfilling Ria's wishes. Lady Thornborough had her granddaughter back and was pleased with her. That was what Ria had wanted. Ria's untimely death had provided a second chance for them both. Lizzie could not allow any regret for what she had done to reach this room on this day.

Freddie had left her in the gutter, but she had survived. Like Cinderella from the fairy tale her mother read to her when she was a little girl, Lizzie now had all those things that had once seemed out of reach.

Except for a handsome prince.

Chapter 18

Martha had once again worked wonders with Lizzie's hair. Her blond locks were braided into an intricate bun in the back, and smooth ringlets framed her face. It had been a trial to be subjected to her brushing, twisting, and pinning, but the end result had been worth it. As Lizzie reached up to finger one of the curls, the diamond and sapphire bracelet shimmered against the dark blue of her gown. Lady Thornborough had insisted she wear it tonight.

Thanks to Mrs. Dodd, Lizzie's gown was at the height of fashion, though the décolletage was not as low as most women's would be tonight. There was a certain amount of propriety that she must maintain. Nevertheless, the V-shape of the neckline did drop low enough to reveal a modest portion of her neck and shoulders.

Lizzie was happy to see that her skin had become paler during her weeks in London. She was no longer "brown as a farm girl," as James had described her.

She studied her hands. Now that she was no longer hauling her own firewood and doing her own washing, her nails were smoother and the cuts and scrapes on her hands had healed. The process had been quickened by the special oils Lady Thornborough had procured for her. They'd been applied and rubbed in by two maids until Lizzie felt like a prized piece of silver that had been polished with the utmost care.

There was a light tap at the door, and Lady Thornborough entered, her dark silk dress shimmering in the candlelight. Her gray eyes shone, set off to best advantage by the gleaming jet-black broach on her dress. "I cannot believe the vision in front of me," she said, her face alight with pride. She placed a gentle hand on Lizzie's cheek. "It's as if the trials of these past few years have been wiped away. You are older in experience, perhaps, and yet still so beautiful. What an enviable advantage for any woman to have!" She continued to inspect Lizzie. "You have your mother's slender figure, although you did not grow nearly as tall as we thought you might." She gently tilted Lizzie's face to one side and studied her profile. "I cannot say that I see much of her face in yours."

Lizzie's chest tightened. Lady Thornborough's attempts to find similarities with Ria's mother would, of course, be fruitless. She stepped back, straightened to her full height, and exclaimed, "I am sure I am quite tall! I shall positively tower over half the men at Lord Beauchamp's ball."

"I doubt that," Lady Thornborough said with a smile. "However, there is no doubt that you have your father's eyes—and his confident look. At times I fancy that I see him in you."

Now here was a topic Lizzie did not wish to avoid. She had gazed at Herbert's portrait many times over the past few weeks, looking for traces of herself in him. "Do I really favor him?"

"There is no doubt in my mind," Lady Thornborough answered.

"Dearest Grandmamma." Lizzie's voice caught in her throat. It was easy to address her that way now. She fully believed she was a Thornborough—not the one everyone believed her to be, but a Thornborough nonetheless.

Lizzie turned to check the mirror one last time, but Lady Thornborough took her by the arm. "You have spent more than enough time on your toilette, dear. The carriage is waiting."

"I blame Martha for my tardiness," Lizzie said gaily. "She spent ages on my hair."

With the barest smile, Martha replied, "It might not have taken so long, madam, if you had remained still."

Lizzie gave an exaggerated sigh. "Isn't that just the worst irony of life? The more excited I am to get out of this chair, the longer it takes."

Lizzie followed Lady Thornborough out the door of the bedchamber and down the hall. She paused as they were about to descend the stairs.

"What is it, dear?" Lady Thornborough asked.

"I've forgotten my fan." She turned back toward her room. "I'll only be a moment."

When Lizzie entered her room, she found Martha sitting at the dressing table, staring pensively at a small framed silhouette of Ria. She jumped up when she saw Lizzie, looking as though she had been caught doing something wrong. Lizzie wondered what train of thought she had interrupted. "I've come back for my fan," she said, trying to keep any unease from sounding in her voice.

Martha snatched it up and placed it in Lizzie's hands. "How careless of me not to notice." She did not meet Lizzie's eye.

"That silhouette never did me justice, you know," Lizzie said. "The artist was far too kind about the shape of my nose." It was true that when Lizzie and Ria were compared side by side in profile, their noses were clearly different. Lizzie had always considered Ria to have the prettier of the two; her own was a tad straighter and longer. "They will pander to one's vanity if they think they will get more money for it, after all."

Martha did not know how to appear to answer this remark, since by agreeing with Lizzie, she would seem to be agreeing that her mistress was perhaps less than beautiful.

"Martha," Lady Thornborough called from the hallway. "I need you to fetch my smelling salts from the parlor."

"Grandmamma, however, is delightfully misguided about my charms," Lizzie said with a playful grin. "She believes the ladies at the ball will faint with envy when they see me!"

Martha's gap-toothed smile reemerged, as did her placid demeanor. Even so, Lizzie worried that she had not managed to entirely erase any doubts that might have been in the old servant's head: from the corner of her eye she saw Martha give one more furtive glance at the silhouette before following her out.

*

"The ladies certainly are taking their time," Geoffrey remarked, looking at his pocket watch yet again. He had been waiting in the Thornboroughs' library with James for what seemed like an age, keenly anticipating seeing Ria again. Each hour he'd spent with her over the past several weeks increased his desire to see her more, like some kind of inverted appetite that grew sharper with each morsel of food.

"Her tardiness is to be expected," James said. "Ria is such a vain creature, you know." He checked his lapel and flicked some minuscule fleck of dust off his coat sleeve as he spoke, causing Geoffrey to wonder briefly who was the more vain of the two.

Geoffrey noticed a slender book that was poking out from under a pile of newspapers lying on the table next to him. He pulled it out and opened it to the title page. It was a volume of poetry by Lord Tennyson. "Is this yours?"

James shook his head. "I find poetry deadly dull, except for a few sonnets that can be read aloud to garner the right reactions from the ladies."

Geoffrey suspected that James's arsenal of poetic overtures was probably small, but effective.

"Ria's been reading that book," James explained.

"Has she?" Geoffrey said, bemused. "I don't recall hearing that Ria cared for poetry."

"It seems to be something she picked up in Australia."

"Picked up?" Geoffrey smiled. "You say that as though poetry were a disease of some kind."

"So it is, as far as I'm concerned."

"I happen to like poetry," Geoffrey said.

"Well, that's one more thing you two have in common, then." He gave Geoffrey a knowing look. "Who knew you and Ria would have so many similar interests?"

"Yes," Geoffrey murmured. "Who knew?" He leafed through the tiny volume. It opened on a poem entitled "Adeline." He began to read.

> *"Mystery of mysteries,*
> *Faintly smiling Adeline,*
> *Scarce of earth nor all divine,*

Nor unhappy, nor at rest,
But beyond expression fair
With thy floating flaxen hair;
Thy rose-lips and full blue eyes..."

Geoffrey scarcely realized he was reading aloud until James remarked, "Now *there* is poetry I could use—if I were courting a blonde, of course."

"With thy floating flaxen hair..."

The author might as well have called the poem "Victoria," he thought with a start.

"Thy rose-lips and full blue eyes...
Take the heart from out my breast."

Just then Ria appeared in the doorway, breathtaking in a shimmering blue silk gown. Diamonds sparkled at her throat and wrist. *"Wherefore those dim looks of thine—shadowy, dreaming Adeline?"* Her blond ringlets bounced a little as she spoke, drawing attention to her violet-blue eyes, which the dress seemed to have brought out and darkened. Her voice, too, seemed deeper. Sultry, almost.

Geoffrey stood up, closing the book, acutely aware his hands were shaking. *Take the heart from out my breast.* He cleared his throat. "I see you know the poem."

Ria nodded. "Edward used to quote it often, except he would change 'Adeline' to 'Ria mine.' He used to say that Tennyson's muse must look exactly like...me." She laughed softly. "I used to chide him for it, but now I would give anything to hear him reading that poem again."

The room grew still. Geoffrey stared at her in quiet fascination. Even James appeared taken aback by the depth of feeling in Ria's words.

He could picture Edward reading this poem to her. Like James, Edward had probably used romantic poetry for the artful seduction of the ladies. But Geoffrey had the sense that, for his brother, things would have changed dramatically when it came to Ria. Edward would have spoken the words with more depth than even the poet himself could have intended. He would have joyfully lost himself in her exquisite beauty.

Even as he was.

Every nerve in his body thrummed with this knowledge. He was beginning to care for Ria in dangerous and forbidden ways. *Be careful, man,* he warned himself. *This is your brother's widow.*

Ria sighed and wiped a tear from her eye. Even in sorrow she was more beautiful than the best poet could describe. Geoffrey was discovering to his profound chagrin that the heart could not be reined in as easily as he had once believed.

"Dear Ria." James took gentle hold of her hand. "You are not alone. You have us." It was a rare display of genuine tenderness from James. Ria gave him a grateful smile.

Geoffrey was tempted to be envious, seeing how much the two cousins cared for each other. He wished he and Ria might one day share that kind of bond, even if all else was denied him. She turned her stunning eyes in his direction, and he tried to do as James had done, to give her some reassurance. "Though Edward would happily point out that I am a poor second, you have me as well."

She shook her head. "You are your own man, Geoffrey. To say you are a poor second is to do yourself a great injustice."

As far as Geoffrey was concerned, the Queen herself could not have bestowed a greater honor.

Lady Thornborough entered the room in time to hear Ria's words. "Who is a poor second?" she asked.

"I am, of course," James said smoothly. "Ria is lavishing praise upon Geoffrey and utterly forgetting about me." He gave a dramatic sigh. "Shall I never get the respect due to me as the head of the family?"

"You?" Lady Thornborough countered. "Head of the family?"

"You see?" James indicated his aunt's incredulous expression. "That is precisely what I mean."

Ria laughed and took hold of James's arm. "Well, you *are* the last man standing. There's something in that."

"That's a girl," James said, patting her hand. "Always looking on the bright side."

Lady Thornborough looked expectantly at James and Geoffrey. "Are we ready to go, gentlemen?"

As they made their way out to the moonlit night, Geoffrey drew nearer to Ria while James assisted Lady Thornborough into the carriage. He said quietly, "You look lovely this evening."

He was rewarded by her smile. "Thank you." Her brow wrinkled just a tiny bit. "You don't feel I am coming out too soon?"

Geoffrey shook his head. "I'm sure that Edward would not have wanted you to remain a recluse."

"Grandmamma assured me of that, too, and yet I am glad to hear it from you."

"Is my opinion really so important to you, then?" How far

they had come since she had first declared that she did not care what he thought of her. Had she changed? Or had something changed between them? *No*, he said to himself once more. *Do not go down that path. Even if her regard for you grows greater, she thinks only of you as a brother-in-law.*

"Geoffrey," Ria said—his name sounded delightful coming from her *rose-lips*—"if I thought my presence at tonight's ball would bring disrepute upon either of our families, I wouldn't go."

"Trust me, there is nothing shameful in your actions."

Geoffrey could not say the same for what was going on in his own mind. He helped her into the carriage, and in the close darkness her rose scent reached him with a more intoxicating pull than ever. He would have to be careful to spend no more time with her this evening than would be considered customary. But he would dance with her. This was allowable, and he had no intention of appearing to spurn his sister-in-law. For the first time in longer than he could remember, the right thing to do was the thing Geoffrey also wanted to do above all else.

Chapter 19

T he reverend Lord Somerville!" The footman announced Geoffrey with a booming voice that carried easily across the din of music and conversation. Lizzie's nerves tingled in anticipation. She must have been gripping James's arm more tightly than she realized, for he gently loosed her hand, giving her a wink as he did so.

"Relax, cousin," he said in her ear. "Everyone will love you. They always have."

"Mr. James Simpson! Mrs. Edward Somerville!" The footman's voice once again boomed across the ballroom.

Lizzie and James stepped forward to join Geoffrey and Lady Thornborough. Lizzie might well have been stepping out onto a stage—and what an opulent stage it was. From the wide landing where she stood, a long flight of stairs led down to an immense ballroom crowded with men dressed in elegant black or in the rich red of army uniforms, and women arrayed in a rainbow of colors, and everyone pausing to look up at her. She had just made a very grand entrance indeed. She was breathless, terrified, and ecstatic.

Brightly lit crystal chandeliers cheerfully laid out everything before her: from the velvet-seated chairs lining the long walls to the additional doors that opened to yet more rooms filled, as far as Lizzie could see, with food-laden tables. Even during her ill-fated months with Freddie, she had never been to an event as magnificent as this. She had never had an entire assembly of gentlemen and ladies looking at her—her!—with such admiration.

"What a crush!" Lady Thornborough murmured.

James looked over the crowd with the air of a king.

"Would you care to wave to your subjects?" Lizzie teased.

James smirked. "Perhaps later. If they are worthy."

They began descending the stairs at a regal pace, with Geoffrey and Lady Thornborough in the lead. Near the bottom of the stairs, Lizzie spotted a half-dozen or so young ladies whom she'd met during her calls with Lady Thornborough. Not surprisingly, they were whispering to one another and sending brilliant smiles in Geoffrey's direction—clearly doing their best to attract the catch of the season. A crazy stab of envy went through her as she realized that they were all quite fetching. Except perhaps for Miss Lucinda Cardington, who was a trifle too red in the face and fanning herself, looking exceedingly uncomfortable.

Miss Emily Cardington was the only lady who had eyes for anyone other than Geoffrey. She peered coyly at James from behind her fan, her eyes shining. Lizzie was dismayed to see James returning the girl's interest with fascination, although at the moment he could do no more than give her a smile and a genial nod. Emily would be out of her depths with him, Lizzie thought. Perhaps she should offer Emily some sage advice. She had no time to reflect on this, however, as they were met at the bottom of the stairs by their host and hostess.

"Lord and Lady Beauchamp, I am so happy to be able to present my granddaughter to you this evening," Lady Thornborough said. The pride in her voice was unmistakable, and it quickly brought Lizzie back to the reason she was here. It was time to do her very best to look, act, and *be* Ria.

Lady Beauchamp, a tall, willowy woman, took Lizzie's hand and said warmly, "How delightful to see you again!"

Again? When had Ria seen her? Under what circumstances? Lady Thornborough had said nothing to indicate there had been a previous acquaintance. Lizzie was aware that she was creating an uncomfortable pause as she tried to think of a response.

"Perhaps you do not remember me," Lady Beauchamp said, perceiving Lizzie's discomfort. "You were only a child the last time we met. Your father brought you to our estate in Lincolnshire, where we had planned a day of riding."

Lizzie's relief at being thus rescued by Lady Beauchamp was quickly overtaken by surprise. Ria hated horses. She never rode, and was uncomfortable even being near them. Edward had often voiced disappointment when Ria steadfastly refused his entreaties to give her lessons.

"The day did not go well," Lady Beauchamp said. "Perhaps you have blocked it from your memory. We put you on Blue Moon, the very gentlest mare we had, but somehow she bucked and nearly threw you off. You were crying and panicking and clinging to that saddle for dear life. Your father managed to get you off the mare, but as I recall, it was a good hour before we could calm you down."

Ria had not related this event to Lizzie, although it was well in line with a remark she once made. *"They are horrid beasts,"* she had said. *"They take one look at me and they just know it's time to have it out. We both keep our distance, and it's a good thing, too."*

However, for the first time Lizzie decided not to repeat Ria's words. For all their similarities, here was one great difference between them. Lizzie was born to ride. Australia had been a land of far too much grief, to be sure. But it was also where she'd ridden a horse for the very first time. She'd taken to it instinctively. It was pure exhilaration to race across the vast grasslands, giving her endless delight and the feeling of absolute freedom. No, she could not give that up. Not for anything. Perhaps, she thought impulsively, it was time for "Ria" to get over her abhorrence of horses. "It is true that horses and I, ah, disliked each other at that time, but—"

"Disliked!" James interjected with a snort. "You were at *war*!"

"Let's just say that during my time in Australia, I was able to arrange a truce. I did some riding there, actually."

It was an enormous risk, she knew, to move in a direction so contrary to Ria's nature. She did not miss Lady Thornborough's look of utter disbelief. But how could she give up riding? She must convince them that, in this one point at least, Ria had changed.

James eyed her curiously. "Cousin," he said with a smile, "I will have to believe that when I see it."

Geoffrey did not look as skeptical as the others. Rather, he looked impressed. "I have an excellent stable of horses, and the countryside around my estate has some lovely paths. Perhaps one day soon we might ride together."

Now Lizzie knew she had made the right decision. What a delight it would be to ride side by side with Geoffrey along a country lane or over a green meadow. "That would be wonderful!" she exclaimed. "When can we go?"

This came out with such artless sincerity that it caused Lady Thornborough to smile. "My dearest Ria," she said. "Unpredictable as ever."

Buoyed by this victory, Lizzie supposed there would be nothing she couldn't handle this evening.

Lord and Lady Beauchamp moved on to greet other guests. Geoffrey, too, was obliged to leave them for a while, explaining that with so many of London's deepest pockets gathered in one place, it was the perfect opportunity for him to make beneficial connections for his charity.

And so Lizzie followed James and Lady Thornborough into the current of people as easily as a twig moving into a stream, happily enduring countless introductions and growing more confident as the evening progressed.

"Are you enjoying yourself?" Lady Thornborough asked her later, once they had found a moment's leisure to sit and watch the dancing. "Are you glad you came out tonight?"

"Oh, yes," Lizzie answered without hesitation. "Everyone has been so kind." Despite Geoffrey's gloomy predictions that she would be scrutinized like an animal in a cage, most people had been politely respectful, offering condolences about Edward and asking only very general questions about her time in Australia.

James had been dancing with a pretty young debutante, and when the dance was over, he led his partner over to meet them. "Do you remember Miss Fitzroy, the little terror who always seemed to be hiding behind the sofa whenever you and the elder Miss Fitzroy attempted to share confidences?"

This bizarre introduction sent Miss Fitzroy into giggles.

"Of course I remember," Lizzie said. "And shame on you, James, for providing such an inelegant introduction." In truth, she was thankful that James kept unwittingly providing the kind of information that enabled her to put faces to the names Ria had given her. "And how is your sister? Is she here?" Lizzie knew she would have to speak to Ellen Fitzroy if she was here tonight, since Ellen and Ria had once been friends.

"She is married now, and at home awaiting the arrival of her fourth child."

"Fourth!" Lizzie exclaimed. "How wonderful for them." She was relieved, too, that this would be one "acquaintance" she would not have to renew this evening. In fact, everything tonight had been surprisingly easy.

The orchestra struck up a waltz. "Please excuse me," Miss Fitzroy said, "but I must be going. I've promised this dance to Mr. Spencer."

"I'll take you to him," James offered. "More than likely we'll find him at the punch table."

Lizzie watched as they skirted the dance floor to reach one of the adjoining rooms.

Lady Thornborough said, "We must also find you a dance partner, Ria."

"I think I would like that," Lizzie replied. She was truly enjoying herself this evening, in a lighthearted way that she had not experienced for a long time.

And then she heard Geoffrey's voice behind her. "Will I suffice?"

Lizzie turned around. How had she gone almost an entire

hour without thinking about this man? Now as he stood there, looking alarmingly handsome, she could think of little else. His dark eyes and the fine cut of his jaw took her breath away. He flashed one of his rare smiles and extended his hand.

Her heart lost several beats as she felt the warmth of his touch through her thin gloves. A joyous, heady feeling pulsed through her—one she had not known for too many years. Yes, she would dance. How had she even considered not coming tonight? How had she not realized she might have given up an opportunity to be in his arms again—if only for a dance?

He led her through the crowd. Lizzie was aware of curious and admiring glances as they passed. When they reached the center of the dance floor, Geoffrey turned to her and rested his hand confidently on the small of her back, setting her alight with anticipation. She brought her hand up to his shoulder, marveling again at how broad it was, and looked into his eyes.

And then they began to dance.

It was the easiest thing in the world to follow Geoffrey's lead. Her steps melted into his as they joined the rhythm of the music. In no time they were gliding expertly around the room as though they had practiced for years. Moving so effortlessly, so beautifully, the whole time Geoffrey's eyes never leaving her face. Perhaps she had had too much punch as well, for she became giddy and light-headed as they swirled around the floor. Geoffrey was a fine dancer. Yet another anomaly of this clergyman turned peer. How many other surprises did he hold? She fervently hoped she would have the opportunity to find out. She felt her heart slipping away to this man more and more with each encounter.

Gradually Lizzie became aware that she and Geoffrey were beginning to receive more than just a few casual glances. "I do believe," she murmured, "that everyone is staring at us." She had leaned in to say this, and now felt the heat of his cheek, so close to hers.

"Does it make you uncomfortable? Do you wish to stop?"

"No," she breathed. "I wish never to stop."

He laughed and whirled her again, and she gave herself up to the pleasure of it. She reveled in the music that moved her soul, in the thrill of being in Geoffrey's arms, in the pleasing sound of his laughter, in the way everything and everyone blurred to a delightful palette of colors as they kept time with the waltz and the beating of her own heart.

It was a perfect night. There was no one in the room but her and Geoffrey; everyone else had faded away, indistinct . . .

Until she saw Freddie.

Lizzie staggered, tripping over Geoffrey as her feet came down in the wrong place.

It couldn't be. It was impossible. Freddie Hightower was dead—Tom had killed him.

She tried desperately to find air, but there was none left in the room. She saw no colors now—only white spots before her eyes.

"Ria, what is the matter?" Geoffrey asked anxiously.

This could not be happening. They had been moving so quickly that her vision must have become distorted. She had only imagined she had seen Freddie. Lizzie willed herself to remain calm and opened her eyes.

Geoffrey held her, his arms providing steadiness and reassurance while Lizzie tried to regain her bearings. She hazarded a look past Geoffrey's shoulder. She was facing the side of the room where the small orchestra was sitting. She thought she had seen Freddie leaning against a door to one of the parlors.

She would have to move, to force herself to turn and look in that direction, to prove to herself that she had been mistaken. She brought her gaze back to Geoffrey's face. "I do feel a bit light-headed. I should perhaps sit down."

"Of course."

She kept her eyes straight ahead as they navigated through the dancers to a row of chairs. When they were seated, Lizzie opened her fan and began fanning herself. "I only need a moment," she said apologetically.

Geoffrey nodded, waiting patiently. Lizzie finally worked up enough courage to peek over her fan and look across the room.

There he was, looking at her so intently that he might have started a fire with the heat of his gaze.

Freddie Hightower was alive.

Chapter 20

An icy horror settled over her. She was looking at Freddie Hightower—how was this possible?

He stood unmoving, his eyes fastened on her with a ferocity she had seen countless times. Impossible to forget.

"Shall I find you a glass of punch?" Geoffrey asked.

"No!" Lizzie shrieked. She saw the alarm in his eyes and the tension in his body, and she forced herself to take a deep breath and speak calmly. She must not let him see that anything was amiss. "Please don't go. Not just yet."

He patted her arm solicitously. "As you wish."

Freddie strode toward them. It took time to work his way across the crowded room, but his eyes were fixed on them, stalking them like prey. Lizzie's mind was whirling in a thousand directions at once. How was he here? Clearly he had recognized her as easily as she had him. Could she convince him she was someone else? Everything Ria had ever shared about her life threatened to dissolve from Lizzie's brain in the heat of

Freddie's gaze. He could expose her. And he would do it in a heartbeat.

She drew in another deep breath, sat straighter in her chair, and poised herself to look as calm as possible. "Geoffrey, I believe a glass of punch would do me good after all."

He nodded and rose. "I shall be back directly."

Geoffrey disappeared into the crowd. Lizzie was alone now, perilously vulnerable, a small ship in a great gale. And still Freddie advanced.

A group of ladies standing nearby parted to reveal that Lady Thornborough was coming to join her, too. She took the chair Geoffrey had vacated, her face lined with worry. "Ria, my dear, are you ill? I saw you falter and leave the dance floor just now. You look as though you've seen a ghost."

So I have. She fanned herself and forced a smile. "I overexerted myself, that's all." She kept her gaze averted from Freddie, but her skin prickled sharply, sensing his approach.

In another instant, he was upon them. "I beg your pardon for the intrusion, Lady Thornborough." He spoke with the cultured, self-confident voice Lizzie remembered too well. "We met at the Harrisons' dinner party last spring."

Lady Thornborough studied him as though trying to recall his name. After a moment she said, "Mr. Hightower, is it not?" There was a cool archness in her voice that was unusual, even for her.

Freddie smiled as though he had received the warmest greeting in the world. He gave a small bow. "At your service, madam."

Lizzie could not allow him to see how badly she was shaken. With great difficulty, she kept her expression neutral and pretended to watch the dancing. But she was intensely aware of his hot gaze upon her.

After the necessary formalities, Freddie said, "I hope that you will forgive my forwardness, Lady Thornborough, if I ask you to introduce me to your lovely companion."

Lady Thornborough turned to Lizzie. "Have you two not met?"

Lizzie forced her eyes to meet Freddie's, fighting back revulsion at the sight of him. Had he recognized her? He *must* have. This request for an introduction was his way of toying with her. She grappled to maintain an outward air of calm. "I believe I have not had the pleasure."

"Well, then, I suppose introductions are in order," Lady Thornborough said. "Mr. Hightower, this is my granddaughter, Mrs. Edward Somerville."

Freddie's eyebrows shot up at these words. Lizzie savored a small burst of pleasure at seeing him put momentarily off-balance. But he recovered himself and gave her a bow. "How do you do, Mrs. Somerville?" He spoke the name stiffly.

Lizzie held out her hand. She was glad to see that it trembled only slightly. It might not even be noticeable. Freddie grasped it and made a small bow over it as he said smoothly, "A pleasure, I'm sure." He held it for a fraction of a second too long, as though trying to inspect it carefully in spite of the silk glove covering it. It took every ounce of her will to keep from wrenching her hand away, to wait until he released it.

He straightened. "I had heard that Lady Thornborough's granddaughter had lately returned to London. From Australia, I hear?"

"Yes, that is true."

"How long were you in Australia exactly?"

His dark eyes bore into her, as they used to when he was

willing her to guess his hand at whist and follow his lead. "My husband and I," she said, deliberately laying stress on the word *husband*, "went to Australia ten years ago."

Lady Thornborough nodded her confirmation, and Lizzie was pleased to see Freddie's look of consternation. Ria had been in Australia for ten years, but Lizzie's fateful affair with Freddie had ended just five years ago. The time gap was clearly puzzling him.

"My granddaughter is a widow now," Lady Thornborough said. "Sadly, Mr. Somerville died two years ago."

Lady Thornborough probably stressed the point of two years having passed to show the propriety of Lizzie's presence at the ball tonight. But she was also helping, albeit unknowingly, to strengthen Lizzie's deception. It would be difficult for Freddie to refute these facts concerning Ria's history.

Freddie turned sympathetic eyes on her, in an expression that Lizzie knew was thoroughly calculated. Everything Freddie did was calculated. "My condolences, Mrs. Somerville. I hope that your return to London may be the beginning of brighter days."

"You are very kind," Lizzie replied, trying not to choke on the words. Her face and arms suddenly ached, as though they had the power to remember and feel all over again the bruises that had once covered them. Bruises Freddie had put there.

"We thank you, Mr. Hightower," Lady Thornborough said, "for taking the time to speak to us." Her words were polite, but her tone implied that the conversation was over, and that she expected him to do the proper thing and move on.

But Freddie did not take his leave. He continued standing there, taking in Lizzie from head to toe as though making an inventory of every feature. A slow flush began to invade Lizzie's face under the scrutiny. She deliberately turned her head away, as though affronted by his rudeness.

Freddie caught her meaning. "Mrs. Somerville, I beg you will forgive my impudent staring. My only excuse is that you have me completely flummoxed. You see, you bear a remarkable resemblance to another"—a faint smirk crossed his face—"*lady* I know."

Lizzie seethed, her fear now tinged with anger. He *was* going to bring it up, and in front of Lady Thornborough, too. She must stop it from going further. She gave one of Ria's high-pitched giggles, so different from her own throaty laugh, and was glad to see Freddie flinch a little at the sound. "Why, Mr. Hightower, how provoking you are. How can you possibly expect to win my regard by telling me I look like someone else?" She arched an eyebrow. "Who was this person anyway?"

An almost imperceptible look of annoyance flashed across Freddie's face. But he said derisively, "No one of consequence."

Lizzie fought to keep her physical reaction to this cutting remark buried deep within her. She turned to Lady Thornborough and said with mocking disdain, "Grandmamma, I do not care at all for this gentleman. He tells me I look exactly like a woman of no consequence!"

Lady Thornborough was not amused. She glared at Freddie, who took the cue and gave Lizzie a contrite look. "I do most humbly beg your pardon. As I look more closely, I can see I was in error. There could be no one on this earth who compares to you."

She gave another high-pitched laugh. "Well, Mr. Hightower, I am in a generous frame of mind tonight. Seeing that we are but newly acquainted, I shall forgive you." Lizzie could hardly believe the way she managed to demonstrate such frivolity when she felt as though she were standing on the edge of a precipice.

Freddie, it seemed, would make every effort to push her right over that edge. "Now that I am in your good graces," he said, "would you do me the very great honor of dancing with me?"

Lizzie knew she must avoid dancing with him at all costs. Even a few moments in his arms might give her away completely. "That is very kind, Mr. Hightower, but…" She tried to think of a way to decline his offer without raising his suspicions.

Lady Thornborough answered for her. "My granddaughter is not well at present. She will not be dancing anymore this evening."

Freddie's pretended gallantry now became all friendliness and concern. "Perhaps you would revive with a bit of refreshment? Allow me to fetch you something to drink."

"There is no need," Lady Thornborough said. "Lord Somerville is returning with it now."

Geoffrey was indeed working his way through the crowd with a glass of punch in his hands. Upon seeing Freddie, he frowned and quickened his pace.

Freddie clearly had no intention of waiting for his arrival. "It has been a pleasure," he said, bowing to the ladies once more. To Lizzie he said, "I look forward to dancing with you another time, when you feel more…yourself." As he left them, he purposefully chose a direction that would prevent him from crossing paths with Geoffrey.

Geoffrey handed the glass to Lizzie, his eyes following Freddie's retreat with a look of distaste. "I see you have met Mr. Hightower."

"Yes, but we did not encourage him to stay," Lady Thornborough said with thinly veiled disdain.

"I am glad to hear it," Geoffrey said.

Lizzie tried to speculate on what Freddie could have done to cause their dislike. Then again, this was Freddie. He was as good at making enemies as he was at charming friends.

Lizzie sipped the punch gratefully. Its alcoholic content soothed her sorely abused nerves as well as her parched throat. "Is there some reason you should not wish me to know Mr. Hightower?"

Freddie had joined by now a small group of men and ladies chatting together on the far side of the room. One young lady in particular could not take her eyes off him. She dropped her glove and he picked it up, kissing it with a flourish before handing it back. The girl blushed so brightly that Lizzie could see her fiery red cheeks plainly, despite the distance.

Geoffrey was also watching this little display. "You see how graciously he acts in polite society. But there is another side of him that is both ungentlemanly and dangerous." His expression was solemn. "Particularly where naïve young ladies are concerned."

"Very true," Lady Thornborough agreed. "No regard for common decency." She lowered her voice. "Several years ago he thought nothing of taking a common girl—a shopkeeper's daughter, or some such—off to Europe."

"Is . . . is that so?" Lizzie stammered.

Lady Thornborough nodded. "He lived with her for nearly a year. I mean, he lived with her *publicly*. He even took her into polite society. Not that anyone there seemed to mind. The Europeans have nothing like the English sense of decorum."

"Perhaps . . ." Lizzie's voice sounded hoarse. She took another generous sip of punch. "Perhaps she thought he would marry her."

"Then she was a fool," Lady Thornborough declared. "She ought to have known such a marriage could never take place."

She ought to have known.

These words burned Lizzie to the core. It was a harsh blow, after Lady Thornborough had taken her in and shown her such kindness. Of course, she had done so only because she thought Lizzie was her privileged granddaughter. Like everyone else in her class, Lady Thornborough would believe that when it came to status, high was high and low was low, and there was no changing it. *The rich and the poor might meet together,* Lizzie thought sourly, *but they never marry.* Lizzie was sorely tempted to lash out in anger. But she knew she must never allow Lady Thornborough to see how deeply her words had hurt her. And in any case, she *had* been a fool. A wanton fool.

"He finally broke it off, of course," Lady Thornborough said. "He was forced to. His mother began the legal process to disinherit him, knowing he would come to his senses if his wealth depended on it. He returned to England and was married within three months—to Helena Graham, the daughter of a wealthy manufacturer."

It was almost too much for Lizzie to take in. "Married? So quickly?" Nothing in his conduct this evening would have suggested that Freddie was a married man.

"His parents were of the misguided opinion that marriage would reform him," Geoffrey said. He threw a disparaging look at Freddie. "Clearly, it did not."

"I almost wish his parents had not interfered," Lady Thornborough said. "He was better off in Europe, cavorting with the sort of people who find no offense in such behavior. The man does nothing but court scandal."

Lady Thornborough's attention was caught by Mrs. Paddington, who was signaling to her from across the room. "Ria, are you well enough for me to leave you for a few minutes?"

"I will be fine," Lizzie replied, thinking that it would actually be a relief to have her gone.

"I'll stay with her," Geoffrey said.

"Thank you, Lord Somerville. I won't be gone long." She gave Lizzie's hand a squeeze. It was meant to be comforting; it was not.

Lizzie watched her go, still reeling from the evening's discoveries. She had come face-to-face with the man who had once nearly ruined her life. She had heard Lady Thornborough's contempt for the woman who had run off with him. To hear herself spoken of as some distant, unknown person, the daughter of a mere "shopkeeper," had rent her soul.

It was a sharp reminder to Lizzie that she must never, ever forget the true state of affairs. She would be the cause of a much greater scandal this time around if she were discovered. She would face far more serious consequences than simply having to find her way home from Vienna.

Lizzie drained the last of the punch from her glass.

Chapter 21

S hall I get you more punch?" Geoffrey asked.

"No, thank you." Lizzie knew her smile was wavering, but it seemed to appease him nonetheless. He took her empty glass and set it on the tray of a passing waiter.

The evening had begun so magnificently, Lizzie thought ruefully. She had made her grand entrance, bluffed her way through every introduction, won everyone's admiration. Tonight should have been a great triumph. How could she have guessed there would be a man here who could quickly turn her world to ashes?

She looked up at the man standing next to her—the man whose company had made the evening all the more wonderful. She desperately wished they could return to that moment on the dance floor before she had seen Freddie. They had moved so well together that Lizzie had forgotten she had any cares in the world. Freddie had brought back her troubles tenfold. The new life she had been carefully constructing now threatened to topple as completely as a house built on sand.

"Geoffrey, may I ask you a question?"

He sat down next to her. "Of course."

"What can you tell me about Mrs. Hightower?"

"*Mrs.* Hightower?" Geoffrey repeated in surprise. "Why do you ask?"

"Curiosity, that's all." With a self-deprecating smile she added, "It's a failing of mine, you know."

"There is not much I can tell you," he said. "She was raised in Manchester and lived there until her marriage." His face clouded. "As I understand it, she was in love with him at first, God help her. But he treated her very badly. It didn't take her long to realize that Hightower had only married her to get his hands on her dowry."

Lizzie felt an immediate empathy for this woman who had also borne the brunt of Freddie's heartlessness.

"Although I mourn for her, at least she is no longer suffering under the weight of his tyranny."

"Mourn...?" Lizzie gasped. "Mrs. Hightower is *dead*?"

He nodded, his brow furrowed. "Mrs. Hightower died under what many people consider to be, well, suspicious circumstances."

"What happened to her?"

"She was with child, nearly ready for her confinement, when she was found dead at the foot of the staircase. The coroner ruled that her fall was an accident, but there are many unanswered questions."

A casual onlooker might never imagine Freddie could have caused the death of his own wife. But Lizzie was no casual onlooker. She knew what lay beneath his outward show. "Do you believe Mr. Hightower was somehow responsible for her death?"

"I don't know. But he had a roving eye, even after marriage. Sometimes he stayed away from home for weeks at a time. It was known among their closest friends that Mrs. Hightower was desperately unhappy. She became prone to dizzy spells and bouts of hysteria. It is rumored that she may have taken her own life. Murder or not, Freddie Hightower has caused nothing but harm to the women unfortunate enough to fall under his power."

"And what became of the woman he took to Europe?" Lizzie was compelled to ask.

He shook his head. "No one knows. Some think she stayed there. Others believe she returned to London and was taken into one of the houses of prostitution."

"Prostitution!" How close she had come to utter, irredeemable ruin. She would have died rather than succumb to that.

"It often happens that way in these circumstances." He spoke so matter-of-factly that Lizzie thought he was dismissing this "shopkeeper's daughter" with the same disregard that Lady Thornborough had displayed. But he unexpectedly let out a small sigh and added, "Poor girl."

"Does her fate really trouble you?" Lizzie asked. She desperately wanted to believe in Geoffrey's compassion, to know that he *would* be troubled by the fate of a woman unknown to him, that he found the ruin of this one poor soul was a tragedy worth grieving for—even one who had been guilty of such wicked behavior.

She was not disappointed. "Of course it troubles me," he answered without hesitation. "Now that Hightower has used her and cast her off, who knows what hell her life has become. She can never return to the life she led before." He scanned the room, and Lizzie followed his gaze as it took in elegant men and women dancing to fine music, jewels glittering in the lamplight, tables laden with sumptuous food and drink. "And even if she could, do you think she would be content to do so after such a taste of wealth and privilege?"

"I think if I were in that position," Lizzie hazarded, "supposing I truly loved him, I would have been most crushed to discover he had merely been toying with me—that I was not the love of his life he claimed I was." This was a dangerous admission, and it was as close as Lizzie dared come to telling Geoffrey the truth.

"You would think of that," Geoffrey said, his expression tightening. "Love always enters into the equation for you, doesn't it?"

It sounded like an accusation. "Geoffrey, don't," she pleaded. Was he about to return to the subject of their first argument, when he had attacked Ria's actions and Lizzie had accusingly replied, *"What do you know about love?"* After the way their hearts had begun to open to each other, such a reversal would be too devastating.

Instead, he surprised her, as he had done so often this evening. "You misunderstand me," he said. "I did not intend to—" He broke off, shook his head, and began again. "I was wrong to belittle you and Edward. You were blessed to have shared such a love." He took one of her hands in his. "What must that have been like, I wonder?"

It was not so much a question as an expression of longing. Lizzie wished she could tell him that many a time she had asked herself the same question. The love she'd seen between Ria and Edward was fathomless and enduring, incomprehensible to her. Having only a disastrous and scarred knowledge of love, Lizzie could not summon up the words to express it. She could only stare mutely into Geoffrey's rich brown eyes and try to stem the tears in her own, leaving him to interpret her silence in his own way.

"Perhaps you will find another love someday," he said.

There was a moment of quiet in the room just then, a brief lull between dances. The rustle of gowns and the low murmur of voices that filled the void seemed muted, as though coming from a great way off. Geoffrey and Lizzie might have been alone, a delicate thread of need holding them together in the stillness.

But then the orchestra began anew, and the room filled with activity, reminding them that they were not alone. They both seemed to realize at the same moment how deeply they'd fallen into their own world. Geoffrey quietly took his hand from hers and ran it briefly over his face, taking a quick breath as though to regain his composure.

Lizzie blinked away her tears. She'd allowed too much of her own heart to surface this evening. It was time to remember that she was Ria Somerville. "I have had my hour, I'm afraid." She tried to keep her voice light as she added, "However, I hear that you are at the very door to matrimony."

Geoffrey shook his head. "Don't believe the prattling gossip you hear in drawing rooms."

"Then you are not about to make an offer to Miss... to some fortunate young lady?"

"No," he said. "Not until love enters the equation."

Was he being truthful or facetious? His expression was inscrutable. She was strangely relieved that he was not engaged just yet, but she found his answer troubling.

Having no idea how to respond, Lizzie turned away and concentrated on watching the dance. A dozen couples stood in two lines facing each other, moving in patterned steps up and down the dance floor. Instantly her eye was drawn to Freddie. He easily kept pace with the sprightly dance, but his upper body moved very little, and his left arm stayed close to his side. She had not noticed this earlier.

"Is there something the matter with Mr. Hightower's arm?"

"He was injured about five years ago, not too long before his marriage. Some sort of wound that never healed properly."

"How was he injured?" Lizzie asked, although she could easily guess the answer.

Geoffrey shrugged. "No one knows for sure. Some say he was shot in a hunting accident, although Hightower was known to be in town at the time. Some say he was in a duel, and that is easy to believe, given his character. He was probably confronted by an angry husband or the father of some young lady he had compromised."

James led a pretty young lady past Freddie and his partner as the two couples turned down the floor. James called out something to Freddie, and he laughed.

"James might know more about it," Geoffrey said. "I heard he was there when it happened. But no one has been able to pry a single detail from him."

Suddenly, a memory of something Tom had told Lizzie rang in her ears. *"Another young man was there with him, for his second. A dandy, he was. Not cut out for a manly art like dueling."*

James was in his element now, amid wealth and easy living. Had he been present at that duel? If so, what had he seen on that cold morning? *"When he saw Hightower bleedin' all over the ground,"* Tom had said, *"he started yelling all hysterical and panicking. I thought he was a-goin' to keel over, too."*

Lizzie had the strangest sensation that the room was beginning to tilt again. Geoffrey took hold of her arm gently to steady her. "Has the dizziness returned?" he asked.

His touch was so warm and reassuring that it was all Lizzie could do to keep from confessing everything right then and there. "I'm just trying to imagine James keeping a secret," she said, forcing a wry smile. "It's an enormous shock."

Geoffrey's eyes crinkled with amusement, and something fluttered in Lizzie's stomach. Not for the first time this evening, she'd wished above all else that she could confide in him.

"Ria, let me take you home. Unless you are resolved to stay until the end?"

Out on the dance floor, Freddie circled his partner and was again facing Lizzie, startling her when he met her eyes. Silently she berated herself for being caught watching him. She forced her gaze to move from his and scan the room, as though looking at nothing in particular, before turning back to Geoffrey. "Thank you. I would be glad to accept your offer."

He stood and offered a hand to help her rise. "Would you like to join me now, or wait here while I call for the carriage?"

"I will join you at the door. I must tell Grandmamma that I am leaving."

Lizzie found Lady Thornborough engrossed in conversation with Mrs. Paddington. Both women eyed Lizzie with concern. "How are you feeling, my dear?" Lady Thornborough asked. "You are looking somewhat peaked."

"The dizziness has returned. I would like to go home right away, with your permission."

"But you cannot go now!" Mrs. Paddington cried. "The evening has barely gotten under way."

"I won't keep you here if you are unwell," Lady Thornborough said. "I will arrange for a carriage to take us home."

"There is no need for you to leave, Grandmamma. I would

hate to inconvenience you. Geoffrey has offered to escort me home."

Mrs. Paddington offered to take Lady Thornborough home later in her carriage, so all was arranged.

As Lizzie walked away, she overheard Mrs. Paddington say, "If only she had married the eldest son, she might be a rich widow now instead of a poor one."

Lizzie made a pretense of pausing to adjust her gloves, curious to hear how Lady Thornborough would answer this inane remark. "My Ria will never be destitute," she said. "I will see to that."

"She is young. Do you think she will marry again?" Mrs. Paddington inquired.

"We mustn't be premature. She is still mourning the loss of her husband."

Lizzie was glad Lady Thornborough did not plan to press her into marriage after all. But Mrs. Paddington had more to say on the subject. "How well she danced with Lord Somerville this evening. What a pity she cannot marry him."

Lizzie found another button on her glove to take her interest while she waited to hear Lady Thornborough's answer. Only a few days before, James had spoken something similar in jest. But Mrs. Paddington was in earnest.

"It is regrettable," Lady Thornborough agreed. She had seemed shocked when James voiced the possibility, but now she spoke as if it were the most natural thing in the world. "Lord Somerville is a worthy man. I believe he was the most suited of the three to inherit the family title. He will manage everything better than either of his brothers could, rest their souls."

Lizzie had the same high opinion of Geoffrey, and after the

events of tonight she could not deny the idea had a particular resonance. He had surprised her many times tonight. It had, in fact, been a night of surprises and revelations.

Freddie was alive, and Lizzie's path, which had once seemed clear enough, was now obstructed and filled with danger. It would now be infinitely harder to keep up her charade as Ria, but it was more vital than ever that she do so. If Freddie was ever able to prove her true identity, he would no doubt divulge the details of her scandalous history. How would Lady Thornborough react if she discovered Lizzie was that wanton shopgirl who had run off with Freddie?

It would be a relief to leave tonight with Geoffrey. But she reminded herself that she must never depend too much on him either. She was beginning to realize how truly isolated she was.

With all these thoughts weighing oppressively on her mind, Lizzie collected her shawl and made her way to the door.

Chapter 22

Lizzie was unable to find Geoffrey among the crowd of people in the entrance hall. Assuming he was still outside sending for the carriage, Lizzie moved to a quiet spot near a large potted palm to wait.

The strains of another waltz drifted from the ballroom. Lizzie closed her eyes and sank into the music, attempting to assuage her buffeted soul in the gently measured meter. She rocked back and forth, moving instinctively in rhythm with the waltz. Such light and uplifting music, recalling memories of the night in Vienna when she'd heard a full orchestra for the very first time. It was so exuberant and joyful, she'd felt as if she were soaring.

"Mrs. Somerville, may I say again what a pleasure it was to meet you this evening." Freddie's unwelcome voice pierced the music and brought her back to the present.

Lizzie's eyes flew open. "Oh, gracious, Mr. Hightower, you startled me." She punctuated her statement with a light laugh. "It appears my silly thoughts were wandering elsewhere."

"I should like to know where they were," he replied. "Any reasonable thoughts should be ashamed to desert your pretty head."

His bland compliments did not fool Lizzie, but they must, of course, charm *Ria*. She tittered again. "Where would you have my thoughts be, Mr. Hightower?"

His eyes glinted. "I would selfishly have them right here in London—perhaps fondly remembering the *new acquaintances* you made tonight. I, for one, am glad to have finally met the charming cousin of my good friend Mr. James Simpson."

Lizzie opened her fan and waved it delicately. "Oh?" she said with the barest hint of disinterest. "I don't believe he ever mentioned you."

"Perhaps not," Freddie allowed. "However, he told me many things about *you*." He spoke casually, but he continued to take in every detail of her appearance. "I shall take him to task, however, for failing to do you justice in his descriptions. Perhaps, since he is like a brother to you, he is unable to perceive certain of your more alluring qualities."

Lizzie gave him a coquettish smile. "I have been informed of your reputation as a ladies' man, Mr. Hightower. Will you attempt to win me over as well?"

"I could gladly give my life to such an endeavor."

There was no denying that Freddie was a handsome man. His smile could melt the resistance of even the most hardened female. Lizzie found it too easy to remember how it had once affected her. Opposing memories fought for preeminence in her heart.

"However, it would be unseemly of me to make too many pleasantries," Freddie said, his look turning sober. "You are, after all, a grieving widow."

His remark unsettled Lizzie, as it was no doubt intended to

do. Had she been flirting too strenuously to be taken for a real widow? Sharply she reminded herself that Freddie was a master at manipulation. "I do grieve," she said with the air of one who is imparting a confidence to a dear friend. "But it has been two years now, and..." She sighed heavily. "I am resigned to it. My dear grandmamma has encouraged me to look to the future."

"Very sensible, I am sure," Freddie said. "Then I shall hold out hope that, at some point in the future, we may share a dance." With a sly smile he added, "I saw you swaying to the music just now. I see you enjoy the music *very* much."

Again, Lizzie easily understood him. Just now he had seen her respond to the music as he had so many times in Vienna. They'd return to their private rooms after a concert, and she would still be in raptures, humming the melody and dancing about blissfully. Lizzie would have to be careful to control this impulse from now on, and to downplay how much the music meant to her.

"The melody is nice enough, I suppose," she said in a casually dismissive tone. "However, I have been feeling faint all evening, and I believe that was the cause of my, ah, *swaying*."

"Then you mustn't remain standing here," he said. "Will you allow me to bring you a chair? Or perhaps take you home? I have a carriage."

Lizzie knew exactly what happened to women who rode home in Freddie's carriage. Fortunately, Geoffrey arrived in time to spare her the necessity of declining his offer. "You needn't concern yourself, Hightower," he said. "I will be taking Mrs. Somerville home. The carriage is at the door."

"Lord Somerville, you've arrived just in time," Freddie said with feigned relief. "I am sure Mrs. Somerville will be most grateful for your assistance."

The two men eyed each other, their mutual dislike easily breaching the thin veneer of polite words.

Freddie looked away first. He bowed to Lizzie. "I shall bid you good evening, Mrs. Somerville. I do hope that we shall meet again soon."

"Thank you, Mr. Hightower. I look forward to it."

Her words may have fooled Geoffrey, for she saw him grimace at this remark. But she had no confidence she had fooled Freddie. With a brief nod and an arrogant smile, he turned and walked away.

Geoffrey offered his arm, and Lizzie took it gratefully. They sifted through the crowd in the receiving hall and walked down the steps to the waiting carriage. A cool breeze welcomed them, tingling along Lizzie's neck and shoulders like a call to freedom. She was making her escape from Freddie.

For now.

She would just have to take each round of trouble as it came.

Geoffrey took the seat opposite her in the carriage as the footman closed the door. When Lizzie was settled, he gave a light tap to the roof with his cane, and the carriage pulled forward.

Through the window Lizzie saw a young woman making her way down the street, wrapping an inadequate shawl around her shoulders, her poorly shod feet slipping on the wet cobblestones. Her heart went out to the girl. *That once was me,* she thought. She remembered walking down these streets, watching the passing carriages, envying the people within. They had not a care in the world, she had thought then. How wrong she had been.

Her musings were interrupted by Geoffrey. "Are you feeling better now, Ria?"

She nodded. "I can breathe again."

"Was Hightower being too forward with you? Did his attentions upset you?"

Yes! Freddie may yet destroy my life, after I thought I was free of him.

She could not say this, of course. "Don't trouble yourself on his account," she said. "The whole evening was...rather taxing, that's all." It was a woefully inadequate description, but she wanted to assuage his concerns.

He did not look convinced. "I hope you will stay clear of Hightower in the future. Do not cultivate his acquaintance."

"Can we please not discuss Mr. Hightower?" she said sharply. Her frazzled nerves could not take much more.

"I will happily comply with that request," Geoffrey said. "But you were enjoying yourself earlier in the evening, I'm sure of it." He gave her a self-effacing smile. "Was it my dancing that did you in?"

This unexpected pleasantry warmed Lizzie's heart. "Honestly, Geoffrey. I believe you have spent too much time with James."

"The man can wear off on people, I suppose," he replied.

"Actually," Lizzie said, "I was surprised at how well you dance. I was not expecting that at all."

"It has been a night of surprises, I think." Something in the way he said this sounded quite different. Wistful, almost.

"Yes, it has," Lizzie agreed. She wondered what about the evening had surprised him.

"I suppose Edward never mentioned that we were all three raised with rigorous lessons in dancing and etiquette. Of course, I was not called upon to use those skills very much. At least, not until recently."

Lizzie saw him tense as he said this, and she knew it was a reference to the loss of his brothers. Her heart did a strange, painful flip in her chest. "You acquitted yourself very well," she said quietly.

He gave her a brief, grateful smile. "Ria, I'd like to ask you something, and I hope you do not think me too forward or impertinent. I'd like to—" He interrupted himself with a grimace. "You can tell me if I've no right to ask this question."

This unexpected change of tack left her with some trepidation, but she said, "Of course. You may ask me anything."

"I want to know—that is, I was wondering—what made you fall in love with Edward? How did you know he was the one?"

The question took Lizzie utterly by surprise. She stared at him, openmouthed.

Still apologetic, Geoffrey continued, "You are no doubt surprised to hear this question coming from me. It's just that with all the talk of marriages this evening, I realized that, well, you and Edward clearly found something, and for the first time in my life I truly want to know what that is."

He looked so vulnerable just then, his face displaying the very same need that Lizzie felt within her soul, the desperate need for someone to confide in. She wished she could delve into this man's heart, return the joy to his face that she'd seen when they'd danced, erase the pain that overtook him whenever they spoke of the past. Above all, she wished she could answer his question. *How did you know he was the one?* She could only repeat the words Ria had used when she had tried to explain it to Lizzie.

"Oh, Geoffrey," she sighed. "It began with William, of course. I did think I loved him at first. You see, I was very young, and he had all that lordly swagger, and I was swept away with the idea of marrying a man with a title. But then, as I began to know Edward, he kept pressing me, asking me did I really love William, and did William really love me. I was indignant, of course. But when I put the question to William, he answered nonchalantly that he was naturally very fond of me and that I was *suitable* enough for a wife. I challenged him and said, can you expect me to pledge heart and soul to someone who thinks I am merely *suitable*?"

A few weeks ago, Lizzie thought, her words might have stirred up a lecture from Geoffrey on the importance of doing one's duty. But something had changed; she could sense it. Tonight she had touched quite a different nerve.

"You were right in what you told William," he said. "I certainly would not wish that for anyone."

The carriage came to a stop. The lights from the mansion shone through the carriage window, illuminating his face. Geoffrey leaned forward and took one of her hands in his. The carriage seemed unaccountably small. Lizzie could not speak, could not think of anything beyond his touch, the solid breadth of him so near her. "I can see now that Edward was truly the wiser of the two." His voice was low, and rough with emotion.

He drew her hand closer to him, and kissed it.

All sound and motion faded to a breathless hush. As Geoffrey's lips brushed Lizzie's thin gloves, she recalled Mrs. Paddington's words: *"What a pity she cannot marry Lord Somerville..."*

What would it be like to be married to this man? How dearly she would love to know.

She reached out with her free hand and gently caressed his hair. He leaned his head into her touch as though seeking more of it.

If only we could stay here forever, she thought. *If only this moment could withstand everything that has happened and all that will inevitably come.*

The footman opened the door, and the cool night air rushed into the carriage. Startled, Lizzie drew back. Geoffrey straightened and dropped her hand. She was sure the footman had seen their closeness and their guilt, but he was too well trained to let on. He averted his gaze and stood back, allowing them room to exit.

Geoffrey stepped down to the street and turned to reach up for Lizzie's hand. Although the mask of propriety had fallen back into place, Geoffrey's touch still did unimaginable things, sending a vibrant rush of desire through every part of Lizzie's being.

He brought her up the steps and into the main hall. Lizzie's head and heart were bursting with all the things she could not say. She murmured, "Thank you for bringing me home."

"It was my pleasure." They were simple words, but Lizzie saw their meaning. "Ria…" He was looking at her with such intense warmth that Lizzie found it difficult to breathe.

"Yes?"

But their solitude was gone. Whatever might have been said in the coach, when their hearts had connected so perfectly, could not be spoken here, in a well-lighted entry hall before the servants. He gave her a small smile. "Good night."

As Lizzie watched the door close behind him, she knew beyond a doubt that she was in love with this man. The knowledge weighed heavily on her, for it only made the decisions before her so much harder.

She made her way up to her room, her heart tossed by wave after wave of contradictory emotions as she considered the terrible choices before her, and where they might lead. She could keep pretending to be Ria, hoping to withstand Freddie's suspicions and questioning. But he would be an ever-present threat, a cloud ready to break open a torrent of misery. If by some miracle she maintained her ruse, she would never be able to reveal her true self to Geoffrey. There would forever be this one last barrier between them. When she had cast herself into the role of Ria, she never dreamed her heart might dare to open again...to the one man who was now denied her.

If Freddie had his way, he would once again ruin her life by his hateful actions. Even worse, Geoffrey's discovery of the truth would come at Freddie's doing, and not by her own admission. This left her with a second terrible choice: to reveal herself before Freddie could do it. That would surely mean losing Geoffrey, for he would learn not only that she had been lying to him, but that she was covering up a disgraceful past as well. She had Geoffrey's esteem now, and his friendship; he was beginning to care for her deeply. All those things would vanish once he knew the truth. Of all the dire consequences that threatened her, this was the worst.

She was gloomily pondering these things as Martha helped her undress and prepare for bed. "I'll bet you were the loveliest lady there tonight," Martha said as she took down Lizzie's hair and began brushing out the curls. "I'll bet you were the grandest success at the ball."

"Was I? I don't know." She truly was Cinderella, she thought bitterly. Her life was returning to ashes.

"Come now, it's not like you to be so modest," Martha said with a chiding grin.

She met Martha's eyes in the mirror. "I'm afraid, Martha. Afraid of disappointing everyone."

"Why, bless me. I never know'd my Ria to be afraid of anything."

"Never?"

"Just look at all the things you've done. Didn't you go all the way to the other side of the world, *and* bring yourself back again? Not many women have that kind of courage."

All the way to the other side of the world. And back again. What good had she gained from either journey? She'd tried to leave her old life behind, only to be brought face-to-face with it again. There was no distance large enough to separate her from her lies.

This led her to the terrible realization of what she must do. She must confess everything. Until she did, she would live in terror of Freddie and in agony over what she had done.

But first, she would get to Rosewood and find the letters that proved who she really was. Thus armed, she would go directly to Lady Thornborough, tell her about the plan she and Ria had devised, and throw herself on the old woman's mercy. She would make sure that Lady Thornborough knew, first and foremost, that Lizzie was her granddaughter. Lizzie clung to the hope that this would give her something to stand on, even after Lady Thornborough discovered she was also Freddie's castoff paramour. Freddie may have changed her plans, but Lizzie would do all she could to ensure that he would never again have the upper hand. Lizzie would reveal herself on her own terms.

Geoffrey would hate her for what she had done, but he would not be able to deny that she had done the right thing by becoming utterly truthful. If she could gain even the smallest measure of his respect for that, she would gladly face whatever else should come.

Chapter 23

"Aunt, you are giving a dinner party next week, are you not?" James looked over the sandwiches on the tea tray while he awaited Lady Thornborough's answer.

"I am. And you cannot back out this time. I promised Lady Shaw you would be there."

James turned his eyes heavenward and said, "Please do not tell me that she will have her daughter in tow."

"For some reason I cannot fathom, Miss Shaw has taken a fancy to you. Even more wondrously, her parents do not object."

James sighed theatrically. "Miss Shaw is unforgivably bland and dull and—"

"*And* she has a very large dowry," Lady Thornborough interrupted. "She has good breeding and all the right connections. You must start thinking seriously of settling down, James. You cannot live your whole life between here and the club."

James did his best to look contrite. "Very well, Aunt. I shall do my utmost to entertain Miss Shaw. I merely meant to inquire whether you might invite Mr. Freddie Hightower to the dinner."

Lizzie's teacup paused halfway to her lips. Her mood was dark, despite the sunlight pouring through the parlor windows. The course of action she'd decided on last night seemed utterly impossible today. Here was the first proof of it. She had planned to avoid Freddie as much as she could—but he would push just as hard to get into her presence.

"Why would I invite Mr. Hightower?" Lady Thornborough asked.

"Because he wants to know Ria better."

"Me?" Lizzie did her best to act surprised.

"He has taken an enormous interest in you. In fact, after you left last night, he questioned me about you in such detail that—forgive me, dear cousin—I grew deadly bored with the subject."

Lady Thornborough's eyes narrowed. "What do you mean, he questioned you *in detail*?"

James shrugged. "He wanted to know the precise date Ria and Edward eloped and how long she's been away." His eyes shone with merriment. "He even asked if I was certain you had really been to Australia!"

"Indeed?" Lizzie did her best to look as though she was as amused as James. "And how did you respond?"

"I told him you declared yourself to have been in Australia, and we have every reason to believe you." He dropped another sugar cube into his tea. "However, I did ask myself why he should concern himself so closely with your history. There is only one answer, of course."

"And what, pray tell, would that be?" Lady Thornborough asked.

"Why, he plans to court Ria, of course."

Lizzie set down her cup with shaking hands. *Courting* was far too polite a term for what Freddie planned to do. *Courting* was something Geoffrey might do, she thought, as he had in that extraordinary moment when he had kissed her hand. What woman could resist such a powerful combination of ardor and respect? Lizzie had no doubts that Freddie had something quite different in mind. Freddie was going to court her the way a cat courts a mouse.

She had no need to voice an objection, however. Lady Thornborough was already doing it. "Mr. Hightower is a dissolute young man, even if he is a widower. How can you think Ria would return his interest?"

"I believe he has changed," James said. "He wants to put some of the more unsavory things of his past behind him. He told me he is ready to settle down, and he needs a good wife."

"I would not be a good wife for him," Lizzie said flatly. Her words drew a quizzical look from James.

"The greater question," Lady Thornborough said crisply, "is whether *he* would be a proper husband for Ria."

"You mean, does he meet the stated criteria? Let's see..." James lifted up a hand to tick off points on his fingers. "He has good breeding, he's well connected, *and* he's rich." He grinned as he repeated his aunt's words back to her.

But Lady Thornborough was not about to be cornered by her own argument. "James, even *you* cannot honestly be so flippant about a man who has been accused of murdering his own wife."

"He was never officially charged with anything," James pointed out. "It was only gossip and speculation, and you know how vicious the rumor mill can be. He has proven his innocence to the authorities. Shouldn't we therefore give him the benefit of the doubt?"

James spoke earnestly, and his argument seemed to be having an effect. A tiny hint of uncertainty flickered in Lady Thornborough's face. Lizzie wished James was not quite so adept at winning over his aunt.

Lady Thornborough rose from her chair. "Very well, I will invite him to dinner."

James hastily stood up also. "Thank you, Aunt."

Lady Thornborough paused at the door. "But I will be keeping a close eye on him. And you. See that you give Miss Shaw the attention she deserves."

Lady Thornborough swept from the room, and James smiled at Lizzie as he dropped back into his chair. "With you and Freddie for company, I shall at least manage to survive the dinner, even if I do have to entertain Miss Shaw."

Lizzie stirred more sugar into her tea, primarily to give herself something to do and cover her agitation. Freddie had taken advantage of James's good nature and had used it to gain his own ends. "If you think Mr. Hightower is such a good match for me, I need to know more about him. How long have you known him?"

James looked at her in surprise. "We met years ago, at school. Surely you remember me talking about him?"

Lizzie and Ria had discussed Freddie, of course, but the name had meant nothing to Ria. Lizzie raised a hand in a gesture of pretended exasperation. "Really, James, you have so many acquaintances. How can I be expected to keep track of them all?"

James laughed in amusement. "I cannot be faulted for having too many friends. Therefore, I blame this lapse on your flighty memory."

"Geoffrey told me Mr. Hightower spent time in Europe before his marriage, and that he took a woman with him."

"The effrontery," James said with mock severity. "I'm sure the reverend Lord Somerville did not approve of that."

"No one did," Lizzie replied. On that point, she was dead certain.

To her surprise, James nodded in agreement. "To be honest, I felt that taking the woman to Europe showed very poor judgment, and I told him so at the time. But he could not be dissuaded. He told me he was *in love.*" James put a hand over his heart to emphasize the words.

"Did he?" Lizzie was astonished. "Do you think he truly was in love?"

"I have no doubt that he fancied himself so. However, he returned to England in the end."

When his mother informed him she would cut him off unless he married Helena and her millions, Lizzie thought darkly.

James looked at her quizzically. "Are you upset about something?"

Lizzie realized too late that she had been letting her anger show. She scrunched her face, as she had often seen Ria do when perturbed. If Freddie thought he was the only one skilled at deception, he was very wrong. "I've been thinking that Mr. Hightower seems rather too fond of dancing. I do hope there will not be dancing at Grandmamma's party. I always trip, and then how shall I make a good impression?"

James laughed. "Do not be uneasy about that, cousin. You already have."

*

Miss Lucinda Cardington was blushing. Her face was such a bright beet red that Geoffrey was beginning to fear for her health.

Their discussion of his work with the Society for Improving the Condition of the Labouring Classes touched upon nothing that should have brought on such a strong reaction. Had it been his mention of working with Prince Albert? Some people were so taken with the importance of royalty that the thought of personal interaction with a prince could send them into raptures. But Geoffrey thought Miss Cardington was unlikely to indulge in such silliness.

Her flush could not have been caused by overexertion. As they strolled in Hyde Park, they moved slowly so that Lord and Lady Cardington, who were walking a discreet distance behind, could keep them in sight. The elder Cardingtons were short and portly, and seemed unaccustomed to long walks.

Fortunately, Miss Cardington had not taken after her parents. She was reasonably tall and very slender. Perhaps too slender. Her hand felt sharp and bony as she gripped his arm. Geoffrey's thoughts went irresistibly to a comparison of how soft and pleasing Ria's touch had been as they had walked together along that same path. Also, Miss Cardington's clean scent with a hint of lavender did not seem to excite him as much as the scent of roses...

"Wouldn't you agree, Lord Somerville?"

He started. Memories of Ria had so filled his mind that he had not been listening to Miss Cardington. Her voice tended to be meek, not really commanding attention. Even so, it was rude of him to allow his thoughts to wander. He gave her an apologetic smile. "I beg your pardon?"

She lifted her free hand and indicated the Crystal Palace. "You were staring at it so fixedly. I was saying that England's status as a world leader is certainly proven by the quality of items on display there. Wouldn't you agree?"

Her thin face was peering up at him now, her eyes a muddy mixture of hazel and brown. So different from Ria's. He could not forget how Ria's violet-blue eyes had sparkled in the light of the chandeliers, how they had danced when she laughed, how they had grown misty when she was pensive. Endlessly intriguing.

He had not seen Ria since the night of the Beauchamps' ball. He'd been constrained by the duties of several parliamentary committees and by the opening of the new housing project. And in truth, he'd been worried by what had passed between them during the carriage ride home. Their attraction had been powerful and undeniable, but he had bared far too much of his heart to her. He could not allow it to happen again. She was his sister-in-law. Edward's widow. Geoffrey told himself that keeping his distance for a time would be a good thing. He needed to clear his head.

Forcing his mind back to Miss Cardington, he said, "Yes, England should be very proud of the Exhibition."

"I find your work extremely interesting," she remarked as they resumed walking. "How rewarding it must be to provide housing for honest and hardworking people. The investors get a solid return on their investment, and so it is a good situation for all parties."

This was not the first time Miss Cardington had shown a knowledge of the Society's work. Geoffrey was grateful for this, since it at least gave them something to talk about. "I see you take a genuine interest in it."

"Oh, yes. I believe it is important for those of us who have been blessed with abundance to reach out and help those who are less fortunate."

"That is true," Geoffrey agreed. "It would be a better world if more people felt—and acted—as you do."

"Thank you, Lord Somerville. I take that as a great compliment."

She blushed again, and Geoffrey finally had to accept that he was the cause of it. He had known for weeks that the Cardingtons hoped to marry her to him. Lady Cardington, in particular, had been none too subtle about it. The charity ball she had organized was a blatant attempt to win him over, but at least it allowed him to raise money for a good cause.

During the time he had spent with Miss Cardington, he noted how shy and awkward she was at social events. More than once she had spilled something on herself—or someone else. Fortunately, she was more relaxed when she was not in a group setting. She was also fairly young. God willing, her awkwardness would lessen with time.

At least she was a good conversationalist. She was fascinated by science and its practical applications. Once she even spoke in great detail of the effects the Lord Mayor's new sanitation plans would have on the health of the London populace. Geoffrey enjoyed speaking with a woman who had more on her mind than gossip and the latest fashions. She even had a good understanding of the Bible. She asked him many questions and seemed genuinely interested in the answers. Geoffrey could not help being impressed at her intellectual curiosity in so many matters.

The more Geoffrey thought about it, the more he realized that there was much to recommend Miss Cardington, and many indications she could successfully fill the role of Baroness Somerville. But would she make a good *wife*? Could he truly and deeply love her? He could not stop thinking about Ria, about the things she had told him during the carriage ride home. If he married Miss Cardington, would he be guilty of marrying someone he thought was only *suitable*?

Geoffrey tried to imagine the two of them together as one flesh. He tried to imagine his heart as wide open as it had been with Ria, remembering the intense pleasure he'd gotten just from her nearness, from kissing her hand, from the way she had stroked his hair. But his mind was a blank. He could only picture Miss Cardington as he saw her now, very prim and proper, stiffly corseted, wearing clothes that seemed somehow wrong for her.

"Lord Somerville?" She was again attempting to recapture his thoughts.

He smiled sheepishly. "I'm afraid I must beg your pardon again."

Geoffrey had discovered that Miss Cardington was sensitive to anything that gave the appearance of a slight. Her smile faded. When the eagerness of conversation left her face, her looks went from passingly pretty to verging on plain.

With forced cheerfulness he said, "I was just remembering that there is a new exhibit that has recently arrived, very late, from France. Would you like to see it?"

Miss Cardington's face brightened, and her eyes managed to evince a twinkle. "I would like that very much."

Perhaps Ria's outlook had been too simplistic, Geoffrey thought. This was more than a question of mere suitability. He would not be guilty of the shallow-mindedness William had shown. Hadn't he already known, long before Ria's return, that he was looking for more than a mere paper doll who was cut to fit society's expectations?

As they crossed the stone bridge to the Crystal Palace,

Geoffrey reminded himself that love was something that grew with time. It often reached its fullness *after* marriage, not before. It might take time, but he was sure that he and Miss Cardington could build a satisfying relationship.

At least, he thought he was sure.

Chapter 24

Lizzie stared in amazement at the giant stuffed elephant. It stood a full ten feet high, but looked taller due to the ornate sedan chair, called a howdah, that had been placed on its back.

Lizzie and James had been at the Great Exhibition for several hours, enjoying the vast array of exhibits from all over the world. Now as they stood in the section devoted to India, Lizzie took in every detail of the magnificent howdah, which was made of colorful cloth and polished silver.

"What an incredible ride that would be!" James remarked. "Perhaps someday I'll go to India and ride on an elephant."

Lizzie laughed. "I can easily imagine you on one of those things, looking as though you were the raja himself."

"Especially if I had a beautiful Indian princess with me," James agreed. "She would be dressed in sheer silks from head to foot, with a very thin veil over the bottom of her face..." He pulled out a handkerchief to demonstrate. "Showing just the top half of her lovely, almond-brown face. Only her mysterious dark eyes would be visible, luring me to give up everything I possessed in order to fulfill her every whim."

Lizzie's laugh turned to a disbelieving chuckle. "I cannot imagine you as a slave to any woman."

He gave her a wink. "That's because I am a slave to them all."

They moved on to other exhibits. The sheer size of the place was breathtaking. Lizzie had initially worried that she might come across someone who would recognize her, as old Ben Weathers had done at the Prince's Cottages, but as the morning wore on and they traveled the vast hall without incident, Lizzie began to relax. Today, when the admission prices were at their highest, very few from the working classes were in attendance.

It was not until they made their way up a wide staircase to the upper galleries and looked over the railing to view the spectacle below that Lizzie thought she spotted someone she knew. A young lady in a drab working-class dress was looking up at her. She looked to be in her early twenties, and Lizzie thought she bore a strong resemblance to Molly, the granddaughter of Ben Weathers.

After the surprise of meeting the girl's eyes, Lizzie looked away quickly. She could not be sure, of course. It had been years since she'd seen the girl. She shook her head and took a breath. She must have imagined it. She'd been thinking too much about Ben Weathers. She turned her gaze back to where the girl had been standing. The sun shone brilliantly through the glass roof, bathing hundreds of exhibits and the colorful clothes of the visitors in an intense, refracted light. The girl in the plain brown dress was gone.

"It's magnificent, isn't it?" James said, mistaking Lizzie's actions as admiration of the view.

"Yes," Lizzie murmured. She looked again at the crowds

below. She thought she saw a glimpse of a brown dress behind a statue. She felt no small sense of irony as she added, "It's almost too much for the eye to take in at one time."

"Interesting that you should say that," James said. "Allow me to show you my favorite part of this entire place."

He led her to a spot that, judging from the size of the crowd, was very popular. The people were inspecting what appeared to be miniature drawings laid against a black velvet backdrop. A small group moved away as Lizzie and James approached, and now Lizzie could see that the items on display were not drawings at all.

Lizzie drew in for a closer look. The images were breathtaking. The one directly in front of her, which showed a woman seated on a plain wooden chair, was more true to life than any drawing. "What are these?" she asked, marveling.

James beamed. "A lot has happened while you were in Australia, cousin. These are photographs." He led her to an object that looked to Lizzie like a simple wooden box. "This captures the true image of the object on what is called a negative, which can then be reproduced multiple times."

James's excitement was plain as he walked her back to the display of photographs. "These are daguerreotypes," he explained. "They have glass negatives." He pointed to the first images they had been looking at. "And these are calotypes, which have paper negatives."

Lizzie nodded, although she could not comprehend his meaning. She examined the photographs with fascination. There were many scenes of trees or buildings or city streets, but it was the photographs of people that intrigued her most.

"It's like looking at the actual person," Lizzie said in awe. "Not just an artist's rendering." She studied the face of the woman in the picture. "I must say, however, the photograph does not flatter the woman the way an artist could."

James laughed. "You have hit the crux of the matter, my dear. These images are just like looking in a mirror. They show the person as he or she actually is."

"What a dangerous idea," said a voice behind them.

"Freddie!" James cried with delight.

While concentrating on the photographs, Lizzie had temporarily forgotten all else. Now Freddie's presence returned all her cares to the forefront of her mind—including her unease about the girl she'd seen a few minutes ago. Was it Molly? It appeared the day was not to be without its troubles after all.

She kept her eyes on the picture in front of her, stealing a few seconds to gather her wits.

"I suspected I might run into you today," Freddie said to James. "I am overjoyed to see you've brought your charming cousin with you."

Lizzie had known she would face Freddie again at some point. This was sooner rather than later, but she was prepared. She *would* keep up her masquerade. She took a deep breath, pasted on a smile, and turned to face him.

He looked her up and down, appraising her bonnet, black shawl, and deep burgundy gown with particular interest, in a way that made her want to slap his face. How dare he look at her like that now—after all he'd done to her? But she would not allow him to take away her self-control. She tipped her head. "Mr. Hightower, how nice to see you again."

Freddie shook James's hand. "Found anything...interesting?" he asked, his voice lewdly suggestive.

"Nothing of *that* variety today," James replied. "But then, I've been busy escorting Ria."

"Of course." Freddie turned back to Lizzie. "James has been finding attendance at the Great Exhibition to be a most efficacious way to meet some of the prettiest—and wealthiest—ladies in England."

"As have you," James countered with a grin.

"True," Freddie agreed. "They have come here from literally every corner of this sceptered isle. As they stand gazing at these magnificent exhibits, it is alarmingly easy to strike up a conversation."

Lizzie tried to tamp down her disgust, and her disappointment in James. She knew James was a ladies' man and an incorrigible flirt, but she did not like to think he was in the same vile league as Freddie. No, she did not believe he would actually leer at a woman the way Freddie was doing right now. His gaze raked over her again. "Of course, with his lovely cousin at his side, I can well understand why James has noticed no one else."

"Why, Mr. Hightower, you are just full of compliments." She transferred her look to James. "My cousin could learn a lot from you. He never compliments me nearly enough."

"I don't need to," James retorted. "There are plenty of volunteers like Freddie to do it for me."

Freddie continued to study her. "I overheard your comment about the lack of flattery in those calotypes. They do give a shockingly accurate picture. But consider this." He leaned in. "The image is preserved forever. How unfortunate that photography was invented after you left England. I should like to have seen a photograph of you from back then."

He was testing her, hoping perhaps that she would show relief that there were no photographs of Ria. "It *is* unfortunate, isn't it?" she agreed. "Ten years ago I was in the bloom of youth. Now I am a poor widow, and so old."

"That's not true," said James. "You are more beautiful than ever. I don't need a photograph to prove that."

"James, you are a dear." Lizzie took his arm. "Now, what were you telling me about calotypes and negatives? I'm such a silly little thing. Whatever you told me went right out of my head the moment Mr. Hightower joined us." She favored Freddie with a bright smile.

Freddie gave a slight nod of his head, as though conceding the first round to an opponent.

James did not need additional encouragement. He launched into a dissertation of the advantages of calotypes over daguerreotypes. Somehow he had amassed a remarkably large amount of information on the subject. At any other time Lizzie might have been pleasantly diverted by this discovery that James, the dissolute playboy, had found something so technical to capture his interest.

But today, Lizzie was more attuned to Freddie while they moved through the exhibit, aware of the way he watched her as she pretended to study the photographs. She kept throwing furtive glances among the crowd, keeping an eye out for the woman she thought was Molly. At least with James lecturing them on the details of what they were viewing, there was no need to make further conversation.

Finally they reached the last of the photographs. "Shall we go for some refreshment?" Freddie suggested. "I imagine you have spent the morning walking all over this overgrown greenhouse. Mrs. Somerville might fancy a rest and something to drink."

James looked chagrined. "Here I've been talking my head off about photography, not perceiving that my poor cousin was fading away."

"I'm not so weak as all that," Lizzie said. "But I wouldn't mind sitting for a few minutes."

They made their way down the stairs and over to the area where the refreshment stands were located. "There is the most delicious lemonade here," James said. "You two enjoy a rest while I get the drinks."

"No!" Lizzie blurted out. James looked at her in surprise. Freddie smirked. "That is, it will take you forever," she amended, pointing to the long line stemming from the lemonade stand.

"I insist," James said. "I shan't be long. I am very good friends with the young lady who works there."

James sauntered off and began skirting the long line. Freddie led Lizzie to a table located under one of the large elm trees. The roof in this section had been designed as a high arch to accommodate the trees. Sunlight poured through the roof and flitted down through the leaves as though they were outside.

Freddie pulled out the chair for her. When she was seated, he pressed his body against the back of her chair. For a few long moments she could feel the warmth of his torso against her back. He had done the same thing the first time he had taken her to dinner at a London restaurant, all those years ago. It had been at the beginning of their disastrous affair. At the time, his closeness had been exciting and inviting. Now, it signaled only danger. It made her shiver. She covered the involuntary gesture with a cough.

He sat down in the chair opposite her. "You are not ill, I hope?"

"Just a dry throat," Lizzie said. "I'm sure the lemonade will cure it."

From her vantage point, Lizzie could see the building's centerpiece: a crystal fountain, fifteen feet in height. Lizzie focused on it, hoping its gentle elegance would help calm her. The water splashed peacefully from the gently fluted top, sparkling like a jewel in the sunlight as it spilled down to the waiting tiers of glass below.

And there, next to the fountain, stood Molly Weathers.

It had to be her; Lizzie was sure of it. She was standing among other visitors who were picnicking at the base of the fountain. Molly pulled out an apple from the basket she was carrying. But she continued to look at Lizzie with real interest as she ate. It could not be coincidence. Were she and her grandfather following Lizzie? Would they try to approach her, embarrass her by insisting they knew her? Or would they try to extort money from her for their silence? She could not truly believe they would do such a thing, but she could not shake the thought.

"Tell me, which of the displays have you enjoyed most?" Freddie asked.

She turned to see Freddie's dark eyes upon her. "I suppose the gems," she replied, still disturbed by the sight of Molly and saying the first thing that came to her mind.

"The gems, of course," he said with a satisfied smile, looking as though she had just thrown him a prize. "The Hope Diamond is quite spectacular, is it not? It was in France for many years, until it disappeared during the revolution. It finally resurfaced in England some years later. No wonder you favor it, *Mrs. Somerville.* It seems you and the diamond share similar histories."

Again the look, the eyes boring into hers. Memories of their time together in France flashed, unwanted, through Lizzie's mind. They had spent two weeks in Paris, before moving on to Vienna. What an irrevocable step she had taken there, in that elegant hotel near the Opéra. But she had been so in love with him then. Swept away by desire and ignorance.

Lizzie forced her breathing to stay even, tempering the panic. She sighed elaborately and shook her head. "I do hope to see Europe one day. Perhaps Grandmamma and I will go there together."

"You would find Paris delightful. I know I did." He took her hand in his. "Perhaps sometime you will tell me the *real* story of all that you did since leaving London."

Her pulse thrummed against the pressure of his hand. "The real story?"

"This little game is…interesting. But we both know you have been to France."

She pulled her hand away and sniffed haughtily. "Are you calling me a liar, sir?"

Amusement flashed in his cold eyes. "I would never accuse a lady of such a thing. Let's just say that women are known to, shall we say, *forget* aspects of their past that they would rather not remember." He leaned back in his chair. "Come now, my dear. Let us have the truth out between us."

She regarded him steadily. "The truth is that you are forward and rude," she said with indignation. "Since you are James's friend, I cannot ignore you. But I must ask you to behave in a more gentlemanlike manner."

He bowed his head. "I humbly beg your pardon, my lady, if I have offended. It certainly was not my intention. I do hope this can be forgotten, and that we can be friends."

His swift reversal took Lizzie off guard. He was a nimble opponent, always keeping his adversary on uncertain ground. What was he up to?

She did not have to wait long for the answer. Freddie looked over her shoulder and remarked drily, "What a pleasant surprise. It appears we may be joined by Lord Somerville."

Chapter 25

I believe I see Mrs. Somerville seated under that elm tree," Lucinda remarked.

She and Geoffrey had just completed a tour of the new display from France. Her parents had separated from them, and they had all planned to meet by the fountain in one hour's time.

Geoffrey's joy upon seeing Ria again was almost immediately doused by his annoyance that she was sitting with Freddie Hightower. Ria had said James planned to bring her here, and yet he was nowhere in sight. Geoffrey would have to give James a serious lecture about allowing Ria to go out unchaperoned with such a man.

He would not have kept away from Ria if he'd known Hightower would worm his way into her life so rapidly. The man had a knack for finding vulnerable women. As a widow with high social standing, Ria would be an appealing target. Geoffrey thought he had given her ample warning about Hightower, and yet here she was with him. Was she really so utterly lacking in common sense?

No, he decided. He could tell at a glance that she was not enjoying herself. She looked exceedingly uncomfortable. Whatever Freddie was trying, Geoffrey would make sure it went no further.

"Shall we go and speak to them?" Lucinda inquired.

"Yes," he replied with determination. "Most definitely."

As they made their way through the crowd, Lucinda said, "I will enjoy talking with Mrs. Somerville again. She came to call last week. She is a kind woman, and has such a good head on her shoulders."

This was high praise indeed, for Lucinda did not open up easily to strangers. Ria must have done something to win her over. He felt an unaccountable surge of pride for Ria's sake. It would be good for them to become friends, he reasoned. After all, they might one day be related, if he married Lucinda. The thought ought to give him satisfaction, but it merely left him with a hollow, unsettled feeling. Ria always left him in an upheaval. He was going through it again now as they drew nearer. She always exceeded his richest remembrances of how beautiful she was.

Ria greeted them warmly and extended her hand to Lucinda. "Miss Cardington, how nice to see you again."

She appeared calmer now, having only small red stains on her cheeks to signal the agitation Geoffrey had seen moments before. Her apparent composure was the only thing that kept him from immediately confronting Hightower about his intentions.

Hightower rose from his chair. He was polite as all of the formal greetings were gone through, but Geoffrey saw that he was irritated by their presence. He was glad of it.

Ria extended her hand to Geoffrey. He grasped it, bringing him just close enough to catch the scent of roses in her hair. He had an urge to close his eyes and breathe in deeply. Realizing

Freddie's sharp eyes were watching, he quickly let go of Ria's hand. He set his face into a stern expression. "Where is James? You said he would be bringing you here."

"He did bring me," Ria replied. "He has gone in search of drinks for us."

At least James hadn't entirely thrown her to the wolves. Or in this case, wolf.

Hightower offered his chair to Lucinda. There was an awkward moment while she was being seated, when her dress caught on a chair leg. Geoffrey was sorry to see her embarrassment at having a bit of leg exposed. But Hightower's wily charm somehow managed to set her at ease. He even whispered a few words that brought a tiny smile to her face.

"I'll just tell James we will need two more lemonades," Hightower said. "I trust I may safely leave the ladies in your care, Lord Somerville?"

"You need have no worries on that account," Geoffrey replied. He did not bother to hide his dislike of the man. It would have been impossible anyway.

Hightower gave him a sardonic grin before going off in search of James.

As the three of them discussed what they had seen during the course of the morning, Ria kept looking back and forth between Geoffrey and Lucinda. She had heard the gossip, then. Was she already picturing him and Lucinda as a couple? How did she feel about it? Geoffrey would have preferred it if she had not seemed so open to the idea. But there was presumably no one in England who did not think it was an excellent match.

Geoffrey noticed that Ria kept glancing over at the fountain. He tried once or twice to follow her gaze, but could see nothing out of the ordinary. Perhaps she was simply enjoying how lovely it was.

James and Hightower returned, each bearing two glasses of lemonade.

"Here we are!" James announced. "Compliments of the Messrs. Schweppes." He handed a glass to Ria, and Hightower gave his glasses to Geoffrey and Lucinda.

"But, Mr. Hightower," Lucinda objected, "you are left with nothing to drink."

"Do not concern yourself, Miss Cardington," Hightower said. "It appears I am the odd man out today. But no matter. I must be going. I have another appointment."

"Surely it can wait?" James asked.

"I'm afraid not." He took Ria's hand. "I look forward to seeing you at Lady Thornborough's dinner party next week."

"It will be a pleasure," Ria replied.

She and Hightower locked gazes, and Geoffrey had the feeling that some intense private message was passing between them. He did not think it was attraction; something in Ria's look made that abundantly plain. Whatever messages they were sending, Geoffrey did not like it. He would not allow Hightower to make inroads of any kind. He could not resist saying, "It appears we shall *all* be at the dinner party."

Hightower turned to assess him. With a knowing look and a nod toward Lucinda, he said, "You will be escorting Miss Cardington, I presume?"

This remark only flustered Lucinda, so Geoffrey answered, "All of Miss Cardington's family will be there."

"Really? How fortunate," Hightower answered without enthusiasm. He gave them all a bow and took his leave.

*

It was with no small amount of relief that Lizzie watched Freddie go. Geoffrey's fortuitous arrival seemed to have hastened his departure. Although she could not forget she would be facing Freddie all too soon at the dinner party, she was grateful for today's reprieve.

Lizzie tried to think of something congenial to say to Miss Cardington, but her mind was filled with less amiable thoughts. Geoffrey had made no effort to see her since the night of the ball. She knew there were many demands on his time, and yet she was foolishly irked that he had managed to find room in his day to escort Miss Cardington on a pleasure tour.

How many times had she returned to thoughts of that night! His look, his words, his touch—these memories sustained her as she kept reaffirming to herself that she was taking the best possible course of action. She was desperate to spend as much time with Geoffrey as she could, to share every possible moment before she must take the steps that would change everything.

Had he been thinking of that night at all? She couldn't tell. His face bore the maddeningly controlled expression she'd often seen on him. Had that moment of deep connection they shared been only a figment of her imagination?

Surprisingly, it was the normally reticent Lucinda who spoke first. "Have you seen the photography exhibit?" she asked. When Lizzie answered in the affirmative, Lucinda's face lit up. "It's one of the most exciting things here, is it not? I believe photography is the next great art form."

James had been idly scanning the crowd, but his attention now settled on Lucinda. "Art form?" he repeated, intrigued. "It is the technical processes that I find so captivating."

"It is a perfect blend of art and science," Lucinda replied. "The ideal metaphor for our scientific age."

Lizzie thought Lucinda looked much handsomer when she was engaged on a topic that interested her. James must have perceived this, too, and he regarded Lucinda with a newfound fascination. In no time, the two of them were ensconced in a discussion that Lizzie found impossible to follow. It seemed to baffle Geoffrey as well, and he gave Lizzie a bemused smile.

"How naughty of James to waylay Miss Cardington's interest from you," Lizzie whispered.

Geoffrey nodded. "We are left on our own, it seems."

He looked more than a little pleased at this prospect, however, and Lizzie took a sip of lemonade to hide the burst of pleasure this gave her. "I am glad you will be coming to Grandmamma's dinner party next week. I have missed—" She pulled up short. "That is, I shall look forward to seeing you again."

Geoffrey guessed what she had been about to say. "Have you missed me? I am sorry I have not been able to call. I have a clerk who has been helping me organize my business affairs, and unfortunately he seems to have overestimated the actual number of hours in a day."

His manner softened as he said this, the hard control she'd seen earlier easing up a bit. Lizzie took a moment to savor looking at him, to drink in the joy of being here with him, one of the few precious moments she was storing away for a much more sorrowful day.

"May I surmise that you were not offended by the things I asked you—about my brothers, I mean?"

"No," she said. "I wanted to share those things with you. However, later I became worried that perhaps they had been unhelpful, stirred up unhappy memories—"

"Quite the contrary," he interrupted. "They helped me very much."

Their conversation seemed like nothing on the surface, within earshot of James and Lucinda. But Lizzie knew the current running beneath their words was deeper than anyone else could imagine.

Geoffrey took her hand. "I think, I hope, we are friends still, Ria."

Friends. Given who she was, both in her real and pretended identities, she could expect nothing more. Something in her heart twisted and tumbled, knowing even this would not last. "I—yes, of course we are friends." She licked her suddenly dry lips and tried again. "I am honored."

Something of her disappointment must have come through in her voice. Geoffrey gave her a quizzical look. He sent a quick glance to James and Lucinda, but they were still deep in discussion. He opened his mouth to speak, but whatever he had been about to say was preempted by the sudden arrival of Lord and Lady Cardington.

"There you are," Lady Cardington boomed. "We have been looking for you this half hour or more." She fanned herself. "The crowds! I did not think there were this many people in all of London."

James helped Lucinda to rise. She extended her hand and said warmly, "I so enjoyed this time together. Perhaps we might talk more at Lady Thornborough's dinner party?"

James gave her a regretful smile, as one might give a child to whom he must deny a requested sweet. "It would be lovely, I have no doubt. However, it is entirely possible Miss Emily will decide to carry the conversation in other directions."

The mention of her sister, who was seeking James's interest for far different reasons, brought a look of annoyance to Lucinda's face. "Emily will be quite cross to discover she missed seeing you here today."

James leaned in and said, as if they were sharing a secret, "Perhaps you ought not to tell her."

"Quite right," Lady Cardington asserted. "It will only put her in a pout, and then she will be insufferable for days."

Geoffrey offered his hand to Lizzie. "Until next week, then."

Lizzie nodded, trying not to dwell too much on the warmth of his hand or the way she felt oddly unmoored when he released it.

Geoffrey took Lucinda's arm, and they followed Lord and Lady Cardington back through the crowds toward the entrance. Lizzie was struck with a pang of remorse as she watched the familiar way Geoffrey leaned in toward Lucinda to catch something she was saying.

"What a charming interlude that was," James remarked.

"Yes," Lizzie agreed, unable to repress a sigh. "It was." One of the few short interludes that were left to her.

She glanced over to the fountain. Molly was still there. She sent a tiny smile in Lizzie's direction, but did not approach. She seemed only curious, not intent on doing Lizzie harm. Lizzie was relieved the girl kept her distance. But as Lizzie and James left the area to continue their tour of the building, she gave Molly the tiniest nod as she passed by. Perhaps, Lizzie thought, she might be able to seek help from the Weathers family if she ended up on the streets after her big unveiling. Assuming she did not end up in jail—or worse.

Chapter 26

"James informs me that you play beautifully, Mrs. Somerville." Freddie Hightower's voice carried over a lull in the dinner conversation. "I hope you will favor us with a tune after dinner?"

Ria blanched.

It was not the first time Geoffrey had seen her look uncomfortable this evening, and he was certain Hightower was the cause of it. Lady Thornborough had seated Hightower at the opposite end of the polished mahogany table that easily accommodated the twenty guests in attendance. Despite this, he had been peppering Ria with questions all evening. If this was his way of winning over women, it was clearly not working with Ria. She answered his questions politely, but often attempted to turn the topic of conversation toward himself or someone else.

She took a sip of wine before replying to Hightower's latest salvo. "I am sorry to disappoint you, but I cannot play this evening. I am too much out of practice. I did not play a note in Australia. I have forgotten the finer points of the instrument."

"Surely it will come back to you," Hightower urged.

Ria set down her glass and gave another of her giggles, the kind that emanated from her only when James or Hightower was around. This kind of behavior seemed to come and go, as though now that Ria was home in England, her younger, sillier self was trying to reassert its dominance over the woman she had become in Australia. "Now that you have put me on the spot, I shall have to practice. But I would spare Grandmamma's guests this evening."

"A wise decision," Lady Thornborough said. "There is nothing I abhor more than badly played music."

"I am disappointed," Hightower told Ria. "However, I will hold you to your promise to play for us soon."

Geoffrey found himself irked at this exchange. Why should Hightower be so intent on hearing Ria play? Only sheer politeness kept Geoffrey from ordering Hightower to stop barraging her with questions. He'd lost count of how many times he'd been required to suppress this urge since the dinner began.

"Perhaps Lord Somerville will read to us?" This suggestion came from Lucinda Cardington. She sent an admiring glance in his direction. "You have a splendid reading voice."

"Thank you," Geoffrey said, grateful for anything to turn the attention of the guests away from the way Hightower was distressing Ria. "You are most kind."

Lady Cardington nodded with approval at her daughter's suggestion. "What a wonderful idea! I am sure we would find Lord Somerville's reading morally uplifting."

"Do not ask Geoffrey to read from one of his old sermons," James said. Smiling at Lucinda's sister, Emily, who was seated on his right, he added, "I refuse to think about weighty matters at a dinner party, when there are livelier subjects to contemplate."

Across from James, Miss Edith Shaw tittered and turned her large eyes to James. "Then what on earth shall we do?" she asked, as though only James could have the solution to such a difficult problem.

Despite his preoccupation with Hightower and Ria, Geoffrey had not missed the fact that both Miss Emily and Miss Shaw had been vying for James's attention all evening. James had so far managed the balancing act with finesse. He now said expansively, "I propose a friendly game of whist—for everyone!"

"Whist?" Ria repeated. She looked as though this idea did not appeal to her.

"Of course!" James said. "Do you remember how many hours we used to while away at that game? And the particular way our tutor punished us when it caused us to neglect our studies?"

"Let me see…" Ria considered the question.

Hightower watched Ria intently, as though her answer were of vital importance.

"Was that the time he put us in opposite corners of the room?" Ria said finally. "Or the time he had us write out our geography lesson five times?"

"What a good memory you have, cousin!" James replied with a laugh. "We certainly got into a lot of bad scrapes, didn't we?"

Ria smiled, and her gaze slipped in Hightower's direction. Hightower's look had been replaced by something Geoffrey would have called incredulity.

James said, "Actually, I was thinking of the day our tutor sent us below stairs to clean the pots. He told us if we were not going to learn our lessons, we may as well join the kitchen help because we were no better than the scullery maid!"

This jab at the servants brought laughter from many of the

guests. Geoffrey did not join in, and he was oddly gratified to see that Ria was not laughing either. In fact, she was frowning.

"That was a superb way to teach a lesson," Lord Cardington said, his portly stomach shaking. "Who was this tutor? I should have hired him for my Emily."

"You know I would learn nothing under the tyranny of such a man, Papa," Miss Emily replied tartly. "I need someone kind and understanding to teach me." She gave James a look that could have melted an iceberg. James responded with a wink.

His gesture must have escaped Miss Shaw, which was probably a good thing. She said, "Oh, I agree with you, Miss Emily. But then, I find studying to be so tedious, no matter who the tutor is."

Geoffrey thought of the dozens of boys in his tiny parish who would have loved to have been under the "tyranny" of any tutor.

"I do not think there is shame in cleaning pots," Lucinda said quietly.

Ria nodded in agreement. "The knowledge of how to clean pots came in handy when I was living in Australia, to be sure."

"All this is neither here nor there," James said. "I believe the subject was whist. So, cousin, I hope you are not out of practice with that, too?"

"Oh no," Ria answered. "Pianos may have been scarce in Australia, but there was certainly no shortage of cards!"

She said this in a lighthearted manner, and everyone laughed again. However, a hint of worry crossed her expressive face, giving Geoffrey the feeling that she was not looking forward to the game.

"I will not have you playing for money," Lady Thornborough said. "Not in my house."

"Then we shall play for points," James said. "For the pure fun of it."

Lady Thornborough rose from her chair. "Well, gentlemen, we ladies shall retire now for some edifying conversation, while you sort out who shall be paired for the card games."

There was a bustle of movement as the gentlemen rose to help the ladies from the table. James assisted Miss Emily, which brought him another adoring look.

Ria linked her arm in Lady Thornborough's, answering some question the old lady was putting to her. Ria's white gold hair, contrasting sharply with her grandmother's dark dress, was the last Geoffrey saw of her as the ladies left the room.

Hightower followed his gaze. "She is an enchanting creature, is she not?" His voice held both appreciation and something else that Geoffrey could not define. "You must be so happy to have your sister-in-law back, even though she brought the sad news of your brother's death."

"I am happy that she has returned," Geoffrey said. "What's done is done, and I pray only the best for her now."

The butler offered brandy, which Geoffrey gladly accepted.

Hightower pulled out a cigar, twirling it in his fingers and savoring its smell. He made an elaborate show of lighting it. "Is it true you never met Ria before her elopement with Edward?"

"It is."

"She seems eager to get to know you now. Her interest in you is unmistakable."

Geoffrey leveled a hard look at him. "I am her last link with Edward. She loved him very much."

James said with a smile, "Freddie, you are jealous because Ria will not act as every other woman does and instantly give you her affections."

Hightower took a long draw from his cigar before respond-ing. "Perhaps she already has."

"What do you mean to imply by that?" Geoffrey asked coldly.

Freddie looked at him over the smoke of his cigar. "It would be natural, would it not? After all, she is a young widow; I am a desolate young widower. We are kindred spirits. Two souls who have loved and lost."

The only time Geoffrey had seen Hightower and his wife together, the man had been barely civil to her. Geoffrey was sure he wasted no tears when the poor woman died. "If you and Mrs. Hightower were in love, you did an admirable job of hiding it."

Freddie's look of contempt was probably aimed at Geoffrey, though it could well have been for his dead wife. "Some sentiments are best kept private."

James either did not see or chose to ignore the growing frosti-ness in the conversation. He said lightly, "You are both wrong. Clearly, Ria is in love with me."

"In that case, I should warn her to be careful," Hightower said. "God knows what will happen to her if Miss Shaw or Miss Emily gets knowledge of it. Hell hath no fury, you know."

Geoffrey threw a concerned glance toward the fathers of the two ladies in question, but thankfully they had not heard High-tower's remark. They were deep in some political discussion at the other end of the table.

"I have my hands full with *all* the ladies," James said with unabashed pride. "It is such a trial sometimes." He took a sip of his brandy. "It would be lovely to marry Ria, of course. But the estate is ailing, and I must find a rich wife. Someone who will be glad for my family connections and bring a sizable dowry to the marriage."

"I am glad to see your priorities are in the right place," Geof-frey said.

James answered the rebuff with an easy grin.

"How about you, Lord Somerville?" Hightower said with a smirk. "It appears the velvet noose is about to close around you. The elder Miss Cardington seems to think she has a claim. Does she meet your qualifications?"

This conversation rankled him, but Geoffrey held his peace. He would not sink to their level of discussing women as though they were cards to be picked up or tossed down.

"Time will tell," he said.

*

Geoffrey found himself partnered with Lucinda at whist, playing against James and Miss Shaw. Hightower had insisted Ria sit with him at the other table. Geoffrey had been unable to object too strenuously to this plan, for fear of hurting Lucinda's feelings. However, he kept a close eye on what was going on between them.

As they played, Hightower kept looking at Ria intently each time he played a card. Ria did not appear to be an accomplished player. If she had played many hours together with James, she must have since forgotten the strategies of the game. She would return Hightower's look, and then glance down at her cards with a completely baffled expression. "Goodness me," she said. "What was the trump again?"

They were losing nearly every hand, despite the fact that they did not have strong opponents. Mr. Shaw always played the wrong suit, and Miss Emily kept sending sidelong glances at James and Miss Shaw, as though trying to size up the competition.

Ria laid down a card that must have been a bad choice, and Hightower tossed his entire hand onto the table in disgust. "It's good we are not playing for money," he said. "I would have lost my fortune twice over by now."

"I never claimed to be a good player," Ria said with a laugh that struck Geoffrey as strained.

"Nor I," said Miss Emily, who looked even more relieved than Ria that the game was over. She stood up and sidled in James's direction. "Lucinda plays the piano beautifully. Perhaps we can have a dance?"

*

Lizzie thought she had been doing so well, deliberately ignoring the signals she and Freddie had developed when they played whist together in Europe. But she had not anticipated having to dance as a result. It would have been better to win at cards than to risk dancing with him. Freddie was gloating as though Emily Cardington had played right into his plans.

"No dancing," said Lady Thornborough, much to Lizzie's relief. "There is no room. But it would be a pleasure to hear Miss Cardington play for us."

Looking embarrassed, Lucinda said, "My sister overestimates my abilities."

"Nonsense," her mother declared roundly. "You play exquisitely."

This hefty claim only made Lucinda look even more uncomfortable. "But I have not prepared anything."

"We have plenty of music," Lady Thornborough said. "Ria can help you." She gestured to Lizzie.

"Of course." Lizzie knew exactly where the sheet music was stored. She'd found it one day while she'd been investigating the house, trying to figure out where Martha had once hidden Lady Thornborough's bracelet. She led Lucinda to the music cabinet.

As they selected the appropriate music, Lucinda said, "Will you help me with turning the pages?"

Lizzie hesitated. She could not admit that she did not read music. She glanced away, only to see Freddie watching and listening, as he had done all evening. All the questions he'd put to her, and the game of cards, had been nothing more than probing, testing, looking for a break in her performance to prove she was not Ria. This evening had already been excruciatingly long, and it wasn't over yet.

She turned away from Freddie and found herself looking into Geoffrey's friendly countenance. He, too, had been watching her. But his attention had been welcome—unlike Freddie's attempts to lay a snare. Over and over again, Lizzie had been drawn to the quiet strength that Geoffrey unconsciously exuded. She reminded herself that she must not lean on him too much. Nevertheless, she was grateful when he said, "I can help Miss Cardington with the music."

This suggestion met with a murmur of approval from everyone. Lady Cardington threw a knowing glance at her husband, as though she took this as further proof of Geoffrey's intentions toward her daughter. It probably was, Lizzie thought, with a stab of jealousy.

Lucinda shyly thanked him, barely meeting his eyes before seating herself at the piano. Lizzie noted that her hands trembled as she arranged the music.

While some of the men busied themselves rearranging chairs, Freddie was again at her side. "I doubt the poor girl will be able to play anything worth hearing. She seems afraid of her own shadow."

"Not everyone likes being the center of attention," Lizzie said. She herself had received far too much of it this evening.

Geoffrey was now standing next to Lucinda, poised to turn

the music. Although there was a modest distance between the two of them, it was painfully easy to imagine them as a couple. Lucinda's continued blushing did nothing to allay that impression.

Lizzie allowed Freddie to lead her to a chair.

"Perhaps Miss Cardington is trembling because Lord Somerville is so near," Freddie said, his voice laced with suggestive tones. "She must be in love. What a fine couple they will make."

Lizzie's envy was heightened by remorse. She would never be worthy to claim this man. She must be forced to endure the advances of a man like Freddie while watching Geoffrey turn his attentions toward another. That was the cruelest punishment of all. But one day soon her dealings with Freddie would be over. "We mustn't be premature," she said. "Nothing is official yet."

"I'm sure it's just a matter of time," Freddie taunted her. He bent over to whisper in her ear, "I can't help thinking, though, that you are the far superior woman. What a shame that the law prevents him from marrying you."

His breath, smelling of brandy and coffee, sent a ripple of disgust through her. "Me? Oh, heavens, no," Lizzie said with a dismissive air, marveling at what a good actress she was. "The law makes no difference in this case. My brother-in-law has no interest in me, nor I in him."

She tried to tame the irrational wish that she could be the one seated at that piano, playing while Geoffrey leaned in to turn the pages. She could imagine the warmth of him as he stood close behind her, the glorious feeling of being all but wrapped in his arms. She fanned herself. "Miss Cardington is clearly the superior talent. I don't play half as well."

"On the contrary," Freddie answered sardonically. "I would say you play rather well."

He leaned back in his chair and said no more. Lizzie pretended to be absorbed in the music. She *had* played well, she thought. She would keep on beating back Freddie's advances, avoiding his poisonous darts until she had played the game her way. Most important, she would never give Freddie the satisfaction of seeing how much she loved Geoffrey. That was one truth that would remain locked in her heart forever.

Chapter 27

Geoffrey walked late into the night, trying to make sense out of what had happened that evening. The streets were quiet now, and he hoped the cool air would clear his head so he could find some answers.

He was aware of Ria's former reputation as a light-headed society miss—her beautiful face and figure had captivated the gentlemen, but she hadn't cared very much for the finer things of the mind. The Ria he was getting to know seemed more sensible and mature. It was true that at times—usually when she was in the company of others—he'd seen a certain shallowness manifest itself. But he sensed that a deeper, quieter person lay underneath. Someone whom, for no discernable reason, she seemed determined to hide.

Would Ria revert to her old ways now that she was back in London? Would she prefer to spend her time with men like James? Geoffrey believed her cousin to be a reasonably good-hearted man at his core, and yet he could not condone James's preference for an idle and irresponsible kind of life. Is that what

Ria wanted, too? After the trial of so many difficult years, was she eager to return to a life of mindless ease?

That moment they had shared in the carriage—that moment that meant so much to Goeffrey—had she already forgotten it? Geoffrey was surprised, and not a little disconcerted, that she'd hardly spoken a word to him all evening. She'd spent most of her time with that abominable Hightower, and what was most galling, she appeared at times to be openly flirting with him. He had not missed the way Ria had laughed at her own silliness while she played cards, or the way she and Hightower had sat together whispering during Lucinda's performance. Why, then, did he still have the sense that she was not entirely at ease around Hightower? He was positive he'd seen a look of sharp discomfort cross her face several times. She was not required to spend time with the man. What had motivated her?

His offer to turn the music for Lucinda stayed on Geoffrey's mind, too. He knew it would only provide more fodder for the gossips. He had not intended that; his offer had been an instant decision, a reflex based on something he'd seen in Ria's expression. Had he been wrong in thinking he'd detected distress there? Or had the distress been simply that she did not want to leave Hightower's side?

This, he thought gloomily, brought him right back to his initial question. Hightower had monopolized her all evening, and she had allowed him to do it. Why?

Given his relative inexperience with women, Geoffrey was tempted to put the evening's events down to his lack of understanding about how these bizarre society games were played. But something in the depths of his being insisted there was more to it than that.

Perhaps *he* was the problem. He had spent far too much time thinking of Ria. She had angered him, worried him, perplexed him, and now she was close to exhausting him. How had this been possible? He had never been a man to let his emotions rule him. Why should things be different now? He should wish to love Ria as a sister. But these were most definitely not the feelings she was drawing from him. He could only be disappointed in himself for this. He had to find some way to regain his equilibrium, and to do what was right.

Slowly he made his way back to his house. Mrs. Claridge must have been awaiting his return; she opened the front door for him. "My goodness, sir, it's not like you to be out so late. You'll catch your death. Don't you know the night air is bad for you?"

He inhaled one last breath of cool air before she closed the door. "Exactly how does 'night' air differ from 'daytime' air, Mrs. Claridge? What sort of dangerous stuff does it contain?"

Mrs. Claridge gave him an exasperated look. "You do ask the strangest questions, sir."

"Do I?" he mused. "I can assure you I have questions far more outlandish than that." He rubbed his eyes, still trying to clear his brain. "Questions for which there seem to be no answers."

Mrs. Claridge folded her hands comfortably in front of her as she regarded him. "It's a good thing you know the One who has the answers, eh?" she said kindly. "If you are troubled, you might well ask Him for help."

It was simple wisdom. And the best. "Right you are, Mrs. Claridge. As always."

"I certainly don't claim that," she returned. "But might I suggest you go to bed, sir? It only makes a person gloomy to be up all night in the shadows. Things often look better in the light of day."

"Thank you, Mrs. Claridge. I shall be off to bed soon."

Nevertheless, Geoffrey knew that sleep was far from him. He went to the library, still continuing his reflections over Ria. She truly was a riddle. How could she be so completely different in public than she was when the two of them were alone? What was driving the two facets of her personality?

He sighed, thought of Mrs. Claridge's admonition, and turned to prayer.

*

The dedication ceremony had drawn quite a crowd.

Lizzie was squeezed in with other invited guests near a small stage that had been set up in front of the new housing project. Behind them, curious onlookers lined the streets, all vying for a better view. Most were gawking at the finely dressed gentlemen and ladies—a rarity in this part of London. Lady Thornborough had been too worn out by the dinner party to come this morning, but she had grudgingly allowed Lizzie to go, so long as she took along Martha and a footman for propriety's sake.

Her first thought on arriving had been to find Geoffrey and speak to him. She'd spotted him near the stage before the ceremony began, but was unable to reach him for the crowd. He'd been surrounded by those who were the primary sponsors of this project, including the Cardingtons. Lizzie's heart gave another jealous lurch as she saw Lucinda's face smiling up into his as they chatted.

Lord Ashley had been waxing eloquent for quite some time about what adequate housing would mean to the deserving workers and their families. It was getting on toward noon, and the day was warm. Trickles of sweat rolled down the back of Lizzie's neck.

"He sure knows how to talk, don't he?" Martha whispered, causing Lizzie to smile.

But the earl was nearing the end of his speech. "And now, I would like to invite the reverend Lord Somerville to give the benediction."

Lizzie was positively enraptured as she watched Geoffrey walk up the steps to the platform. He looked so handsome, so dignified. He looked out over the crowd, and his eyes seemed to catch hers almost immediately. He could do no more than give her a brief smile, but Lizzie did not miss the sincerity behind it. He was glad she was here. She smiled back broadly.

"In the name of God and Our Lord...," he began, his voice strong and clear.

Everyone bowed their heads, including Lizzie, although she could not resist glancing up a few times just to look at him. About the third time she did this, something else caught her eye. To her far right, Molly Weathers was standing just behind the barrier that had been erected for the invited guests, looking straight at her.

"Please," Molly mouthed, her eyes beseeching. She held up a basket of apples, and Lizzie understood. Molly wanted to speak to her, but would not risk embarrassing her.

Lizzie bowed her head again as Geoffrey finished his prayer. For the first time in longer than she could remember, she found herself praying, too. *Please, Lord,* she thought fervently. *What should I do?* Lizzie was not sure if she would recognize an answer. But she knew she had to find out what Molly wanted.

She dabbed lightly at her face with a handkerchief, trying to remain patient while Lord Ashley gave a few more closing remarks. At last, it was over. There was a round of applause, and the crowd slowly began to disperse.

"Wait here," Lizzie told Martha. "I want to buy an apple from that girl over there."

"I can do that for you, madam," Martha said in surprise.

"No, I want to do it. Please wait here. I won't be long."

"Yes, madam," Martha said, reluctantly obeying. "Mind your reticule; I've spotted more than one unsavory type wandering about."

Lizzie pressed her way through the crowd, looking around to be sure no one who knew her was close by. She could not afford to have anyone overhear their conversation.

"Buy an apple, madam?" Molly said deferentially as Lizzie approached.

"Yes, thank you." She pulled out enough coins for a dozen apples and dropped them into Molly's palm.

Molly's eyes widened. "Thank you, madam."

She held Lizzie's eyes for several long beats. Lizzie did not dare speak. She wanted to reach out to Molly, to apologize for how she had treated her grandfather. It was tempting, but too dangerous. She could not risk exposing herself, not yet. She hoped her expression told Molly everything she could not say. At last, Lizzie felt she must move on. She turned away.

"If you please, madam."

"Yes?" Lizzie turned back, realizing she had not taken the apple.

She now saw that Molly's hand held both an apple and a folded piece of paper.

"If you please," Molly said again, very low, "I have a letter from Tom."

Her words sent Lizzie reeling. *A letter from Tom?* She knew she should be pretending ignorance, but she didn't have the strength. "Tom is dead," she whispered. She looked at the paper with a kind of incredulous hope.

"He's not!" Molly said, her eyes shining. "This came enclosed in another letter to my family, explaining that he had survived a terrible shipwreck and was desperate to find you. He thought you might be in London, and he begged us, as dear old friends, to do all we could to find you. As soon as we received this letter, Grandfather knew the woman he'd seen in Hyde Park had to have been you after all."

She slid the smooth apple and the rough paper into Lizzie's hand. Wonder, joy, and terror came with it. Was Tom really alive?

"I shan't trouble you again, madam. I can see you're in a good place now, and I wish you well. But my family and I . . . well, we were sure you'd want to know."

"Thank you," Lizzie rasped. *For giving my brother back to me.*

Molly gave her a brief smile and a curtsy, and walked away. With great difficulty, Lizzie summoned up the presence of mind to slip the letter into her reticule. Slowly, numbly, she made her way back to the spot where she'd left Martha. Geoffrey was there now, too. And—because the world could not get any more dangerously unbalanced—so were James and Freddie. They were all looking at her, in their different ways and for entirely different reasons. It was like the heat of a hundred suns beating down on her. She practically gasped, finding no air at all.

"Dear Lord, the heat is incredible," James said. "I shall never forgive Geoffrey for bringing us to Spitalfields when we should be lounging under a tree in Hyde Park." Seeing the apple in her hand, he added, "I see you are in need of refreshment, too."

"Have you been here long?" Lizzie asked hoarsely. They must have seen her with Molly. Had anything looked amiss?

"We've just arrived," Freddie said. "Sorry we missed the fun. James seemed to have been mixed up about the time." As he said this, he threw a glance toward the street corner where Molly had been standing. It looked casual enough, but it filled Lizzie with dread.

She was in a waking nightmare now. The most fantastic, topsy-turvy kind of dream, where nothing was solid, all was shifting, constantly re-forming into shapes that would dissolve as soon as she reached out to touch them.

"Perhaps coming out here was too taxing after such a late night," Geoffrey said with an apologetic look at her.

"No," Lizzie assured him with a tremulous smile. "I'm glad I came." *If joy laced with fear could be called "gladness."*

The next hour was the longest Lizzie had ever endured. When at last she was home and Martha had helped her change into a more casual day gown, Lizzie was able to be alone. With trembling hands, she pulled out the letter and began to read.

My Dearest Lizzie,

If this letter makes it into your hands, I can only imagine your surprise and wonder. Yes, I am alive. Somehow I made it to shore, to a lonely stretch of land where I was found, half-dead, by some Aborigines. By the time I'd recovered and made my way back to Bathurst, you were gone. Rev. Greene says you've gone back to England, so I'm sending this in care of Ben Weathers, in the hope that he can find you.

Oh, Lizzie, you don't know the heartache I've been through. I don't blame you for selling everything, thinking I was dead. But why did you leave? I have an inkling you were too taken by Ria's stories. Don't put your faith in them. No good can come of stirring up the past.

As soon as I can collect passage money, I'll come back to search for you myself. For now, I send this letter on the fastest possible boat, and have the audacity to pray to God (despite all I've done) that it reaches you. If it has, write to me right away and tell me where to reach you. You must know that I am in agony until I hear that you are safe.

Your loving,

Tom

Lizzie cried.

She cried with all her heart and strength, long and desperately. She cried for joy that Tom was alive, and in despair of ever seeing him again.

How could she even think of revealing herself now? If she did, Freddie would hound her about Tom's whereabouts. She would never give him this information, but he knew she'd been in Australia, and he would know where to begin his search. He would undoubtedly go after Tom and seek retribution. She had been willing to risk many things for herself, but how could she risk her brother's life after all he'd done for her? She would have to break off all ties with her brother, for his own sake. Tom was alive, but he might well be lost to her forever. Lizzie thought she understood now what Geoffrey had been going through on the day she met him. Like him, she had now lost a brother twice.

Chapter 28

Miss Emily Cardington had Lizzie cornered at the refreshment table. She was flushed and her eyes sparkled with joy. "I am absolutely ecstatic!" she exclaimed.

It was the Cardingtons' charity gala—the final event before Lizzie and Lady Thornborough left London, and Lizzie was doing her best to take in Emily's silly chatter, even as she was counting the hours until she could escape. She was on a knife's edge, caught between elation at her brother's miraculous survival and a new fear for his life. She had to get away—far from Freddie, far from the endless demands placed upon her in town. She needed time to think, to decide what she should do.

Just one more night, and I will be gone. If I can just get through this night.

"I danced with James," Emily said, bringing Lizzie's thoughts back to the party. "It was heaven." She pulled Lizzie away from the group of ladies near the table and spoke to her in a confidential tone. "And after the dance, James and I went out to the terrace—just to cool down after the dancing. It's so dreadfully hot in here."

She blushed, and Lizzie imagined that Emily and James had done more than breathe in the fresh night air. Lizzie suspected the girl was getting in over her head, and she knew all too well where such things could lead. "Emily, I don't think it was wise for you and James to be outside alone. Someone might misconstrue your actions as improper."

"Really?" said Emily with an impish smile. "Then wait until I tell you whom we saw out there." She glanced around to make sure no one could overhear. "Lucinda and Lord Somerville were seated together on a bench in the far corner, where it is very dark and they were nearly hidden from view."

A sort of numbness traveled over Lizzie at hearing this news. "Go on."

"Well, that's all there is," Emily admitted. "They were only talking. But James and I could tell they were talking very earnestly. Don't you see? He was probably *proposing marriage!*"

No, Lizzie thought desperately. *Not tonight.* Her heart was already pushed to the brink.

Emily had practically squealed—a sound that drew disapproving glances from two elderly ladies who were standing a short distance away. She fanned herself and took several deep breaths, which enabled her to speak again in a quieter tone. "Perhaps they will announce their engagement tonight."

Lizzie had known it could happen, of course. But the knowledge could not prevent the strange lurch her stomach was taking right now. "It might not be a proposal. Just because they were talking together…"

"James was convinced that it was," Emily insisted. "And he seemed curiously put out about it."

"Did he? Why would he be against the match?"

"That is exactly the question I asked myself," Emily said with a little nod of her chin, as though she and Lizzie were both very clever people indeed. "And I have divined the answer. If James intends to ask for my hand..." She took Lizzie's free hand into her own. "I do hope that is the case, don't you?"

Lizzie blinked. Her mind was so agitated it took a few moments to realize Emily had asked her a question. She nodded vaguely. "Of course."

"You are a dear," Emily said, squeezing her hand so hard that Lizzie had to work hard to keep from spilling the punch that was in her other hand.

"Go on," Lizzie prompted. "If James asks you..."

Emily's smile widened. "He is always joking about what a bore Lord Somerville is. Perhaps he does not want Lucinda to marry him, because then when James marries me, they will be brothers-in-law!"

"Really, Miss Emily," Lizzie said, trying to keep the impatience out of her voice. "Why should James be concerned about that? There are far worse things than having Lord Somerville for a brother-in-law."

"You would know," Emily said. "I mean, since he actually is your brother-in-law." But her attention was already elsewhere. She excused herself and hurried toward a group of young ladies—no doubt to apprise them of her sister's pending nuptials.

Lizzie made her way through the crowded ballroom and found an unoccupied chair on the far side. She leaned back in her chair, watching the dancers without really seeing them.

Was Geoffrey about to marry Lucinda Cardington? He'd shown every indication that he was courting her, of course. Lizzie should not be surprised if he announced his engagement. Only, somewhere in the depths of her heart, she *was* surprised. Sorely disappointed, too. It was wrong of her to feel that way. It was not as though she could ever claim Geoffrey's affections—not now, and certainly not once the truth about her was known. Why, then, did the last ounce of hope on this subject painfully refuse to leave her?

"My dear Mrs. Somerville, what are you doing hiding in this corner?"

She turned to see Freddie. The man whose presence brought on all her thoughts of despair.

"You have been avoiding me all evening. I am beginning to feel genuinely slighted." He held out his hand. "Shall we? It's a waltz. I happen to know that you dance the waltz very well."

"Oh? And how would you know that?"

"I saw you dancing at Lord Beauchamp's ball, of course."

Of course.

"It was there," Freddie continued, "that, as I recall, you promised me a dance."

There was no way around it. She would have to dance with him. She must do all she could to make it convincing. *One more night.*

As she stood, she gave one of Ria's silly giggles. "Then I must dance with you, mustn't I? It wouldn't do for a lady not to keep her word."

His smile was friendly like a fox. "No one would ever accuse you of not being a lady."

Lizzie took his arm. A small thrill went through her as she touched him. Not from infatuation, as had once been the case. It was more like the jagged heart-pounding awareness of being too close to a dangerous animal. His hand closed over hers, and he led her to the dance floor. His hand found the spot on her back where it had rested hundreds of times, and they began to dance.

Lizzie danced a half pace out of step with the music. Twice she "accidentally" failed to follow Freddie's lead, causing her in the first instance to step on his foot, and in the second to collide with another couple. Each time she laughed and apologized, while Freddie eked out false reassurances and picked up the step again.

Lizzie had worried that it would be a fight to keep from falling into his smooth lead, allowing the music to carry her away as it had so often when they had danced. But, in fact, it was easy to do, knowing that with every step, she was fighting for her life. And for Tom's.

Freddie was putting on quite a show, doing all the things that he would have done if, in fact, he'd been dancing with Ria Thornborough.

But still Lizzie could tell he was not convinced.

When the music ended, he released her and gave her a bow. She saw irritation in his eyes as he straightened. "I don't know when I've had a more charming dance partner."

"Mr. Hightower, you are too kind. You may yet win me over with all these compliments."

"You are not so easy to be won as that," he said. "You are a fortress to be won. A prize. I intend to scale your walls."

He lifted her hand to his lips, his eyes meeting hers as he did so. The gesture took her back instantly to the night when Geoffrey had done the same. This time there was no joy. No breathlessness. Only the cold, hard knowledge that she was playing a most dangerous game.

She was aware of heads turning, of people watching, whispering. "Perhaps I shall enjoy being won over," she said with a flirtatious smile. *Let them whisper,* she thought. *It can only help me. They think I am Ria, and I will beat Freddie at his game.*

From the corner of her eye, Lizzie could see that Geoffrey was among those who were watching them. She was surprised and shamefully happy to see that Lucinda was not with him. The moment Freddie kissed her hand, Geoffrey began stalking—actually stalking—toward them.

"Might I have the next dance?" Geoffrey said. His words were civil, but the look he gave Freddie relayed something more akin to cold fury.

Freddie did not appear inclined to fight this particular battle. He let go of Lizzie's hand, saying easily, "Until the next time, then." With a curt nod to Geoffrey, he turned and walked away.

Instead of escorting Lizzie to the dance floor, however, Geoffrey led her out a set of French doors to a stone terrace. The cool breeze felt startlingly good after the heat of the ballroom and the exertion of her charade with Freddie.

"Are we not going to dance?" It was not difficult to feign annoyance. Her feelings were in such chaos that she did not know how or what to think. Especially when Geoffrey was this close. Was he going to tell her about his engagement to Lucinda? She could not endure a discussion of Geoffrey's wedding plans just now. Her heart was too fragile.

"Ria, do you have any idea what you are doing?" Geoffrey said, practically biting out the words.

Lizzie looked at him, realizing with shock that the anger clouding his face earlier had not been solely for Freddie. He was, in fact, angry with *her*. It was not enough to have to flirt with Freddie; she would now be tasked with facing Geoffrey's ire. No doubt he would say she was not behaving in a seemly manner. Not being a proper widow.

Or had she actually made him jealous? This thought gave

her an irrational burst of hope. It would mean he had deeper feelings for her after all. She had to know.

*

Geoffrey looked at Ria expectantly, waiting for a response.

"I believe I was dancing with Freddie," she said. "Now I am standing outside with you. Does that answer your question?"

Geoffrey tried to control his anger. All he had gleaned from his prayers and reflection was that somehow Ria needed him, needed his help. This he would willingly give. But how could he help her when she seemed so determined to do herself harm?

He took her by the arms, doing his best to keep from shaking her. "I saw the two of you in there. I warned you before that he is dangerous. He preys on women he knows to be vulnerable. Clearly you are in his sights."

"I am well aware of the sort of man he is," she said, giving him a defiant look. "I thank you for your concern, but I am able to handle myself. Perhaps you should be returning to Miss Cardington. She has set her sights on you; that is plain."

"Lady Cardington has been doing the hunting, not Lucinda. She—"

He stopped short, realizing with dismay that he had used her Christian name, implying a greater intimacy with Miss Cardington than, in fact, existed.

Ria noticed it, too. "Lucinda?" she repeated, a note of inquiry in her voice.

He shook his head and began again. "*Miss Cardington* is a very admirable lady, and she is pliable enough to acquiesce to her mother's schemes."

Ria gazed up at him, her violet eyes reflecting fire from the torchlight. "Is that what you want? Someone who is pliable?"

"No! I am not at all sure she is the right woman for me."

"She is not," Ria said in a pained voice. Her words shocked him. She looked as though she had surprised herself as well. "I'm sorry," she said. "That was wrong of me."

He realized then that he was still holding her arms. But she had stopped trying to resist him. He relaxed his grip, but could not bring himself to let her go.

She lowered her head and leaned in, closing the gap between them ever so slightly. Geoffrey found his head instinctively lowering toward her hair, seeking the soft rose scent that always seemed to linger about her.

She lifted her face at that precise moment, and her cheek brushed against his. Their eyes met. He knew then that he would be forever powerless to fight against her pull. It was delicate and unseen and yet as unstoppable as the moon's draw on the tide.

Her lips parted, an unconscious request that he could not deny. He bent his head and kissed her.

It was startling, that first touch of his lips on hers. He realized then that he had been wanting this from the moment he had laid eyes upon her. Even bruised and bleeding in the street, she had drawn him to her with that curious mix of strength and vulnerability that he had never seen in any woman.

Ria made a small noise, whether in protest or in compliance, he did not know, but he could not stop and she did not pull away. Her hands came up around his neck, her mouth now seeking his, kissing his lips, his cheek, his chin. It was too good, too satisfying, too right.

Right? He was kissing his brother's widow! And yet he could

not resist kissing her once more, knowing the sweet richness of it would haunt him forever.

At last he found the strength to pull away. "We must stop." His voice held no conviction.

She tried to pull him to her again. "Please..."

"Ria!" He said it too roughly, causing her to wince.

The heat from their kisses faded into the cool breeze.

Grabbing what self-control he had left, he said, "You know why we can't do this."

Her hands fell to her sides. "Yes, I know why," she said with a shaky attempt at a laugh. "I cannot imagine what you must think of me."

He wanted only to take hold of her, to kiss the contrite expression from her lips, replace it with the desire he had seen there moments before. It took more strength than he ever thought possible just to stand motionless, to keep some distance between them.

Ria turned away and walked to the stone railing lining the terrace at the edge of the lamplight. Geoffrey glanced quickly toward the French doors leading to the ballroom, belatedly aware that they might have been seen. Thank heaven they seemed to be alone.

He followed her to the railing. There they stood, unspeaking, gazing out over the garden below. A full moon flooded the landscape with silver light. The effect was achingly beautiful, deceptively peaceful. Music and laughter drifted from the ballroom.

Ria was trembling, but Geoffrey did not trust himself to reach for her, to comfort her. He could tell from the way she held herself that she was not asking for solace. They must keep as much distance between themselves as possible.

Guilt overtook him. How had it happened? He had only been

trying to warn her about Hightower. Surely *this* was not what the Lord had in mind. But she had been too irresistible. *How easily sin does beset us,* he thought.

"Ria." Her name seemed to bruise his dry throat as he said it. "I cannot even begin to apologize. It was unforgivable of me to take advantage of you as I did."

"No." Her voice was barely audible. "You did not take advantage." She turned to face him. "I *wanted* to kiss you. I wanted—"

I wanted you.

She did not have to say it aloud. Her expressive eyes, so earnest under those delicate brows, spoke more loudly than any words.

The realization shook Geoffrey to the center of his soul. Plenty of women had wanted him for his money, his position, even for his honorable reputation. But never had he been convinced that a woman simply wanted *him*.

Fool, he reprimanded himself, recalling Ria's former harsh words. *What do you know about love?*

Not much, apparently, if he could fall so irrevocably for the wrong woman at the wrong time. "Ria. We can't let this happen again." He was appalled at the harsh tenor of his voice, but told himself it was for the best. It might shake both of them into their right minds.

Her gaze fell, the longing now veiled. "It will not happen again. I leave for Rosewood tomorrow, and who knows how long it will be before we see each other?"

Two couples spilled onto the terrace, chatting gaily, disrupting any further chance to discuss the matter privately.

"We should go in," Geoffrey said.

Ria nodded.

They reentered the brightly lit ballroom. Ria did not meet his eye, nor did she see his bow as she left him.

He should have been glad that she was so willing to do the right thing. He should have been proud that they were going to put this moment behind them.

He should have been.

"Geoffrey, there you are."

Geoffrey turned to see James approaching, accompanied by Freddie Hightower. "Come with us," he said loudly. His face was flushed from drinking. "We are just going outside for a smoke."

"It appears Geoffrey has just come from the terrace," Hightower said with a smirk.

Geoffrey was sorely tempted to curse. The man must have seen him and Ria come in together. He could only thank God that Hightower hadn't seen what had transpired outside.

"Well, then," said James, undaunted. "He gets to go again!"

James was clearly feeling the effects of too much punch. He grabbed Geoffrey by the shoulders, nearly stumbling as he did so. Geoffrey set him to rights and, seeing there was no way around it, accompanied the two men outside.

Hightower pulled three cigars out of a coat pocket. "Looks like I'm buying this evening."

Geoffrey would have refused, but instead indulged in the minor pleasure of going against Hightower's expectations. He accepted the cigar.

"What were you and your dear sister-in-law doing out here on the terrace?" Hightower asked.

Geoffrey was determined to stay on the offensive. "I was warning her about you, as it happens."

"How brotherly of you. I believe you are too late, however."

"Too late for *what*?"

"Gentlemen, I think it's time I told you a little story," Hightower said. He lit his cigar and took a long pull on it. "Ria and Edward ran away ten years ago. They were not seen or heard from since."

"We know that," Geoffrey said impatiently.

"Yes, but it has bearing on what I am about to tell you. Here it is, gentlemen, plain and simple. About seven years ago, I fell under the spell of a charming young woman. A blond lady she was, with amazing violet-blue eyes that could reach out and snare you from fifty yards."

The implication was clear. But how could he be talking about Ria? Seven years ago she was in Australia. Wasn't she? Every time he'd seen her with Freddie, he'd been certain there was something going on between them. Something that went beyond the surface. "And just where, exactly, did you meet this lady?" Geoffrey demanded.

"I saw her in Hyde Park one fine Sunday as I was taking a stroll. She was so beautiful that I could not resist speaking to her."

"You approached a woman with no introduction?"

"Freddie, how impudent," James said with a grin.

"The lady was willing to speak to me," Freddie replied. "And when a lady is willing..." He took another puff on his cigar and blew out the smoke with a self-satisfied air. "The long and short of it was that we struck up a very nice acquaintance. When I told her I was leaving for Europe on a grand tour, she begged me to take her along."

James gave him a smile. "She begged you, did she?"

"She *begged* me." Freddie relaxed against the railing and focused on the dancing inside as though he were seeing and reliving his *grand tour*. "We had a most agreeable time, of course."

Geoffrey gripped his cigar tightly. The thought that Freddie could speak of his lustful affairs so casually rankled him for more reasons than he would admit. "What does this have to do with Ria?"

"Come on, man," Hightower said impatiently. "Don't be so deliberately obtuse. Ria has been gone for ten years. During that time, I spent nearly a year with a woman who was her exact double. I have not seen that woman since the day she and a so-called brother—who, by the way, looks nothing like her—took themselves off to God knows where. Now Ria comes back and tells you she's been in Australia all this time. She says Edward has been dead for two years, but she doesn't seem to be mourning him much. My guess is that he's been dead for much longer than that, and that our lovely Ria has been engaged in a few more occupations than just sheep farming."

Geoffrey threw his cigar away sharply, his anger rising. "How dare you insult Ria!" Every nerve was in revolt against this man who had not the slightest idea of common decency.

Hightower met his wrath with a look of smug satisfaction. "I suppose you feel it your duty to defend her honor? What will you do? Challenge me to a duel?" He laughed derisively. "I can tell you *that's* been tried already."

Geoffrey grabbed Hightower's coat, forcing him from the railing.

A look of panic flashed across Hightower's face, but he said coolly, "I cannot believe you would stoop to violence, Somerville. Have you already forgotten everything you stood for as a clergyman?"

"A clergyman," Geoffrey said fiercely, gripping Hightower tighter and shaking him, "stands up for what is right."

"Does he?" Hightower returned. "Well, then, perhaps you had better give up your claim to the title. I can't help but suspect you've been stepping over that line between right and wrong."

Geoffrey was a hairsbreadth from punching Hightower when James pushed himself between them. Apparently the altercation was beginning to bring him back to sobriety. "Gentlemen, calm yourselves. Do you want everyone to know what you are doing out here?"

Geoffrey let go of Hightower. He took a step back, upbraiding himself for losing his temper, and silently cursing the man who had deliberately caused him to do it. He would not allow the man to dictate his actions.

Hightower straightened his coat and his cravat. "I thought you would see reason," he said, his smug expression returning.

Geoffrey kept himself in check. "I merely realized that your suggestion is preposterous," he said evenly. "Why would Ria have come back to London, but not tell anyone she was here? It must have been someone who looked like her."

"Now *there's* an interesting supposition," Hightower said. "If there is a woman who looks so much like Ria that one could pass for the other..." He tilted his head toward the ballroom. "Then who is the woman inside?" He turned to James. "You're Ria's cousin. You were playfellows growing up. You are the only one of us who actually knew Ria then. Is that woman Ria?"

James looked completely taken aback. "What an outlandish question. I should think I know my own cousin. She talks like Ria, remembers the silly games we used to play together. She knew the names of all the old servants who have been with us since we were babes."

"And does she look *exactly* like Ria?" Hightower asked.

"She was a mere girl when she left. She is a woman now."

"So there *are* differences?" Hightower pressed.

"Freddie," James warned, "I will not allow you to go around publicly insinuating that my cousin is not who she says she is. It would ruin her reputation, and it would utterly crush Aunt Thornborough."

"I do not care a whit about your high-and-mighty aunt," said Hightower caustically. "However, I do not intend to tell anyone. I shall bide my time. If I discover she is *not* Ria, then she and I will have unfinished business to attend to."

The sinister edge to Hightower's voice was unmistakable. At moments like this, Geoffrey could believe every one of the whispered stories about what Hightower had done to his wife. The thought that Hightower might attempt some physical harm to Ria was far more harrowing than Geoffrey's previous concern that the man was simply dallying with her. He was not about to let anything happen to Ria.

Geoffrey walked away without another word, leaving the other two men on the terrace. He searched the ballroom and adjoining rooms looking for Ria. He had to talk to her, to see her once more. Hightower's words had launched dangerous ideas into his head, and he needed to reassure himself, regain solid footing.

But she was already gone.

Chapter 29

The carriage slowed as it entered the long drive to Rose-wood Manor. Lizzie was taking in little of her surroundings, however; she was trying to sort out the tangled web her life had become. Months ago when she'd envisioned this day, she'd seen herself firmly ensconced as Ria and poised to prove she was a Thornborough. She seemed to be reaching that goal. How could she have foreseen all the events that would make this a hollow victory?

Soon she would have to make a choice. She had to rethink her decision to reveal herself, now that she knew Tom was alive. There seemed to be no good way out. Amid the multitude of her concerns about Tom, Freddie, and the letters had been the most perplexing thing of all: what was happening between her and Geoffrey.

During the long drive from London, Lizzie had relived those moments in the moonlight with Geoffrey a thousand times: the warmth of his arms around her, his kisses filled with a heady blend of tenderness and desire. He was in love with her—she was sure of it.

He had to be feeling guilt over his attraction to his supposed sister-in-law. *We can't let this happen again,* he had said. Lizzie had readily agreed. She did not want him to stay away for fear that it might go further. She wanted more than anything to see him again.

"Ria!" Lady Thornborough brought Lizzie's thoughts back to the carriage. "You have not heard a word I've spoken."

Had Lady Thornborough been speaking to her? She looked guiltily at the old woman sitting next to her.

"Your head appears to be in the clouds," Lady Thornborough chided. "Perhaps you should bring it down to earth. We are nearly to Rosewood."

"I'm sorry, Grandmamma." Lizzie gave her an apologetic smile. Truly, Lady Thornborough ought to have been her first concern. She had promised Ria that she would do all she could to make Lady Thornborough happy. Was she at least accomplishing this? She could not resist asking, "Grandmamma, are you happy with me?"

The question came out sounding a bit forlorn, and it clearly took Lady Thornborough by surprise. "Goodness, child. Whatever brought that on?"

"I want to be a good granddaughter to you."

"Of course I am happy with you. What a strange question." Her voice was brusque. Lady Thornborough was not one to show emotions easily, as Lizzie was discovering. Her thin lips turned to a hint of a smile. "I will admit," she added, "that you are not such a handful as you used to be."

Lizzie put her arm affectionately through Lady Thornborough's. "You say that as if it were a bad thing," she teased.

She sighed and squeezed Lizzie's hand. "You are not as light-hearted as you once were, but given all that has happened, it's understandable. Perhaps, in time…"

"Perhaps," Lizzie agreed, not wanting to disturb her with doubts. Trouble was, Lizzie did not know how much time she had left.

She turned her gaze to the carriage window. Now she took note of the stately oaks lining the drive and the mansion that was rising up before them as they drew closer. Rosewood Manor looked exactly as Ria's mother had painted it all those years ago. The immense stone building stood like an elegant old lady, trimmed with a multicolored coat of rosebushes and laced with vines bursting with vibrant blooms. All was loveliness and serenity. To think of growing up in this place! Even Ria's effusive praise had been inadequate. It was beyond words.

Lady Thornborough said, "Are you content, my dear?"

"It is so lovely," Lizzie murmured, her troubles temporarily assuaged by the peaceful landscape. "So lovely."

"Well, then, it's true that absence makes the heart grow fonder. You used to complain about this 'sorry old place' where there was nothing to do and no company but the dogs."

"Did I?" Lizzie was unable to keep the surprise from her voice. The carriage passed a charming rose-covered trellis that provided just a glimpse of pathway beyond. Lizzie imagined it leading to a garden overflowing with roses of every conceivable color. "How foolish I was."

The wheels crunched on the gravel as the carriage moved at a stately pace. At the sound of their approach, two dozen servants spilled out the front door and formed two rows on either side of the entrance, the men on one side and the women on the other.

"I expect you'll see some familiar faces there," Lady Thornborough said.

A tall woman of about sixty walked down the line of servants, making sure everyone was in their place. She was a thin woman with an angular face and a large nose. She wore a plain black dress, and a bundle of keys hung from her side. This had to be Rosewood's housekeeper.

Lizzie took a deep breath. Now was the time to say something. If she was wrong, Lady Thornborough could correct her before she made a fool of herself in front of the servants. It was also a chance for her to show some of the lightheartedness Lady Thornborough seemed to wish for. "Mrs. Carter is older than I remember, but she certainly hasn't managed to find any more meat for her bones."

"Indeed," said Lady Thornborough with a short laugh. Lizzie laughed, too, although the game of coming up with names no longer thrilled her as it once had. Now it was just a necessary and unavoidable task.

The carriage came to a stop, and a footman opened the door. Lady Thornborough stepped majestically from the carriage, and the servants applauded their welcome.

Once the applause had died down, the footman helped Lizzie from the carriage. She took her place next to Lady Thornborough and surveyed the two lines in front of them.

All was silent.

Lizzie stood on the gravel drive as nearly thirty pairs of eyes studied her.

Her heart seemed to tick off the seconds as the silence lengthened. All at once it was broken by a collective intake of breath, followed by vigorous applause and cheering. Lizzie beamed, nodding her head in acknowledgment of the greeting as Lady Thornborough had done. Her gaze landed on the housekeeper. "Mrs. Carter," she said, "I'm so glad to see you again."

The woman stepped forward and inclined her head. "Welcome home, madam."

Every servant bowed or curtsied as Lizzie and Lady Thornborough proceeded down the row. Lizzie kept a congenial smile on her face as she searched her memory for any descriptions Ria had given her that might help her put names to the faces.

One man caught her particular interest. He was short and wiry and clad in a rough tweed suit and thick boots. He held a worn cloth cap in his calloused hands. He was nearly bald, and the few remaining wisps of reddish gold hair at the back of his wrinkled head were fading to gray. A strong smell of tobacco emanated from his person, underlain by a scent of horses.

"Hello, Mr. Jarvis," Lizzie said.

The man smiled widely, showing teeth badly stained from too much smoking. "A pleasure to see you again, madam, I'm sure."

With so much uncertainty about what she would do and so much hinging on her decisions, Lizzie thought riding might provide some relief from the worries pressing in on her. She longed for the freedom of once more riding swiftly over an open field. "I am happy to report, Mr. Jarvis, that I have recovered from my fear of horses, and I am anxious to learn to ride. Perhaps one day soon you might introduce me to one of your good mares?"

Jarvis's yellow smile managed to grow even wider. "I have just the one. A beautiful bay mare, plenty of spirit, but easy to handle."

Lady Thornborough took Lizzie's arm. "Come, dear. I am exhausted and I need my tea."

When they reached the entry hall, they stood for a few moments to accustom themselves to its dimness after the bright sun. Once Lizzie's eyes had adjusted, she took in all that was around her. They were standing on a magnificent tiled floor of contrasting black and white stone. To their right, a grand staircase swept upward to a spacious landing. Every side of the broad hall was lined with large oak doors leading to other rooms. The entrance hall alone was larger than most of her previous homes. Even the five-story town house in London could not compare to this. *Oh, Ria,* Lizzie thought, *your descriptions did not do justice to the place at all.*

"Grandmamma, I want to reacquaint myself with the whole house right now—every inch of it!" Lizzie exclaimed.

"Come upstairs and wash up first," Lady Thornborough directed. "You will have plenty of time to look around after tea."

"I feel compelled to point out, Grandmamma, that if you had acquiesced to riding the train, we could have been here hours ago."

"Those smoky, dangerous things?" Lady Thornborough made a noise that in a person of less regal bearing might have been described as a snort of derision. "There are some who would say I have already lived a long and productive life; nevertheless, I plan to do everything in my power to extend it further."

Lizzie was growing very fond of these bits of humor that sometimes managed to escape Lady Thornborough's frosty exterior. At least, Lizzie thought with a twinge of guilt, her love for the woman was one thing that was *not* a pretense.

Lady Thornborough was all business again as she asked the housekeeper whether their luggage had arrived.

Mrs. Carter nodded. "Yes, my lady. Hortense has seen to your gowns. They are pressed and laid out for this evening."

Hortense was Lady Thornborough's lady's maid. She had taken the train along with a few manservants in order to see to the luggage. "That reminds me," Lady Thornborough said. "Martha has been delayed in London. She was a bit under the weather and unable to travel. We expect her in about a week, but in the meantime we will need a lady's maid for Mrs. Somerville."

"Of course," Mrs. Carter replied. She indicated a servant who looked no more than twenty, who was standing just inside the hallway. "Mary is skillful at hair dressing and keeping the wardrobe in order, and does a fine job helping out when we have guests. Might she do?"

Mary gave Lady Thornborough and Lizzie a shy smile.

"I'm sure she will do just fine," Lady Thornborough said matter-of-factly. She beckoned to the girl. "Please come with us now, Mary. I'm sure Mrs. Somerville could use your help."

When they reached the wing where the sleeping rooms were located, Lady Thornborough said to Lizzie, "You will be in your old rooms, of course."

"Rooms?" The word was out of Lizzie's mouth before she could stop it.

"I'm speaking of the nursery, too, of course. Perhaps you will find a new use for it as a library or sitting room. We will redo it as you see fit. I know you always loved the view from there."

Mary went ahead to open the door for her.

Lizzie stepped through the doorway into the room where Ria had spent so much of her childhood. The room had a high ceiling and two large windows, giving it an airy spaciousness. Two large wardrobes lined one wall, and a vanity table stood near one of the open windows. As Mrs. Carter had indicated, one of her dresses had been pressed and set out on the bed for her.

Lizzie wandered around the room, her fingers gliding gently along the soft counterpane as she passed the bed on her way to the open window.

No wonder Ria loved the view. It was spectacular. Rolling green hills as far as the eye could see, dotted with small stands of trees and crossed here and there with roads and footpaths. In a nearby pasture, four horses munched on grass, lazily enjoying the sunshine. One chestnut mare with a white blaze on its nose lifted her head up, sniffing the breeze. It turned, and Lizzie could have sworn the mare was looking directly at her.

"Who are you?" Lizzie said softly, as though the creature could hear her. It was as much a question for herself as for the mare.

"I beg your pardon, madam?" Mary asked.

Lizzie turned away from the window. "It's nothing."

She inspected the rest of the room while Mary set out her comb and brushes on the vanity table. She opened the door on the far side of the room and peered in.

The room that had been Ria's nursery was, like her bedroom, large and airy. Its warmly painted walls and polished floorboards gave it a welcoming air. Small tables and chairs stood near a generously large fireplace. Ria may have complained about Rosewood, but Lizzie felt her presence here even more than she had in the London home. She went to a bookcase filled with children's books and read a few of the gold-embossed titles on the spines. So many books! All belonging to just one child. *Oh, Ria,* she thought, *what wealth you had. What I wouldn't have given to grow up here.*

Lizzie chided herself for that thought, reminding herself that she'd been raised in a loving family, something Ria claimed she'd never had. She thought of her parents, of the love she was sure had been between them. Sam Poole must have loved his wife very much indeed if he had forgiven her for such a great sin as she'd committed.

A new idea surged into Lizzie's mind. She had believed it impossible for Geoffrey to love her if he knew about her past. However, if Sam had forgiven Emma for her indiscretions and had even taken in her daughter as his own, might there not be hope for Lizzie? Would Geoffrey's love be strong enough to withstand so many terrible revelations?

If Sam had done it...

Had he, though? Had everything really happened as she and Ria had surmised?

Lizzie turned her attention to the place where Ria had told her the letters were concealed. They were behind a loose board in the wainscoting near the window. Eagerly she scanned the wall. It looked smooth and continuous, showing nothing that would indicate an opening to a secret compartment.

"Of course it wouldn't," Lizzie said under her breath. "That's why it's a *secret* opening."

She hurried over to look at it more closely, but was almost immediately interrupted by Mary, who appeared at the door with a hairbrush in her hand. "If you please, madam. Lady Thornborough gets ever so cross if she is kept waiting for tea."

So close, Lizzie thought. *I'm so close to knowing the truth.*

Suppressing her frustration, Lizzie followed Mary back into the bedroom and closed the door behind her. She would have to wait until she was alone before she could search the nursery more fully.

While Mary was tending to her hair, Lizzie kept returning

again and again to the idea that she might somehow find a way to tell Geoffrey who she really was, and that she loved him. Her foolish heart conjured up scenes where Geoffrey forgave her wholeheartedly and took her gladly into his arms.

She tried to be rational, to replace those pictures with one that was far more unsparing. With Freddie an ever-looming threat, and her desire to protect both Tom and Lady Thornborough, Lizzie might well remain trapped in her deception forever. A life shared with Geoffrey was a dream she might enjoy in solitude but that could never become a reality.

Chapter 30

Lizzie rose before daybreak. She was not sure she had even slept. She had been waiting for the moment when she could search the room in the light of day, but before the servants began their rounds.

She had been unable to do anything the day before except accompany Lady Thornborough on a tour of the house and spend the evening with her. Even after the long journey, the old woman had stayed up surprisingly late, and Lizzie felt bound to sit up with her. Today she knew she would have few moments when she wasn't surrounded by servants. If she wanted to investigate the nursery alone, this was her best chance.

Lizzie found her dressing gown and slippers and then opened the door to the nursery.

She walked to the first window and looked outside. These windows enjoyed the same overlook of the pastures as those in her bedroom. The predawn glow cast a soft light on the mist-covered fields.

Lizzie dropped to her knees and began to feel the wainscoting. She carefully tugged at each section in exactly the way Ria had described. But nothing moved.

She worked her way past the first window and toward the second, her anticipation growing. She had to know the truth about herself. If the worst happened, she could at least claim some justification for calling herself a Thornborough. She also wanted very much to know if her mother had truly had an affair with Sir Herbert, and if Sam had somehow forgiven her. Lizzie wanted to believe such a love was possible in this world.

She kept moving, faster now, tugging hard, willing with her whole soul for something to move. Her frustration increased as each board remained stubbornly in place. What if someone had found the loose board already? What if it had been repaired, and the contents behind it were now sealed forever?

She was forced to pause when she heard steps in the hallway. The housemaid was coming to build up the fire, sooner than Lizzie had anticipated. She would be worried if she did not find Lizzie in bed.

Lizzie ran to the nursery door. She threw open the door only to find herself staring into a maid's shocked eyes. Lizzie put a finger to her lips, then spoke quietly. "It's all right. I couldn't sleep. I...I thought I'd search through some of my old books for something to read."

"Shall I light a fire in there, madam?" The maid kept her voice low to match Lizzie's.

"No need. You may tend to the fire in my room, as usual. I'll be in directly."

"Yes, madam." The maid curtsied and continued on, but did not bother to hide her puzzled expression.

Lizzie closed the door and returned to her search by the window. "It must be here," she kept repeating to herself. "It must."

She was nearing the end of the wainscoting when finally a board moved beneath her hands. She pulled it harder, jubilant when it came off. Behind where the board had been, there was a gap in the plaster, just as Ria had described. It had not been repaired. The letters would be there. The letters *must* be there.

Lizzie flattened herself on the floor to get a better look through the opening. Inside was very dark and she could see nothing. She slipped her hand in and began to feel around, hoping she would not come upon some bug or mouse that might have taken up residence there.

The space was long and narrow, following the line of the thick exterior wall. Lizzie reached even farther, her arm straining into the space. Her hand brushed against dust and grit, but little else. Fighting disappointment, she shifted her body into awkward positions in order to reach in as deeply as possible. "Please," she whispered. "Please be here."

At last her hand hit upon something. It was a smallish lump that was pliable like cloth and gritty with dirt. Breathless with anticipation, she took hold of the object and gingerly pulled it forward. It took some work to get it through the gap and into the open.

She was looking at a square packet about the size of a small book, wrapped in cotton cloth and tied with brown string. It was covered with a thick layer of dust, evidence that it had lain in that secret place for a very long time. These had to be the letters! Here, at last, would be some answers.

Lizzie fumbled with the string in her haste to untie it, loosing a small shower of dirt. When she finally got the string off, the cloth fell away to reveal a small, leather-bound diary.

A diary?

Lizzie fought off a surge of disappointment. "No," she groaned. She'd risked too much for this moment. This could not be all there was. She lay back down and reached into the opening again, grasping into every possible corner, unable to believe there was nothing else in there. But her fingers found only more dust.

She could hear the sounds of the maid stirring the fire in the next room, followed by gentle clinks as she finished her task and put the fire implements back on the metal rack. What if the maid decided to come in here after all? Lizzie could not risk being found like this.

With a frustrated sigh, she pulled her arm back out and sat up. She used her hand to sweep the loose dirt back into the hiding place before setting the board back in its place. Satisfied that she had left nothing that would catch the eye of a casual viewer, she stood up and brushed a few remaining pieces of dirt off her dressing gown.

She moved to the door adjoining the bedchamber. She peeked in and saw the maid exiting through the other door to the hallway. The maid had done as she'd asked and moved on.

Lizzie moved to the chair by the fire and placed her feet near the grate, glad for its warmth after the chill of the nursery. She contemplated the diary in her lap. What could have happened to the letters? She tried, desperately, to think of possible answers, but could come up with nothing. Might the diary contain a clue?

She opened the diary and flipped through its pages. The entries were dated at about the time Ria met Edward. They contained the typical musings of a love-struck young girl, bringing Ria back to life for a time in a way that gave Lizzie both sadness and pleasure.

Eventually she noticed that two small envelopes had been tucked inside, near the back. Could these be the letters Ria had told her of? Ria had spoken as if there was a whole stack of letters, not just two. Lizzie pulled them out and examined them. Each one had the same address.

To Mr. B.W.
Sennoke Post Office
To be left until called for.

Lizzie's heart jumped. It was her mother's handwriting—she was sure of it. Her mother had a particular way of writing her *b*'s and *d*'s tall and straight, in a way that left them curiously at odds with the rest of her more conventionally slanted letters.

With shaking hands, Lizzie carefully unfolded the brittle papers and read the first letter.

March 18, 1823

My Dearest Bertie,

I can only surmise that you have not come because some unforeseen circumstance has hindered you. I pray that this is only a temporary delay and that I will soon be in your arms again. It is true that I had been ill for several weeks, including the morning we last met. But I am recovered now.

Could you not send me some word? P. tells me you no longer have messages for him to deliver. He tries to make excuses for you, but they are weak, and not in keeping with your strong character. I must see you soon, for I have vital news to tell you.

I will wait for you every day at our usual time and place.

Until then, I remain, as ever,

Your Rose

Ria had told Lizzie that the letters were to "Bertie" from "Rose." She had said Bertie was one of her father's nicknames, and that the *W.* in the address stood for his middle name, which was Wilson. She further insisted that "Rose" must have been what Sir Herbert called Lizzie's mother, even though her Christian name was Emma. *"We are Thornboroughs,"* Ria had said. *"Our estate is covered in roses. It's an obvious choice."*

Lizzie was convinced of it, too, now that she had seen her mother's handwriting. With dread for what she would find, Lizzie read the second letter.

March 28, 1823

My Dearest Bertie,

My heart threatens to turn traitor, telling me you never intended to do right by me. For my own sanity I must refuse to believe it. However, if it is true, I beg that you will burn all my letters, so that no one but ourselves will ever know what a terrible fool I have been.

R.

Lizzie allowed the letters to fall to her lap. She did not need any more letters to know exactly what had happened to poor Rose.

Tears began to trickle unbidden down her cheeks. She knew from firsthand experience what her mother had suffered. She, too, had borne the devastating blow of a love that is not returned, the bitter despair when reality crushes the naïve belief that love conquers all.

"Oh, Mother, I'm so sorry."

Lizzie wiped uselessly at the tears as she was forced to confront the harsh fact she had shrunk from since the day Ria had told her about the letters: just like Lizzie, her poor mother had been cruelly cast aside by a man she thought had cared for her. She had been foolishly searching for true love, only to be burned by the fires of passion.

The biggest difference was that Lizzie had never—thank God—found herself in the desperate straits her mother had been in. From time to time when Lizzie was a little girl, her mother called her "my little thorn." If Lizzie was Herbert's illegitimate daughter, her mother had good reason to call her that.

Emma had died during a terrible cholera epidemic when Lizzie was twelve years old. If she'd lived longer, would she have been able to warn Lizzie against making such disastrous choices about men?

Lizzie dried her eyes and read the letters again, doing her best to review their contents with reason and logic. In the end she had to accept that, although they might be construed as damaging to the Thornboroughs, they could offer no real evidence of the thing Lizzie most desired to prove. There was no way to show for certain that "Bertie" was Herbert Thornborough, or that "Rose" was Emma Poole, or that Rose had even been pregnant, despite the fact that the letter said she had "vital news" to relate. Above all, there was nothing to connect Lizzie with any part of the whole sad story.

Why had Ria been so certain these letters were proof of their kinship? Lizzie chided herself for even wondering. Ria had, typically, jumped to conclusions, making large leaps of logic about things that could never be proven. And Lizzie had been foolish enough to believe her—to the end that she had come all the way back to England. To be sure, when Lizzie had left Australia, she'd thought nothing was left for her there. She had not known her brother would survive a terrible shipwreck, or that her actions would once again put him in harm's way.

Lizzie considered the faded letters, written so long ago. She'd been looking for undeniable proof, something that would sustain her, or even protect her, from whatever was to come. But these were proof only to her. She alone knew the handwriting on these letters belonged to her mother. Beyond that, she could prove nothing.

Lizzie went to the window. Dawn lit up the diverse colors of the landscape, from the rich green meadow to the oak leaves now kissed by fall into glorious gold. Like the seasons, her plans had changed yet again. She must remain at Rosewood, far from London, and take on Ria's identity so completely and unassailably that Freddie could do nothing. She would do what she could to protect her brother. She would give as much love and respect to Lady Thornborough as she could, as she had originally promised Ria.

And she would forget that she had ever hoped to love again. She would never show Geoffrey her true feelings for him.

Everything about her life was a lie now, and she regretted it more deeply than she had ever imagined, down to the very depths of her soul.

"Please forgive me," she said softly. It was a prayer, but to whom, she had no idea.

Chapter 31

H ow long do you think James will need in order to take her photograph?" Lucinda asked.

From their vantage point on the hill, Geoffrey and Lucinda had a clear view of James and Emily by the river. James kept placing Emily in various poses, but with each passing moment, she grew more and more fidgety.

"I have doubts that he will manage it at all. I don't believe Miss Emily will be able to stay still for the time it takes to complete an exposure."

The two were out of earshot, and for that, Geoffrey was thankful. Not because he had any great desire to be alone with Lucinda, but because James's prattling and Emily's simpering laughter in response to everything James said were beginning to wear on him.

"I'm so glad you were able to come," Lucinda said. "The place was very dull before you and Mr. Simpson arrived." Lucinda, who normally did not mind quiet, seemed nervous today, attempting to fill in any silences with attempts at small talk.

But Geoffrey knew it was time for more than idle conversation. It was time for the discussion he had been putting off for too long. "Miss Cardington...," he began.

She turned her face toward him. "Yes?"

He had been preparing for this moment for several weeks now—ever since he had made up his mind what he should do. But now that he was looking into Lucinda's expectant face, he found himself tongue-tied. This was not going to be easy.

"Yes?" she repeated gently. Her eyes were bright, her face alight in the afternoon sun.

Geoffrey and James had been at Stanford Park, the country estate of Lord and Lady Cardington, for nearly a week. Geoffrey knew they were expecting him to offer for Lucinda's hand; they had made very little effort to conceal it. But the time had come to be honest. He could not marry Lucinda. He took her hand in his. "We have spent a lot of time together over the past several months."

She gave a tremulous smile. "Very pleasant times."

Her mind was, of course, moving swiftly in the wrong direction. Geoffrey knew he had better speak fast or be forever bound to the wrong person. But he had to tread lightly as well. He had no idea how she would react. She seemed quiet and sensible, but what if the disappointment drove her to hysterics? It was a daunting thought. Geoffrey reminded himself of his own certainty that he was doing the right thing, that the Lord surely had something better in mind for both of them.

He took a deep breath, sent one last, silent prayer heavenward, and said, "Miss Cardington, I admire you very much. You are a kind woman, with many talents. And your father has been most generous with his support of the Society."

Her smile faded a bit at the unexpected mention of her father. "I am glad you think so highly of us."

"I do," Geoffrey affirmed. "I want you to know that I will always hold you in the highest esteem. I hope that we may always remain good friends."

The smile was gone now. "Friends," she repeated. Her brow furrowed. "Have I done something to displease you?"

"Not at all."

"Someone in my family, then?"

She was thinking of her mother. She had to be. But Geoffrey did not want her to think Lady Cardington's peculiarities had influenced his decision not to offer for her. "Please do not misunderstand me." He tried to begin again. "You are a woman of kindness and integrity—"

"So," she said, her eyes registering confusion, "kindness and integrity are not what you are looking for in a wife?"

"Of course it is. But I—"

"You want more."

She said it with such a downcast air that Geoffrey felt himself the worst possible kind of rogue, to hurt her in such a way. He was tempted to propose, simply to redeem himself.

Lucinda sighed. "It's a relief, to be honest. I think I…" She gave a nervous cough. "I would prefer not to get married." She looked at him guiltily as she said this, as though she were making a terribly shocking confession. He had no doubt she was telling the absolute truth.

Geoffrey was completely bewildered. He had been the golden marriage prize for so many months that it never occurred to him

Lucinda might want something different. How quickly had his hubris grown. It was a good reminder to him that pride goeth before a fall. With an abashed smile he said, "I would have been a disappointment, then?"

She shook her head, smiling in a way that suddenly made her more attractive. "It is my own shortcomings that I am too aware of. Trying to hold my own in society, giving fancy parties and knowing whom to invite to them. Having all my actions observed and commented upon. Although my dear mama cares only to see me marry into the peerage, the thought terrifies me."

"Does she know how you feel?"

"Certainly not!" She said it with such melodramatic horror that Geoffrey wondered if she had a hidden sense of fun. "I never had the strength to stand up to Mama, as I'm sure you are aware." Her gaze shifted to James and Emily, who were still caught up in their own playful banter. "If I do not procure a husband this year, it is my sister who will be most upset with me, I fear. It will delay her own marriage, for Papa wishes me to be settled first."

"She is only sixteen—far from being on the shelf."

"I certainly hope I can get her to see it that way." She sighed. "Everyone is relying on me to get married. I know I shall be a great disappointment to them."

"Don't be so sure of that," Geoffrey encouraged. "You may yet find someone whom you truly do want to marry. And in any case, I do not think it is wise for us to live our lives based entirely upon what others expect of us." Geoffrey surprised himself as he said these things. It dawned on him that he had been trying to live up to others' expectations far more than he had realized. "Surely there is a better way."

"I imagine that way requires a great deal of fortitude," Lucinda mused. "It's very hard to go against the current of people's expectations."

"So it is. However, you are stronger than you think."

She looked at him, considering. "Of course, you will say that we should be most concerned with what the Lord expects of us."

He pretended to look surprised. "Why, I hadn't thought of that."

She laughed.

They regarded each other with easy warmth, Geoffrey's esteem for her mingling with a newfound respect. Eventually it dawned on him, however, that things were growing too quiet. Not even the distant chatter of James and Emily could be heard. He turned his head toward the river.

Lucinda followed his look. James and Emily were nowhere to be seen. "Oh, dear," she said. "It appears I must go rescue my sister. Lord knows what trouble they may be getting into."

As they rose to begin their walk down the hill, Geoffrey took hold of her arm one last time. "Lucinda, I pray you will find every happiness in your future."

She rested her hand on his. "And I shall be praying for yours as well."

And so they descended the hill, arm in arm, as true friends.

Chapter 32

Unwatched, the garden bough shall sway,
The tender blossom flutter down,
Unloved, that beech will gather brown,
This maple burn itself away.

Lizzie sat under the large old oak, reading Tennyson's poem and thinking about Ria.

The landscape here, just as in the poem, had continued its pattern in timeless harmony with the seasons, regardless of those who had come and gone.

Till from the garden and the wild
A fresh association blow;
And year by year the landscape grow
Familiar to the stranger's child.

Lizzie could well see herself as the "stranger's child." The landscape was indeed familiar to her now. Nearly a month had passed since she'd given herself wholly to her new life, and her days were growing into a comfortable pattern. She and Lady Thornborough would eat meals together and spend the evenings by the fire. Occasionally they would go out to dinner at a nearby neighbor's home. Once they had even attended a small dance, and Lizzie had enjoyed the music and dancing and the lively conversations with the local gentry. Most of these were people Ria had known only casually, so Lizzie was able to "reacquaint" herself with them with relative ease.

In the afternoons, Lady Thornborough was usually occupied with the business of the estate. This was Lizzie's favorite time of day. She often spent it out of doors, where she could pass the hours unhindered with her thoughts.

She once again scanned the page whose words she knew by heart.

> *As year by year the labourer tills*
> *His wonted glebe, or lops the glades;*
> *And year by year our memory fades*
> *From all the circle of the hills.*

She looked out across the endless, timeless landscape. Although Ria and Edward were gone, she could keep their memory alive here for just a while longer.

Her gaze settled on the bay mare tethered some yards away, a lively creature with an easy temperament who had become Lizzie's steadfast companion. Lady Thornborough had procured a riding master to come and give lessons to Lizzie several times a week. All had been amazed at how quickly she had learned to ride. The riding master had already declared her competent enough for short outings on the estate. Though she was usually accompanied by a groom or Mr. Jarvis to assure her safety on the horse, she was sometimes able to ride out alone so long as she did not stray too far. She could not let them know that she had ridden much farther distances in Australia. Nor had she told them that one day last week she had used the opportunity to ride to the post office in the nearby town of Sennoke to post a letter to Australia.

Writing that letter had been Lizzie's greatest trial thus far. It had taken her multiple tries and an ocean of tears to compose it. She knew she had to tell Tom she had taken on Ria's identity. He would be so angry with her, but she could see no way around it. She told him she had a new life here, and she was happy. She begged him to stay in Australia, that coming back would be ruinous to them both. After much debate with herself, she decided not to tell him Freddie was alive. This would bring him back to England for sure, and renewing a feud with Freddie would jeopardize his life and his freedom—the things she was trying hardest to protect.

The letter had skirted another very important fact. Lizzie supposed that, if she tried, she might have found a way to leave England—to secretly slip away and return to Tom in Australia. She knew Tom would want her to do this. Her reason for staying in England was not the new life she was building, as she had told Tom in the letter. It wasn't even her growing affection for Lady Thornborough.

It was Geoffrey.

Geoffrey filled her waking thoughts and moved through her every dream. Tom had been a loyal and loving brother, and their fellow settlers in Australia had been kind in a rough, plain sort of way. But no one had filled the yearning in her heart that had been real and palpable. Not until Geoffrey. Even if she could never be more to him than a sister-in-law, this was inexplicably preferable to leaving him behind forever.

The mare lifted her head and whinnied, attracted by something on the hill.

"What is it, Bella?" She turned to follow the horse's gaze. Even as she did so, she had a kind of tingling, prescient awareness that a man would be there. She knew exactly who it would be. There, standing at the crest of the hill, as though she had conjured his presence with her very thoughts, was Geoffrey.

*

The moment Geoffrey laid eyes on her, he knew he was a fool for coming here. She was the very picture of loveliness as she sat reading, deep in contemplation, under a tree on the hillside. Sunlight filtered through the thinning leaves, causing a play of light and shadows upon her face and her golden hair. Irresistibly, he thought of how she had felt in his arms when he had danced with her, and when he had kissed her.

He had spent far too many hours thinking of that evening. He kept telling himself it was something that was best forgotten—for both their sakes—and yet deep down he longed to know why she had returned his kisses so eagerly. Was she falling in love with him? It seemed incredible even to contemplate.

Ria stood up and hastily brushed the grass off her dress as he moved to close the gap between them. From a distance she had appeared serene, but now as Geoffrey drew closer, he could see that her face reflected deep sorrow.

He was unprepared for the hesitancy that overtook him. He stopped a few feet away and bowed. It seemed an absurdly formal gesture in this natural landscape.

"Geoffrey," Ria said, her voice filled with wonder. "What are you doing here?"

He tried to discern from her expression whether she was pleased to see him. She seemed so, smiling even as she brushed a few tears from her eyes. He did not answer her question, but only remarked with concern, "You've been crying." He offered her a handkerchief, which she accepted. "Were you thinking of Edward?"

She appeared so pained by his question that he immediately regretted asking it. She turned away and dabbed at her eyes. "Yes, I suppose I was."

He reproved himself heartily. How could he have entertained the idea that she might love him? It might be years before she recovered from the heartbreak of Edward's death. Indeed, she might never recover. She had looked to Geoffrey for strength and comfort, no more. That kiss under the stars had been the unfortunate result of her reaching out to him for solace. He would do well, he reminded himself sharply, to keep that in mind.

"I ought to be happy here," Ria said, indicating the bucolic landscape around them. "I should be content to be home." She sighed so deeply on the word *home* that it made her voice shake. "Yet it is here that I feel their loss even more."

Her words confused him. "*Their* loss?"

The injured look crossed her face again. "I mean Edward, of course, and...my parents."

He took a step back. "I apologize for interrupting your reverie. Perhaps you would prefer to be alone."

"No, please don't go. I am glad for your company." She indicated the book in her hands. "Lord Tennyson's poems seem to have taken my thoughts into an overly melancholy direction."

Geoffrey nodded. "Our Poet Laureate does have rather a somber side."

She smiled. "Grandmamma told me that she had invited you. She will be so happy you're here. Have you seen her yet?"

"Yes, I just came from the house. James is with her now."

"James!" Her face lit up, and once again Geoffrey was seized with that jealousy reserved for anyone who could claim her warmest thoughts. "How on earth did you cajole him to come out here to do his duty to his family and his estate?"

Her reference to *duty* made Geoffrey realize how differently he felt about that word than when he'd first met her. But then, she'd made him look at everything differently. "James wanted to come. We both did."

"I'm so glad." She loosed the horse's reins from the fence post. "Will you be staying long?"

He tried to gauge her interest in the question. It seemed only casual, however. "I must leave day after tomorrow."

"So soon?"

His heart leaped, unaccountably, at her unguarded statement. "Would you be happy if I stayed longer?"

"Of course," she said with a bright smile. The smile that pulled him in every time. Was she thinking of their kiss at all? For a moment Geoffrey thought he saw the look she'd given him in the moonlight. But she turned and deftly slipped under the horse's neck to the other side, then coaxed it to a walk. "Perhaps we might do some of that riding we once spoke of," she said. "Bella is a wonderful horse, and I've come a long way in my riding."

If she was thinking of what had happened between them,

she was making good on her promise that it would not happen again. Or had the event truly slipped from her memory?

"That would be wonderful, I'm sure," Geoffrey said.

They walked together, with the horse between them. "There is an excellent field for riding," Ria said, pointing. "At the far end is a lovely glade for a picnic."

She was clearly doing her best to keep the conversation in neutral territory. He reminded himself that he should do so as well. He had to remember that even if she could recover from Edward's death and find a way to love him, such a love would be impossible for them to act on. She was, and would remain, his sister-in-law only. And yet, he was not yet ready to let the matter rest entirely. "Ria, I feel I should apologize to you for my conduct the last time we met."

There was silence from the other side of the horse. Then Ria said shakily, "It was my fault. I should apologize to you. Here I am, your brother's widow, and all but throwing myself into your arms. I promise you that it will not happen again."

He came around to the front of the mare, forcing Ria to face him. "I would like to ask you one question, and I promise you it will remain between us. I do not intend to allow anything more to happen . . . that is," he faltered, "I know the honorable thing to do and I will do it. But you said that night that you *wanted* me to kiss you. Why?" Ria attempted to turn away, but Geoffrey reached out and took her hand. "Please tell me. I have to know."

Ria stood very still. Her lips fluttered with quick, shallow breaths, and Geoffrey wanted more than anything to lean in and kiss them, to crush her body to his.

The mare whinnied, breaking the silence. Ria stepped back. "It was a mistake," she said quietly. "You said so yourself."

"Yes," he agreed. "However, that still does not answer my question."

Ria flashed a brief, apologetic smile and reached for the reins. "Perhaps some questions are better left unanswered."

*

Lizzie was barely able to think or speak during dinner. She was so intensely happy that Geoffrey had come, she could do little else but watch him. She loved the line of his short, neatly trimmed side whiskers as they followed the upper part of his jaw; the way a stray lock of hair fell just slightly over the left side of his high forehead; the way even his hands had a certain mesmerizing grace as he ate his food or brought a glass to his lips. Above all, she loved the moments when his rich and unfathomable eyes held hers. It was powerfully strange, to be aware of so little else in the room except him.

James monopolized the conversation, regaling them with stories of what he had been doing since leaving London. He had been making the rounds at the country homes of several friends, including a week with the Cardingtons. Inspired by the exhibit at the Crystal Palace, Miss Lucinda Cardington had purchased a camera, and James and the two sisters had roamed the countryside seeking suitable subjects.

"Miss Emily was put out by all this photography business at first," James said with a chuckle. "But we enjoyed ourselves so much that she ultimately forgave us for making her march all over Hampshire."

Lady Thornborough made a tsking noise. "I cannot believe the Cardingtons allowed such a thing."

"Lady Cardington was less than enthusiastic," James admitted. "However, the arrival of Lord Somerville lent some dignity to the affair and appeased the great lady considerably."

Geoffrey visited the Cardingtons? This took Lizzie by surprise. Was he perhaps planning to pursue a match with Lucinda after all? Lizzie had not thought it possible after what he had said at the ball, but perhaps she had been mistaken. It was not a pleasant thought.

Geoffrey merely said, "Lord Cardington has been working with me on the housing projects for the poor. I had some fundraising plans to review with him, so I accepted an invitation to visit."

"That is his official statement, and I cannot get him to declare otherwise," James said. "Neither, unfortunately, can the elder Miss Cardington." He made a sound that was a sly imitation of Lady Thornborough's disapproving tsking noise. "All of London society was crushed when there was no announcement of an engagement for the most eligible peer in the realm."

"We do not stoop to gossip in this household," Lady Thornborough reminded her nephew.

"How can it be gossip, Aunt, if the person being spoken of is here in the same room?"

"Really, James, you are most trying," Lady Thornborough huffed, although she could not hide her own curiosity about the matter.

"I take no offense," Geoffrey said. "The London season afforded me many lessons in how to inure myself to the endless stream of gossip."

Lizzie asked tentatively, "So you will not...that is, there is no understanding between you and Miss Cardington?"

Geoffrey considered her question with a slight smile. "An

interesting turn of phrase, that. We do have an *understanding*. That is to say, we understand each other very well. However, we will not be getting married."

This news sent a flash of elation through Lizzie's insides, as did the particular way he looked at her as he said it. Geoffrey had made it plain that they could never repeat what had happened on that night. And yet he was unattached to anyone else, and he was taking time to visit Rosewood. Furthermore, his actions that afternoon had convinced Lizzie that their kiss had affected him deeply. All of these things rekindled her foolish dreams.

Lady Thornborough said to Geoffrey, "It is fortunate for us that you did visit the Cardingtons. You have managed to find James and bring him to Rosewood. He has many things here to attend to."

"From what I can see, you were doing an excellent job without me," James declared.

Lady Thornborough did not deign to answer his remark, but again addressed Geoffrey. "What a pity that you must leave in two days. I was hoping you might at least stay through Sunday. Our Mr. Hollis is a most learned man, and his sermons are always educational. Also, his sonorous voice is quite different from our previous vicar, whose warble could barely reach to the back of the church. I am sure you would enjoy it."

Lizzie wondered whether Geoffrey's own rich voice had been honed from his years of giving sermons. She would like to have seen him give a sermon. What kinds of things had he preached on? Had he been strict, reproving, judgmental? Before she met him, she would have guessed that was true, having only the knowledge gleaned from Edward to go by. But now she truly wanted to believe he would speak on compassion and kindness instead. Whichever it was, he most likely had his parishioners eating out of his hand.

"I will be sorry to miss it," Geoffrey said. "Perhaps I may come another time? It is, after all, less than half a day's ride to my estate."

"You know you are most welcome anytime," Lady Thornborough assured him.

"What shall we do this evening?" James said. "Have you managed to practice your piano, Ria? Perhaps you can play for us?"

Lizzie tried to stifle a grimace. "I confess I have not."

"Naughty girl," James teasingly scolded. "Aunt tells me you have been out riding every day. I am glad you are benefiting from your newfound friendship with horses, but shouldn't you be practicing the finer arts as well?"

"I like being outdoors," Lizzie said, defending herself. "There will be time enough for indoor pursuits when the weather turns cold." And time enough, she thought, to find some way to obtain surreptitious music lessons. With an exaggerated lift of her eyebrows, she said haughtily, "And you, sir, are no person to be lecturing me about responsibilities!"

"Right you are!" James laughed. "I have perceived yet another way you have changed during your absence, cousin. You are much better at winning verbal jousts."

"Thank you." As Lizzie smiled triumphantly, she caught Geoffrey's eye. He seemed to be suppressing a bit of a smile.

Lady Thornborough, however, was frowning. "I was not aware that *winning verbal jousts* is a goal toward which a lady should aspire."

"No, indeed, Grandmamma," Lizzie said demurely, but braving another quick smile to James.

James sighed in resignation.

"Lord Somerville, perhaps you will tell us about your time in Devonshire?" Lady Thornborough asked. "I understand you are celebrated for your efforts at educating the children and for establishing a medical clinic. I'm sure we shall be greatly edified by an evening of instruction on doing good to one's fellow man."

James rolled his eyes. "There is nothing more enthralling than discussing poor, sick people."

"I would love to hear about Geoffrey's work," Lizzie said.

"Would you really?" He looked pleased.

Lizzie nodded. "You might give us ideas for ways we could help the less fortunate folk who live around here. Perhaps we could even take a ride to some of the surrounding cottages while you're here. I've been wanting to meet more of our tenants."

"I was, in fact, just thinking," Geoffrey said, "that I might be able to stay through Sunday after all."

"Splendid!" Lady Thornborough said with hearty approval.

James did not seem to share in this moment of good feeling. He merely said, "Here's another way in which our Ria has changed—she loves charity work now." He tilted his head and narrowed his eyes as he studied her. "She's left off the piano for charity and horses. How odd."

Chapter 33

Lizzie lay awake in the darkness, unable to sleep, her mind filled with all that had happened that day. Geoffrey's arrival had stirred the longings that she had tried to set aside, the hope that one day she would find a way to get to the truth, and truly win his heart.

Geoffrey had given riveting accounts of Devonshire and his work there. The joy on his face as he discussed teaching his poor parish children to read, opening up a world for them they would not otherwise have had, was thrilling to her heart. She thought she would happily have done the same, if given the opportunity.

She could imagine morning walks with Geoffrey along the steep paths in the wild landscape he had described. Just the two of them, far from the pressures of society, with time and space to talk without hindrance. If only they had met in different circumstances, all these things might have been possible. *No,* Lizzie corrected herself; they would never have met under other circumstances. She'd been a poor shopgirl, living in an entirely different world than his. Now their world was the same, but they could never fully share it.

What was he doing now? she wondered. She pictured him stretched out in his bed, his limbs relaxed, his hair tousled. It was an irresistible vision that made her whole body tremble.

Her thoughts kept returning to their encounter on the hillside that afternoon. Geoffrey had come so close to kissing her again. He would surely have done so, if Lizzie had allowed it. But she knew that she could not be cavorting with her "brother-in-law," no matter how much she longed to. The truth was that she had had to withdraw, the temptation was too great, and she knew if she kissed him again, nothing could stop her from being swept away by her feelings for this man.

With these thoughts tumbling through her mind, Lizzie was likely to get little sleep this night. She left the bed and went to the window. With a gentle tug she eased it open, just enough to allow fresh air to sift gently into the room and cool her overheated body. She stood there for several minutes, admiring the play of moonlight on the serene fields below. Now as the still of the deep night enveloped her, she regretted that she had denied herself the pleasure of his kiss.

Throughout the evening, Lizzie was sure their brief interlude this afternoon had been uppermost on Geoffrey's mind as well. It was mostly in a quick glance or a fleeting expression, but she received his meaning as clearly as if he had spoken it aloud—as though he had audibly declared his desire to be back on that hillside, pulling her into his arms. Thank goodness Lady Thornborough hadn't noticed the way she and Geoffrey had been trying to suppress their unspoken emotions. James had observed something, however. Lizzie was sure of that. He missed nothing—especially when it came to attractions between men and women.

As they had said their good-nights, Geoffrey had held her hand for a moment too long, looked into her eyes with such questioning earnestness that she had found it nearly impossible not to say what was on her mind. She wanted to tell him how much she cared for him, how happy she was that he had come to Rosewood, and how wonderfully alive she felt in his presence. Instead, she had merely murmured her good-nights, her body shaking from the effort of hiding her true feelings as she turned away.

Now she stood here, counting the hours until she might see Geoffrey again. He had spoken of being an early riser, of taking long walks in the morning. Lizzie would be up with the dawn, prepared to go out, in the hopes of catching him alone. She knew she was courting danger, but she had to be with him.

She considered that she might distract herself by doing some reading. The ready use of candles long into the night was a luxury she had never known before. Throughout most of her life, candles had to be carefully conserved, being too costly to use other than when strictly necessary. She'd mostly used the cheaper taper candles that did not burn long and did not provide good light for reading. The long-burning wax candles were an indulgence she had enjoyed often since returning to England.

She turned away from the window, lit a candle, and searched for her volume of poetry. It was nowhere to be seen. She tried to think of where she might have placed it, and realized the last time she had been reading it was earlier that day, just before Geoffrey met her in the meadow. She must have placed the book near the door with her bonnet and shawl when they had come in. She had been so preoccupied with Geoffrey that she hadn't given the little book a second thought. Since the book had not been returned to her room, Lizzie concluded the servants must have either left it by the door or placed it in the library. After a few moments' hesitation, she decided to go down and look for it. No one would be about at this hour; she could quickly retrieve the book without fear of being seen in her nightclothes.

She put on her dressing gown and a pair of soft slippers, then went to the door and gently turned the latch. The door opened without a sound. She widened the gap just enough to peek her head out. There were no lights visible from under any of the other doors. The house was very quiet. She fancied she heard the great clock in the parlor striking two o'clock. Yes, she was sure of it. The sound was faint, but clear.

She closed the door behind her with care, and made her way down the hall.

*

Geoffrey surveyed a row of books on one of the library shelves. There were plenty to choose from, but he paused when he noticed Ria's worn book of poetry lying at the far end of the shelf, looking out of place among the more finely bound volumes. He was about to pick it up when he heard the library door open behind him.

He turned, startled, and was completely unprepared for what he saw. He held up his candle to get a better look. "Ria? Is that you?"

"Geoffrey." She breathed his name with a soft air of delight. "I thought I saw a light in here."

She lingered at the door, as though unsure whether to enter.

Her hair was down, loose and flowing. The high lace collar of her nightdress was just visible above her tightly sashed dressing gown. The draft from the hallway caused his candle to flicker and throw shadows across her lovely face, which only seemed to lend her an air of mystery.

"I couldn't sleep," Geoffrey said, as though in answer to her unstated question. He gestured toward the bookshelves. "I thought some reading might help."

"I seem to have found myself in the same predicament," she said with a rueful smile.

"And what has kept you awake, I wonder?" he asked, knowing too well why *he* was here. He had not been able to get her out of his thoughts.

"My mind was so full after our conversation this evening that sleep seemed quite out of the question."

"Was it?" he said, unable to hide his surprise. "Must have been all those tedious details I related at dinner."

"Please do not apologize. I enjoyed it very much." She took a small step forward and said haltingly, "I want you to know how happy I am that you have come to visit."

"I am glad to hear it," he said.

"And isn't it strange that we should meet here, like this?"

"Yes." Geoffrey set his candlestick on a small reading table, largely because he knew his shaking hand would give him away if he kept holding it. To be alone with Ria like this had such an unreal quality that he thought perhaps he had drifted off to sleep and was now in the middle of an exquisite dream. He took a deep breath. "Well, we'll just get our books and be on our way."

She laughed softly. "Are you worried for my reputation?"

"Of course."

He could just make out the corners of her mouth as they lifted into a smile. "Perhaps it is *your* reputation we should be concerned about," she said, her voice lightly teasing. "It is unseemly, sir, to be seen without your coat and cravat. What would James say?"

Only then did Geoffrey realize how disheveled he must look, wearing only his trousers and a loose-fitting shirt. He was in stocking feet, too, having left his boots in his room so as to make no sound as he descended the stairs to the library. He reached up to close the opening at his shirt collar, feeling foolishly self-conscious as he did so. "I really must apologize for—"

His words died on his lips as her eyes met his. The look she gave him held such love and longing that he knew in an instant what he had only dared hope was true.

Geoffrey had always done the right thing, the proper thing. Especially where women were concerned. His attempts at courtship with Lucinda were proof of that. But his soul had always cried out to find a love that was deep and true—a love that was nothing short of the melding of two minds and two hearts. He had never been able to give this hope a voice or a name, having no idea how he would even recognize it. Now, as he looked at Ria, he knew with absolute certainty what it was.

In two strides he was across the room. He took her in his arms and she looked up at him. Something like fear tangled with the yearning in her eyes. He could not bear to see it, so he did the only thing that would stop him from looking at her. He kissed her.

Her lips were as full and soft as he remembered. She returned his kiss with an eager boldness that almost made him take an involuntary step back. But he soon gave himself over to the pleasure of it and took her fully into his arms. Her hands came up and gently grasped his head, her fingers working through his hair. After a time, her lips moved away from his mouth and began to caress his cheeks. At last her head came to rest on his shoulder, and she gave a deep sigh of contentment. They stood wrapped in each other's arms for what seemed like an eternity. *Dear Lord, how could this be?* No matter what the law decreed, holding her like this was so right.

A dangerous idea began to form in Geoffrey's mind, growing swiftly until he felt that nothing else mattered. "Ria," he murmured, his voice tender. "Dearest Ria. You must marry me."

Chapter 34

The sound of Ria's name brought Lizzie back to her senses and made her fully and shamefully aware of what she was doing. She could not remain like this, lost in Geoffrey's embrace, no matter how badly she wanted it.

She removed her hands from Geoffrey's shoulders, but he continued to hold her close. "Don't move, my love. This is where you belong." He let out a deep breath. "Always."

"Geoffrey, we cannot—"

He cut off her objection with a brief, warm kiss. "We can, and we will. We can get married in Europe. It is legal there."

"But your title...your responsibilities..." A dreadful realization began to settle on her of the mischief she had unwittingly inspired. "You will be ruined."

He took her face in his hands, his dark eyes burning into hers. "Do you love me?" His voice was fierce, possessive.

She longed to say yes; she did love him with all her heart, could easily picture giving herself to him completely. Her eyes stung with the knowledge that in doing so she would, in the midst of all her lies, be speaking the absolute truth. But how could she?

A desperate thought came upon her that if she did marry Geoffrey and they ran away to Europe, at least they would be far from England, far from Freddie's threat. It was so tempting to think it could be that simple. But it wasn't.

She could not marry him as Ria, and not only because of the shame and scandal it would bring upon him. It would be a travesty of the legal bond, because she would be lying about her identity. Far worse, she would be wrongly entering into a church sacrament, making a false vow in a holy place…She would not be guilty of *that*, despite all the terrible things she had done. They would not truly be married. She could not bring such a thing upon Geoffrey.

But neither could she confess to him who she truly was. She had determined that she could not do it. The specter of Freddie and what he might do always loomed over everything.

She managed, in spite of every impulse to do the opposite, to pull away. She took a few steps back and said quietly, "Love cannot be the deciding factor here." She gave a bitter, hiccupy sort of laugh. "You must be amazed to hear those words coming from me."

"I do not wish to begin another discussion of love versus duty," Geoffrey insisted. "I want only to talk about us. The duty we have to our own hearts."

How sad, Lizzie thought, that they should be taking different sides of that argument now. She was giving up all she held dear because of duty to her family—to keep Tom safe, and to keep scandal and shame from the Thornboroughs.

It was too dangerous to be here with him, in the soft candle-light, discussing love and the future as though both were available to them. If she had truly been Ria, she might have done it. She knew the law regarding in-laws was unreasonable. But she was not Ria. She could only spend her life pretending to be Ria, and accept that she could never have this man.

Another thought, far less welcome, entered Lizzie's mind. It was the bitter memory of what had happened the last time a man had promised to take her to Europe and marry her. "You may feel differently about all this in the morning," she said, and she meant it. She knew Geoffrey might be sincere now, as they held each other in the moonlight. It was easy for their love to seem like the only important thing in the world. But he could easily have a change of heart once he viewed their situation in the cold light of day. "I must go," she said. "Someone may find us here, and that would be unpardonable." She turned for the door.

"Wait!" Geoffrey said. "You cannot leave now. There is more to be said, surely. Ria?"

"We have said too much already." And with those words she fled the room.

*

Geoffrey paced for hours in the library, thinking about what had transpired between him and Ria. He knew what he must do. He would take Ria to Europe and marry her there. The scandal in England was unavoidable, but people of high reputation had been agitating for years to change the particular law that now stood between them. Geoffrey decided that once he and Ria were wed, he would join this cause and use whatever influence and resources he could muster in an effort to get the law repealed. If this was not successful, he and Ria might have to stay in Europe indefinitely. But they would be together.

He would press his suit until she agreed. He knew without a doubt that this was what he wanted. He only hoped there was enough of the younger, impulsive Ria left in the mature woman to take such a step.

She wanted this, too; he knew it, despite her objections. Every time they were together, he knew she, too, felt the undeniable bond between them. And how could she have kissed him the way she had if she did not love him?

His candle had burned out long ago, but now the room was beginning to grow even darker. He walked to one of the large windows and pulled back the curtain. The moon had set, and the night was shifting to the flat darkness that blanketed the landscape just before dawn. With the coming of the day, others would be waking. The servants would be slipping into rooms to rebuild the banked fires. Each passing minute would increase the likelihood of his meeting one of those servants in the hall. If he did, they would wonder why he was up so early, wandering the house in such a state of undress.

He found another candle near the fireplace and lighted it so that he could make his way back to his room. As he did so, Ria's small book of poetry caught his eye once more. From the moment she'd entered the room, she had so captivated his thoughts that he'd forgotten all about it. He picked it up. He would return it to her at breakfast. In the meantime, it would be one way to keep some part of her close until he saw her again.

He did not encounter anyone in the hall. He breathed a sigh of relief as he closed his own door behind him. He had not been in bed long before a manservant came in to tend the fire. As soon as he was alone again, Geoffrey got out of bed. To pass the time before his valet arrived to help him dress for breakfast, Geoffrey sat by the fire and opened the book he had brought back from the library. Why was Ria so drawn to these poems?

Something fluttered to the floor as he began to turn the pages. He looked down to see a letter, a square of white lying in sharp contrast to the dark hearth rug. He reached down and picked it up. Although he was not an astute judge of handwriting, it looked as though the address had been written by a man's hand. Geoffrey stared, disbelieving, at the name on the envelope.

The letter was addressed to Lizzie Poole.

An old man in Hyde Park had called Ria by that name, he remembered uncomfortably.

He set the book aside and unfolded the letter.

The handwriting was rough. The writer was inexperienced with pen and ink; there were thick blotches all over the paper from a poorly trimmed pen. But the words jumped off the page with crystal clarity.

My dearest Lizzie...

...you don't know the heartache I've been through...

...I have an inkling you were too taken by Ria's stories...

I'll come back...

Your loving,
Tom

Geoffrey gripped the letter so tightly that it crumpled between his fingers. He might have tried to tell himself there must be some other reason she had a letter addressed to Lizzie Poole, except for one very important line:

Too taken by Ria's stories.

It would appear this woman had plied Ria for a myriad of

details about her life and remembered them well, to the end that she'd been able to pass for Ria. It seemed too fantastic to believe, but somehow she had done it. Where was Ria in all this? And where was Edward? What else had this Lizzie Poole lied about?

He barely restrained himself from throwing the letter into the flames. If only it could be that easy. If burning the letter could erase the truth it contained, Geoffrey knew he would do it in a heartbeat. Anything for her. And that was his downfall. He was ensnared by a woman as surely as any fool ever was.

From the moment he'd seen her, he'd been captivated. She had drawn him in with her beauty, her warmth, her fiery independence. She had seemed, ironically, so genuine compared to so many women he knew. And whenever she was near him, when she was in his arms...

He stood up and began pacing the room, his mind assaulted by questions.

Why was she here? What could she possibly be after? Money was the obvious motive for such a scheme. After all, she had taken up Ria's position in society, accepted Ria's inheritance. She might even have asked for a widow's dower eventually. And yet last night she had refused his offer of marriage, which would have made her very rich. Of course, their "marriage" would have been a complete farce, since she was not Ria. She had to have known that.

Did she wish to bring disgrace to the family? If so, what possible reason could she have? If she had run away with him, she could have brought plenty of scandal to both their families. More than anything Ria and Edward had done. And yet, again, she had refused him. Did she have particular reasons for remaining in England?

And who was this Tom? Her lover? Her husband? How many men had she had?

To whom had he opened his heart, his very soul?

Hightower's words came back to him with a raw ugliness that made his blood run cold: *"A blond lady she was, with amazing violet-blue eyes that could snare you from fifty yards...And when a lady is willing..."*

Geoffrey slammed the letter on the table and took a step back, staring at it with disgust. There could not be *three* people in the world who looked like Ria. Had the woman he'd fallen in love with been Hightower's mistress? The thought filled Geoffrey with a revulsion so solid and physical he thought he might literally retch from it.

He wanted to race to her room, kick down the door, and demand an explanation. But he held himself in check, telling himself it would do no good to put the house in an uproar before he could get the truth from her. He would undoubtedly see her again at breakfast. He had time for a brisk walk before then, and he needed it. He needed to clear his head and regain his self-control before confronting her. Jealousy, rage, and self-recrimination were fighting for control of his heart and mind, threatening to drive him mad.

And in the center, like the eye of the hurricane, stood Ria.

No. Not Ria. Lizzie.

Chapter 35

When Lizzie entered the breakfast room, Geoffrey greeted her with chilly politeness that made her immediately wary. Had last night's ardor cooled so quickly, as she'd feared it would? She returned his greeting with equal mildness, hoping his aloof manner was due to the presence of the servants. She was too nervous to look at him directly, too afraid that she would see what she was sensing, that he had already regretted all he had said. From the corner of her eye she detected a faint blush, barely perceptible above the line of his side whiskers. Clearly he was agitated.

They sat alone at the table.

"How odd that Grandmamma has not come down to breakfast," Lizzie said, trying to keep her discomfort from showing in her voice. Lady Thornborough's presence might have helped reduce some of the awkward tension.

"She has sent word that she will be spending the morning in her room."

Geoffrey's voice—indeed, his whole manner—was overly restrained.

"Oh dear," Lizzie said. "I hope she is not ill." She did not think Lady Thornborough was ever ill, but in her nervousness she said the first thing that popped into her head.

"It is an early cold, I expect. James once told me she usually catches cold around the time of the first frost." He set down his fork and looked at her directly for the first time since she'd been seated. "Perhaps you recall this, too, given your *excellent* memory?"

Startled, she met his hard gaze. Whatever she had expected to see—tenderness, regret, or guilt—she saw none of these things. She saw only a tightly banked anger. She cleared her throat, which was suddenly far too dry. "Of course," she managed. "Grandmamma's early colds. I had forgotten."

His eyes narrowed, and Lizzie's confusion increased. Her seemingly innocuous words had, if anything, stoked his anger.

The butler set down Lizzie's plate and filled her teacup. She took a sip of her tea, wishing for the thousandth time that Ria had preferred coffee in the morning. She could have used its stimulating power to brace her.

Breakfast became an agony, trying to make polite conversation as the servants came and went, when all the while she could see Geoffrey seething beneath his stiff exterior.

When it was finally over, Geoffrey said, "Will you be so good as to take a walk with me?"

"Yes," she said with brightness she did not feel, "I shall be delighted." She knew they needed to have it out, to discuss matters more fully and reasonably. Even so, there was still so much she could *not* tell Geoffrey, much as she longed to. She was oppressed under the weight of all the lies she could not leave behind.

The morning mist was dense as they made their way down a narrow lane that led away from the house. It shrouded the pastures that lay on either side of the hedgerows, leaving Lizzie with the impression that she and Geoffrey were entering their own private cocoon.

They were far from prying eyes or ears that could overhear their conversation. Yet Geoffrey did not speak. He walked beside her, his mouth set in a hard line. Here it was, then. The reconsideration in the hard light of day, just as she had anticipated. It was heartbreaking, no matter that it was for the best; Lizzie would foolishly have him still wish for their marriage, even if it could never happen. Perhaps he did not love her after all. Perhaps it had been only a temporary infatuation. One whose folly he now saw too clearly.

They continued in silence for some time. Why would he not speak? Finally she ventured, "I believe we ought to discuss what happened. You're angry, as you have every right to be. You probably think I have betrayed Edward."

He laughed, but it was a coarse and humorless sound. "You have betrayed more people than Edward." He turned then, and took her by the arms. His face was inches from hers, as it had been only hours ago. But this was no lover's embrace. He was finally releasing the pent-up emotions she had glimpsed at breakfast. Anger and revulsion now seemed to roll off him in equal measure. "What is your game exactly?"

She looked at him, uncomprehending. "Game?" Her voice came out in a rasp.

This only enraged him more. "Be honest for once. What are you after? Is it money?"

"No!" The word came out with effortless sincerity. How

could he think such a thing? What terrible conclusions had he been drawing?

His grip held. "You want to ruin me, then. Bring scandal and disgrace to my family."

Lizzie shook her head. "No," she said again, fighting to keep her voice calm. "No one else need ever know what happened last night. It is—and will remain—solely between us. I do not blame you for hating me, but you can walk away now and no one will ever be the wiser."

"Is that really what you want? You want me to just walk away?" His hands tightened around her arms, bringing her a hairsbreadth closer. His eyes locked on hers, dark and unfathomable. For one sliver of an instant Lizzie thought he was going to draw her to him.

But he released his hold and drew back, leaving Lizzie's arms tingling and her heart bereft. He pulled a folded paper from his coat pocket and held it out. "Perhaps you would care to clarify exactly *whom* I would be walking away from?"

Lizzie took the paper. It was the letter from Tom. Clearly, Geoffrey had read it.

Lizzie took a step back, as the world around her seemed to shift into odd angles and leave her only vaguely aware of which direction was up. She found herself against a low stone wall, which she leaned on gratefully for support.

She tucked the letter into the pocket of her dress. It would be pointless to ask where he had found it, or to reprimand him for reading it. Nothing would change the fact that the time had come for complete honesty. She took a long, slow breath, looked unflinchingly at him, and said, "My name is Elizabeth Rose Poole."

It was actually a relief to say it out loud. The taste of her own

311

name on her tongue was a simple pleasure she'd been deprived of for too long.

Geoffrey stood motionless. Although his eyes remained fixed on her, Lizzie saw with relief that his posture was no longer as aggressive. Rather, he received this information stoically, like a person who has been expecting bad news but is still unprepared for it when it comes. "You are not Ria," he said, sounding as though he still could not believe it. "How could you have done it? How did you fool everyone so completely? How on earth did you think you would get away with it? How—"

"I will explain everything," she interrupted, "if you will allow me to speak."

His mouth closed again into that thin, hard line. With great effort, it seemed, he gave a curt nod and said, "All right. I am listening."

"My mother, Emma, grew up just a few miles from here, in Sennoke. My father—that is to say, my legally recognized father—was Sam Poole. Before his marriage, he had spent five years as a valet for Sir Herbert Thornborough."

Geoffrey's face registered a brief flash of something that might have been understanding, but he quickly shuttered it. "Do you believe this earns you some kind of connection to the Thornboroughs? Is this why you feel justified impersonating another woman?"

Was he going to deny what was so evident that Lizzie was certain he had seen it himself in a split second of time? She lifted her chin defiantly. "Yes. I believe there is a *direct* connection."

"That is a serious accusation. The implications—"

Lizzie gave a brittle laugh. "I am aware of the implications. Every one of them."

"Does Ria know you are here, pretending to be her? Where is she?"

"Ria is dead," Lizzie said.

Her unsparing answer left Geoffrey speechless for several long moments. But he rallied and said in an accusatory manner, "Exactly *how* did she die?"

This was too much. She would not be accused of killing her dearest friend—her sister. Shakily, Lizzie stood up. "She did not die by my hand, if that's what you wish to imply. I did everything in my power to keep her alive."

"Did you?" he challenged. "And why should I believe that?"

"It is the truth!"

"So you have finished telling lies now? Then tell me this. What has become of Edward? Is he dead or isn't he?"

Despite his harsh tone, Lizzie saw a flicker of anguish in Geoffrey's eyes, as though hoping against hope that his brother still lived. She chastised herself for not clarifying this point at the beginning. "Everything I have told you about Edward is true," she said evenly. "I wish with all my heart it could be otherwise. Edward was a good man."

It was an attempt at comfort, but it seemed only to reignite his anger. "How do you dare judge the goodness of anyone?"

"Please, Geoffrey." She reached out to take him by the arms. "Listen to me before you pass judgment. Once you have heard me out, you may do as you see fit. In spite of how it must appear, I wanted only the best for our families."

His arms were rigid beneath hers. She might have been holding one of the steel girders at the Crystal Palace. "*Our* families?" he repeated coldly.

"Look at me, Geoffrey. Look at my eyes, my face. How else

could I look so much like Ria? How could her closest family members have mistaken me for her? I must be a Thornborough. It cannot be denied."

He tried to turn his head away but she forced him to look at her, willing him to acknowledge that he saw the truth of her words. At last she felt him relax slightly.

"I will hear you out," he said with forced calm. "But I make no promises as to what I shall do or not do with the information."

She nodded, releasing his arms. He leaned against the low wall, watching her, his eyes wary.

"Six years ago," she said, "my brother Tom and I left London for Australia."

"Your brother!"

She looked at him in surprise. "Yes. Tom is my brother."

Geoffrey shook his head, as though he could not quite believe it. "That letter was from your *brother*."

"Who did you…" Lizzie stopped herself in mid-question. She had read Tom's letter a thousand times, knew every word by heart. Tom's loving words could easily have led Geoffrey to an entirely different conclusion about the man who wrote that letter. It seemed Geoffrey was only too ready to put Lizzie in the role of dissolute woman. Who could blame him?

She pulled her thoughts from that unhappy tangent. "Tom and I met Edward soon after we arrived in Sydney. He was naturally intrigued by how similar I looked to Ria. He'd been sent to hire new workers, and he immediately offered us a place. From the moment Ria and I met…" Lizzie broke off, her voice cracking. She paused to regain her composure. "From the moment we met, we became great friends. In time we began to piece together that we must be sisters, too. Our meeting seemed fated somehow." She sighed. "Everything else I told you about our lives was true, including…" She stopped again.

"The robbery and the shooting," Geoffrey prompted. "It happened all as you said?"

"Yes."

Another flash of pain crossed Geoffrey's face, and he looked away. "And Ria?" he asked. "What became of her?"

"A few weeks after Edward's death, Ria discovered she was with child."

Geoffrey groaned softly, as though guessing where Lizzie's narrative would lead.

"We were worried because Ria had had two miscarriages already. The doctor ordered her to remain in bed. This distressed her to no end, for she was normally such an energetic person. To cheer her up, I got her to tell me everything about her life in England. We would talk together for hours. It made her happy to relive so many fond memories."

"So that is how you were able to step so easily into her shoes."

"Yes. She had described everything in such detail that I truly did feel as though I were coming home again." Lizzie half expected Geoffrey to balk at this, but he said nothing. "As you have no doubt guessed, Ria's lying in was difficult. She was still in shock from losing Edward, and she was desperately missing her family in England. She made me promise that if anything happened to her, I would return and try to make amends for her. I assured her that she and her baby would make it home. But that was never to be." Lizzie was unable to keep her voice from wobbling as she finished. "The child was stillborn."

Geoffrey pulled a hand over his face. "Dear God."

"That was the last straw for poor Ria. She had overcome so

many setbacks, but to lose her child was more than she could bear. I saw her wasting away, day after day, despite all I tried to do for her. The doctor said that complications from the birth killed her, but I know she died of a broken heart."

For several moments, neither of them spoke. Only the call of morning birds filled the air. Lizzie was grateful for this brief respite between the release of the burden of lies and the weight of the consequences that would surely follow.

"Why did you not tell us these things from the beginning?" Geoffrey asked. "What did you hope to gain by this deception?"

"I was keeping a promise to Ria."

"What?" Geoffrey said harshly. "You can't mean she *wanted* you to do this."

"Yes!" Lizzie said defensively. She explained quickly, before Geoffrey could argue. "During this time, Tom was in that ship-wreck that he spoke of in the letter. I thought he was dead. I tried to keep the news from Ria because she was in such a deli-cate state, but she got wind of it anyway. I really am terrible at keeping secrets," she finished with an ill-advised attempt at wry humor.

Geoffrey did not respond to this. He said only, "What does this have to do with you pretending to be Ria?"

"Ria and I were now on our own, having lost the two men who meant the most to us in the world. Ria insisted—made me promise—that I should take up her identity. 'I am giving you my family,' she said. '*Our* family.'"

"That's insane!" Geoffrey fairly exploded.

Lizzie flinched, but said nothing. She knew she was speaking the truth.

"It would appear that Ria was every bit as foolish as I had

thought her to be. More so, in fact. How could you have gone along with this?"

"If you had been at the end of the world, left with nothing, with your heart and soul wracked to its very limits, you might have an inkling of why I did it." She spoke forcefully but without rancor. "I do not say that I never felt guilty about it. But it was the promise I had made. Also, it was very important that I get to Rosewood."

He looked confused at this. "Here? Why?"

"Ria told me about a cache of letters hidden here that would prove I am Herbert Thornborough's natural daughter. I wanted to get the proof."

"And do you have this proof now?"

"No. That is, I found two letters, and they are ... inconclusive."

Geoffrey made a small noise, as though she had confirmed his reasons for being skeptical of her story. "You cannot continue this charade any longer. You must tell Lady Thornborough who you really are."

"Yes," Lizzie agreed. "I must." It would be a relief to tell Lady Thornborough everything. All her efforts to "become" Ria had in the end done nothing but chafe against her very nature and hurt those she most loved. She was ready to make what amends she could and reclaim her life, miserable though it was.

Only the question of what to do about Tom still gnawed at her. She would have to persuade him to leave Australia for America, or anywhere else that would keep him beyond Freddie's reach. He would once again be forced to give up everything for her sake. But would he do it? She desperately hoped he would not return to England to fight Freddie again.

There was nothing for it but to shore herself up for whatever lay ahead. She began to turn back toward the road. "In fact, we should probably return now."

Geoffrey held out a hand. "There is one more thing I would like to ask, before we go."

She paused and looked up at him. "Yes?"

Geoffrey opened his mouth, then closed it again. Once again she saw the heightened color in his cheeks, the tightness around his eyes. Another moment passed. At last he said, "You never said what you had been doing *before* you and Tom sailed to Australia."

A chill began to weave through Lizzie, as though the morning mist had found its way down the back of her neck. "What I did before leaving London has no bearing on this story," she declared.

"I believe it does." He stood very stiff, clenching his hands in a manner Lizzie had seen before, when he was trying to keep his emotions in check. "Before you went to Australia, did you *know* Freddie Hightower?" He put an ugly emphasis on the word.

Lizzie stared at him in silent defiance. She should have known he would find out about Freddie. He would have soon, in any case. Nevertheless, she could not bring herself to answer his question.

She did not need to. He knew. She could see it in the horror and disgust crossing his face. "I offered you marriage," he said as though it were an accusation. "I was willing to ruin my reputation for a—"

"Don't say it," she cut in angrily. "Do not say the word. If you recall, I turned down your offer. I never intended to marry you."

"You never intended..." His face twisted in contempt. "That is to say, you were content only to lead me on?"

"I did not ask you to come to Rosewood," she shot back. "You came of your own volition. And I most certainly did not intend to find you in the library last night—where, I might add, you were all too willing to toss aside your own honor and integrity. I denied you because I *loved* you. You may condemn me for a lot of things, but let me remind *you* of something, *Reverend Somerville*. Let he who is without sin cast the first stone."

It gave her strength to see him recoil at these words. Today their souls were laid bare. This was the truth of who they were. She was a fallen woman and a liar. He was a man who had allowed himself to be separated from the lofty ideals he claimed to uphold.

She prepared herself for another attack, but Geoffrey seemed to have no more fight left in him. He turned away. The sun was beginning to clear away the mist, and he leaned heavily on the low stone wall, looking out across the endless fields.

It was as she had feared from the beginning. Despite her hopes and dreams to the contrary, she and Geoffrey would never be able to find an equal ground of love and respect. She had thrown herself into last night's embrace precisely because she had been aware, in the deepest recesses of her heart, that it would be the last.

Slow, silent tears began to fall down Lizzie's cheeks.

*

Lizzie was not entirely sure how she and Geoffrey made it back to the house. They had at some point turned as if by mutual consent and began walking, keeping a safe distance between themselves as they retraced their steps up the narrow lane.

They reached the wide gravel drive just in time to see Lady Thornborough's carriage disappearing down the road that led to town. Lizzie approached Mr. Jarvis, who was still standing near the front door. "Has Lady Thornborough gone out?"

"Yes, madam."

"Do you know where she has gone?"

"Gone to the station, madam."

"To the *railway* station? She never takes the train."

"It is unusual," Jarvis agreed. "But she was in a great hurry."

Lizzie and Geoffrey entered the front hall to find James descending the wide staircase. "Hello," he said cheerfully. "Have you two been out for a walk already? You look quite done in."

"Do you know why Grandmamma has gone to London?" Lizzie asked.

He shrugged. "No earthly idea." He pointed to a letter on the side table. "Auntie left a note for you, though."

With a tinge of trepidation, Lizzie picked up the letter and opened it.

My dear,

I am going to London on urgent business. Something has come up that demands my immediate presence. I shall return in a few days. Stay close to home while I am gone. I will speak to you immediately upon my return.

The note held only a vague salutation, and no signature. Lizzie was mulling over whether there might be any significance to this when James said, "Well? What has she to say?"

Lizzie looked up from the letter. "She has gone to London."

James clapped his hands together, smiling. "Well, then. We shall make a merry party while she is gone. You, Ria, shall play hostess. Do you feel up to that, dear cousin?"

"We cannot stay," Geoffrey said curtly. "It would not be proper. There is no chaperone."

Geoffrey had a good reason for requesting a chaperone, Lizzie thought wryly, although it was completely unnecessary. She was sure nothing untoward would be happening in this house tonight.

"We don't need a chaperone," James declared. "We are family, are we not?"

Geoffrey grimaced at that remark. Lizzie thought he might still have his doubts about whether she was a Thornborough, but he knew she was not his sister-in-law. She was afraid he was about to tell James where they really stood on the matter of "family."

To her great relief, he chose not to. "As *cousins*," Geoffrey returned, "you two are considered eligible for marriage."

James snorted. "Nonsense. Ria is like a sister to me. And you are her brother-in-law, so there's no need—" He cut himself off in mid-sentence. He looked from Geoffrey to Lizzie with a curious expression.

We must appear a strange pair, Lizzie thought. Her face was swollen from crying, and Geoffrey's was solemn and haggard. James might be inferring any number of things from their disheveled appearance. Heat crawled up her face, and she braced herself for one of his highly inappropriate remarks.

But he simply said, "I see you have made up your mind on the subject, Geoffrey. However, since this is my house, I have no qualms about remaining. Martha has gone to town with Lady Thornborough, but I will station a lady's maid at Ria's side night and day if that is what's required to keep the gossip hounds at bay."

Apparently Geoffrey did not intend to argue. "You may do as you see fit, of course," he said dryly.

"Can you not convince him to stay, Ria?" James asked.

Lizzie did not trust herself to speak. She turned away to hide eyes that were again brimming with tears, and to avoid James's curiosity.

"James," said Geoffrey, "will you please have my valet sent upstairs? I will need him to begin packing my clothes."

James sighed in resignation. "As you wish."

James called a footman over and delivered the necessary instructions to prepare for Geoffrey's departure.

While James was thus occupied, Geoffrey said quietly to Lizzie, "I trust you will speak with Lady Thornborough as soon as she returns, and that you will inform me when you do?"

Lizzie nodded. "Of course."

"I do not need to remind you that if you do not handle this right away, I will do so—and I will personally make sure the authorities become involved in the affair as well."

How far they were from where they'd been just a few short hours ago, Lizzie reflected. How unutterably sad, too, that Geoffrey's reaction to the truth had been so entirely in line with all her fears. But she would not cower before his threats or his scorn. "Rest assured, sir, that I have every intention of keeping my word."

She knew Geoffrey caught the hostility underlying her words. He looked about to reply in kind. But he stopped himself. He turned toward the stairs.

"One moment, if you please," Lizzie called after him.

He paused.

Lizzie slowly removed the ring—Edward's ring—that had been on her finger. She walked to Geoffrey and held it out. "I believe this is rightfully yours now."

Geoffrey took the ring. His expression remained hard and unreadable. Once more he turned away, and went up the stairs with a purposeful stride.

An hour later, Lizzie watched from an upstairs window as James accompanied Geoffrey out the main door. Two footmen were just completing the task of securing Geoffrey's trunks to his carriage. James and Geoffrey exchanged a few words and shook hands.

Even with all that had happened, Lizzie would have given anything to have seen Geoffrey look up, to give some sign that he still loved her, somewhere deep in his heart. Could his love really have vanished so swiftly and completely? She had been bracing herself for it for weeks, but she still could not accept it. "Please look up," she whispered. "Please."

But he did not look up. Without even a trace of a backward glance, Geoffrey stepped into the carriage and was lost from Lizzie's view.

Chapter 36

Lizzie sat at the piano, her fingers soundlessly stroking the tops of the ivory keys. It was comforting, as though she were somehow closer to Ria by sitting here.

She studied the open sheet music before her. The collage of strange marks and lines was like some kind of bizarre, esoteric language. *This must be how illiterate people feel when they see words in a book,* she thought. *They marvel at mysteries known to others but not to themselves.*

These pages were as incomprehensible to Lizzie as her own life. She could neither understand nor explain how she had come to this point of being trapped in a vise of her own making. She was about to do the one thing she had been wishing for—to reveal herself to Lady Thornborough, to become completely honest, to be rid of her lies. But still she shrank from this task, knowing the trials that lay ahead.

Lizzie had been sorely tempted to run away immediately, without facing Lady Thornborough. She could have disappeared in London and made her way back to Tom somehow. But it would have been a coward's way out. Above all, she had given her word to Geoffrey, and although she could never hope to regain his love, she would from this point forward strive to live virtuously. Perhaps if she did so, the Lord would help her through the terrible things that were sure to come. She would discover if, like Saint Paul, the past could finally be put behind her.

"You do not seem to be practicing, cousin."

James's words broke her reverie. She turned to see him leaning casually against the door frame, observing her intently.

She straightened and blinked back the tears. "You startled me. I thought you went down to the village for the afternoon."

"I did." He sauntered into the room. "The afternoon is far gone."

"Is it?" Lizzie glanced at the large grandfather clock and was surprised to see that it was nearly five o'clock.

"How long have you been sitting here, mooning over the sheet music and doing nothing?" James playfully chastised.

"Too long, it seems," Lizzie replied with a sigh.

"You will be glad to know I received a note from Aunt, informing me she will be returning day after tomorrow on the three o'clock train—if, and I quote, 'the train does not explode or get derailed by a stray cow.'"

He grinned, and Lizzie offered a weak imitation of a smile in return. "I think I know where you get your sense of humor, James."

"I'm glad to see you smile," James said comfortably. "You have been much too melancholy of late. For the life of me, I cannot figure out why. I cannot bring myself to believe you have been agonizing so over Geoffrey—he hardly seems worth it."

This casual mention of Geoffrey was suddenly and inexplicably too much for Lizzie's bruised heart. She broke into a sob, knowing she was immensely foolish but unable to stem the tears that streamed down her face.

James sat next to her on the piano bench and placed an arm around her shoulders. "It's all right," he murmured soothingly, offering her a handkerchief. "It's all right."

He allowed Lizzie to cry herself out. "You and Geoffrey had a falling-out, didn't you?" he asked, once her sobs had subsided into a few hiccups and sighs. "Whatever this rift is between you, I'm sure it can be mended. We'll invite him back, and—"

"No!" Lizzie interrupted. "He will never come back."

"I cannot believe that. Any fool, including me, can see how much you care for each other. How could he stay away?"

This started a fresh flow of tears, which Lizzie tried ineffectually to mop up with the handkerchief. "I'm sorry, James, but I cannot explain it to you now. I must first speak to—"

Lady Thornborough? Grandmamma? Lizzie no longer knew how to refer to her.

James gave her a friendly squeeze. "I'll wait. In the meantime, how about we play a little duet?"

Lizzie threw a dark look at the ivories that had seemed so comforting a short while ago. "Do not start nagging me again about this cursed piano."

"Just one," James urged. "One of those easy little duets we used to play to cheer us up whenever we were sad."

"Duets?" Lizzie had no idea what James was talking about. Ria never mentioned playing the piano with James. She sniffled and wiped her eyes again, trying to clear away the fog of grief so she could think.

"Our favorite was one of those Brahms lullabies, remember?" He seemed so sincere, and hurt almost, that she had forgotten.

"Of course," she murmured faintly. "But I have no heart to play just now."

Despite the fact that she was refusing, her answer seemed to satisfy James immensely. "That's all right, my dear," he said with a smile in his eyes. "We'll do it another time."

*

Geoffrey let his mare run the last quarter mile to the house. The animal stretched out beneath him, happy to be given free rein, knowing her bed and meal were close at hand.

Geoffrey was glad to concentrate wholly on the rhythmic movements of the horse as trees swept past him in a blur. This, at least, was the advantage of his new station in life. He had a stable full of fine horses, and they were only one of the many pleasant diversions available to him.

He was going to need every possible distraction in order to forget Lizzie. So far it had been impossible to keep her out of his thoughts. She was with him night and day, a dull ache in his heart he could find no way to assuage.

The worst of it was, of course, that she might never be entirely out of his life. Lizzie seemed to have won a genuine affection from Lady Thornborough during her months of masquerading as Ria. If the old woman became convinced that Lizzie was indeed a Thornborough, she might well accept Lizzie into the family. Once Lizzie told her what had happened to Ria, Lady Thornborough might be desperate to keep her only surviving grandchild, despite the trick Lizzie had played on her.

If that were the case, they would be bound to meet from time to time, especially during the season. He already knew that every time he saw her, he would remember afresh the way he had once loved her. He'd trusted her, and she'd repaid that trust with lies. Why had she not come to him? Why had she not trusted him enough to tell him the truth?

Whether or not he ever saw her again, one thing was certain. She was seared on his heart forever. He could only hope for the years to lessen its sting, as a scar might fade with time.

He prayed that God would forgive him, both for what he had done and for what he had been fully prepared to do. He knew dozens upon dozens of Bible verses about God's loving kindness and mercy; yet he found it hard to believe any of them just now. And when it came to forgiving others, he'd discovered, to his mortification, that it was a far easier thing to preach than to practice.

He had received no news from Rosewood in the three days since he had left there, leading him to assume that Lady Thornborough was still in London and Lizzie had not yet been able to speak with her. He had no doubt that once the old woman was apprised of the state of things, there would be an uproar that all of England would hear.

His mare slowed to a gentle trot as they approached the main entrance of his manor house. A groom stood at the ready as Geoffrey brought the horse to a halt. Geoffrey dismounted and handed over the reins.

"There is a guest waiting for you, sir," the groom informed him.

"A guest?" A surge of dread mingled obstinately with hope. If Lizzie had come here . . .

But a quick glance around the courtyard confirmed there were no additional carriages. The guest had arrived on horseback, and must therefore be a man. "Who is this guest?"

"Mr. James Simpson, sir."

Geoffrey actually swore under his breath. He saw the groom's eyebrows rise a fraction, but he didn't care. Save Elizabeth Rose Poole, James was positively the last person Geoffrey wanted to see right now. No, that wasn't true. He wanted to see Lizzie just as fervently as he despised her—more proof that he was a senseless fool. He wiped the sweat from his brow and took the steps to the front door.

James had made himself comfortable in the study. Geoffrey found him seated in one of the overstuffed chairs, his dusty boots propped carelessly on a velvet footstool. James had also helped himself to the brandy. He lifted his glass as Geoffrey entered. "There you are. I've been waiting for ages."

Geoffrey tossed his riding coat on a chair and poured a glass of water from one of the decanters on the wooden sideboard. With a quick nod to the glass in James's hand, he said, "I trust my brandy has made the waiting worth your while."

James tipped the last drops of amber liquid into his mouth and set the glass on a side table with an air of satisfaction. "Well, it certainly took some of the boredom out of it."

"Why are you here, James?" Geoffrey sank wearily into the chair next to the one James occupied.

James regarded him with a touch of amusement. "I see we've decided to dispense with formalities."

Geoffrey leaned his head back on the chair and rubbed his eyes. Already fatigued from lack of sleep, he'd been brought to near exhaustion by his long ride. He was in no mood for sparring. "You always said you hated standing on ceremony."

"Yes, Ceremony hates it when you stand on him," James quipped.

Geoffrey turned his head just enough to shoot him a warning glare.

James threw up his hands in surrender. "All right, I will get to the point. I've come to talk to you about Ria."

To hear Ria's name spoken aloud—a woman whose life had ended so tragically, only to be dishonored by Lizzie's deception—raised all of Geoffrey's anger afresh. He made up his mind he was not going to aid her lies in any way. "Ria is dead." He spoke the words forcefully, expecting James to recoil in shock.

A look of genuine sorrow crossed James's face, but not surprise. "I was afraid of that."

"Why?" Geoffrey sat up. "What do you know about this?"

"I don't really *know* anything," James replied. "I have only suspicions. Perhaps you should tell me what you know first."

Geoffrey was about to protest, but he held his peace when he saw that James was not playing games. His look held a gravity that Geoffrey was sure he'd never seen in the man before.

"Let's begin with your statement that Ria is dead," James prompted. "I had been holding out hope for a different answer. I assume the woman I have been calling Ria for these past few months is, in fact, someone else?"

"You assume nothing! You know it!" Geoffrey stood up and towered threateningly over James. "Don't deny it. How long have you known? Since the night that bastard Hightower made his lewd insinuations?"

James raised his hands in a mildly defensive gesture. "Let's discuss this rationally. Shouting will not help."

Geoffrey took several deep breaths and curbed his desire to throttle the man. "Very well."

James sat back in his chair. "The truth is, I had my suspicions before that conversation with Freddie. I grew up with Ria; we were as close as any brother and sister could be. This woman who arrived from Australia knew many things that only Ria could have known. And yet something about her was not right. Or more correctly, not Ria."

"Why didn't you confront her about this?" Geoffrey tried in vain to curb his frustration. "Why did you allow her to continue this charade?"

"I had no real proof," James said reasonably. "I was not about to trouble my aunt until I had something concrete—especially since I had no answer as to where the real Ria was. I wanted to find that out first. I was, in fact, on the verge of asking this woman straight out who she was—confidentially, of course. That was one of the reasons I came to Rosewood. But it seems you have already made the discovery. Please, tell me what has happened."

This explanation appeased Geoffrey somewhat. He could see some sense in it. He sat down, but did not speak right away. He took several moments to formulate what he would say. "The last night I was at Rosewood, I . . . borrowed a book of hers." Nothing would induce him to give the details surrounding his "borrowing" the book. James had undoubtedly drawn his own conclusions about the two of them anyway. He wished James could have acted sooner, before he'd made such a complete idiot of himself with Lizzie.

"Go on," James said.

Geoffrey told James about discovering the letter from Tom, and how he had confronted Lizzie the next day. He related her explanation of who she was and why she had been perpetrating this deception. "It's preposterous, of course," he finished.

"Why do you say that?"

"It's obvious!" Geoffrey fairly shouted. "Apart from everything else, she claimed she was looking for letters that would confirm she is Sir Herbert's illegitimate daughter. Conveniently, however, she was unable to produce such letters. She claims she found them, but they proved nothing."

"What did you do then?" James asked.

"I insisted that she tell Lady Thornborough who she was. I made it clear that if she did not, I would expose her and possibly bring action against her."

"She agreed to this?"

"She has no choice!"

"I don't know about that," James countered. "Given her physical similarity to Ria, I believe her story that she is related to us. As we are a proud and somewhat belligerent family, I would have expected more fight from her. Some protest, perhaps."

"Oh, there was fight in her." Geoffrey's exasperation rose as he recalled her vehement words. "She—" He shook his head. Even now he could hardly believe it.

"She what?" James prodded.

He would persist, Geoffrey thought with irritation. "She quoted scripture at me." As he spoke, he gave James a look that virtually dared him to make a joke of it.

"Easy, my friend. I know you are upset." James rubbed his chin in contemplation. "Don't tell me, let me guess. It was something about 'casting the first stone.'"

Geoffrey looked at him, incredulous. "How on earth did you guess that?"

"My dear Geoffrey, it's a personal favorite of mine."

Seeing that Geoffrey's self-control was about to evaporate, James moved swiftly to the sideboard and poured them each a brandy. He brought the glasses over and handed one to Geoffrey. "We are both facing great losses, my friend," he said, his voice now serious. "I have grown fond of this Lizzie Poole, but I grieve for my dear Ria. My aunt will take all of this very hard. And you—well, you feel betrayed by someone you were beginning to care for very much."

Geoffrey was about to utter a sharp denial of this, but James lifted up a hand to stop him.

His expression was warm and compassionate. "Geoffrey, I believe you and I need to discuss, in earnest, what should be done."

Chapter 37

The hands on the clock stubbornly refused to pick up their pace, despite the multitude of times Lizzie checked it. And there was still one more day before Lady Thornborough's return. These days of waiting had been interminable, spurring Lizzie's anxiety to have everything out in the open once and for all. She felt like a condemned prisoner who's decided it's better to face the ax than to remain in its dread.

She did not even have James to distract her. He had left the house at an uncharacteristically early hour, leaving a message that he had estate business to attend to and would return in time for tea.

Lizzie was so wrapped up in her thoughts that she never heard the approach of a carriage on the front drive. She was surprised when the parlor maid entered with news that a guest was downstairs, asking for her. "Who is it?" she asked.

The maid held out a silver tray, and Lizzie read the card that was upon it. *Mr. Frederick Hightower.*

Lizzie started up from her chair, panic rising. She could not see him alone. She knew what he was capable of. She had to avoid that at all costs. "I cannot receive him without James or Lady Thornborough," she said. "It would not be proper. Please inform the gentleman that there is no one at home."

"Too late for that," Freddie said from the doorway. "I took the impertinent liberty of showing myself up." He gave a short, dignified bow, which Lizzie knew was primarily for the benefit of the maid. "I hope, Mrs. Somerville, that you will forgive my gross lack of manners. But it is imperative that I speak with you."

From the moment he had first approached her at Lord Beauchamp's ball, Freddie had always put an odd inflection on her name, and today was no different. And as before, it only added to her irritation. "I cannot imagine what urgent matters we would have to discuss."

With a significant look at the maid, who was still befuddled by this breach of protocol, Freddie said, "It is a matter of great delicacy."

"Very well," she said. She had been playing the part of Ria for several months now. She could continue on for another hour or so, despite anything he might try. However, she would make sure they were not left alone. She addressed the maid. "Jane, will you bring up tea?"

It was too early for tea, but Lizzie needed the security of having the servants nearby. She would think of ways to keep them coming and going from the room as much as possible.

"Right away, madam." Jane gave Lizzie a small curtsy and moved toward the door. Freddie handed her his hat and cane as she passed. She accepted these with another curtsy and left the room.

Freddie advanced several steps, but Lizzie knew she could not afford to have him too close. She quickly returned to her chair by the fireplace. She motioned to another chair, which was at least five feet away.

"I beg you will be seated, Mr. Hightower." She pulled out her handkerchief and made a show of wiping her nose. "I am not well, which is why I asked Jane to state that I was not at home. I was not planning to receive guests today."

Freddie sat down on the edge of the proffered chair, but his cold eyes held hers intently. "You needn't put on all those polite airs. I know you would be far more comfortable just telling me to state my business and then get the hell out."

"Mr. Hightower!" It was not difficult to sound shocked and offended. "What language."

He ignored her protestation. "I think, Lizzie, that it's time we finally got things straight between us."

Lizzie touched her handkerchief to her nose once more, primarily to buy a few moments of time. She could not, would not allow Freddie the slightest foothold. "I do not know why you persist in calling me by another woman's name," she said icily.

"Do you not?" His tone was mocking. "Let me clarify. As you are aware, from the first night I saw you at Lord Beauchamp's ball, I was struck by your amazing resemblance to a woman I used to know." A slow smile broadened his features. "A woman I used to know intimately."

Lizzie sighed dramatically. "We have been over this before, and I am at my wit's end. You have the word not only of myself, but of my nearest relations. Why can't you accept it?"

He leaned back in his chair, as though relaxing for a long visit. "I just couldn't seem to rid myself of doubts. I had to be sure, because this woman and her supposed brother—I have my doubts as to their exact relationship—nearly succeeded in killing me. Needless to say, this is not something a person can forget easily."

Lizzie steeled her face to show nothing but disdain. "You are attempting to involve me in events that occurred while I was not even in the country."

"James and Lady Thornborough may be willing to accept your story at face value," he replied with a dismissive gesture. "Even that idiot Somerville. I suspect they do it to protect their precious family reputations. It is certainly easier than actually sending someone to verify whether the events occurred as you claim they did. But I saw no reason that I should not do so." He pulled a piece of paper out of his pocket, unfolded it, and made a show of reading its contents.

Lizzie stared at him, trying to discern whether Freddie was attempting to bluff the truth out of her. He had to be. She could see that Freddie was holding a piece of newspaper, not a letter. "You are wasting both your time and your money," she said. "And in any case, you cannot possibly have heard back already. It takes three to four months just to get there."

"Right you are," Freddie agreed. "I was prepared to wait. How fortuitous, therefore, that I have uncovered some remarkable information in the meantime."

He paused for dramatic effect. *He always loved drama,* Lizzie thought. She had to find a way to defuse the situation. Jane should be returning soon with tea, which would provide an interruption and buy Lizzie some much-needed time. Lizzie strained her ears, hoping to hear the servant's tread on the stairs. But she and Freddie were very much alone.

He waved the paper in his hands. "Last week I spotted a small but fascinating article in the *Times* about a shipwreck that occurred not too long ago off the Australian coast."

Lizzie was stunned. She could not even open her mouth to speak.

Freddie kept talking, referring to the newspaper. "It's an amazing tale, really. All were lost except a man and a racehorse. Both made it to a desolate piece of shoreline, where the Aborigines kept them for weeks before they were able to struggle in to Melbourne. A great fire swept through the region during that time and devastated the countryside, which only added to their woes. At one point they'd taken refuge in the middle of a river to escape the flames."

Lizzie had heard of the horrific wildfire that had destroyed vast tracks of land around Melbourne. It had happened a week or two before her departure. Her brother had gone through all of that! But she could not let on. It took everything within her to say in a disinterested tone, "I fail to see what that has to do with me."

"That's because I haven't gotten to the best part," Freddie said. "Here's the line that got my attention: 'The man was one Tom Poole of Bathurst.'" He indulged in a self-satisfied smile. "It appears that a journey to Australia may be soon in the cards for me."

No! Lizzie wanted to shriek the word. Instead, she covered her face and coughed into her handkerchief. She would not, could not, let Freddie see her fear. "You may do as you like, Mr. Hightower," she said acridly. "I should, in fact, be happy if you would take yourself off to Australia as soon as possible."

He waved off her insult as if he were swatting away a pesky fly. "Did you know that the *Times* receives copies of *all* the Australia newspapers? Occasionally they pull information to reprint in the *Times*, like they did in this article. The rest they archive. I didn't know that myself until I made the acquaintance of a man who works there. It was easy enough, for ready cash, to do a little research among those musty old newspapers, and I didn't have to go back too far before I discovered that Ria—the *real* Ria—is dead."

Lizzie stood up. "That is utter nonsense." She spoke more loudly than she'd intended to, in a vain attempt to make her voice forceful and confident.

"Is it?" Freddie returned. "Not according to this particular death notice from the *Bathurst Free Press*. I copied it carefully, word for word: 'Died. At Bathurst, on the thirtieth of December, aged twenty-seven years, Victoria, beloved wife of the late Mr. Edward Smythe, who was killed by bushrangers last summer. She is deeply lamented—'" He tossed down the paper and stood up. "I think you know the rest."

Lizzie moved behind her chair and grasped the back of it, as though it might afford her some protection. Freddie rounded it easily, bringing him menacingly close. "I was wrong, you see, about one thing. Here I thought the precious Victoria Thornborough had gone about playing the harlot in Europe for a few years before making her escape to Australia. Instead I discover she is dead and being impersonated by a common whore."

"That's enough!" Lizzie shouted. "How dare you insult me in my own house."

She attempted to skirt the chair and move toward the door, but Freddie caught her by both arms. "*Your* house! You have no more right to be here than a stray dog."

"Let me go!" She attempted to wrench free from his grasp.

His arms gripped her as tight as iron bands. "Be still!" he ordered. He brought his face very close to hers.

Lizzie could smell liquor. It lay upon him in multiple layers, a repulsive mixture of recent and stale odors. It was unbelievable to think she had ever loved him. How had she ever been so deceived?

He brought his lips to a spot just under her right ear. She thought at first that he was attempting to kiss her neck. She shrank back, expecting to feel the unwanted contact of his lips to her skin. But she felt only the warmth of his breath. "You always have that scent of rosewater, Lizzie. In your hair, especially." His voice was deceptively soft. "I would know you anywhere. Even blindfolded."

She was unable to move, frozen like a lion's prey.

"Come on, girl," he whispered gruffly. "How about a little taste of that thing you do so well."

His lips came down on hers in a harsh, demanding kiss. She struggled, pushing against him. He laughed and held her tighter. "That's a wench," he said with approval. "I always loved your feistiness."

He managed to kiss her again, despite her efforts to resist. She was repulsed by the taste of stale tobacco and the lingering scent of alcohol. Without warning he violently pushed her away from him. She stumbled backward at the unexpected freedom, toppling onto the floor. The shock of the fall took the breath out of her.

Freddie stood above her, looking down. "You managed to fool everyone else, but you could never fool me." He reached down as though to help her up, but she scrambled away from him, silently cursing her tangle of heavy skirts.

Grabbing on to the arm of a chair, Lizzie managed to get to her feet. She shook out the folds of her dress. "You are no gentleman, sir."

He shook his head. "I might accept such a chastisement from a *proper* lady."

Lizzie eyed Freddie warily, expecting another attack. He merely stood looking at her with an insolent expression. "Fear not, *my lady*. You may go on with your little charade for as long as you like. I will tell no one."

Despite his casual tone, he was clearly tensed for another pounce. Lizzie saw with alarm that he had placed himself between her and the door.

"Why would you stay silent if…if you believe I am not Ria?"

"Still hedging, are we? No matter." He straightened his coat and collar. "When you think it through, it really does no harm. James is still the heir to Rosewood. If 'Ria' is alive, it takes nothing from James except a little spending money, which the fellow will only lose gambling anyway. And the old lady can still have someone to call her granddaughter. She might as well die happy."

"Then why are you here?"

He laughed. "With your usual straightforwardness, you come right to the point." He let his gaze fall over her, studying her with a particular gleam in his eye. "I have missed you, Lizzie. Missed your feminine charms. I knew you would be *grateful* to me for not exposing you."

The suggestion behind his words was clear, and Lizzie went cold. She could actually have sworn the temperature of the room had dropped. "You expect me to make some sort of confession, and then give myself to you? I must condemn you to disappointment."

"Afraid of ruining your reputation?" he said derisively. "Don't worry, there is a way around that problem, too. You will have to marry me."

"That," she said with venom, "will *never* happen."

He took a menacing step toward her. "You will categorically deny that you are Lizzie Poole? In spite of the clear evidence I can lay out against you? Would you prefer to go to prison, then? Or perhaps they'd throw you in Bedlam for being out of your wits." With a humorless grin he added, "Or perhaps they'd transport you to Australia so you can join your brother in chains."

She drew herself up to her full height. She would bluster her way out of this, no matter what. She strode purposefully toward the door. "Let me go, Freddie," she said between clenched teeth. "Or I shall scream bloody murder and you will be exposed for the villain you are."

He reached for her as she passed, but she shoved him with surprising force, throwing him against the doorjamb. By the time he regained his balance, she had reached the head of the stairs. For a moment she thought her bravado had worked. But he caught up to her and grabbed her from behind, placing his hands with greedy familiarity around her waist. "If you do not come back into that study right now," he threatened softly, "it is *you* who will be exposed."

Lizzie did not budge. They stood there together, locked in mutual defiance and fury.

"Let her go, Hightower." A cool, authoritative voice came up the stairs.

Lizzie had never heard a more welcome sound.

But Freddie's grip on Lizzie did not slacken. "This is not your affair, Somerville."

"I beg to differ."

Lizzie saw Jane now. She was standing at the foot of the stairs, staring up stupidly, unable to move. Geoffrey's hat and gloves were still in her hands. She must have been in the process of receiving him when Lizzie and Freddie had burst out of the study.

Geoffrey began to make his way up the stairs. "I said, let her go."

"Oh, yes, my lord," Freddie replied with facetious deference. He made a pretense of stepping back, but as Geoffrey reached the landing, he pushed Lizzie to the wall, wheeled around, and hit Geoffrey hard in the jaw.

The force of the unexpected blow sent Geoffrey backward. He lost his footing and tumbled down a half-dozen steps before managing to grab the railing. He took a quick gulp of air and then raced back up the stairs with a burst of speed that caught Freddie unprepared. In an instant the two men were locked in battle.

Lizzie was trapped against the wall as the two men fought before her on the landing, giving and receiving fierce punches, rolling dangerously close to the stairs.

"Jane!" Lizzie cried. "Get help!"

But the maid stared dumbfounded at the fighting men, unable to process Lizzie's words into coherent thought or action.

"Get help!" Lizzie repeated. "Find the footman!"

Her words finally got through. Jane thrust Geoffrey's hat and gloves onto a table and hurried out of the hall.

Freddie gained the upper hand. He managed a wicked blow to Geoffrey's gut and began to punch repeatedly at his bloodied face. Lizzie threw herself at Freddie, grabbing for his right arm in a frantic attempt to stop the terrible blows.

Freddie was no better than an animal now. He left off beating Geoffrey just long enough to grab Lizzie by the front of her dress, picking her up and tossing her away as though she weighed nothing at all.

She crashed hard into a large, ornate mirror, which shattered with an appalling noise. She collapsed in a stream of broken glass, her head slamming hard against the wooden floor.

She lay, stunned, unable to move, as though some unseen force were pinning her to the floor. She still had her hearing, though, and could register the multitude of sounds around her: the scuffling of the two men fighting, shouted curses, a groan as a punch found its mark. The voices of James and other men she could not identify soon rose up from the entryway and added to the confusion. And then, in a moment, everything went silent, and Lizzie thought she had lost her hearing, too.

Until she heard the sickening thud of a body hitting the floor somewhere below.

Chapter 38

For the second time, Lizzie thought how odd it was to be waking up in a strange room, her body aching, with no memory of how she had gotten here. Through half-open eyes, she saw sunlight slanting through heavy curtains in a manner eerily reminiscent of the day she had found herself in Ria's old room in London.

Slowly Lizzie realized her surroundings were not so unfamiliar after all. This was the room she had occupied since coming to Rosewood. The feather bed held her in a gentle embrace like an old friend. She lay still, unwilling to move, savoring the comfort it offered to her sore body. But then a vibrant memory cleared the mist from her brain: the terrible fight between Geoffrey and Freddie.

Lizzie struggled to sit up, crying out involuntarily as her head complained in protest. She caught sight of Martha on the far side of the room. "Where is he?" she exclaimed, her throat dry with panic. "Where is Geoffrey?"

Martha hastened to her. "Don't fret yourself, miss. Lord Somerville is not here, but he is well. He and Lady Thornborough have gone to London."

Geoffrey was well. Lizzie thought her heart might burst with joy. But she knew she had heard something—or someone—fall from that landing. Hesitantly she asked, "What has happened to Mr. Hightower?"

Martha's grim face displayed the answer, even before she said, "Mr. Hightower is dead, miss."

A strange mixture of relief and anguish flooded Lizzie's soul. She was free from Freddie, and from the torment of what he might do to her or Tom. But at what price? A terrible thought presented itself to her—what if Geoffrey was held responsible for Freddie's death? What if he was in London because the police had arrested him for murder? "It was an accident, Martha!" Lizzie cried, as though Martha were both judge and magistrate. "Lord Somerville never intended—he would never—"

Martha patted her hand. "There, there, Miss Lizzie, don't fret. No one has accused Lord Somerville of any wrongdoing. It was clear he was only trying to protect you."

Miss Lizzie. Martha's use of her real name rang loudly in Lizzie's ears. She said tentatively, "Did Lord Somerville tell you who I am?"

"Yes, miss. But there was no need."

Lizzie gaped at her. "You knew?"

"Well, I didn't know who you were exactly, but I was ready to wager you wasn't Miss Ria." She studied Lizzie. "When you first arrived in London, all sick with fever, it was me that got you out of that filthy dress and cleaned you up. Do you remember?"

Lizzie nodded, remembering how she had woken up in a

clean nightdress and been overtaken with worry about what had become of the bracelet.

"As I was tending to you," Martha continued, "I discovered something peculiar. A large scar on your right knee, what had been there from your tree-climbing days as a child, was completely gone."

Lizzie knew that scar; she had seen it while attending Ria at childbirth. "How astonishing that you should remember that, Martha."

Martha gave a little nod of her head. "I said to myself, what a wondrous place Australia must be, if it can completely heal such a nasty scar."

"But you didn't really believe that, did you?"

"No, but it got me thinking."

Lizzie recalled Martha's early admonitions that Lizzie should take care not to hurt Lady Thornborough. "I did wonder, Martha, if you suspected something."

"I was watching you carefully, to be sure," Martha acknowledged. "But it was not my place to say anything. As time went by, Lady Thornborough was so happy with you that I was glad I held my tongue. There are stranger things in heaven and earth, I said to myself. It was possible the scar really had healed."

Lizzie smiled with gratitude, her eyes blurring with tears. "Ria always said you were the most wonderful woman in the world."

Martha showed a gap-toothed grin. "It's a good thing her ladyship ain't here. I would hate for her to hear you say that."

The mention of Lady Thornborough sobered Lizzie quickly. "Do you know why she has gone to London?"

"She told me there were details regarding Mr. Hightower's death to attend to, as well as other legal matters."

Other legal matters. That had an ominous sound. "She must be furious over what has happened. Perhaps she plans to bring the authorities back for *me*."

Lizzie half expected Martha to bolster her with another round of reassurances, but the servant's face was suddenly impassive. "I don't know what she intends to do. Of course, she would not be confiding her plans to me."

"Did she leave any word for me?" Lizzie asked hopefully. "A note, perhaps?"

Martha shook her head.

"How about...Lord Somerville?" She had to ask, although she could guess the answer.

Martha gave her a sympathetic smile. "They had to leave very quickly. There was no time to write a letter. I'm sure we will be hearing something soon."

But Martha's prediction was unfulfilled. No letter appeared. With each passing day, Lizzie grew more worried. She kept calling to mind the fact that Geoffrey had returned to Rosewood, perhaps to see her, and that he had fought Freddie valiantly for her. But the slim reassurance she gleaned from these facts could not outweigh what now appeared to be a stony silence.

The lack of contact from Lady Thornborough was equally distressing. Perhaps she was planning to do more than merely toss Lizzie out of her home. Perhaps she was even now arranging legal recourse against her. Every hour brought Lizzie closer to what she had begun to think of as the day of reckoning.

She reminded herself that she should concentrate on regaining her health. She would need it soon, regardless of what happened. But she could only sit, hour after hour, fretting over the mistakes she had made and the hurt she had caused. *Oh, Ria,* she found herself murmuring many times, *why did I agree to your request?* But in the end she had only herself to blame. She had known, but had never once admitted to herself, that this plan would be folly.

After a week of such thoughts, she finally came round to remembering the vow she had made that, from this time forward, she would strive to live honestly and virtuously. She called to mind the comment Rev. Greene had made many years ago— that the Lord would forgive those convicts if they sought Him. Might He not do the same for her? Even if, as the captain had wryly pointed out, men did not forgive. *Dear Lord, you are the searcher of hearts, the great healer. I will trust in you.* Her heart's burden seemed to ease a little as she prayed.

She had barely reached "Amen" when she heard the sound of a carriage on the drive. She ran to the window, anxious to set everything straight, to do anything in her power to make amends.

She opened the window in time to see James helping Lady Thornborough out of the carriage. James looked up and, seeing her at the window, signaled for her to stay where she was. She held her breath, waiting for Geoffrey to step out of the carriage, longing to see him again. But the footman closed the carriage door, and the carriage pulled out of the drive. There were no other passengers. Her heart, which had begun to lighten only moments before, now sank in disappointment.

When James finally appeared at the parlor door, she rose and ran to him, breathless with a thousand questions. "James, what is happening? Will Lady Thornborough not speak to me?"

"Calm yourself, my girl," James said cheerily. "Auntie needs time to rest, that's all. The train ride has taken a toll on both her nerves and her creaky old joints."

"Where is Geoffrey? Is he well? Does he—"

"All these questions about everyone else," James interrupted, pretending to look hurt. "Are you not glad to see *me*?"

Lizzie took a deep breath, genuinely chastened. "How right you are, James. I must apologize to you, too. What I did was terribly wrong. I took advantage of your goodwill."

"I think it is I who should be apologizing to you," James said. "If I had spoken to you sooner—really spoken to you, I mean—your nasty encounter with Freddie might have been avoided."

It took a moment for these words to sink in. Her eyes widened. "Did you know I wasn't Ria? How long have you known?"

"Why don't we sit down," James admonished, leading her to a chair. "You look very pale. Although I understand that is the fashion for young ladies, I must say it does not suit you."

She sank into the chair, and James took another nearby. "Now let us talk freely," he said. "You are not the only one who can pull the wool over someone's eyes, Miss Lizzie Poole. When I told you I was going out to tend to some business, I was, in fact, taking my horse as quickly as I could to Geoffrey's estate. You see, by then I had concluded that you were not Ria."

How had he guessed—what had confirmed it? Lizzie thought back to their discussion before James had left, and realized the answer. "The duets," she said.

James grinned. "Precisely. I made up that tale to see if you would fall into my little trap. You did, and very nicely, too. I can't even play the scales, much less a duet."

Lizzie shook her head in disbelief. "Yet you said nothing."

"I decided the most important thing was to bring Geoffrey back to Rosewood so that we could all sit down and discuss the matter together. I did not know that Freddie was at that same time setting things up so that you and he could have a little tête-à-tête."

"*He* set it up?"

"Yes." James's expression was solemn. "He thought I was still in Hampshire with the Cardingtons. He arranged a meeting in London with Aunt Thornborough to draw her away from here. He did not, needless to say, keep that appointment."

"I can hardly believe she agreed to meet him," Lizzie said. "How did he convince her?"

James shrugged. "I will let Aunt Thornborough tell you about the particulars."

"You mean...she plans to speak to me?"

"Of course!" He slanted a look at her. "I will be honest with you—she was deeply hurt when Geoffrey filled her in on who you were, and when we had to tell her about Ria's fate."

"I wanted to tell her myself," Lizzie said sadly. "I had every intention of doing it. I wanted to explain things properly."

"I believe you. You will have time to do that, don't you worry. Auntie does not plan to have you thrown into prison just yet."

His words gave Lizzie comfort, as they were meant to do. Lizzie's fears returned to Geoffrey. "Geoffrey isn't in trouble over Freddie's death, I hope? I have heard talk of an autopsy, and even an inquest."

"There was an autopsy," James confirmed. "But the matter ended there."

"But how can that be?" Lizzie asked, still unwilling to believe it.

"The autopsy brought to light some information that changed the probable cause of death. Freddie had an internal disease, you see. His health was not as sound as one might have guessed by looking at him. The fall merely exacerbated an already fatal state of affairs. The coroner was of the opinion that even without the fall, Freddie's liver would have killed him within six months."

"His liver?" Lizzie thought of the smell she had detected when he attacked her. It was the indication of heavy, habitual drinking. When she and Freddie had been together in Europe, his drinking had seemed only occasionally excessive. It must have since become far worse. Lizzie thought back to her recent encounters with Freddie in London, realizing that never once had he appeared entirely sober. Worse, he had been a vicious drunk, as Lizzie had painfully experienced. "I cannot say I am surprised, although it seems cruel to say so, now that he is dead."

"You speak only the truth," James said. "I must confess it has been an important lesson for me. We were friends for many years, yet I refused to acknowledge how he was changing. He had not always been so foul-natured and cynical."

"Yes, I know," Lizzie murmured.

James lifted an eyebrow. "So you did know him before? You were the woman he took to Europe?"

"Yes." Lizzie was not going to shirk the truth now. "And now you know the whole shameful truth about me. I was nothing but a rich man's dalliance. As my mother had been before me."

Her words were filled with bitter self-reproach. But James did not offer either rebuke or pity. He simply said after a few moments' reflection, "Do you know, I believe Freddie's better qualities began to fall away at about the same time he was forced home from Europe and into a marriage he did not want. It was a harsh awakening to the fiscal realities of life."

His observation made Lizzie wonder if perhaps Freddie had once loved her after all. Suppose, as James was quietly suggesting, he had not wanted to give her up but had been unwilling to risk his financial security. Lizzie could see how such a decision might cause resentment to grow like a cancer, eventually obliterating whatever decency he had possessed. "Money will always trump true love, will it not?" she said sourly.

"In his case, yes." Seeing Lizzie's bleak expression, James reached out to gently tilt her chin upward. "Don't you start down that road of thought, young lady. I believe life has better things in store for you."

"You always see the bright side of things, don't you, James?"

"Oh, yes. Anything else is a dreadful waste of energy."

Lizzie managed a smile, and braved a question she'd been wanting to ask. "James, were you with Freddie on the night of the duel?"

"So it *was* a duel, then," James said. "I always suspected as much. How quaintly old-fashioned."

"But you weren't there?"

"Me? No. The season was over by then, and Aunt had dragged me to Rosewood to oversee some repairs. I believe it was Richard Spencer who was with him. But everything was so hushed up that I'm not even sure of that."

"I'm so glad it wasn't you."

"Me too, my girl, me too. How extraordinary that it was you Freddie ran off with," James mused. "If I had met you then, seen your incredible resemblance to Ria, everything might have turned out quite differently."

"Thank you, James. For giving me back at least a shred of my self-respect. No matter what happens now, I will always be grateful to you."

"I'll hold you to that," he said with a grin.

Chapter 39

James escorted Lizzie to the downstairs parlor. Lady Thornborough sat stiff and regal in her high-backed chair, looking as though she were the Queen herself. She regarded Lizzie severely. Without preamble she said, "You have lied to me, Lizzie Poole."

Lizzie bowed her head. "Yes. I humbly beg your pardon. There is no excuse for what I have done, but I—"

"You think you can simply request my forgiveness, and then it is done?"

Lizzie stole a glance at Lady Thornborough. Her face was stern and unyielding. "I have no right to ask forgiveness," Lizzie said. "But I want you to know that I did it for Ria's sake." Seeing the look of pain on Lady Thornborough's face, she hastily added, "Ria asked me to come here. I was determined to be a good granddaughter to you. I told myself I had good reason to do what I did, but I see now that I was wrong."

"Are you truly repentant," Lady Thornborough asked, "or do you merely regret having been caught?"

Lizzie lifted her head. This accusation she could, and would, answer with all sincerity. "I do not regret that the truth has come out. I regret that I have hurt you. I have grown to love you, you see." Lizzie's heart felt raw as she laid it bare before the woman.

"Lord Somerville informs me that you were quite adamant about your perceived connection to this family."

"Yes. I still am. But I make no claims. I deserve nothing after the way I betrayed your trust."

There was a very loud silence after Lizzie spoke these words.

At last Lady Thornborough said, "You do not try to justify yourself?"

"Clearly I strayed far from the right path, and from my best intentions. However, I am determined to live honestly from this day forward, and that includes accepting all responsibility for what I have done. I ask for no pity, for I know I do not deserve it."

"It is true that you deserve no pity," Lady Thornborough said, her voice still hard.

Lizzie braced herself. They could send her off in chains right now, and she would be satisfied that at least she had been able to state her apologies, even if they had not been accepted.

"You might earn it, however," the old lady added, her voice still crisp, but not quite so razor sharp.

Was she really being offered a chance to make amends? A glimmer of hope lit in her heart. "Name it, I beg of you. Anything, and I will do it."

A hint of a smile appeared on Lady Thornborough's face. "I will tell you what you must do. You must come here, and kiss your grandmamma."

Shock and confusion coursed through Lizzie all at once. Her

knees threatened to give out, and she grabbed on to James's arm more tightly.

"You heard her," James urged. "It is never a good idea to keep Auntie waiting."

Lizzie raced to Lady Thornborough, nearly toppling the chair as she threw her arms around her.

"What in heaven's name?" the woman said with a gasp.

"I'm so sorry for everything," Lizzie cried, peppering her cheeks with kisses. "I do love you. I loved Ria, too. I loved her better than a sister. Whatever I can do, somehow I will make things right—"

"Perhaps," Lady Thornborough wheezed, "you could start by removing the choke hold around my neck."

This comment made Lizzie realize how much force she had been applying. Slowly she untangled herself and stepped back.

"That's better," Lady Thornborough said, readjusting her shawl. "Sit down, child. We have much to discuss."

Still dazed, Lizzie complied.

Lady Thornborough picked up a piece of paper that had been lying on the table next to her. She adjusted her reading glasses and read over it very carefully. Finally, she set her cool gray eyes on Lizzie. "I have a letter here, Elizabeth, from your father."

"My...father?"

"Yes. Your father. Herbert Thornborough." She held up a hand to keep Lizzie from replying. "You thought the letters that might prove the truth of your parentage were lost. They were not. I have them."

This cannot be happening, Lizzie thought. How long had Lady Thornborough known the truth about her? Had everyone seen through her charade and allowed her to play the part anyway?

"The letters," Lady Thornborough continued, "have been stored at my solicitor's office in London for safekeeping."

"I don't understand," Lizzie said. "Ria told me they were here. She had seen them herself."

"I found them after Ria ran off with Edward," James explained. "I was searching for any clues I could find about their possible destination." He gave her a playful grin. "I knew where Ria kept her diary, so I went looking there first."

Lizzie shook her head in resignation. "She really had no secrets from you, did she, James?"

He looked pleased with himself. "Not a one."

"You cannot have found the diary, though. I found it myself, undisturbed in the very back corner."

"That is correct, but I did find a packet of letters. After I read them, I gave them to Aunt."

"It was an unusual display of wisdom on your part," Lady Thornborough told him. To Lizzie she said, "I told James at that time that we would speak no more on the matter, since it had nothing to do with the problem of Ria's elopement. It was an unfortunate aspect of the family history that was best forgotten."

"You knew?" Despite her earlier feelings of contrition, Lizzie now felt stirrings of resentment. "You knew of my existence and yet you considered it something that was *best forgotten*?"

"That is what I told James," Lady Thornborough answered brusquely. "The letters stated nothing outright about a child. I did not feel it wise to enlighten James, since I could not trust him to keep the matter to himself."

James sighed dramatically. "I would love to deny this, but I fear it is all too true."

"But you *can* keep secrets," Lizzie declared. "And you must have made the connection between those letters and the rumors about Father's valet. That day in Hyde Park when I asked you about the affair, why didn't you tell me you knew about the letters? If you believed me to be Ria, you would have known I was aware of them."

"But you didn't know that *I* knew about them. I meant what I said then about not dredging up the past. I had no idea you were—forgive me, dearest—the *product* of that affair."

Lizzie looked at Lady Thornborough. "But *you* knew about me?" she persisted.

Lady Thornborough indicated the paper in her hand. "This is a document your father left with his solicitors before his death. In it, he states with unwavering clarity the circumstances surrounding his involvement with Emma Poole, the trouble she found herself in, and how he allowed his valet to take the blame for it. He also explains how he gave this valet a certain sum of cash to set himself up in London, and how he always took an interest in you, albeit from afar."

From afar.

"In this document," Lady Thornborough continued, "he stated that upon Sam Poole's death, you were to be notified of an annuity that he had set aside for you. The problem was, by the time he died, you had disappeared from England."

It's true, Lizzie thought. Her father had died while she was in Australia—another of her bitter regrets.

"The money has sat, in trust, in the event that you might one day be located."

"He set aside money for me?" Lizzie asked incredulously.

"Yes. Despite how it may seem, I believe he cared for you very much."

A tiny part of Lizzie's heart seemed to unclench. He *had*

cared for her after all. Perhaps the scowl on his face as he had hurried Ria away on that long-ago day was not disgust, as he had pretended. Perhaps it was the anguish of having a daughter he could not acknowledge. The anguish that another man was raising her as his own.

Lady Thornborough studied her intently. "I assume you will claim the money?"

Lizzie could hardly formulate a response. All this time she had pretended to be another heiress, not knowing she had a right to claim an inheritance of her own. It was tempting, of course. But something still troubled her. "How can I accept this now, after what I have done? I would have to disclose how I lied to you and to all of London society."

"You fear the consequences, of course."

"No. I would gladly face the public shame that I deserve, if it could be done without bringing hurt or scandal to you. But it cannot, and that is my main concern."

Lady Thornborough smiled. "That is why it seems your most recent injury will be a boon to us, my dear. I have Dr. Layton's firm medical opinion that the blow you suffered in London caused you more harm than was at first supposed. It gave you a sort of temporary amnesia. You came here to deliver the bracelet for Ria, but then you became disoriented by the blow and began to think you *were* Ria—especially when we all thought you were, and behaved as such toward you. This latest fall has happily brought you back to your right mind."

"By Jove!" James said, slapping his knee. "What a coup, Auntie!"

Lizzie looked doubtfully at Lady Thornborough. "Will anyone believe that?"

She smiled confidently. "I have been a woman of my word for

nearly seventy years. In addition, we have Dr. Layton's official diagnosis. No one will dare to contradict it."

James snapped his fingers, his mind clearly working as though the three of them were planning strategy for some kind of game. "We must also say that after we discovered our error, we had to keep humoring you until we were able to bring you back around to your right mind, lest we bring more damage to your already tortured psyche."

"Indeed." Even Lady Thornborough seemed amused by this idea.

"But this will still bring disgrace to the Thornborough family," Lizzie insisted. "You will have to acknowledge publicly that Sir Herbert—your son—"

"Clearly Herbert himself wished to acknowledge it," Lady Thornborough said. She sighed. "I cannot say I relish being fodder for the malicious gossip that will inevitably arise. However, the unfortunate truth is that scandal is nothing new to our family. More to the point, all the parties who could be most hurt by it are dead." She held out her hands to Lizzie. "Except for you and I, of course."

Lizzie knelt by the chair and took the hands the woman had proffered.

Lady Thornborough smiled down at her. "There is only one course of action, so far as I can see. I will formally acknowledge you as my granddaughter, and we will get you that annuity." With a glance at James, she added, "Rosewood estate is still entailed to the male heir. I cannot change that."

"I shall take great pains to treat it well, Aunt," James vowed. "I know you think me quite inadequate to the task, but I have a tremendous urge at present to mend my ways."

Lady Thornborough looked unconvinced. "Let us hope your

good intentions do not fade. You have a lot to learn, and you must do it quickly, for I will not be here much longer to carry these responsibilities for you."

"Please don't say that," Lizzie exclaimed. "We will have many years together, I am sure."

She patted Lizzie's hand gently. "As I was saying, Rosewood and the income from the lands must go to James. However, my personal funds are mine to do with as I please. And I plan to settle that upon you."

It was too much good fortune. Lizzie reached up to hug her grandmother tightly, and neither of them was able to speak for a very long time.

"Why is it," James finally remarked, "that women always cry when they are happy?"

Lizzie straightened and began to wipe away her tears. Now that the first flush of joy had passed, she found her thoughts returning, as they always did, to Geoffrey. "It is a bittersweet happiness," she said. "I am grateful for your willingness to do these things for me. But surely Lord Somerville would never agree to such a plan."

"Perhaps you should ask him yourself before drawing that conclusion," Lady Thornborough said.

Lizzie laughed in disbelief. "How am I to do that?" He was showing no signs that he wished to speak to her.

Lady Thornborough's mouth widened in an uncharacteristic grin that was almost like her nephew's. "It's simple, really. He is waiting for you under the old oak tree."

*

The autumn sky was bright and clear as Lizzie raced down the path. She breathed in deeply of the scent of wood smoke mingled with the crisp air, moving as fast as her dress and shoes, which were unsuitable for out-of-doors, would allow. She slowed to a stop at the crest of the hill, caught her breath, and scanned the valley below.

Geoffrey was leaning against the fence and looking in her direction, waiting for her. He smiled and extended his hands. Lizzie ran to him, conscious of very little else until she felt his warm arms holding her tightly.

*

Geoffrey held her close, immeasurably happy to have her in his arms again, this time with no lies and no barriers between them. He had come so close to losing her, and he would never let that happen again. "Lizzie," he murmured. "My dearest Lizzie."

She sighed against his chest. "It feels good to hear you call me by my real name. I've been Ria for so long, I thought my true self was lost forever."

"Lizzie." He brushed his lips over her hair, taking in for the hundredth time her gentle rose scent. He laughed softly.

"Is my name so humorous?" she asked.

"Not at all, dearest. I was just thinking to myself that a rose by any other name would smell as sweet."

She laughed. "You know I love a man who is a poet."

"Besides all that," Geoffrey said, "there is a very important reason I am glad to call you Lizzie Poole. It means I may ask you to marry me."

Lizzie stiffened and made a move to pull away, shaking her head in disbelief. But Geoffrey kept her close with one hand, his other reaching to caress her face as he repeated the words that had been haunting him since the day she uttered them in Lady

Thornborough's parlor. "How many women can say they are married to the man they love, desperately and passionately, and that her husband *worships* her?" He regarded her quizzically. "I assume you do love me, desperately and passionately?"

Absurdly, all she could say was, "You...worship me?"

He chuckled. "Not, of course, in the same manner that I reserve for our Lord," he said, feigning a note of defensiveness. "However, I believe He will not take me to task for doing no more than repeating the words of my beloved."

"I am your beloved," she breathed, as though hardly daring to believe the words.

"My dear, you have not answered my question."

"But...after all I've done..."

"We have both done things of which we can be heartily ashamed. I suppose that only proves we are human."

"But...my past. The lies. My less than stellar pedigree." She looked at him, her face stricken with pain.

Her look cut Geoffrey to the heart, because he knew his words had put that sorrow there. "Lizzie, I have had plenty of time to reflect on the terrible things I said to you."

She shook her head. "They were well deserved."

"No." He touched a finger to her lips. "Hear me out. In time I came face-to-face with the brutal truth that there was only one thing standing between me and the woman I loved more dearly than anything on this earth."

She looked at him, her eyes questioning.

He said, "It was me. I hated myself for having fallen so far short of the ideals I had so proudly believed myself to uphold. It blinded me to everything else."

"You are the most honorable man I know," she protested.

He shook his head. "I was in as great a need to receive forgiveness as to give it. Christian charity covers a multitude of sins—and we are *all* in need of it."

"But there are many in this world who will not be so charitable," Lizzie pointed out, "if they should discover the truth."

"Hightower is dead," Geoffrey said with finality. "No one beyond our family knows the darker details of your history. You lived an honest life in Australia with your brother before you came to England. That is all anyone needs to know." He reached up with his thumb and brushed away a stray tear from her eye. "As for that 'pedigree' you mentioned earlier, you are the granddaughter of Lady Thornborough. That should be good enough for anyone." He paused. "And if it isn't, you need only consent to be my wife and you will also be a baroness. That will most certainly stop the mouths of the critics."

She sniffled, her eyes lightening.

Geoffrey felt his own heart lifting as he saw the hope growing in her eyes. "Lizzie, you were very brave to come to London."

She shook her head. "Brave? Or foolish?"

"It's no easy thing to cross the ocean as you did, and you could not know what awaited you here. You risked a great deal. You also brought me news of Edward. You answered questions that had been plaguing me for years, and in that way you gave my brother back to me. You're a strong woman, Lizzie Poole. You've got a hard head, but it has served you well."

Lizzie let out a tiny laugh as she gingerly touched her temple. "Yes, it would appear my hard head has saved me more than once."

He clasped her hand and placed it over her heart. "But what's in here is soft. It is filled with kindness and virtue."

"Virtue," Lizzie repeated with quiet disbelief. "I have not been accused of having that for many a year."

"Well, my love, I understand it may be hard for you to accept. But accept it you must. I myself have learned a hard lesson from this. I was too ready to judge you once, but no longer. I will defend your honor and virtue against any and all comers."

She brought his hands to her lips. "So you have already."

He inhaled sharply at the delicate touch of her lips on his hands. He pulled her close to his own heart, and kissed her.

Society beauty Maggie Vaughn is horrified
to find herself engaged to a gold prospector from humble
beginnings. But what begins as a marriage of convenience
may blossom into a true affair of the heart...

A *Lady* Most Lovely

Please turn this page for a preview.

London, August 1852

A ren't you the man who rode a horse twenty miles to shore after a shipwreck?"

This was just one of the many inane questions to which Tom Poole had been subjected this evening. Apparently everyone in London had heard his story—or some wild, exaggerated version of it. "It was only seven miles," he said, barely glancing at the man who asked the question. "And I didn't *ride* the horse."

The offhand way he said this may have sounded to a casual observer like false modesty. But that was not the case at all. Truth was, his real attention was held captive elsewhere by the most beautiful woman he'd ever seen.

She was breathtaking—tall and stately, with every feature that Tom had always found desirous in a woman: gleaming dark brown hair, high cheekbones, and a full, sensuous mouth. A generous portion of her smooth, ivory skin was displayed to great advantage by the low-cut neckline of her emerald-green gown. Tom had spotted her the moment she'd come in. He had been quietly observing her for an hour, even as he'd been taken by the elbow and introduced to every other person in this overcrowded ballroom. She, however, had remained far away—unreachable, like a star or a distant planet.

Tom had come to the soiree as a guest of James Simpson, his sister's cousin. James had already informed him that the beautiful woman in question was Miss Margaret Vaughn, and that she and her fiancé were the guests of honor tonight. Even after he'd learned she was engaged, he could not curb his desire to meet her, to get closer to her.

He must get James to introduce him.

"You mean, you didn't ride to shore on a wild stallion?"

Wild stallion? With great effort, Tom pulled his eyes away from Miss Vaughn and tried to focus on his inquisitor—a man who, although he must have been the same age as Tom, was much shorter and a good deal more rotund. He'd been introduced to Tom as Mr. Carter, and he was typical of so many men Tom had met over the past two weeks. They were self-indulgent, self-important gentlemen who would not have given him the time of day seven years ago. Now Carter's weak, watery eyes were focused on him with complete fascination.

"The horse was not wild," Tom corrected him. "It's a Thoroughbred." It was a fine racehorse, too, Tom added to himself, although it would never be used for that purpose again. It was Tom's personal horse now.

"That's not the way I heard it," Carter persisted. "Heard he could barely be contained in his stall during the voyage to England."

"The horse is, understandably, leery of ships," Tom allowed. That wasn't even the half of it, of course. It was a wonder they'd gotten the horse to England at all. But now that he was on dry land, the stallion wasn't too difficult to control. Not that Tom was about to confide this information. The closest Carter ever got to a horse was probably sitting in a finely appointed carriage. Tom's gaze drifted back toward Miss Vaughn. She looked so poised, so cool and collected, as though she didn't realize the crowd of people in the room had sucked all the air out of it.

It was hot in here, and Tom's collar chafed. All his clothes, from his elaborately knotted cravat to his trim-fitting coat and trousers, were far too confining. He was still adjusting to the sheer volume of clothing worn by the upper classes. In Australia he'd rarely needed more than a simple shirt and trousers, which left him free to do the physical labor his work required. He tugged a little at his cravat in an attempt to loosen it, even though he could imagine the look of disapproval this would bring from his new valet. Stephens was not just a servant but also a mentor. He was teaching Tom how to dress and how to allow others to do dozens of things for him that any man should be able to do for himself.

He'd also been getting lessons on deportment from his dear sister. Indeed, Lizzie was an important reason he had returned. For a time she had thought him dead, and he had thought her lost to him forever. Their reunion had been one of the happiest days of his life.

In addition to the joy of seeing his sister again and the plea-sure of meeting his new brother-in-law, Tom had been excited to see London again. He'd always loved the energy of the noisy, foggy, messy, bustling streets. Admittedly he was seeing a new side of the city now that he'd made his fortune. He'd been dirt poor when he'd left, laboring just to survive, living in parts of London that nobody in this room was aware even existed. Or at least, they did not acknowledge it if they did. In the past he'd been on the outside looking in, seeing the elegantly dressed men and women in their carriages, their well-lit houses, the elaborate rituals involved in "taking the air" in Hyde Park. Now he was one of them. Well, not exactly *one of them*. Perhaps *among them* would be a better way to describe it.

"What was it like to be held by wild natives?" Carter prompted. "They kept you for months, didn't they?"

Again Carter had it wrong. "I stayed with them for about a month," Tom said, trying to curb his frustration at having to carry on this conversation. "They tended my wounds and helped me recover."

This drew a look of disbelief from Carter, who evidently preferred to visualize Tom being held prisoner at the point of a spear.

Despite the differences between himself and the Aborigines, it was here in London that Tom felt like he was truly among a different race. England was two countries, rich and poor, with the boundary lines clearly marked. And without question, the queen of this foreign race was the statuesque brunette now gracing the room with her sweeping gaze. He had heard she was worth millions, and he believed it. She carried herself with the air of one who has whatever she wants at her fingertips.

Carter was not done yet with his questioning. "Is it true that the Aborigine women walk around all day without a stitch of clothing?" he asked with an ugly leer. He didn't understand. No one here did. The Aborigines had their own customs, their own kind of dignity. And yet to these rich Londoners, they were mere savages. Or animals.

Tom clenched his fists, and with great effort resisted the urge to punch this smug idiot in the mouth. He was finding it mighty hard to remember what Lizzie had been teaching him about how to behave in "polite" society. *Polite*. He suppressed a derisive laugh at the thought.

Fortunately, James joined them, walking up just in time to hear Carter's last remark. "Carter, you've plied Tom with quite enough questions," he admonished. "You cannot keep him cornered here all night. Besides," he added with a wink at Tom, "Tom is needed elsewhere. I've been asked to introduce him to Mr. Denault and Miss Vaughn."

"Thank you," Tom said, once they were clear of Carter, "for rescuing me from that fool."

"I had the impression I was rescuing Carter from *you*," James replied. "You looked ready to throttle him. Not that I would blame you if you did. He is an absolute bore."

They began working their way across the crowded ballroom. "Who asked you to introduce me to—" Tom was about to say "Miss Vaughn," but stopped himself. It wouldn't do to look too excited at the prospect of meeting a lady who'd already been promised to another man.

"You did, of course," James said lightly.

"Me?"

"Well, you've been staring at her all evening."

"Has it been that obvious?" He felt foolish now, caught mooning over a woman who was unattainable. And yet it had been a very long time since a woman had taken such complete hold of his attention. Longer than he could remember.

"I'm sure it was perceptible only to me," James assured him. "But then, I tend to notice these things."

Tom could not help but grin at this remark. In the short time he'd known James, he'd become well aware of the man's tendency to be a matchmaker—so long as he himself was not one of the interested parties. James was a confirmed bachelor, for sure.

He also knew everyone in London, it seemed. Tom tilted his head in the direction of Denault. Clearly Denault was one of those polished and suave society men who always drew the attention of the fairer sex. There was a small cohort of young ladies clustered around him right now. "He is very rich, I hear."

"Indeed."

"Was it inherited?" He figured Denault was like so many of the privileged class whose money was handed to them from birth.

"Not at all," James said, surprising him. "He's from an old family, well-connected, but not as wealthy as it once was. He made his fortune on some lucrative railroad investments in America. Only returned to England a few months ago."

They were still a distance away when a portly elderly gentleman drew Miss Vaughn and Denault together and loudly proclaimed his intention to toast the couple.

"That's Mr. Plimpton," James informed him. "He's one of the pillars of London society—and he'll be the first to tell you so. He's a good man, but a bit of a blowhard."

Plimpton proceeded to make a speech about how this would be one of the most important weddings since the Queen's own marriage fifteen years before. When Plimpton finished his speech, Denault was immediately approached by two remarkably pretty ladies who had been fluttering around him earlier.

Tom wondered that such a thing did not seem to annoy Miss Vaughn. But she was sipping her champagne with equanimity and listening to Plimpton as he began prattling on about something else. She seemed not to have even noticed these attempts to lure her fiancé's attentions elsewhere.

But she *did* notice as Tom and James approached; Tom was sure of it. He could tell by a slight shift in her posture, an extra alertness in their direction, even though she kept her eyes fixed on Plimpton. He felt a surge of excitement at this realization.

Suddenly, Tom was far too conscious of his tight collar, his heavily starched shirt, and his overpolished boots. In fact, everything he had on was completely foreign to him. He told himself this must be the reason he felt as though he were moving through heavy sand.

James extended his hand in greeting to Denault, whom he evidently knew well. Denault greeted him warmly. Miss Vaughn excused herself from Plimpton and came to her fiancé's side in time to return James's greeting.

"I'd like to introduce you to my new cousin," James said, bringing Tom forward. "This is Mr. Thomas Poole."

"Tom," he corrected. "Just Tom."

"Tom Poole?" Denault repeated. "The man who made a fortune in the gold mines?"

News certainly traveled fast in the rarified society that was the London elite, Tom thought again. Faster than the wildfires in Victoria. "I see you have heard of me."

"Heard?" Denault echoed. "You might buy and sell the Crown now; that's what I've heard. You're a lucky man." There was admiration in his eyes.

There was a glint of avarice as well. Tom had seen it in plenty of people, from the dirt-poor, ex-convict gold miners in Austra-lia to the well-to-do here in England. The upper classes he now moved among might abuse him behind his back for his lowly origins, but to his face they could only compliment him for hav-ing so much money.

"It was a lot of work," Tom pointed out, as he had done too many times tonight already. "I was fortunate to lay claim in the right place, it is true, but the gold don't mine itself."

"Of course, of course," Denault said, waving off Tom's remarks. He turned to his fiancée. "Miss Margaret Vaughn, may I present—"

She cut him off as she extended her hand to Tom and said, "How do you do, *Just* Tom?"

Her eyes held his, displaying a hint of something that might have been a challenge. There was fire under the exterior of this icy beauty. Tom could sense it with every fiber of his being.

Her remark was meant to sound like a pleasantry, but Tom picked up a hint of derision as well. Calling him as she did by his Christian name, even in jest, she might have been speak-ing to an errand boy or a servant. The thought, ironically, cued something his sister had taught him to say during introductions. "Your servant, madam."

He grasped her hand, and a curious thrill ran through him. Had she felt something too? Her eyes seemed to open a bit wider. They were an amazing color—deep green, lined with yellow-gold toward the center. Her gown was nearly the exact same shade, bringing out her eyes with startling clarity. Tom's lessons in etiquette completely left him and he forgot what he was supposed to do with her hand. So he continued to hold it, savor-ing its warmth and the opportunity it afforded him of being so close to this woman. He was fascinated by the strength and fire in her gaze.

"Will you be in London long, Just Tom?" she asked. She sounded a bit breathless.

"I…" He faltered like an idiot. What was happening to him? Suddenly he felt as unsteady as if he were back on the stormy seas. *Keep your wits about you, man.* "I will be in England for the indefinite future."

"How wonderful." Her gaze held his. "We shall be glad to get to know you better."

Somehow he remembered to release her hand.

"Indeed we shall," Denault broke in briskly. "Mr. Poole, perhaps you and I might meet at my club on Thursday? I've a business proposition for you."

Tom knew he should have expected this, even from a man as rich as Denault. Everyone, it seemed, wanted to discuss business ventures with him. So far, he'd deflected or turned down every offer for such a meeting. He could have found some reason to avoid Denault, too, but somehow found himself agreeing to the appointment instead. He had an unreasonable urge to get to learn more about Denault, to discover what kind of man could capture a lady like Miss Vaughn.

"Will Miss Vaughn be joining us as well?" Tom asked.

Denault threw a condescending look to his bride-to-be. "Heavens, no," he said with a laugh. "Women aren't allowed at the club. And besides, she has no head for business, poor thing."

Something like annoyance or anger flashed across Miss Vaughn's face. It was brief, and she quickly suppressed it, but it did not escape Tom. He suspected that this woman, who was an heiress in control of her own millions, was plenty capable of handling business affairs. Why did she not correct him? Tom was aware of the adage that when a man and woman were married they became "one person, and that person is the husband." Even so, he found it difficult to imagine Miss Vaughn in the role of a meek wife.

She seemed to be going along willingly, however. She smiled and said, "I could not possibly join you in any case. I am far too busy right now. The wedding is next week, and there are still a thousand details to arrange."

At the mention of their wedding, Miss Vaughn and Denault exchanged a glance so intensely amorous that Tom wondered if he'd been mistaken about her earlier show of irritation. He was even tempted to be jealous, although he had absolutely no right to be. She was betrothed to this man, and it was evidently a propitious match. Certainly there was nothing he could do about it.

She turned her attention back to Tom. "Do you plan to settle in England, Mr. Poole?"

"Settle?" Tom repeated. He did not know if he would ever settle anywhere.

"Earlier this evening I saw you observing all the ladies in the room very intently." She had been watching him, just as he had been watching her. Tom found this knowledge incredibly intoxicating. "You are perhaps searching for a wife?" she concluded.

"No," said Tom. He could not possibly picture himself married to any of the simpering ladies he'd seen here tonight. He'd thought Miss Vaughn was different, but after seeing the way she acted around Denault, he was beginning to wonder. "I might have to return to Australia for that. The ladies there have far more strength and backbone."

"Do they?" she said. Tom didn't realize he was giving her a

challenge until he saw her accept it as one. She rose up a little taller, and her eyes narrowed almost imperceptibly. Her gaze swept over him from head to foot, as though taking his measure. He withstood her scrutiny with confidence; the unsteadiness he'd felt earlier was gone. "Everyone in Australia seems quite… resourceful," she said at last, smiling a little on the last word. "Including you. I should like to hear more about this famous shipwreck you were in."

For the first time this evening, the mention of the shipwreck did not annoy Tom. He did not try to analyze why. "I'd be more than happy to tell you about it. It's such an amazing story that at times I have trouble believing it myself."

"Paul, dear," Miss Vaughn said without even looking at her fiancé, "I am absolutely dying of thirst." She held out her empty champagne glass in Denault's direction.

Denault looked at it in surprise, as though her request had taken him off guard.

"That's an excellent idea," James interposed. "Don't worry, Denault. We'll keep her company while you're gone."

Denault glanced from Miss Vaughn to James, and then to Tom. Was there mistrust in his eyes? Could Denault possibly feel threatened by Tom, by his fiancée's apparent interest in him? Tom actually found the thought somewhat appealing.

"I have a better idea," Denault said. "I am sure you are famished, my dear. Why don't we both go to the supper room?" He took hold of Miss Vaughn's elbow, as if to lead her away. With a nod to Tom and James he said, "If you gentlemen will excuse us."

Miss Vaughn gently extricated herself from his grip. "I only asked for something to drink," she said in a low voice, her voice a shade too brusque.

Denault looked annoyed. "Yes, my darling, but you've eaten nothing this evening. We cannot have you fainting away from lack of food." His words were solicitous, but he spoke them through clenched teeth. It was more of an order than an expression of concern. She gave him a frosty look in return.

Yes, there was something amiss, Tom decided. Some kind of trouble beneath apparently smooth waters. Perhaps Miss Vaughn and Denault were not as madly in love as they wished to portray. Of course, being *in love* was no requirement for marriage— certainly not among the upper classes. Even a commoner like Tom knew that. Why, then, should they pretend?

He could see her wavering, undecided. Clearly it was not in her nature to be docile. He found he would dearly love to know what was going on in that head of hers right now.

"I do hope we shall meet again, Just Tom," she said.

"Mr. Poole is currently residing with Lord Somerville," James said. "I believe you both live on the same street. We will be glad to pay you a call."

"Please do," she said. "And soon. I should like that very much."

Funny, Tom mused, that she was willing to receive visitors, when earlier she had sounded as if she had no time for anything except her wedding preparations.

Denault took her elbow again, and this time she did not demur.

As he watched her retreating form, Tom's gaze fastened on a stray curl that had made its way down the back of her slender neck. It was without a doubt the most beautiful neck he had ever seen.

And Tom knew that he was dangerously and completely in love with her.

THE DISH

Where authors give you the inside scoop!

♥ ♥ ♥ ♥ ♥ ♥ ♥ ♥ ♥ ♥ ♥ ♥ ♥ ♥ ♥

From the desk of Margaret Mallory

Dear Reader,

I've been startled, as well as delighted, by all the positive comments I've received regarding the deep male friendship—the "bro-mance"—among my four heroes in the Return of the Highlanders series. If my portrayal of male camaraderie rings true at all, I must give some credit to my younger brother, who always had a gang of close friends running in and out of our house. (This does *not*, however, excuse him for not calling me more often.)

Looking back, I admire how accepting and utterly at ease these boys were with each other. On the other hand, I am amazed how they could spend so much time together and not talk—or talk only very briefly—about trouble in their families, divorces, or other important things going on in their lives. They were always either eating or having adventures. To this bookish older sister, they seemed drawn to danger like magnets. And I certainly never guessed that the boys who shot rubber bands at me from behind the furniture and made obnoxious kissy noises from the bushes when I went out on dates had anything *useful* to teach me.

Yet I'm sure that what I learned from them about how male friendships work helped me create the bond among my heroes in the Return of the Highlanders. These four

Highland warriors have been close companions since they were wee bairns, have fought side by side in every battle, and have saved each other's lives many times over. Naturally, they are in each others' books.

Ever since Duncan MacDonald's appearances in *The Guardian* and *The Sinner*, readers have been telling me how anxious they are for Duncan's own book because they want to see him find happiness at last. We all love a tortured hero, don't we? And if any man deserves a Happily Ever After, it's Duncan. In truth, I feel guilty for having made him wait.

Duncan, in THE WARRIOR (available now), is a man of few words, who is honorable, steadfast, and devoted to duty. With no father to claim him, he's worked tirelessly to earn the respect of his clan through his unmatched fighting skills. His only defeat was seven years ago, when he fell hard for his chieftain's beautiful, black-haired daughter, a lass far beyond his reach.

He never expected to keep Moira's love past that magical summer before she wed. Yet he accepts that his feelings for her will never change, and he gets on with his duties. When he and his friends return to the Isle of Skye after years spent fighting in France, every stone of his clan's stronghold still reminds him of her.

Moira's brother, who is Duncan's best friend and now chieftain, is aware that Duncan loves her, though they never speak of it. (Thanks to my brother and his friends, I do know it's possible for them to not talk about this for seven years.) When the chieftain hears that Moira may be in danger, he turns to the man he trusts most.

The intervening years have not made Moira trusting nor forgiving, and the sparks fly when this stubborn pair reunites. After the untimely death of her abusive husband, these star-crossed lovers must survive one dangerous adventure after another. They will find it even more daunting to trust each other and face the hard truths about what happened seven years ago.

I hope you enjoy the romance between this Highland warrior and his long-lost love—and that my affection for the troublesome boys who grow up to be the kind of men we adore shines through in the bro-mance.

I love to hear from readers! You can find me on Facebook, Twitter, and my website, www.MargaretMallory.com.

Margaret Mallory

♥ ♥ ♥ ♥ ♥ ♥ ♥ ♥ ♥ ♥ ♥ ♥ ♥ ♥ ♥

From the desk of Jennifer Delamere

Dear Reader,

Have you ever wished you could step into someone else's life? Leave behind your own past with its problems and become someone entirely different?

I'm pretty sure everyone has felt that way at times. When you think about it, the tale of Cinderella is such a story at its essence.

When I was in college, I saw a film called *The Return of Martin Guerre*, starring the great French actor Gérard Depardieu. It was actually based on true events in medieval France. A man has gone off to war but then stays gone for over a decade, essentially abandoning his wife.

One day, though, he does return. The good news is that, whereas the guy had previously been a heartless jerk, now he is caring and kind. The wife takes him back, and they are happy. The bad news is that eventually it is discovered that the man is not who he claims to be. He is an impostor.

Ever since I saw that movie, I have loved stories with this theme. One thing I've noticed is that so often in these tales, the impostor is actually a better human being than the person he or she is pretending to be. In the case of *Martin Guerre*, Gérard's character *wants* the life and the responsibilities the other man has intentionally left behind. The movie was remade in America as *Sommersby*, starring Richard Gere and Jodie Foster. Richard Gere's character grows and *becomes* a better man over the course of the events in the film. He does more for the family and community than the real Sommersby ever would have done.

Please note that a sad ending is not necessarily required! There are lighthearted versions of this tale as well. Remember *While You Were Sleeping*, a romantic comedy starring Sandra Bullock? Once again, she was a better person than the woman she was pretending to be, and she was certainly too good for her fiancé, the shallow man she thought she was in love with. In the end, her decency and kindness won over everyone in the family. They were all better off because she had come into their lives, even though she had initially been untruthful about who she was. And—what's most important for fans of romance!— true love won out. While Sandra had initially been starry eyed over her supposed fiancé, she came to realize that it was actually his brother who was the right man for her.

The idea for AN HEIRESS AT HEART grew out of my love for these stories about someone stepping into another person's shoes. Lizzie Poole decides to take on another person's identity: that of her half-sister, Ria, whom she had no idea existed until they found each other through an extraordinary chain of events.

Lizzie is succeeding in her role as Ria Thornborough Somerville, a woman who has just been widowed—until she falls in love with Geoffrey Somerville, the dead husband's brother. And aside from the fact that it would have been awkward enough to explain how you had suddenly fallen in love with your brother-in-law, in England at that time it was actually illegal: The laws at that time prevented people from marrying their dead spouse's sibling. So Lizzie is left in a quandary: She must either admit the truth of her identity, or forever deny her love for Geoffrey.

In a cute movie called *Monte Carlo*, a poor girl from Texas (played by Selena Gomez) impersonates a rich and snobbish Englishwoman. During her week in that woman's (high-priced, designer) shoes, she actually ends up helping to make the world just a bit better of a place—more so than the selfish rich girl ever would have done. She finds a purpose in life and—bonus!—true love as well.

Maybe I'm so fascinated by these stories because of the lovely irony that, in the end, each character actually discovers their *true* self. They find more noble aspects of themselves than they ever realized existed. They discover that who they *are* is better than anyone they could *pretend* to be. They learn to rise up to their own best natures rather than to simply be an imitation of someone else.

As the popular saying goes, "Be yourself. Everyone else is taken."

Jennifer Delamere

♥ ♥ ♥ ♥ ♥ ♥ ♥ ♥ ♥ ♥ ♥ ♥ ♥ ♥ ♥

From the desk of Roxanne St. Claire

Dear Reader,

I'm often asked if the fictional island of Mimosa Key, home to beautiful Barefoot Bay, is based on a real place. Indeed, it is. Although the barrier island is loosely modeled after Sanibel or Captiva, the setting was really inspired by a serene, desolate, undiscovered gem called Bonita Beach that sits between Naples and Fort Myers on the Gulf of Mexico.

On this wide, white strip of waterfront property, I spent some of the most glorious, relaxing, deliciously happy days of my life. My parents retired to Bonita and lived in a small house directly on the Gulf. On any long weekend when I could get away, I headed to that beach to spend time in paradise with two of my very favorite people.

The days were sunny and sandy, but the best part of the beach life were the early evening chats on the screened-in porch with my dad, watching heartbreakingly beautiful sunsets, sipping cocktails until the blue moon rose to turn the water to diamonds on black velvet. All the while, I soaked up my father's rich memories of a life well lived. And, I'm sorry to say, a life that ended too soon. My last trip to Bonita was little more than a vigil at his hospital bed, joined by all my siblings who flew in from around the country to share the agony of losing the man we called "the Chief."

My mother left the beach house almost immediately to live with us in Miami, and more than twenty years passed before I could bear to make the drive across the state to Bonita. I thought it would hurt too much to see "Daddy's beach."

But just before I started writing the Barefoot Bay series, I had the opportunity to speak to a group of writers in that area of Florida, and I decided a trip to the very setting of my stories would be good research—and quite cathartic.

Imagine my dismay when I arrived at the beach and it was no longer desolate or undiscovered. The rarefied real estate had transformed in two decades, most of the bunga-lows replaced by mansions. I didn't have the address, but doubted I could find my parents' house anyway; it couldn't have escaped the bulldozers and high-end developers.

So I walked the beach, mourning life's losses, when suddenly I slowed in front of one of the few modest houses left, so small I almost missed it, tucked between two four-story monsters.

The siding had been repainted, the roof reshingled, and the windows replaced after years of exposure to the salt air. But I recognized the screen-covered porch, and I could practically hear the hearty sound of my dad's laughter.

I waited for a punch of pain, the old grief that some-times twists my heart when I let myself really think about how young I was when I lost such a fantastic father. But, guess what? There was no pain. Only relief that the house where he'd been so happily retired still stood, and gratitude that I'd been blessed to have had him as my dad.

And like he had in life, my father inspired me once again. For one thing, despite the resort story line I had planned for the Barefoot Bay books, I made a promise to keep my fictional beach more pristine and pure than the real one. I also promised myself that at least one of the books that I'd set on "Daddy's beach" would explore the poignant, precious, incomparable love between a father and a daughter.

That book is BAREFOOT IN THE RAIN. The novel is, first and foremost, a reunion romance, telling the story of Jocelyn and Will, two star-crossed teenagers who find their way back to each other after almost fifteen years of separation. But there's another "love" story on the pages of BAREFOOT IN THE RAIN, and that's the one that brought out the tissues a few times while I was writing the book.

The heroine is estranged from her father, and during the course of the story, she has to forge a new relationship with the man she can barely stand to talk to, let alone call "Daddy." Unlike my father, Jocelyn's dad can't share his memories, because Alzheimer's has wiped the slate clean. And in their case, that's both a blessing and a curse. Circumstances give Jocelyn a second chance with her father—something many of us never have once we've shared that last sunset.

I hope readers connect with Jocelyn, a strong heroine who has to conquer a difficult past, and fall in love with the catcher-turned-carpenter hero, Will. I also hope readers appreciate how hard the characters have worked to keep Barefoot Bay natural and unspoiled, unlike the beach that inspired the setting. But most of all, I hope BAREFOOT IN THE RAIN reminds every reader of a special love for her father, no matter where he is.

Roxanne St. Claire